THE GARDEN OF BEFORE

A SEQUEL

RYAN LESLIE

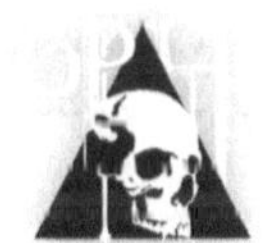

A QUICK REFRESHER...

For a summary of the events of book 1, *The Between*, please visit:
HTTPS://RYAN-LESLIE.COM/REFRESHER-FOR-THE-BETWEEN

BEFORE

The Montclair twins ran through the forest as fast as their fifteen-year-old legs could carry them. The bony hands of branches grabbed out as they sped past. Rocks jutted from the ground, threatening to twist their ankles. Would-be trails turned into dense dead-ends waiting to swallow the girls whole. But nothing could catch Lark and Zee Montclair. Not in the woods where they moved like two mountain lions.

Lark—*Lauren*, but nobody called her that—jumped over the remains of a fallen tree and shot through a grove of aspens, their pale bark making them look like zombie trees among the ponderosa pines. After a hard cut to the left where she nearly stepped on a terrified ground squirrel, she emerged back on the trail in front of her sister.

"Caught you, rabbit," Lark said with a quick smirk over her shoulder.

"I let you catch me," Zee said, returning the smirk. "Now it's your turn to be the rabbit. Run, rabbit, run!"

Lark upped her pace and took a glance at the smartwatch on her left wrist. 6:10 mile pace, heart rate 140. Too fast to maintain for more than another mile or so, but she'd let Zee be the one to cry *mercy*. Besides, the rabbit had to run for its life. If the rabbit quit, the rabbit died.

To their right, through about fifty feet of trees, a two-lane highway ran parallel to their path, an asphalt river carving its way through the Rocky Mountains. Their grandmother had told them to stick to the path that followed the road; it was too easy to get lost out here, and some trails led for fifty miles or more across the Continental Divide.

When the trail began to climb, Lark felt the thinner air pull at her. Each breath became more strained, and her hamstrings and glutes burned. But the cool, dry air made up for that, at least in part, compared to their home in New Orleans, where the summer heat and humidity made running miserable. She'd take the thin air any day. Besides, when they got back home next week for the start of their sophomore year in high school, they'd hit the first cross-country team run with oxygen-rich blood and run circles around the other girls. All the boys, too.

"You're a sneaky rabbit!" her sister yelled from behind her.

Somehow, amid thoughts of home and high school, Lark had drifted from the main trail and led them away from the mountain road.

"You sound like you're falling behind," Lark said between heavy breaths.

"Never!" Zee cried in return.

When the new path broke into a rocky clearing, Lark recognized a boulder, its flat side carved with initials. They had hiked this way with their dad a few years ago, back when he would come with them to their grandmother's cabin during the summer. He hadn't come in the last two years. "You two are big enough to fly there on your own," he had said. But that's not why he stayed behind. Lark and Zee could read their dad's thoughts as if they were printed on a screen on his forehead. After the fire, their dad couldn't go back to any of the old familiar places. The happy memories weren't happy for him. And so, he moved to the East Coast while they stayed with their mom in New Orleans.

"Water break!" Zee yelled. "The rabbit survives. Well done!"

Lark had been wanting a rest for several minutes now, but her sister's acquiescence gave her a burst of energy. She jumped off a rock, caught a low-hanging branch, and pulled herself up into a tree, all in a quick motion.

"Show off," Zee said. Zee—*Zenia*, but nobody called her that—squirted two shots of water into her mouth followed by another two on top of her brown, ponytailed hair. Then another squirt up at her sister.

"Hey! Watch it! You're gonna feel awful when I slip out of this tree and break my skull open on that rock," Lark said.

Zee put her hand on her hip and gave Lark a thoughtful look. "I guess I'll have to bury you and then live two lives, pretending to be both of us. School will be a trick. I'd need offsetting schedules." She narrowed her eyes and giggled. "Tony will be easy to fool. He always thinks I'm you, anyway."

Lark pulled a pollen-filled bud off the tree and threw it at her sister. "I was thinking about breaking up with Tony. You can have him."

"Off to another boy, eh? You've had, what, five boyfriends already in high school? And I've never made it to date number three with anybody. Dating is gonna be the best thing about living a double life after you fall and spill your brains out. I get to be the prude and the easy girl both. I'm gonna date half the school pretending to be you. I'm gonna give your name a rep-yoo-tay-shun."

Lark dropped back to the ground, letting loose a puff of brown dust. "Looks like I survived, so no double life for you. Now it's your turn to be the rabbit again. Don't trip and die, because I don't know how to play the clarinet and so I could never pull off the whole double-life thing. Plus, your life is boring without all the hot sex."

Zee's eyes went wide. "You and Tony?"

Lark sprayed her sister with her own water bottle. "In his dreams. Now get running, rabbit, or I'm going to catch you and eat you all up."

Zee hesitated before continuing on the trail that led away from the road. She was the cautious twin, after all. But off Zee tore, and Lark gave everything she had to keep her sister in sight. Twice she slipped on loose rocks. All joking aside, getting injured out here would be a mess. Who knew if anyone else would pass this way the rest of the day. Or even the rest of the week.

Ahead, Zee crested a slope, scaring a fawn out of the brush to their right. Lark wanted to watch as the fawn bounced its way through the trees, but Zee was nearly out of sight. Lark sped after her sister, never once questioning whether Zee knew where she was going. Zee wouldn't get them lost. Lark, maybe, but not Zee. Zee was always in control.

<hr>

Three years earlier, before the divorce but after the fire and all that was lost, Lark sat across from her therapist wishing it were possible to split herself in two. One half could sit here, pretending to listen, answering the same questions asked of her every week, while the other half was free to be anywhere else. The problem— aside from not being able to split herself in two—was that she had no place else she dreamed of being. After the fire, the world had become a dim, ruined place, where the sun no longer shined as bright.

"What about basketball or volleyball?" the therapist asked, probably for the second or third time.

"What?" Lark said. "Oh. I don't like team sports." She didn't like sitting in this dark office, either. The armchair she sat in was too big, her feet dangling unless she scooted to the edge of the seat. There was also the smell. Earthy, smoky, and bitter. *Did it come from the room or from the middle-aged, muumuu-wearing therapist?* Lark wondered every time she came here. Besides the smell, the air had a heavy feel, like it took more effort than usual to walk through it, and more effort to make your words come out of your mouth. Zee had said she felt the heaviness, too—that it was the weight of all the problems and pain that had been released in this room. Lark didn't believe such a thing could be true, but she had no better explanation.

Worse than the too-big seat, the smell, and the room's heaviness was the empty chair next to her, where her sister should have been. It was the therapist's suggestion that the twins meet for their sessions separately. Her dad said it was so the therapist could charge double, which started another argument with her mom.

"How about tennis?" the therapist asked. She was seated in an identical chair across from Lark without so much as a table to separate them. "Tennis is a great individual sport."

"If you like it so much, you should play it then," Lark said, channeling something Zee would say.

The therapist looked up and twisted a lock of her curly dark hair around her finger, appearing to give Lark's suggestion real thought. "I probably should. But we're looking for something that would be good for you, not me. This is to help you."

"I don't care about tennis. I don't like sports."

"Let's not make this about sports, okay Lauren?"

"Then what is it about?"

The therapist leaned forward. "It's about release, using physical activity to get the clutter out of your mind. You have a little beehive of anger and anxiety inside. I see you fidgeting there—it's okay, don't try to stop just because I mentioned it. Imagine what it would feel like if that buzzing went away, even if only for a little while. That's what I'm trying to help you do."

A knock came from the office door.

"Oh, the time got away from us, didn't it?" the therapist said, looking at her watch but not really looking at her watch.

Lark stood without saying anything in response and shuffled to the door.

"Think about it, Lauren, please. Think about finding an outlet."

Her mom and Zee were on the other side of the door. As Zee passed by to take her own turn with the therapist, the twins grabbed each other's hands and gave a small but solid squeeze.

On the drive to their rental house, their mom made two wrong turns despite having lived in New Orleans her entire life. The girls said nothing. They didn't even have to look at each other to share a thought. Some part of their mom had been lost, had faded away after the fire. You could almost see through her if you looked close enough. It was more than the forgetfulness and the constant state of distraction. She was like a wraith. The strength had left her body, and she needed help opening jars and lifting grocery bags. The twins were the ones in therapy, though. Maybe what was lost in their mom could never be found again.

She did show brief flashes of energy, but only in arguments with their dad. And that afternoon, when they pulled into the driveway where he was giving Ross's big wheel, salvaged from the fire, to a little neighbor boy, their mom came to life in a glowing rage.

Lark hadn't noticed her mom's knuckles turn white on the steering wheel. The screech of the tires and sudden jerk of the seatbelt snapped her out of a colorless daydream. Their mom left the car door open. The flood of screams and cursing seemed louder somehow in the car than it could've been outside. Their father wilted, looking occasionally at the horrified neighbor boy who was backing away from the big wheel like it had burst into angry flames.

Zee had already jumped out of the car and was trying but failing to calm their mom down. Lark also stepped between their parents, not really understanding why or what she hoped to accomplish. But being between them made Lark a vessel for their mom's fury. It flooded and filled her until something broke, and her own anger flowed loose toward her dad.

She screamed all the words their mom had said and then more.

He was the one who had left the stove on.

He was the one who should have run back in.

He was the one who left Ross inside.

Ross was dead because of him.

The words left her lips, and then the world stopped. Cars stopped moving. Pigeons nearby froze with their heads turned toward Lark. No more yelling from their mom. The neighbor boy had been backing away, and now he stood as if turned into a little statue. Zee stared at Lark, eyes wide, mouth open as if she were going to speak but had lost the words. Their father looked like he had been speared through the heart.

When the world moved again, it moved silently, starting with their father wordlessly entering the rental house, leaving the front door open, leaving the big wheel–Ross's big wheel–on the driveway. Their mother stared blankly at each sister and then walked away, neither toward the car nor the house but down the sidewalk, headed nowhere. Zee grabbed Lark's hand, pulled Lark into a hug, and began shaking with silent tears.

Lark felt nothing but absence. She wanted to cry and share the moment with Zee like they shared everything. She wanted to hate herself for the words that had escaped her mouth, but those words were no longer hers. They now lived invisibly in the world, floating forever nearby.

"Take the big wheel, please," Lark said to the neighbor boy.

He grabbed the handle and began dragging it down the sidewalk in the opposite direction that her mom had walked. The plastic tires cried against the concrete.

The trail turned downward suddenly, and Lark's right foot slid out from under her as the rocks on the path came loose. She only kept from falling by catching a low branch with her hand, a reflexive move that felt like it briefly pulled her arm out of its socket. But that was better than the alternative. By the time Lark made it back to the path—this was a path, wasn't it?—Zee had disappeared below where the path curled behind a dense thicket.

There was no catching Zee now. She'd always been the better distance runner, conserving her energy for a final push at the end. Lark, on the other hand, treated every moment of a race like the final seconds before the finish line. She always wanted to be in the lead, to be the rabbit, faster than all the wolves chasing her. In the spring's cross-country season, Lark had placed at or near the top in all the two-mile events. The twins had run two three-mile races and had alternated victories. The five-mile races were where Zee was unbeatable.

How far had they run today? Lark looked at her wristwatch, but its screen was black. Tapping got no response.

"You win, rabbit!" she yelled, examining her palm where the branch had torn her skin. "Hey, rabbit?" She looked up and, seeing no sign of her sister, yelled again. "Zee! I want to head back!"

She took a sip of water, expecting to see Zee come around the thicket below at any second. When Zee didn't appear, Lark tapped at her watch a few more times and then began to retrace her steps over the small ridge she had just cleared. The mountain woods stretched out in all directions without any sign of a path. *Where did the path go?* But she hadn't been following a path. She had been following her sister. Zee wouldn't have veered off the path. Right?

"Zee?"

The cool and quiet numbness—this was why Zee ran, not a feeling so much as an absence of feeling. Her coach called it the runner's high, but to Zee a high would be something, and this feeling was pure nothing. No pain, no tiredness, no invading thoughts, only motion and wind and silence.

The snap of a twig broke the silence, but it couldn't break the numbness. The snap was Lark, not far behind. Zee didn't speed up or slow down, letting her body run as it wanted to, at the speed that would preserve the numbness for as long as possible. She navigated slopes and turns without thought.

Loud crunches came from behind her, suddenly so close Zee swore she felt Lark's hand brush the back of her shirt. The rabbit's panic broke through the numbness. With a burst of adrenaline, Zee pushed harder. The woods looked like they cleared ahead, up another hundred feet or so.

"If I make it to the ridgeline, the rabbit escapes!" Zee yelled without looking back.

Lark didn't answer, but the crunches on the ground were as

close as ever. *Putting everything she's got into one last effort to catch the rabbit*, Zee thought. *Sorry, sister!* When Zee cleared the woods, it felt like slipping through a barrier into a different world. The Rocky Mountains spread out to her left and right as far as she could see, a hundred miles or more. She turned back, expecting to see her sister emerge from the woods right behind her. When her sister didn't appear, Zee made a little self-satisfied chuckle and began preparing some jabs and taunts for Lark. The rabbit could be a little bitch sometimes when she won.

After a few more seconds, Zee's grin began to sour.

"Come on, slowpoke!" she yelled. She hadn't realized Lark had fallen so far behind. Why hadn't she said something? "Did you slip and crack your skull?" She had meant that to be funny, but when her own words returned as echoes, they didn't sound funny at all. She had strayed from the main trails, drifted away from the road, and now...

"Lark!" she yelled, from on top of what felt like an empty, endless world.

Lark sat on a moss-covered boulder, mind racing. Not the steady type of racing she was used to, but a frantic, whipsaw race from one thought to another and another. She had spent the last few minutes yelling until her throat burned. The only explanation that made sense was that she had gone the wrong way, thinking she was following Zee but maybe even running the complete opposite direction. How long had she run without sight of Zee? Two minutes? Three? Surely Zee would've stopped after getting too far ahead. Why hadn't Lark yelled for Zee to slow down earlier? It wasn't competitiveness. She didn't care who won the stupid Run Rabbit Run game. Not really. And what should she do now? She probably could retrace her path, but that would leave Zee alone, so maybe Lark should stay put, right here on this rock.

She took a deep breath, preparing to yell for Zee again, but something acrid in the air caught in her throat, causing her to cough so hard she had to stand up and bend over. When the coughing fit stopped, she calmed her angry throat with the last of her water and used the back of her hand to wipe away the tears that'd filled her eyes. They burned, and the tears came back. Something was in the air. A haze she could taste and smell. A darkness like a film covering the world. A burning.

Maybe it's a campfire, she thought, but she had passed a big Smokey the Bear sign admonishing would-be fire-builders at the trailhead. No one would build a campfire out here during the middle of the day. It was the middle of the day, wasn't it? She tapped hard on the unresponsive screen of her watch and resisted the sudden urge to take it off and hurl it into the trees.

The sky had turned the color of old asphalt, in part due to the haze, but there was something more to the darkness. A storm cloud rolling in over the ridgeline? It was too early for the sun to have set. Way too early.

Lark looked back at the way she had come. That's where she should go now—retrace her steps until reaching the path. Wait for Zee there. Zee would go back to the path, also. The path was the only way back.

As she had these thoughts, she instead started walking the other way, toward the source of the smoke. The smoke wrapped around her and pulled. *Zee is this way*, it seemed to say. And so, she let it lead her deeper into the woods.

<hr>

Zee had just reached the top of a boulder on the ridgeline when she saw and smelled the smoke coming from a deep part of the woods, far from the path she had taken to get here. The air carried, too, the sound of Zee's name, a lingering echo of her sister's voice. But no sight of her sister.

"Lark!" she yelled in return. "Lark, where are you?"

A sudden gust of wind kicked up dried leaves and nettles. She turned her head and closed her eyes, debris hitting her skin like little probing insects. The smell came next. A stinging, burning smell. When she opened her eyes, day had become a starless night. How was that possible? What little light there was came from the dimly glowing circle in the sky, but whether it was the moon behind a thin layer of clouds or the sun through heavy smoke, she couldn't tell. The only other light came from a smoldering amber glow in the woods at the source of the smoke.

ZEEEEEE! came a voice from the glow. The voice sounded scared and familiar.

She started toward it, her heart thrumming so quick and hard that she put her hand to her chest as if she could calm it, as if it were a small, scared animal, as if it were a rabbit. And a thought occurred to her that made her heart beat faster still.

The game hadn't ended. She was still the rabbit.

LAAAARK!

Lark heard the voice, a voice she knew, and stared in disbelief at where it had come from. In a clearing ahead, she saw a house that couldn't have been there. A house on fire. Their house on Chestnut Street in New Orleans with the magnolia tree out front and the swing hanging from that one thick branch perpendicular to the trunk—like it existed only to hold a swing.

The tree was on fire.

So was the swing, rocking back and forth, empty.

LAAAARK! came the voice again. Ross's voice. From inside the house.

And then she heard her own voice, screaming at her father. "You should've run back in! You left Ross inside!" Over and over again, her voice screamed those words. She whirled around, expecting to see herself standing nearby. Instead, she saw nothing. Only darkness, as if the mountains themselves had vanished, or as if she had somehow been transported into an abyss with only the burning house at its center. She reflexively put her hand to her mouth and found that she was the one screaming.

She ran toward the house's open front door.

Zee saw her sister enter the black maw of a burning skull. That's what the house had become—a skull. All of it ablaze except the dark eye sockets of two upstairs windows and the mouth that was the front door.

"No!" she screamed at her sister for rushing in, at the house for being where it shouldn't be. She had to run in after her sister, but her legs wouldn't move.

In one of the windows, in an eye of the skull, she saw her sister's form.

"Lark! Get out of there!" Zee's cry filled the abyss.

ZEEEEEE! came the voice again.

Not Lark. Ross. Little, eight-year-old Ross, who had been gone for over three years.

ZEEEEEE!

Her voice became a whisper. "Ross? Oh Ross, no!"

Lark had seen the inside of the burning house in her nightmares. Now, her nightmares had come alive. The orange glow of flame covered the entryway walls. The tile floor reflected the burning ceiling, making the porcelain look like it was burning as well. The French doors to the right led to the dining room. Ahead lay the kitchen. But Lark's only interest was the stairs leading up to the bedrooms on the second floor. The path to and up the stairs looked clear, but the top of the stairs was obscured in smoke.

LAAAARK! came Ross's voice from somewhere above.

Lark took the stairs two at a time, the hot air in her lungs feeling like it was boiling her insides. She pushed through the smoke with her sweat-soaked shirt pulled over her mouth and nose. When she reached the top, the smoke swirled in the hallway and then cleared. It pulled unnaturally under the doors, leaving the path to the one closed door at the end of the hall exposed. Little snaking flames writhed on the walls but didn't seem to burn them, as if they were prop flames on a movie set. Lark stopped, confused, but then Ross's voice screamed out from behind his bedroom door.

LAAAARK! HURRY!

She ran to the door, grabbed the handle, and tried to turn it. "It's locked, Ross! Open the door! I'm here!" Lark twisted with all her might, and when that failed, she began ramming into the door with her shoulder, all the while screaming, "I'm here! I'm here, Ross!"

The door swung open as she was about to crash into it. Her momentum took her inside, but it wasn't Ross's room.

A man in a hooded cloak stood among overturned pews in the middle of a small chapel. Several bodies lay on the floor in pools of blood. Lark was flooded by terror, but just as quickly, the terror retreated to the back of her mind, replaced by an overwhelming need to serve the hooded man. The room changed, its colors inverting. The wood of the pews and the chapel walls shifted from brown to an ashy gray. The dark red pools of blood became blue like pools of bright summer sky. Light became dark. White became black.

The hooded man turned and looked at her with color-inverted eyes: white irises surrounded by black. He seemed surprised, or perhaps amused, with the hint of a smirk on his thin, pale lips— lips almost as white as the bone white of his skin.

"And who are you, little one?" the man asked in a voice of gravel and honey.

"I'm Lark," she heard herself say. A part of her screamed silently to run away from him, but that part seemed silly, didn't it? Why would she run from him?

He greeted her with a slight tilt of his head and a mirthless grin. "Nice to meet you, Lark. I have many names, but the one that is most important here is *Malluma Sinjoro*, the Dark Lord of Chaos. That's a mouthful, isn't it? You can call me Sin." He nodded toward the bodies on the ground. "They died trying to protect me. And now I have no one left to protect me. No one but you, Lark."

One of the bodies—a man wearing a bloodstained T-shirt,

trousers, and a strange, spiked collar—twitched and then gasped. Before Lark knew what she was doing, she ran to him and brought the heel of her right shoe down hard into his head over and over until the unexpected spark of life was extinguished. A voice inside her head screamed at what she had done, at the sickening crunch of bone and meat, but that voice wasn't in control of her body.

"Ah...Well done. Today is my lucky day," Sin said, "because I have found such a savage little bird." He made a sound that was equal parts laugh and growl. "And it's your lucky day, too. I think that collar will fit you. Why don't you try it on?"

As soon as Sin suggested it, trying on the collar became the most obvious and natural thing in the world to Lark. She knelt and turned the dead man's head to get a better look at the collar. She had blood on the bare skin of her knees and now on her fingers, but she acted as if she didn't notice or care. The voice inside her head continued to scream.

The collar covered about an inch of the man's neck and seemed to be woven from strands of metal wire. Most of the strands were dull gray, but a single strand in the middle of the collar, encircling each of the seven spikes, flickered occasionally like the filament of an incandescent light bulb. The clasp on the back of the collar was nearly invisible, but Lark's hands pinched and twisted in just the right way to make it come loose.

The collar felt surprisingly light in her hands. She turned it over, rubbed a finger on one of the spikes, and then, on a whim, fastened it around her own neck.

The collar came to life.

A thick black substance poured out of it, coated her like a second skin, then solidified and formed plates and ridges until it looked like an alien suit of armor. Spikes, like those on the collar, grew out of the armor. While she stared in disbelief at her now covered body, the air began to blur and...

...the world was replaced by a million dreams, a million flashes of another life, where she ruled over a crumbling city from a crumbling castle surrounded by a sea of sand, where she gathered armies of men and giants and beasts and sent them out to kill, where her thoughts

*radiated out from her body with the force of iron... She dreamed of a wake of blood and chaos, of destruction trailing behind her... She dreamed of a word, a name—*malespero*—that tied together all the dreams...*

...and a lifetime and a split second later, she stood again in the chapel with the cloaked man. The strange inversion to the world's colors had ceased. The blood on the ground was again red, as it should be. *The* malesperos *get comfortable with blood*, a voice in her head said. Or was it her own voice?

"What happened to me?"

Sin looked her up and down. His eyes burned. His lips curled into a smile. "My savage little bird, you are now a servant of Chaos, like me. You have become the *malespero*." He walked to the other end of the chapel, stepping over the bodies with indifference. "Now follow me. I will take you to your new home in the Ruins."

"But my sister..." Lark began. What had happened to Zee? Was she still in the mountains? Had she entered the burning house also?

For the second time, Sin appeared surprised and amused. "Was your sister with you before you came through the door?"

"We got separated. I think I—"

"Is she your twin?" he interrupted. "Answer me. This is important."

"Yes."

An irritated scowl flashed on his face. "Then she will be pulled here soon, too." He pointed to the door that still led to the burning Montclair house. "Close and lock that door. We have a change of plans. I'm going to leave you now, little bird. And when I do, count to... fifty, just to be sure. Then you can open the door. Don't let your sister in a second earlier, no matter what. Do you understand?"

"I understand the instructions but not the reason," Lark said.

"Because you are now a servant of Chaos like me. You are... unaffected... by my aura—this color-inverting area surrounding me wherever I go. Your sister, however, will be affected if I remain nearby. She will go mad and attack the first person she sees, much like you attacked your *malespero* predecessor. What do you think would happen then?"

Lark's eyes widened as she realized his implication: Zee would attack her with the same bloodthirst Lark had felt moments ago. She jumped and slammed the door. It had no lock, so she leaned her weight into it and held the knob.

"Good," he said. "What is your sister's name, little bird?"

"Her name is Zee," Lark said. "Zenia."

"Like you, Zenia is fortunate. See the woman with the dress?"

Lark followed his gaze to a body on the floor with long, blood-covered blonde hair. A piece of the woman's skull was missing. The dress, a gleaming, diaphanous white gown, was somehow unspoiled by the carnage and dirt of the room.

"The dead woman was the *gardistaro*, a servant of Order. Tell Zenia to put on that dress. She will be the next *gardistaro*. These roles will make you powerful and help you survive. For a while, anyway."

Lark looked down at the armor she wore. Every aspect of it conveyed a sinister purpose in stark contrast to the white dress the man intended for Zee.

"Servant of Order? A minute ago, you said I served Chaos."

"Ahh. You're a clever one. Yes, it will cause... tension... that the two of you serve opposing forces. But, if you survive for any time at all, you'll quickly find that it is better to have power here than to lack it. We have talked for too long. I must leave. I will find you again soon, little bird."

"Wait," Lark said. The look from Sin told her quite clearly that he was not a man accustomed to being told to do anything. Still, she continued, "What happened to my brother's room? I heard him and I ran and—"

"All an illusion meant to lure you here," Sin said, and his expression softened. "Just as I was lured here long ago, too. We have fallen through the looking glass into a place called the Between. It is said that no one can escape, but I believe I know of a way. We will talk more of this soon. Until then, take care of your sister. Survive. Grow powerful. And destroy any who threaten you. Be ruthless, little bird."

As Zee finally convinced her body to step toward the burning house, it seemed to stretch out and pull away from her. It warped and shrank as if the reality it occupied was being sucked through a hole. Within seconds, the house was gone. A rippling oval about twenty feet tall stood at the center of where the house had been, casting a strange blue glow, pulling at her.

Zee felt her eyes start to roll back and her legs go limp. Her thud on the hard obsidian black ground woke her back up. She had begun to pass out. Now, she was sliding toward the oval, toward the hole, and the ground was so slick that she couldn't stop herself.

She frantically clawed at the ground, and when that didn't work, she pressed herself flat. The friction from her shoes and her sweat-soaked shirt slowed and then finally stopped her. She lay there, splayed out on her stomach and motionless for a minute or more. She tried to look back at the oval—the hole in the air—and even the slightest twist of her neck was enough to set her loose and sliding until she dragged herself flat once again.

All around her she saw only darkness. Behind, the hole rumbled with a deep, static hum. She tried to make sense of what had happened. Getting too far ahead and losing her sister on the mountain trail. The bitter smoke and the darkening sky. The house—their family home—burning in the mountain woods. Ross's voice calling to her. Seeing Lark enter the house, and then the house disappearing as if it was sucked into the hole that now tried to devour Zee.

She caught herself again losing consciousness, slipping. A jolt of adrenaline snapped her back, but almost immediately, her newfound energy was gone. She was exhausted. Physically from the run, from the panic, and now from tensing every muscle to keep still. But to keep still to what end? All around her was nothingness. Whatever the hole was, it had taken her sister. To be with her sister—even if the hole was death—was better than being here, alone.

A peaceful lightness came over her. She felt herself begin to slide, but the sliding no longer caused panic. She turned to look at the shimmering blue oval—a portal, perhaps. Her long hair had come loose, and it now stretched out toward that portal, tunneling her vision toward whatever lay on the other side. But it was an exit from the darkness. Zee got her feet under her, and without giving it more thought, ran toward the hole, toward her sister, and jumped in.

She hit something hard and became stuck in the air, the glow of the portal almost blinding around her. Except for the lack of heat, it felt like being on the surface of the sun, crushed by its overwhelming gravity, surrounded by white, fiery light.

And then she was falling, first one way and then another.

She looked up and saw Lark holding open a door, a door that led to the blinding light Zee had emerged from. She scrambled to her feet and went to embrace her sister, but found Lark wearing a strange, armored suit covered with spikes.

"What are you wearing?" she started to say, but her words vanished as she turned about to see the room.

"We're not in Colorado anymore, Zee," Lark said with the cold detachment that usually only came out in the therapist's office.

Zee backed away from her sister. Something about Lark had changed, almost like a shadow had been cast upon her, following her as she moved. A shadow without a source. And her eyes burned with intensity. Zee broke eye contact and turned her head, but all that did was force her to take in the room. A chapel so decrepit and broken that whatever god had been worshiped here must have long forsaken it. The bodies on the ground. The blood —more blood than she had ever seen. The floor, half covered with it. The bodies drowned it in.

"What is this place, Lark?" Zee tried to ask, but the quivering of her voice made the words almost unintelligible. The room began to spin. Zee knelt and put her hand on the ground, but it didn't stop the feeling that she'd become dislodged from the space around her. Closing her eyes made it worse, but once they were shut, she became too scared to open them.

<hr>

Lark went to Zee and put a hand on her shoulder—a distant gesture, but it was all she could do to push through the strange dark cloud in her mind. Something had changed in her when she put on the collar. With her free hand, she probed at the clasp that held it closed around her neck. She wondered if she could remove it, but the dark cloud devoured the thought before it could linger, before her body could act. Her focus, then, came back to her sister and the instructions from the man who called himself Sin.

"Put on that white dress, and everything will be fine," Lark said.

Zee opened her eyes, making a point not to look up at Lark, and then scanned the room until she found the blonde woman's corpse.

Lark felt a shudder ripple through Zee's body.

"He said you had to put the dress on... or you would die," Lark said. The words sounded deranged even to her own ears. She tried to explain—about the flashes of dreams when she put on the collar, about the spiked armor that had formed around her, about the man with the aura that inverted the world, about the feeling of power that now filled her like a hive of bees buzzing and eager to be released.

"I don't understand any of this," Zee said in a whisper.

Neither do I, Lark thought. While her sister's mind was full of unanswered questions, Lark's mind had too many answers—answers that seemed to come from the memories of others. Just then, a thunderous boom echoed through the room, sending ripples through the syrupy blood on the ground. It sounded like a giant church bell. Whatever the noise was, it triggered memories of fear in Lark's mind.

"We have to leave before it gets here," Lark said, although she didn't know what *it* was. It had something to do with the bodies on the ground. *The Košmaro!* a voice in her head said.

Lark grabbed her sister's hand and yanked her toward what looked like the main entry of the chapel at the far end beyond the pews. "Wait," she said as they reached the door. She ran back to the woman in the white dress and proceeded to strip it off her with no care whatsoever to the woman's body, to the unnaturally pristine garment, or to the blood she splattered as she yanked and pulled.

With the dress in hand and a chunky glob of bloody pulp running down the left side of her face, Lark smiled at her twin sister. "Okay. You can put it on when you're ready. Let's get out of here. Oh… and you're still the rabbit."

CHAPTER 1
A KNIFE THROUGH THE HEART

It always felt like the dead of night in the Grand Staircase. If there were clocks on its black stone walls, their hour, minute, and second hands would all point straight up, to the number twelve perched like a gargoyle atop the clock face. But there were no clocks on the walls in the Grand Staircase. Only sconces with slender finger-like candles, and far too few of them. Candles that barely illuminated the cold black handrail and obsidian steps that twisted, above and below, into darkness.

Paul had taken the habit of counting out loud each step as he descended the stairs.

"Four hundred and twelve," his voice echoed through the giant stone cylinder. "Four hundred and thirteen."

He didn't know—he never knew—how many steps there would be. The number changed each time. Once, it had been as few as twenty, and another had been almost two thousand. Paul counted as an inoculation against madness; whether it worked or not was still up for debate.

The Grand Staircase allowed for travel from one world of the Between to the next. Alone, Paul descended toward the Garden of Before, the fourth world of the Between, a world he had only read about but had never reached in each of his previous, failed expeditions.

At a count of five hundred and ninety-nine, just over ten minutes after Paul had begun his descent, light emerged at the bottom.

Sunlight.

Paul stood on the landing that extended outward from the final step of the staircase with his hand shielding his squinting eyes, the sun warming his skin. A thought occurred to him. Was this the same sun that shined down on him back home in the sky above Austin, Texas? Everything else about the Between—its laws of nature, its creatures, even the people with familiar names and faces—they were all different, alien. But the sun above seemed to be the same. Like the number of stairs he had traversed in the Grand Staircase, this piece of information—assuming it was true that this sun was *the sun*—had no real utility beyond anchoring an unmoored mind drifting toward madness.

Madness was the Between's quiet killer. So, Paul embraced any defense he could find against it.

He looked out and for the first time saw the Garden of Before.

***

What makes a plot of land a garden? Is it defined by the effort invested into its development and maintenance? Does a garden have to be intentional: a forced region of order, a bulwark against the ever-encroaching chaos of nature? Or can a garden be a product of nature? A place of serene beauty born of no plan, shaped without a hand tending its soil or pulling its weeds?

Nothing about the Garden of Before looked like it had been crafted or designed, yet it was hard for Paul to imagine that nature could create such a place. Rolling hills covered with red wildflowers extended out from the staircase in all directions. Green and brown vines snaked through the flowers like veins through the inner flesh of a great beast. To Paul's left, which he thought of as west irrespective of whether that was correct or not, the vines grew and twisted together into spiraling towers, creating what resembled a miniature Seussian city. To the east, the blood red flowers gave way to tall orange grass that swayed and pulsed in the breeze. In the north, purple-leafed trees peaked above the nearby hills. One hill in particular was large enough that Paul spent a moment considering what to call something that was too big to be a hill yet too small to be a mountain. This dwarf mountain, or whatever it was, had a beautiful waterfall cascading down its rocky face to a stream below.

Each time the breeze changed direction, it brought with it a new mélange of complex smells. It reminded Paul of the unexpected fragrance shop he and his wife, Julie, had found on the stairway up to Prague Castle in the Czech Republic. The shop had been filled with glass decanters of gold and amber liquids. The fragrance maker offered to concoct a unique scent for each of them, and when they happily agreed, he began a funny little ritual, waving combinations of glass stoppers in front of their faces to fill the air with effervescent olfactory creations. Perhaps most memorable to both Paul and Julie was that the fragrance maker's pants had been unzipped, gapingly so, while he performed his wafting dance.

Somewhere in the mix of floral and vegetal scents, Paul detected the unmistakable vetiver note that had been the heart of Julie's custom fragrance. As quickly as he smelled it, the breeze took the scent away and replaced it with something foreign and bitter.

Paul caught himself reminiscing, took a deep breath, and tried to maintain focus on what he was doing and the world around him. The slightest misstep in the Between could be fatal, and no place in the Between was more dangerous than an unfamiliar world.

Focus, Paul. Focus.

According to the FAQ, the Garden of Before "stretched out infinitely in all directions across space and time." Infinite space he could understand—at least conceptually. He assumed it meant that if he traveled in a straight line through the Garden's fields of flowers and vegetation, he'd never reach an end. The fields would go on forever. The meaning of infinite time, on the other hand, was less clear. Didn't all worlds stretch out infinitely across time? Or, if not infinitely, at least book-ended by the Big Bang on one side and the heat death of the universe on the other?

But time behaved differently in the Between than it did in the real world, or what Paul thought of as the real world. His first few days in the Between took place in mere minutes back home. Indeed, when his partner-in-crime, Jay, emerged at Paul's Central Austin home only an hour or so after Paul did, Jay claimed to have been gone for weeks and had the scruffy beard to prove it.

Paul assumed the FAQ's language about time was hand-wavy mumbo jumbo made more inscrutable by a lousy translation from the original Esperanto. He learned within his first ten steps into the Garden how wrong he was.

Footworn paths led north, south, east, and west from the Grand Staircase. Perhaps two hundred yards or so in each direction was an obelisk of glass or crystal. It was hard to tell from this distance, and the FAQ gave very little detail, but each one appeared to be about fifteen or twenty feet tall. What the FAQ did say was that similar obelisks could be found occupying nodes on a giant grid of paths throughout the Garden. Each obelisk reflected light from the sun and from its hyaline twin. They were painfully bright and difficult to look at directly.

Paul decided he had hesitated long enough and set out down the path leading north, trying to follow the FAQ's instructions. As usual, its guidance was cryptic:

> It doesn't matter which way you go. All that matters is that you walk in spirals. Straight paths lead first to confusion, then to madness, and finally, to death.

Walk in spirals? How? The answer seemed relatively clear. The patchwork nature of the gardens reminded him of the sitting room maze in the Between's first world, the Patchwork World. Just like in that maze, he found himself faced with four choices at every node.

To walk in a spiral, he would simply turn the same direction each time. North then east. East then south. South then west. West then north. That route should lead him directly back to his starting point, to the foot of the Grand Staircase. But he suspected the weird mechanics of the Between would cause that path to lead him *elsewhere*. Paul's goal was to find the one obelisk that differed from the others. The nexus, as the FAQ named it, appeared to be a fifty-foot-tall black obelisk, but it wasn't a physical object. It was a void of some kind at the precise center of the Between, where all the overlapping outworlds intersected. Paul had become increasingly obsessed with the nexus, certain it held the answers to the Between's mysteries.

And those mysteries gnawed at him. He had no hope of escaping the Between, not with the Silver Spiral on his forearm. Not after seeing Jay and Supriya revert to their roles as *stelisto* and *gardistaro*. He wasn't here to escape. He was here to find an explanation, and if he died looking for that explanation... well... at least death would come while he stared into the Between's metaphorical eyes instead of being run down like a scared animal.

"I am the seeker," he said aloud. "I am the *serĉilo*."

With a swell of confidence, he walked forward, slow and steady. Almost immediately, something felt wrong. He looked back on the short distance he'd traveled and saw a desiccated body on the path—mostly skeletal remains in scraps of tattered cloth. The skeleton obviously hadn't been there a moment ago. He would've seen it, would've had to step over it. Strangely, though, he *did* feel like he'd stepped over something.

But how could he have stepped over a skeleton without noticing it? He turned back toward the north, toward the obelisk that was his first destination. Reflected light from its glassy exterior glared at him. He could make no sense of the skeleton or its sudden appearance, so he pushed it out of his mind and continued toward the obelisk.

About halfway there, he saw something—no, some*one*—at the obelisk, partially hidden by the glare.

"Hello?" he said.

The figure stepped to the side of the obelisk. It was Paul himself, wearing the same clothes he had on now: white T-shirt, jeans, hiking boots. The other Paul was staring at him, studying him, but without any surprise evident on his face. As if the other Paul had expected to see himself approaching on the pathway. Then, the other Paul's eyes grew wide, and he looked to his side, either at the obelisk or something behind it. "Shit!" the other Paul yelled, turned, and began scurrying down the path to the north—a path obscured both by the obelisk and the downward slope of the hill beyond.

For a few seconds, Paul's mind refused to process what he had seen, and then a torrent of explanations came flooding through, causing his legs to go weak and a cold sweat to break out on his skin. It was a shapeshifter or mimic, some vile creature masquerading as him, and he had to kill it before it killed him and took his place! Or was it another Paul—an alternate Paul from an alternate outworld—who had found his way here as well? But at the exact same time, wearing the exact same outfit? That was too much. A copy, then? A reflection of some kind? The implications were too dizzying to explore. The only thing he knew for certain—and he wasn't sure why he knew this—was that he couldn't let himself get away.

"Wait!" Paul yelled at the other Paul, but the other Paul vanished from sight. So, he chased, without giving any thought to why or what he would do if he caught himself. By the time he reached the obelisk, the other Paul had made it halfway to the subsequent obelisk to the north, where the purple-leafed trees grew thicker together.

"Wait!" he yelled again, but the other Paul didn't slow. If he continued to chase him, he'd be moving in a straight path, precisely what the FAQ instructed not to do. He stopped and tried to calm himself before he did something reckless. And in that moment, he thought he understood what was happening. He was seeing himself...a minute or so in the future. If that were the case, then...

He looked back, and just as he feared, he saw his past self near the Grand Staircase, beginning to walk in his direction. His past self got a curious look on his face, paused, and turned to see a long-dead skeletal corpse on the path behind him. Then, just like Paul—the real, in-the-present Paul—had experienced it, he turned back toward the obelisk and saw himself.

Paul stared at his past self incredulously. And then he saw the corpse begin to twitch. The tattered cloth started to recompose, and flesh began to appear on the bones of the skeleton. Past-Paul, oblivious to the skeleton rising to its feet behind him, continued to stare at Paul.

"Hello?" Past-Paul called.

Paul was about to scream to warn the past version of himself, but as the air filled his lungs, he realized the warning was unnecessary. The skeleton hadn't caught him, so it wouldn't catch Past-Paul. But what happened to the skeleton? An icy chill ran down Paul's spine. He turned to his right as if drawn by the weight of a presence close by, and the skeleton was almost on top of him.

"Shit!" he exclaimed. Without considering what he was doing, he took off on the path leading north, exactly as he had watched himself do not even a minute before. Over his shoulder, he could see the skeleton following him, only it wasn't a skeleton anymore. The muscle and flesh had grown back over most of the exposed bones, and the tattered clothing had continued to repair itself. Same white T-shirt. Same jeans. Same brown hiking boots. Wisps of brown hair waving about the top of its head, and its eyes— green eyes just like Paul's—staring back at him as it staggered, following.

It was another Paul—or a future Paul. *His* future. *Fuck.* Did that mean that he was going to die no matter what he did? How was that possible?

The dead Paul was walking toward him, jaw hinging up and down as if it were trying to speak. It didn't have its hands stretched out to grab Paul, zombie-style. Instead of looking hungry and growling *BRAINS!*, it looked confused and maybe even sad.

Still, Paul wasn't taking any chances. He turned back toward the north and started to run, ignoring the voice in his head screaming that he was going the wrong way. He could see a future-Paul—or maybe it was the same future-Paul he'd been following—continue past the next obelisk surrounded by strange trees that looked like upside-down octopuses with white, quivering tentacle-limbs.

Straight paths lead first to confusion, then to madness, and finally to death.

The words from the FAQ echoed in his head. He had already passed confusion and was knee-deep in madness. If he didn't turn off the straight path soon...but if he could see himself continuing forward, was it even possible to change course?

At the next obelisk, he turned right toward what should've been east. Down the east path he saw exactly what he had seen to the north: future-Paul running ahead through the octopus plants. He turned back to the left, back to what should have been north, but instead he saw Past-Paul running toward him with Dead-Paul shuffling close behind.

He spun around, looking down one path and then another. Every time he turned, he saw a different path than he expected. Either the world around the obelisk was shifting, or he truly had gone mad.

A voice, gruff, low, and animal-like, called out from his left. Beyond the octopus plants stood one of the creatures that Jay had called *ganglions*, with too-long arms and spidery fingers. It wore a long coat and a black bowler hat tipped down low, covering half of the creature's bulging, oversized eyes.

"Come this way, human," it said. "The *naĝanto* is already hunting you." It beckoned with its spidery fingers and then cackled. "Continue to wander, and it will find you and devour you. Ruki will save you from yourself."

Paul took a step backward, away from the creature. He had

encountered ganglions before in the City Above, the Between's third world. None of those encounters had been pleasant. And a pack of them had chased Jay right before the run-in with the *Kosmaro*. But this ganglion—Ruki, it had called itself—wasn't chasing him now. It was offering to save Paul from something that *was* chasing him.

"What is the *naĝanto*?" Paul asked. The name sounded familiar. He knew he had seen it in the FAQ, but he couldn't remember anything about its entry.

Ruki shook its bulbous head. "The *naĝanto* swims in the Garden looking for helpless fish to eat. Are you a little fishy, human? Let me help you, fishy-fishy."

That toothy grin told Paul all he needed to know about Ruki's trustworthiness. Paul turned south, or what he thought was south. He was about to begin down that path when the ganglion called out to him again.

"No-no-no, don't you go that way, fishy. To go back the way you came is to un-live your life."

"I didn't come this way," Paul yelled back.

The ganglion shook its head and flashed a smile full of long, sharp teeth. "You are all turned around. Twisted in body and twisted in mind! Look again down that path and tell Ruki you don't see your death."

Paul turned away from the ganglion and now saw his dead self shuffling toward him. Dead-Paul was trying to speak, jaw working up and down, but no sound came out of his mouth. Dead-Paul's muscle and skin had largely re-formed, leaving him looking like a week-old corpse instead of the skeleton he had been only minutes before. The T-shirt he wore had a dark bloodstain covering its left half.

"You see, don't you, human?" the ganglion said. "Let Ruki guide you. Ruki knows the Garden. Ruki will help you escape the *naĝanto*. Ruki will show you Fangblossom."

Fangblossom? What the hell was Fangblossom? Paul had perused the whole FAQ, and he was certain he had never read that word before. Fangblossom. It sounded like something out of *Little*

Shop of Horrors. "Why should I trust you?" Paul asked, turning back toward the ganglion named Ruki.

"Because you do not trust yourself, fishy. Come. Let me show you Fangblossom. Fangblossom holds the answers to whatever you seek in the Garden."

"I doubt that. Thanks, but no thanks."

Paul looked back toward the approaching Dead-Paul, which was now only twenty feet or so away, those so-familiar green eyes pleading with him. But pleading for what? Down the path to his right—he no longer had any idea which cardinal direction that was—he saw a path of trampled yellow flowers leading to yet another obelisk. An empty path. Was emptiness a good thing or an indicator of oblivion? In the opposite direction, he saw a living version of himself walking. A small red creature with wings and a long, swaying tail was following him. A *diableto*? Paul had read that these little mischievous devils were obsessed with murder and death, but he had never encountered one before.

"Well, I'm certainly not going that way," he muttered. He took a step toward Ruki, whose eyes seemed to glow at Paul's choice.

"Yes, yes. Come. See Fangblossom."

Paul took another step.

Ruki's eyes grew wider still. "Dawdle-dawdle fishy, and your past will catch up to you. If your past passes you, then what present can be left? Hurry and come."

A scuffing sound approached from behind. Dead-Paul shuffling in pursuit? Paul resisted the urge to look over his shoulder and instead began walking toward Ruki. "What is this *Fangblossom*? And why should I see it?"

Ruki hopped from one foot to the other in a giddiness that made Paul think he had made a very bad mistake. But he couldn't turn back now, could he? Not without encountering his dead self —and that seemed about the worst thing imaginable.

The ganglion adjusted his bowler hat and said, "Fangblossom is a little girl. The sweetest girl in the Garden. Sweeter than the purple flowers that grow near the exit staircase." It stopped its giddy hopping, and its eyes flared with a sinister look. "Flowers you will never smell. An exit you will never see."

Paul spun around. Walking toward him was not the dead version of himself that he expected. It was, instead, the *diableto* he had seen down the other path. Paul took a half step backward, but that direction took him toward the ganglion, and so he stopped, frozen as the little red creature approached.

Behind him, Ruki's raspy voice said, "Ah, my sweet little girl approaches. This is Fangblossom!"

"What the hell is it?" Paul asked Ruki. To the little creature, he said, "Are you a *diableto*? I mean you no harm."

"*It*? Did you call me an *it*? I'm not an *it*. You're an *it*!" the *diableto* named Fangblossom said. She looked like the love child of a cherub and a devil. Somehow both adorable and terrifying at the same time. When she got within ten feet of Paul, Fangblossom unfurled her wings and began hovering in the air so that her head was at the same level as his. She wore a broad smile that was contradicted by massive pairs of upper and lower fangs. Likewise, her puppy dog eyes were soured by irises the color of blood. As she continued speaking, her long tail swirled behind her like a flyfishing line in mid-cast. "You're a mean, nasty creature, calling me an *it*!"

"What?" Paul stammered. "I... I didn't mean anything by it. I've never seen a...uh... *diableto* or whatever you are."

"You continue to insult her," Ruki said and then added a menacing snicker. "I thought you were deserving of help. We should have let the *naĝanto* eat you, but it will not get the chance."

Paul turned back toward Ruki, who had silently closed the distance between them and was licking his lips. Paul swung back toward Fangblossom, mind reeling through possible next actions. Should he apologize? Run through the brambly plants next to the path? Or should he—

Fangblossom's tail whipped forward and struck Paul's chest like a little hammer. He started to yell at her, more surprised and angry than hurt. But all that came from his lips was a stuttering gasp. He looked down and saw that the tail's barbed tip had speared him through his chest. He sank to his knees. The little devil yanked her tail back, and a spout of blood followed, creating the same stain he had seen on the shirt of Dead-Paul just moments ago.

"I only help nice creatures who offer me something sweet... like MURDER," Fangblossom said as the energy drained from Paul's body, and the light was absorbed by darkness—a darkness that became everything and then nothing.

CHAPTER 2

ANOTHER OF LIFE'S LITTLE
ENDINGS

Out of the darkness, three words appeared.

YOU HAVE DIED

Paul slammed the laptop closed so hard he heard its screen crack. That sound jolted him back to the awareness of his surroundings. No longer in the Between. It was surreal how playing the command line game had become so immersive that he'd been losing himself in it, almost like it transported him back to the actual hidden world he had stumbled upon through the door buried in his backyard.

But he hadn't been back in the flesh. Every fiber of his being shook with fear at the idea of actually returning. The Between had pulled Jay and Supriya back within days of the fight with the *Kosmaro*. At first, they periodically returned to Texas and what Paul thought of as the real world, but the intervals dragged out until Paul no longer thought he would see them again. The last time had been, what, a month ago? Maybe more? And before dawn this morning, Corinne had left as well, saying goodbye only to Julie.

Paul put his hands flat on his desk to keep the room from spinning. It was the big oak desk in his hospital office, which was converted from a patient room decades before. The temperature never rose above 65 degrees, no matter how many space heaters he and his officemates used.

He absently twisted the snakelike bracelet around his left wrist —a peculiar piece of jewelry that had prompted many questions from his colleagues despite his efforts to keep it hidden. "I got it in Santa Fe recently," was his unconvincing response. He couldn't very easily tell them what it really was: the Silver Spiral, the artifact of the *serĉilo*—the searcher. He didn't want to be the *serĉilo*. Try as he might, he couldn't remove the bracelet. Not without cutting off his hand, anyway. So, he still was the *serĉilo*. And either through the bracelet or through his role as the *serĉilo*, the Between pulled at him to go back.

"What was that noise, Paul? It sounded like something breaking. It wasn't your laptop, was it?" Ramona Buck, the hospital's chief operating officer, appeared in his doorway, her arms folded across her navy suit jacket. Ramona was somewhere around Paul's age of thirty-two. Maybe a year or two older. She was tall and slender, being a marathoner with finish line photographs covering the walls of her office, and was the single loudest person Paul had ever met. Her laughter could wind its way from one corner of a hospital floor to the other. And when she was angry, everyone in the neighboring counties knew about it.

Paul was about to respond when he noticed someone else outside his door, pacing behind Ramona. Then the pacer stepped into view, and a voice in the back of Paul's head started yelling out warnings, much as it had when he had encountered the ganglion moments ago in the game—the ganglion that had lured him to his death.

The other person outside Paul's door was Lawrence Filby, the regional human resources director, a wide, balding man in his fifties who always seemed to be sweating, even in the frigid lower-level offices.

Without invitation or even a word of response from Paul, Ramona and Lawrence entered his office. Lawrence sat, opened a notebook, and took a pen from his rumpled shirt pocket. Ramona only uncrossed her arms briefly to shut the office door.

The voice in Paul's head grew louder, and he had the sudden urge to run. But there was nowhere to run. He was trapped.

"Paul, why were you not at the finance review this morning?"

He started to respond, but she talked over him.

"You didn't complete your forecast by the deadline on Tuesday, and now I'm the one who looks bad to corporate. No, strike that. The whole hospital looks bad because of you."

"I thought the finance review was next Tuesday. Isn't it always the third Tuesday of the month?"

Ramona shook her head and stared at him.

"This Tuesday *was* the third Tuesday of the month," Lawrence Filby said and then moistened his lips. He held a hand up to keep Ramona from peppering Paul with more questions and then said, "Paul, please tell me again how you got that swirling injury on your forehead."

Paul touched his forehead where the *Koŝmaro* had carved a spiral with the long, black talon of its index finger. "I... uh... I fell. Like I told you before."

"It's not just the strange injuries," Ramona said. "Have you looked in the mirror, Paul? Your clothes are all wrinkled and stained. You're missing deadlines. Not responding to emails. Not showing up to meetings." She pointed at the small pieces of glass next to his laptop. "And did you just break your computer? Is that what that crashing sound was?"

Paul rubbed his face. "My hand slipped. I mean, I didn't... I wasn't trying to break it. I shut it too hard by accident."

Lawrence Filby shook his head.

"I know I've been distracted because of the fire," Paul said. "I guess I'm still having a hard time processing it all."

Now Ramona was pacing, and for what seemed like a solid minute, no one spoke. Finally, she stopped and looked directly into Paul's eyes. "Paul, you're fired."

The words hit him like Fangblossom's barbed tail in his heart.

I'm what? he tried to say, but the words wouldn't come out.

"Thank you, Ramona. I can take it from here," Lawrence said.

Ramona Buck left Paul's office, shutting the door behind her. While Lawrence recited severance details and pushed forms in front of Paul, Ramona's voice echoed through the hospital hallways as she spoke to everyone she passed. The last thing Paul heard was the echo of her laugh.

Standing outside of the hospital under the glaring eye of the August Texas sun, Paul called Julie on his phone. They had lost everything when the *Kosmaro* followed him from the Between, through the iron door buried in their backyard. Their small bungalow house was now a pit of char and ash, surrounded by a ring of chain-link fence covered with yellow *DANGER!* signs. Their homeowner's insurance policy didn't cover destruction by giant reality-warping demons. Both their cars, nestled away in the house's garage, had been turned to slag when the *Kosmaro* died in a miniature supernova of white-hot flame. Their auto insurance, surprisingly, had provided them with a single rental car while the nature of the "accident" was investigated.

Julie drove the rental, dropping Paul off at the hospital in the morning and picking him up after she finished work in the late afternoon. Rather than wait several hours for her to arrive on schedule, he needed her now, needed to see and touch and hear her. Needed proof that she, too, was still present in his life after everything else had vanished or been destroyed.

After several rings, the call went to her voicemail. He called again, and again she didn't answer. He texted, *Need you to call me. Important.* And waited. Then texted again. *Jules?*

An hour passed with no response. At first, he thought she must have been tied up in a meeting, but Julie was the most phone-reliable person he knew. If she didn't respond given a reasonable amount of time, it was because she couldn't...or had chosen not to.

He considered calling a taxi, but with their bank account dwindling—not to mention the sudden loss of his income—he didn't want to spend a dime he didn't have to. So, he texted Julie, *Got fired. Walking to the hotel. Maybe a walk will do me good. Love you.* Then he started walking.

The two and a half hour walk in the afternoon sun while wearing a wool suit did not, in fact, do him good. Nor did the empty hotel room when he arrived. Nor did Julie's continued lack of response to his calls and text. Nor her absence that evening.

He sat on the edge of the hotel bed, not knowing what to do next. For all of Paul's life, he'd had a plan. Now there was nothing. He looked up and stared at his own colorless reflection on the dead television screen.

"She's gone," his reflection said. He turned away from it, but even with his head buried under the pillows and his hands pressed against his ears he could hear the voice. His voice. "She's gone."

CHAPTER 3
A MONSTER IN HUMAN FORM

Three days earlier, Corinne sat on the edge of the bed, listening to Paul and Julie go through their morning routine in the adjacent hotel room. She stared at the closed door connecting their two rooms as if she were staring at Paul and Julie themselves. In her mind she saw them quietly making coffee and breakfast, eating while mindlessly scrolling on their phones, brushing their teeth, et cetera, et cetera, barely saying a word to each other, just as they would barely speak during the car ride to the hospital where Paul worked.

When they left, it became only marginally quieter—as quiet as a morning could get at the ThriftySuites Extended Stay Hotel on the busy Interstate Highway 35 south of downtown. Heavy feet still pounded on the ceiling above her, children cried, and televisions blared through paper-thin walls.

She opened the door to Paul and Julie's room. Like hers, it was almost bare. All the Prentices' worldly possessions had been destroyed, and now they had nothing. Like Corinne had nothing. She poured the remaining coffee into a cheap porcelain mug and grabbed the sugar-topped blueberry muffin they left out for her.

She turned back toward her room and found another Corinne standing a few feet away, also with a mug of coffee and a muffin in hand. The rooms each had a wall mirror mounted on the adjoining doors. Corinne had removed hers and placed it facing the wall in the closet. The mirror in Paul and Julie's room, however, still hung on their door. Every morning before the coffee kicked in, she forgot about this, and every morning she felt the same shock, confusion, and ultimately disgust that the image before her was her own reflection.

Julie saw it happen several days back, on a Saturday or Sunday. Paul had gone somewhere, maybe to the grocery store, so it had just been the two of them.

"Is that why you took the mirror off your door?" Julie had asked, gray eyes fixed on Corinne's own. No small talk. No warning signs from the little, buzz-haired woman that those gray eyes were about to pierce directly into Corinne's soul.

Julie didn't have to say that Paul conveyed everything Corinne had told him. The anorexia. The career-ending ballet injury. The pain meds, and then stronger meds, and then more meds but now from forged scripts. Finally, the heroin. The look in Julie's eyes said she knew all this. Everything.

Corinne let her lack of response be the answer.

"Do you want me to take the mirror down?" Julie asked.

"No. It's not your problem, it's mine."

Julie narrowed her eyes as if she were evaluating Corinne's words. Then she gave a nonchalant shrug and said, "Well, I don't know what you see. But what I see in front of me now is the face of a woman who put herself between a demon and the rest of us. I see a woman who hasn't been broken by what she's gone through and isn't going to be broken by whatever this is."

Now, alone, standing in front of her reflection, Corinne saw only the toll the past had taken on her. The dark circles under her eyes. The two parallel creases in her forehead. The mottled, sun-damaged skin. She wished the mask she wore in the Between had stayed with her here in this world that wasn't her world. Wearing that mask, she wasn't Corinne Pelletier; she was Skull Girl, a ruthless survivor. The longer she went without the mask, the further away Skull Girl felt, and the more trapped she felt in the skin of Corinne.

She could see how emaciated she still was even after weeks of eating real food and not constantly running for her life. She also saw arms that could be thinner, despite being almost nothing but muscle and bone. Cheeks that weren't sunken in enough. Thighs that would betray her on the scale that sat in the corner of the ballet practice hall, a practice hall she hadn't seen in almost a decade and that she would never return to.

Some monsters she could kill, others she could escape, but the most frightening ones were inside her, and the more she sat alone in that hotel room, the more those inner monsters began to prowl and hunt.

She put on some cheap cargo pants, a white tank top Julie had picked up at Target, and some chunky combat boots Paul got her to replace the pair she had taken from a corpse in the Between.

A quick stop in the bathroom, leaving the light off and never facing the mirror, and then she was out, walking through the streets in South Austin without any destination in mind. Since coming to this hotel with the Prentices, she'd spent her days wandering while they were at work. She carried no money because she had none. Paul left a small stack of twenty-dollar bills on the kitchen counter and invited her to take what she needed, but the stack remained untouched.

Despite being penniless, she would occasionally have lunch in restaurants—never the same ones, always with table service, the more crowded the better. She would eat half her meal and then ask someone at a neighboring table to watch over her plate while she ran to the restroom. By the time people realized she wasn't coming back, she was blocks away.

She justified this and the occasional petty shoplifting by reminding herself that this wasn't her world. That justification worked fine for Skull Girl but not so fine for Corinne Pelletier. And the more that Skull Girl retreated inward, the more that guilt followed Corinne on those walks like a second shadow. As her guilt grew, she found herself stealing more and doing it more recklessly. She asked herself why she was doing this and came up with two answers. The first: self-flagellation. That one was obvious. She was a bad person who did bad things and deserved to wear the guilt of those deeds like a mantle of heavy chains. The second pushed her into thoughts she'd been failing to avoid. This all had to end, one way or another. Maybe she was trying to force an ending. Maybe some part of her wanted to be caught, arrested, and put into a cage. Whatever happened, she couldn't keep on living in a cheap hotel room paid for by Paul and Julie, couldn't keep wandering the streets aimlessly every day.

But what were her alternatives? Try to make a life in this world? There was already another Corinne Pelletier here some-where—that is, unless she had died, which was entirely possible if her life had mirrored Corinne's own. Either way, she couldn't be herself here, and she had no idea how to be someone else. The only alternative was to return to the Between like Jay and Supriya had. But that would be suicide, and if she wanted to go that route, there were less painful ways to do it.

So, her aimless walks continued.

Until that morning, when something *did* happen.

She entered a convenience store to acquire a pack of gum. Stealing things turned out to be much easier than she would've thought. It didn't require sleight of hand and magician-like dexter-ity. The clerk in this store—a man in his late forties or fifties, possibly the owner—had likely seen it all. And she was the only customer in the store. She greeted the clerk and walked purpose-fully toward the back to scan the limited section of household goods.

"Looking for something?" the clerk asked.

"Allergy eye drops," Corinne replied. "Whatever is in the air is killing me. Is it oak pollen?"

"Oak pollen is in March and April around here," the clerk said. Then he turned and looked at the shelf behind the register where the eye drops were kept—small, expensive, and high risk of theft. "We have Visine, Opticon, and... uh... let's see here."

Corinne walked toward the counter, grabbing and pocketing a

single pack of gum from the shelf on her left, and said, "Anything with an antihistamine?"

The clerk looked back over his shoulder and said, "It looks like we only have these two. If you want something else, there's a Walgreens down the road."

She thanked him, wished him a nice day, and went to leave. As she reached for the door, a man on the other side pulled it open and held it for her, less out of politeness than simply to avoid a collision.

Corinne froze.

It was Matt Waggoner, her former dealer and quasi-boyfriend. His teeth were unnaturally white except for a yellow-stained circle right in the front where he sucked in cigarette smoke. He smelled like cheap cologne and gasoline.

Corinne felt like an animal trapped in the corner of a cage while a hand reached in to grab her. If everything rotten about her past life had been compressed into human form, that form would be Matt Waggoner. What was Matt doing over here? He haunted the East Side, over where 7th hit 183.

"In or out, lady," Matt said without any sign that he recognized her.

Over his shoulder, she saw her own reflection in the glass door. Dark shadows encircled her eyes, a painted skull beginning to emerge on her face. Her right hand reflexively grabbed one of the knives she kept on her belt, but that belt and the knives were back in the hotel closet. She jumped through the doorway and backed away from him, heart racing.

Matt gave her a dismissive scowl and was about to proceed into the store when a curious look took his face. "If you need something to calm you down, I got better stuff than you'll find in here."

Those words were as sharp as any blade.

Outside, a woman stood by the door, shivering despite the late summer heat. She looked like she might have been beautiful once. Early twenties, hair not washed in days, maybe weeks. Dirty nails. Bruises all over her pale skin. The woman looked like a younger version of Corinne at her worst. Just Matt's type. "C'mon, Matt. Let's go," she said.

"Don't you fucking tell me what to do," he replied.

Corinne continued to back away through the parking lot—only she wasn't Corinne anymore. She was Skull Girl. Skull Girl didn't care that this world's version of Matt didn't recognize her. The Corinne of this world, for better or for worse, had apparently never fallen in with Matt. He wasn't a threat. But to Skull Girl, he was a monster.

Matt disappeared into the store. Corinne hustled through the parking lot while keeping eyes on the door. The Corinne part of her mind, now relegated to the back, was trying to process what it meant that Matt hadn't recognized her. Skull Girl ignored all this, scanning the nearby area for possible weapons. It was always better to run than to fight, but not all fights could be avoided.

Something familiar in her periphery caught her attention. Parked in front of a fire hydrant was a beat-up yellow 1991 Honda Civic del Sol, with a mismatched green left front fender. Matt's car. The same car or at least the parallel version of the car she had ridden in countless times, with the same worn-through cloth seats, the same pine tree air freshener hanging from the rearview mirror, the same hole in the dash where a car stereo had been ripped out, and the same 8-ball knob on the gear shifter.

Before Corinne knew what she was doing, she had reached through the targa top and opened the driver's side door. She pulled up the corner of the floor mat and found the car key where Matt always put it rather than carrying it with him. His reasoning had never made sense to her. Something about him just borrowing the car and it not really being his, even though he had been driving it for months. That, or maybe it was one of Matt's many obsessive-compulsive quirks—not wanting anything in his pockets. Whatever the reason was, it didn't matter. All that mattered was that Corinne was now in the driver's seat with the engine rattling, ready to escape.

The woman near the door noticed Corinne and screamed

louder than should have been possible from her skin-and-bones frame. "Fuckin' bitch is stealing your car, Matt! MATT!"

The store's glass door flew open, and Matt came running out. Running right at her. It would've been easy to drive straight ahead. He never could have caught her. But that's not what Corinne did. She turned the car toward him, dropped the clutch, and floored it, hopping over the curb. He tried to jump out of the way, but his forward momentum caused him to slip on the asphalt instead.

The car's bumper struck him in the hip and slammed him down like a rag doll on the pavement. His body made two thumps against the undercarriage, and then, with a hard swerve to the left, Corinne had the car back on the road and was speeding away. She glanced in the rearview mirror to make sure the monster was dead, but the mirror had been tilted toward the driver's side. Instead of Matt's corpse, she saw herself, no skull painted on her face.

For the next two days, Corinne stayed in her room, waiting for the police to knock on the door or kick it in. But the only knock had been from Julie, checking on her. Corinne said she wanted to be left alone, and Julie obliged.

Corinne had ditched the car a few miles away with the key in the ignition and blood still smeared over the left headlight. She didn't care about herself being caught. But there was another Corinne in this world who shared her fingerprints and didn't deserve to be connected to Matt's death, so she had used her shirt to wipe her fingerprints from the steering wheel and other places in the car she had touched. Quick and mechanical, as if she had done this before.

She expected to feel guilty but instead found a hole within herself where the guilt was supposed to be. Corinne had killed before while in the Between. Cold, necessary deaths that somehow didn't count, just like killing *this* Matt somehow didn't count. But it should have, right? Running Matt down with a car wasn't self-defense, and who was she to play judge, jury, and executioner?

She didn't eat for two days. Her hunger slid away easily. It knew it wasn't wanted. After hunger came the familiar, hazy euphoria she'd been cocooned in during her ballet days. She pulled the mirror out of the closet and propped it against the wall, then stripped out of her clothes and stood before it.

Her eyes tried to turn away, but the Skull Girl part of her wouldn't let them. In that moment, trembling and staring at her own emaciated form, it was as if she truly split in two. Skull Girl was no longer the cold and dark side of Corinne Pelletier but a separate being that had emerged from her flesh. The *Dia de los Muertos* mask began to form on her face. Not the paint she had applied that night long ago while sitting atop the parking garage, the paint that the Between kept fresh day after day. No, this mask was deeper than paint, staining her skin all the way through to her bones. The stain began to spread down her neck. The white bones of a skeleton came first. Then an orange and golden glow around the bones, tongues of flame by the hundreds. Rose vines with blooms and bleeding thorns came next. Finally, the inky darkness covering the rest of her.

The mirror reflected both bodies, like two film cells laid atop one another. If Julie had been standing next to her, Julie would only have seen Corinne's naked flesh—not the stained, blazing image of *Santa Muerte*, our Lady of the Holy Death. Corinne knew this, but it didn't make the stain of death any less real.

The image of herself as death brought with it a clarity she had been looking for but had thus far never found. She had always felt haunted, or maybe a better word was *cursed*—cursed by the universe, where the shiny objects of happiness and meaning would be dangled in front of her, and just as she was about to grab them, they'd be yanked away. Her spot within a prestigious New York dance company had been revoked after she had blown out her Achilles tendon in her final college show, and the ballet career she had worked so hard for, wrecked her body for, had been taken from her. And then, after building a new and unexpected career as the publisher of an art magazine, the same demon came for her again. The lingering pain from her dance injuries had led to a drug habit that had grown so wildly expensive and all-encompassing that it brought financial ruin to everything she had built. The collateral damage extended to almost everyone she knew. And finally came her time in the Between, where each person she met she eventually saw destroyed—sometimes mentally first, but always physically. Until she had nothing and wanted nothing, knowing that anything she touched would be cursed. Corrupted.

She had to go back into the Between. Not because it was pulling her back in like it had done to Jay and Supriya, like it was trying to do to Paul. Skull Girl wasn't a role from the Between; it was a role that had originated within her. She had to go back because the Between was the only place that *deserved* her presence, her corruption.

She heard a cabinet close in the Prentices' room next door and felt like she had been jarred out of a deep, dream-filled sleep. In the mirror, she no longer saw her second stained skin. She turned the mirror toward the wall and quickly put her clothes back on, laced up her combat boots, and filled her backpack with all her meager worldly possessions. Then she opened the door.

Julie, standing in the kitchen in a dark blue robe, nearly dropped the glass she was filling with water in the sink. The clock on the oven showed it was 4:28 a.m.

"Sorry. I didn't realize what time it was," Corinne said.

"Something on your mind?"

"I have to leave."

Julie stared blankly at Corinne for three full seconds and then nodded slowly, as if she had expected something like this. "I have this feeling I want something stronger than water for this conversation. Too early for coffee? I can make some scrambled eggs as well if you're hungry." Without waiting for an answer, Julie began preparing an early breakfast.

Corinne sat on the counter—the little half-kitchen had no table and chairs—and watched as Julie got the coffee started and cracked eggs into a glass bowl. Julie's silence was worse, somehow, than her usual piercing questions.

"I have to go back," Corinne said once the whisked eggs were poured into the frying pan.

Julie's eyes turned back toward her. "Why would you go back after everything you and Paul have told me about that place?" Julie only ever called the Between *that place.*

"Because I can't stay here, Julie. I don't mean here with you and Paul. I mean this world. I feel..." She paused for a moment, trying to find the words. "I feel like there's a darkness that follows me, and it's followed me here."

Julie turned back to the cooktop and nudged the solidifying yellow mixture with a wooden spoon. "A darkness that follows you? Like, has literally followed you here, like some kind of monster?"

"No, I think I am the monster."

At this, Julie turned and, without warning, pulled Corinne down from the counter and wrapped her up in a hug that was several sizes too big to have come from Julie's little frame. "Honey, you're not a monster."

Tears began pouring from Corinne's eyes, and the strength left her body. "I am, though. I am."

"No, you're not."

Corinne pushed Julie back. She would have told Julie everything that had happened with Matt to prove that she was, indeed, a monster, but that brief hug—the first caring physical contact she had felt in years—left her unable to speak.

Julie stepped back to her and again pulled her in, and this time Corinne held on to her and cried silent, body-shaking tears until long after the coffee maker finished and the eggs became burned and ruined.

Paul, in the neighboring bedroom, slept through all this, including the smell of fresh coffee and a second—this time, edible—batch of eggs.

Corinne ate her eggs, and when Julie pushed her own untouched plate in front of Corinne, she ate those as well.

"I have something to show you," Julie said and handed her phone to Corinne.

The phone's screen displayed Corinne's face, painted in the *Dia de los Muertos* style of *Santa Muerte*. Although similar, the photo's painted mask used different colors and was less intricate than Skull Girl's face. The photo was from a Facebook album belonging to Corinne Pelletier—this world's Corinne Pelletier.

"What the fuck, Julie? What the ever-loving fuck?"

"Keep scrolling," Julie said with the hint of a smirk.

Corinne's hand shook. The mask might look different, but the darkness had extended to this parallel Corinne as well. She reached a finger toward the screen, to swipe to the next photo, and saw the stain of the blazing bones begin spreading over her hand. She swiped—and almost dropped the phone. The painted face was still there but part of a bigger picture where she was handing out Halloween candy from a porch. Two little skeletons, girls with her own unmistakable dirty-blonde hair, stood next to her, gripping her dress, smiling at the camera.

The next dozen photos were of this little painted-skeleton family out in neighborhood streets with costumed heroes and monsters in the background. In one photo, a man she didn't recognize with a mask and wig that looked like Beetlejuice had his arm around Corinne and the two girls; the other arm was extended to take the picture selfie-style.

While Corinne continued to scroll through the photos of this world's Corinne, Julie said, "Sometimes the world feels very small. Your twin, here, and I have a mutual friend in common. Several, in fact. She's the principal at a small charter school. Married. Two kids, as you can see. The house looks like it's in Round Rock or Cedar Park."

Corinne couldn't take her eyes off the phone. She flipped quickly through the photos, seeing a kind of curated, reverse chronology of her doppelganger's recent life history.

"I don't see a lot of darkness here," Julie said.

"So she made better choices than me."

"I know your story, Corinne. Enough, anyway, to say bullshit to that. Some bad things happened. Life didn't turn out the way you wanted. But you talk as if you deserved it, somehow. Like you were fated to a dark end."

Corinne looked up at Julie. "What difference does it make that she didn't turn out like me? How does that change anything about my situation?"

"It changes whatever you want it to change, Corinne. If you're committed to finding your death by going back to *that place*, then I suppose it changes nothing. But that's your choice, not the universe compelling you."

"What if I don't want to live in the fucking suburbs and have a normal life?"

"You're not fated to that life, either. Can you get back to your world? Paul and Jay came back out the same door they went in through. Can you do the same?"

Corinne looked down at Julie's phone, as if it might hold the answer to the question. It didn't, so she handed it back. "I tried, initially."

"And then you gave up?"

"No. Well, maybe. For a while I was just trying to stay alive. I got good at that. Better than everyone else." Corinne got up and poured more coffee for them both. "It was easier for Jay and Paul. The door in your backyard led to a maze-like place. It's confusing, but once you understand how it works and where the dangers are, it's easy to navigate. My entry led to the ruins of a city in a desert. I was lucky to escape it, and I haven't been back. I'm not sure I could find the tower where my door was, or that the door would even still be there." More to herself than to Julie, she added, "Maybe with Supriya's help, I could ..." She shook her head. "The *malespero* rules the Ruins. It's too dangerous."

Julie stared with those gray eyes. When Corinne said no more, Julie said, "If it can't be done, it can't be done."

"Now you're just being provocative."

"That's what I do best. If I can't talk you out of going, you should at least go to live and not to die."

It was a quick goodbye. Corinne thanked Julie for everything and declined the offer for a ride back to the remains of the Prentices' house. The morning walk—all two hours of it—would do Corinne good.

Julie seemed to sense that Corinne didn't want another hug and instead held her hand out, which Corinne briefly squeezed.

The sun had not yet come up when she left.

CHAPTER 4
FIRST MOTHER

Later that morning, Julie sat in a rented Chrysler, engine running, air conditioner on full blast. She tried to point the vents so that they blew cold air down her shirt sleeves, to dry the sweat that had soaked through her clothes, but one of the vents wasn't cooperating. It was broken and pointed down unless she held it up.

After dropping Paul off at work, she drove to their old Central Austin home—or what rubble and ash remained of their old home. She hadn't meant to come here, but before she knew it, she had crawled under the orange-netting-wrapped fence littered with *DANGER!* signs.

She had stayed away for weeks, in part to avoid reliving that night in her memories, although that seemed to happen anyway, usually right before she was about to fall asleep. Her main reason for avoiding coming back was the profound sense of loss she felt when she saw the empty space where the house had been. Not long before all this happened, she had told Paul that material things didn't matter to her. Yet now that virtually all of their material possessions had been lost, her feelings didn't match her prior words. Some of those objects—those *things*—were imprinted with memories, most of which were shared memories between her and Paul. Souvenirs from their travels together. The shirt he had been wearing when they first met. The photo album Paul's grandmother had made of their wedding.

Paul's grandmother had since died. The photos had been taken with her film camera and had no digital counterparts, and now the album was so utterly gone it was as if it had never existed in the first place. As if the scenes it had captured hadn't happened.

The worst loss of all had been her platinum and diamond wedding ring. It had been sitting on a small melamine tray on her bedside table, and the heat of the fire warped the tray until it folded in on itself, turning into a protective shell—a small black charred egg. That egg had been sitting under the summer sun these past weeks, blending in with the rubble. How many police, firefighters, and insurance adjusters had stood right next to it?

Maybe it's what called her back this morning. Could an object do that? After what she had seen that night, she no longer knew what was and was not possible.

All that mattered now was that she had the ring back on her finger where it belonged. She promised herself that she would stop taking it off at night, that the ring would never leave her finger again. The future may have become uncertain, but the ring could be one small, stable thing she could count on.

Strangely, she had found another ring as well, one made of onyx or obsidian. It was completely unfamiliar, yet its dark shine really had called to her, or so it seemed. It looked like a circle of petrified, intertwined vines, one of which seemed to glow ever so slightly, as if it contained a filament of an incandescent light bulb. The black ring must have been stepped on countless times in the aftermath of the battle with the *Kosmaro*. It was a wonder she had seen it. It had seemed to glow for a moment, as if that little filament had flared, or perhaps it had been the sun's reflection. In any case, it had called to her, so she put it into her pocket and took it with her back to the car.

The black ring was now in her left palm, although she didn't remember taking it out of her pocket. It was as if her thoughts of the ring made it manifest itself in her hand. She could tell it was too large to fit on the ring finger of her right hand, yet it slid perfectly onto her right middle finger.

She held her hand up to examine the ring and saw that the smeared dirt was gone. Even between the twisting vines, where she hadn't been able to reach, was all clean somehow. The ring sparkled in the daylight—no, too bright to just be reflecting; it was shining with its own light, the filament casting the interior of the car in its glow. Then, barbs started digging into the flesh of her finger, little thorns on the vines that couldn't have been there before but were now pressing in, sending jolts of icy pain up her arm, into her chest, and into her mind and ...

...The world was replaced by a million dreams, a million flashes of another life, other lives, where her children were dying all around her, their bodies mangled and torn, but their little precious souls stayed intact, crying out for her to rescue them, to collect them and keep them safe, so safe that they could never be mangled and killed again, protected by iron, replacing weak flesh, iron that couldn't run away, her children all lined up neat and safe and protected and everlasting, oh the countless children, ever more children falling and needing their souls collected, the bell calling her, the Koŝmaro, to collect and collect and collect her poor children, her poor children...

The vision ended, and Julie's clothes and skin were now dry. She was shivering. She turned off the air conditioner and then turned the car's engine off as well.

She knew immediately what had happened. The spiral of metal on Paul's forearm, what he called an *artifact* from the Between—the black ring on her right middle finger was one of those same *artifacts*. The Silver Spiral, Paul had said, made him the *serĉilo*, the seeker, whether he wanted to be or not. Did that mean that she was now the—

Her mind wouldn't let her finish that thought. In panic, she tugged at the ring, tried to ignore the pain as it dug itself into her flesh as if to resist her attempts to remove it. It wouldn't budge.

She got out of the car, circled around the door, and tried putting her finger in the space where the door met the front fender. It was awkward on the driver's side; she would have to push with her left arm crossed in front of her, and maybe she wouldn't create the force needed to... to do what she had to.

Leaving the driver's side door open, she ran to the passenger side. Yes, much better. This would work. She put her right middle finger in the door jamb and readied herself, left hand grabbing the end of the door, her heart thudding in her chest, her muscles shaking but ready. She hesitated briefly; her body wasn't designed to do this to itself. But the image of the towering *Koŝmaro* holding Paul's body before it, scratching a spiral into his forehead—that, and the wave of panicked horror that came with it, overrode any mortal psychology. She wouldn't let herself become that thing.

She slammed the door as hard as she could, sending the planes of metal together as if they were blades on shears. Every part of her being strained to turn away, but she made herself watch. She saw how easily the metal severed the flesh and bone of her finger. She saw the finger and the ring vanish behind the closed door as blood began to spout from the stump on her hand where the finger had been.

But she saw more as well.

Overlaid on the wounded hand, she saw another hand: bigger and beastlike, with fingernails that resembled raven beaks. When the door had closed on this hand, the door itself—an overlaid version of the door—buckled and bent, leaving the beast hand unharmed and still wearing the ring, now larger to fit the larger hand. She saw this beast hand and dozens, no, hundreds of other versions of her hand, some harmed by the car door, but most were not.

She pulled her hand away and stared at the way reality seemed to vibrate and shift around it. Although she had seen her finger severed and the ring removed, that alternative hadn't come into being. The warping aura that had protected the *Koŝmaro* many nights before was now protecting her.

Because she was the *Koŝmaro*.

On the other side of the street, from within the living room of Min-woo Kim's house, a man watched as Julie slammed the car door again and again. Her silhouette had darkened to almost black, and the air around her crackled and shifted. Each slamming of the door did nothing to her, to the monster she had become. It only ruined the door further until finally she pulled it open, and it ripped off its hinges.

The man watched as she screamed a thousand screams at once, beast, human, and everything in between. Unlike the previous *Kosmaro*, whose silhouette looked almost insectile with its spider-like hands, Julie's *Kosmaro* took the shape of a minotaur with a pregnant body.

"Ah. Fascinating," the man said to himself. His heavy accent turned the word *fascinating* into the hiss of a snake. Then, he said, "Do you know why she picked this specific form?" almost like he was asking himself a question.

Although no one else stood with him, another voice answered. It sounded nearly identical to his voice with the same accent, yet with a sardonic tone the man lacked. "I couldn't begin to guess. You will tell me, of course. You are itching to tell me."

"You know me well," the man answered. "It is the form of *First Mother*, a wooden statue that Paul bought for her as a present. A very fitting form for Julie, if you have been paying attention."

"I have not," the other voice said.

The man gave an annoyed scoff.

Out in the street, Julie, or the thing Julie had become, was still howling.

"That's enough," the man said. He reached into the air and curled the fingers of his hand as if grasping something that hung before him. Then he pulled downward, and a deep, resonant ring came from a bell down in the earth, behind the safety fence surrounding the Prentice home.

Julie's howling stopped. The warping void-silhouette of the minotaur stood up straight and began walking in the direction of the bell. It tore apart the safety fence as if it were nothing more than a paper nuisance, opened the iron door in what had been the Prentices' backyard, and climbed down below.

A self-assured chuckle came from the man, and then it became a wheezing cough. He gripped the nearby desk with wrinkled, bony fingers. A tremor ran through his arm.

"If we stay out any longer, we will not have the strength to return," the other voice said. It, too, sounded raspy and pained.

"Soon. We will return soon. They are all back except the *serĉilo*."

Julie, in the new minotaur form of the *Koŝmaro*, threw aside a bookshelf and crouched down to enter the rough rock tunnel leading from the underground chamber to the Between. The only thought in her mind was of the bell, echoing every several seconds. Each echo rippled with a gravitational force, pulling her, compelling her onward. When she opened the door to the sitting room, she saw what the bell had been drawing her to.

Blood everywhere.

Matted in the velvet Damask patterns on the walls.

Dried pools on the floor, soaked into the rug. Splattered on the ceiling.

A body laid behind the sofa—only the legs were visible, twisted unnaturally. Julie let out a primal scream, the scream of a mother seeing the wrecked body of her own dead child. She rushed to her child and cradled its cold form against her body. Rage and sadness radiated from her, warping the world around her.

Who had killed her child? Her child!

The face of the dead man in her arms was both unfamiliar yet somehow the face of a child of her own flesh. She'd given birth to that child—nursed, protected, and loved him. All for nothing now that he was dead.

But how could this child be mine? a voice in her head asked. A horrible question. She wanted to tear the voice out from her mind... but it was her own voice. She tilted her head back and let out a beastly howl that split the sofa and knocked the nearby lamp over. When the lamp hit the ground, the light vanished, and the room became black.

Still, she could see. Either her beast eyes could see in the dark, or the weird warping aura around her had created its own light. A translucent copy of the lamp still stood, illuminating the room, even though the lamp lay broken on the ground.

Another light source, this one much dimmer, came from the forehead of the dead man in her arms. It was his soul, the soul of her child, waiting for her to free it from its lifeless shell. In her right hand, a basket appeared, woven with knotty ebony-dark branches, the interior padded by a ringed bed made of leaves and moss. This is where she would keep her child's soul warm and safe.

The soul pulsed from within the corpse's skull, begging to be saved. The fingernails of her minotaur form weren't as razor sharp as the talons of the previous *Koŝmaro*, but they were sharp enough to carve a spiral into the corpse's forehead and for her to press her index finger through its center and into the skull where she could hook the soul and pull it free.

Once released, it looked like a small star that threatened to fade out. She hurriedly placed it in the basket, and warmth filled her. Her child was safer now in her possession, but it still wasn't safe enough.

A vision filled her mind: the Underworld's dark body of water next to the shore covered by iron statues. The soul in her basket belonged in one of those statues. Only the statues could keep her child safe. Some of the statues already held a soul, a soul that she had placed within them. That thought made her happy, made her feel like a good mother, but her memories of the statues felt foreign, as if they belonged to someone else.

She stood and placed the basket into a pocket in the air next to her where the ripples of her aura made it invisible. Only she could grasp it, its gnarled threads made for her hand alone. She did this without thought and suffered a brief moment of panic upon seeing her empty hand afterward. She reached back into the pocket, and her hand reemerged with the basket. It felt natural yet so alien to watch.

The bell beckoned again, and her giant horned head swiveled to look in the direction that the bell demanded. Another of her children had been slain. Another soul needed her protection. With a snarl, she tore open the door in front of her and moved into a pristine copy of the sitting room she had just been in. She navigated the maze without thought as the bell pulled her toward the next body, and then the one after that, and the one after that.

So many deaths. So many of her children torn apart by slash wounds up and down their bodies. Every corpse felt like a tragedy, another of her children that she had failed to protect. All she could do now was harvest their souls, protect those little remaining stars from any other harm. And so she collected them until her basket was full, then sat and hugged her basket, singing a quiet lullaby to the babies in her arms while tears rolled from her eyes.

Sometime later, she felt the little thorns on the basket's woven branches digging through her jeans and into the flesh of her legs. They were her legs. Julie's. Human. Not the giant minotaur legs of the *Koŝmaro*. The past several hours felt like a smear in her memory. She had cried body-wracking tears over the deaths of her children, and while the sadness still clung to her like a walked-through spider web, she knew that none of the souls in her basket belonged to any child of hers. She and Paul had no children.

The twisted ring on her right middle finger flickered in the darkness, and she looked up at an unfamiliar room. Paul had told her about the sitting room maze. The first few bodies had been found there, and she remembered every detail of the space: the velvet wallpaper, the stained oak floors, the Persian rug, the sofa. But as her grief had grown, she lost herself in a frenzy, going from body to body, and that frenzy took her out of the maze, to someplace else entirely.

To here: the dark inside of a ramshackle church. Wooden pews, only half of which still stood. Broken glass and dust covering the floor. Ahead, an altar with a lone candle provided the only light, flickering and threatening to go out.

With effort, she moved the basket to the floor and rubbed her legs where it had left impressions in her skin. Her hands wouldn't stop trembling. It wasn't only her hands—it was her whole body, shaking in fear.

She pressed her eyelids closed, and through sheer force of will, stopped her body from shaking. "This is not productive," she whispered to herself. Other thoughts tried to push their way to the front of her mind—*Where am I? I'm going to die!*—but she turned her mind into a slippery rock and watched those thoughts slide off and away. It was a technique she had learned in a yoga retreat several years back that had become almost second nature through practice. Nothing could scale the rock unless she let it.

"That's better."

She stood and took a deep breath. The air was cold and stale, as if it had sat undisturbed for a long while. She smelled a hint of something burning, at first thinking it must be the candle, but it smelled more like smoldering leaves. The smell was familiar, but in her exhausted and confused state, she couldn't place it.

Her phone showed no service, but at least it could be used as a flashlight. She swept the little light around the single room of the church. There were two exits: a sagging archway behind the altar that led to darkness, and, at the other end of the church, a closed wooden door. Footprints in the dust connected the two doors, but whether they were made recently or years ago, Julie couldn't tell.

In her mind, the image of the *Kosmaro*'s ring sliding onto her finger kept replaying and replaying. She allowed herself a few seconds to let in all the feelings she had been keeping at bay—the fear, the panic, the confusion. The dread. The overwhelming dread that she was alone and trapped in hell.

This is what Paul must have felt, she thought. And suddenly the lyrics from a Death Cab for Cutie song, "I Will Follow You into the Dark," came to her mind. Paul loved the song and always seemed to get uncharacteristically verklempt when it came on. In the song, the singer tells his love that when death claims her, he will enter the darkness with her so she is not alone. Was that what was happening here? Paul had been in the dark, captured by this place, leashed with that spiral bracelet around his arm, and now Julie was leashed, too. She would see what he had seen, feel what he had felt. She had followed him into the dark, and that gave her current experience a sliver of meaning.

Meaning was humanity's superpower. With meaning, people could endure the harshest pains and the greatest evils. With meaning, strength is ever replenished. Without meaning, without purpose to give context to struggles, you wither and collapse.

She decided to open the door to the church and see where it led. But what about the basket? A noise that sounded like paper tearing came from behind her. She turned and saw that the closed door was now a shimmering portal to somewhere brighter, somewhere with white marble walls and statues.

The *gardistaro* glided in through the portal with an unnatural smoothness. She stood tall and regal in a diaphanous dress that looked like it had been taken from Aphrodite's wardrobe. In stark contrast, the body draped by the dress was big and muscular. The *gardistaro* was a common presence in the foreign memories polluting Julie's mind, and upon seeing her, those memories came to life—warnings chattering away in Julie's head. The loudest of these—*Careful with her! She will steal your children!*—jarred Julie, and for a moment she didn't recognize the woman. Then she saw the chrome robotic leg beneath the dress.

"Supriya!"

"Do you seek answers?" replied the *gardistaro*.

"What do you mean? It's Julie, Supriya. Paul's wife."

The glassy calm on Supriya's face showed no change. "Do you seek answers?" the *gardistaro* asked again.

Julie didn't have time for this shit. She took off one of her running shoes and threw it at Supriya, hitting her right on the forehead. "Oh, fuck. Sorry! I didn't mean to—"

The *gardistaro* was gliding forward now. Her eyes had grown wide, and her hands began dancing in the air.

The chorus of memories in Julie's head knew what was happening even though Julie herself didn't. The *Koŝmaro*'s distortion field snapped into being right as little squares of elsewhere began appearing, intersecting with Julie's body. Her left hand severed at the wrist then vanished as it fell through a tiny portal. But her hand somehow simultaneously remained attached and unaffected. The other little portals likewise tried to slice her body apart, but in the distortion field, the attacks had no effect.

The minotaur within Julie began to take control, and she felt herself grow into its huge silhouette.

Julie's sudden transformation into the *Koŝmaro* broke through the *gardistaro*'s calm. She turned and in two steps was in the portal where the church's door had been, but then slid to a stop and spun around on the marble floor beyond.

"Julie Prentice?" It was Supriya's singsong voice.

The giant void-silhouette of the *Koŝmaro* walked toward the portal, crushing a pew in its path. The field around the creature caused alternate versions of the room to flash in and out of existence. It reached toward the portal with its hand as if to grab Supriya from the other side. When the dark arm of the *Koŝmaro* crossed the plane of the portal, the distortion field sizzled and flickered. The beast at its center flashed through form after form: the pregnant minotaur, the spider-clawed *Koŝmaro* that had hunted Supriya before, a wolf-like creature on all fours, and countless others. Julie's human form overlaid them all, her face wracked with confusion and pain.

Then the *Koŝmaro* pulled back its arm, and both the dark beast silhouette and the warping field vanished, leaving Julie Prentice heaving deep breaths. Every few seconds, her form jittered unnaturally, as if the order of time around her became momentarily jumbled.

"My god, it is you," Supriya said. She rushed back through the portal and reached out to embrace Julie, but another of those jitters caused Supriya to yank her hands back. "You are the... You are the *Koŝmaro*! How did... No, it makes no difference. We are all doomed, Julie. I wish you had escaped, but you haven't. None of us have. I am more *her* now than I am me. You will be lost soon, too."

"Did you kill my children?" Julie asked, looking confused as if she hadn't heard a word.

Supriya stepped back, cautious, and some of the steely demeanor of the *gardistaro* returned. "Your children? Ah... The deaths that continue the cycle. Without a *Koŝmaro* to harvest the souls, the bodies have piled up. You see them as your children—how strange and how awful."

"Did you kill my children?" Julie asked again. This time her voice rippled with an echo, and the jittering of her figure intensified. Her gray eyes flared.

"She didn't," came a voice from a shadowy corner of the room. The *stelisto* stepped forward, but the darkness clung to him so that his face and hands were barely visible. The blade in his right hand pulsed once with blue light as if to announce its presence—or its hunger. The *stelisto* faded back into shadow, and then, without any apparent movement, he emerged from a dark alcove behind the altar, a good ten feet or more away from where he had been.

"Leave, Jay," Supriya said. "Before someone gets hurt."

"I would never hurt Julie. Despite what Paul did to you, Supriya, my love. How he shot you in the field." The wicked smirk on the *stelisto*'s face softened, and the shadows seemed to retreat. He blinked rapidly and then his whole body seemed to loosen up.

Jay leaned on the altar as if it had been put in the church just to let him slouch there at that moment. "God damnit, Julie. It got you, too," he said, West Texas drawl more pronounced than it had been seconds ago. "Is Paul with you?"

Julie looked back and forth between Jay and Supriya and then she, too, seemed to snap out of the role she had become. "No," she said. "I didn't mean for this to happen. I don't know why I put the ring on. Paul is at work. At least he was this morning."

"Old Paul is missing out on the fun as usual," Jay said. He

briefly gave Supriya a thoughtful look and then, with a flash of his eyebrows, he said to Julie, "We should stay together, the three of us, until we get you out of here and safely back to Paul."

"No, Jay," Supriya said. "I told you to stay away from me."

"Babe, I'm fine. I'm in complete control. You know I am." Jay stood up straight and put one hand on his hip. Either the candle had gotten dimmer, or the shadows had started inching back across him again.

Supriya turned her head toward Julie but kept her eyes on Jay. "I can lead you back out. He won't be coming with us."

Jay started to protest, but Julie interrupted. "I need to take this basket to the statues first, I think." The words seemed to make sense until she heard herself say them aloud. She wanted to go deeper in the Between? That's not at all what she wanted.

"I'm not taking you to the Underworld, Julie."

"I will," Jay said, and now the red cast of his eyes had returned, as though something else lurked beneath his goodwill.

"You need to leave before you cause more bloodshed," Supriya said.

At the word *bloodshed*, memories flooded into Julie's mind, memories of the *stelisto* slaughtering her children—how he would hide in the shadows and become one with the darkness, emerging to sink that blue blade into unsuspecting victims.

"You're the one who killed my children." Julie's voice began to reverberate, and the air around her rippled.

Jay stepped backward into the shadows. His voice came from a different corner of the room, and mid-sentence, it echoed from yet another place of darkness. "You and I are a pair, and you don't even know it. I slay, you harvest, and the machine keeps humming along. Embrace your role, Julie. It was made for you, like mine was made for me."

She grabbed a broken pew and, with beastlike strength, hurled it into the corner where the voice had last come from. Wood exploded in a cloud of dust, and laughter sounded from behind her.

"Don't forget, I've killed one *Kosmaro* already."

Another pew smashed into the wall where these words came from. The giant minotaur silhouette, now superimposed over Julie, let out a howl that shook the church. The roof above splintered and sagged, threatening to collapse.

Jay's laughter, the *stelisto*'s laughter, seemed to come from all the darkness at once.

"Stop, Jay!" Supriya screamed, but before she could say more, the void eyes of the *Koŝmaro* turned to her.

Supriya fell to one knee and grabbed at her hair.

"YOU HELPED HIM KILL MY CHILDREN!" the *Koŝmaro* shrieked in a chorus of layered voices. The dark beast Julie had become walked toward Supriya. Through the *Koŝmaro*'s eyes, Julie could see the faint glow of Supriya's soul within her skull, a soul that needed to be taken out of that weak flesh and kept safe in an iron statue in the Underworld. Julie reached a hand to grab Supriya's head but hesitated. She remembered locking eyes with the *Koŝmaro* herself that night when the whole world had changed. She remembered the terrifying visions it made her see, of the Underworld, of the doom of being locked away in a solitary iron prison in a constant state of fear and pain—the pain that fueled the great engine of the Between.

In that moment of hesitation, fire erupted from her right, fire in a jet that seemed to come from the *gardistaro*'s portal where the church door should have been. Suddenly the whole interior of the church was ablaze. The fire couldn't touch Julie, protected within the *Koŝmaro*'s reality-warping aura, but what about her basket and the souls?

She turned and saw that the black wood of the basket was burning. "NO!" she screamed. A single step toward the basket, and her aura engulfed it, eliminating the flames and all traces it had left on the basket. Another jet of fire came from behind her, forming a glowing red bowl as it sizzled against the edge of her protective shield.

Julie nestled the basket safely in the extradimensional pocket within her aura and turned toward the source of the assault. Corinne, face covered by a white-painted skull, had one arm wrapped around Supriya, dragging her backward toward the gateway, and in Corinne's other hand, she held the same red cylinder that Julie had tried to use against the prior *Kosmaro*.

Corinne was here? Well of course she was! She had said this morning she was going to find Supriya in the hopes that she could help her get home.

Within Julie, a battle raged. The *Kosmaro* part of her should have won this battle with its sea of voices imploring her to kill the *gardistaro*, to destroy the murderer of her children. The Julie part of her, the one sole voice within that sea that was truly hers, was getting overwhelmed. The *Kosmaro* would take its pound of flesh and seize the soul from the *gardistaro*, from Supriya Reddy. Julie could as easily stop herself from breathing as she could stop herself from acting as the *Kosmaro*. If she couldn't stop herself, perhaps she could delay the inevitable.

"*GARDISTARO*, YOU WILL FREE CORINNE FROM THIS PLACE," her voice boomed and echoed, "AND UNTIL THEN, I WILL NOT HARVEST YOUR SOUL." She made no such promise to the *stelisto*. With the darkness in the church chased away by the fire, Jay had nowhere to hide and must have already fled.

Corinne, with Supriya now pulled into the gateway, lifted her head and started to turn toward the *Kosmaro* upon hearing its words. But she knew better than to meet its void stare.

Supriya made a dismissive wave with her hand, and the gateway vanished, leaving Julie in the burning old church, alone. She was Julie for a few seconds more before the sea of voices took over and transformed her fully into the singularly focused *Kosmaro*.

The giant void-beast set out toward the shore of iron statues next to the black sea in the Underworld of the Between. It knew the way there.

CHAPTER 5
ROCK BOTTOM

Paul huddled against a concrete column under the Pleasant Valley bridge, the rain falling so hard it seemed to form walls on either side of him, shutting away the outside world. He hadn't meant to spend the night under a bridge, but there was a first time for everything. Probably not the last, either, unless someone or something killed him in the night. And that wouldn't be so bad, now, would it?

He dug into his backpack and pulled out a bottle of whiskey. In a single swallow, he finished its remains. He cocked his arm to throw the bottle at another of the bridge's concrete columns, wanting to feel the brief flash of destructive satisfaction, but the bottle slid out of his hand, and the moment slipped away just like the last several weeks had.

Leaving his key in the door, he had walked out of the hotel room a vague number of hours before without a destination in mind. Less than $200 in his pocket. The sum total of his worldly possessions. No job. No wife. No money. At some point, the night decided it needed to rain on him also. Near Rosewood Avenue on the East Side, he ducked into a liquor store to dry off.

"You're getting water everywhere, man," the clerk said. "Either buy something or get moving."

Paul pointed to a bottle he recognized on the shelf behind the clerk. "How much is the Yamazaki?"

The clerk eyed him suspiciously and said, "One-fifty. Plus tax."

Paul slapped down everything in his pocket. "Keep the change."

He sought cover from the rain under the bridge crossing at Rosewood Park. Several hours later, the empty whiskey bottle sat unbroken a few feet from him, the rain still fell, and the ground grew wetter. The only light came from lightning flashes that burned through his closed eyelids.

And then one flash kept shining. He turned his head away and raised his arm to block out the light, but it burned through.

"You can't sleep here," a voice said, hard to make out over the sizzling percussion of the rain on the bridge above.

The flashlight's beam lowered, allowing Paul to see the silhouette of a policeman standing about ten feet away. Behind the man sat an idling patrol car, its headlights carving a tunnel into the night beyond the bridge and the empty stretches of the park.

"Let me see your hands, buddy," the policeman said. "I can help you get to the shelter or the hospital. I just need to make sure you don't have any weapons. You high? Drunk?"

"Hospital?" In Paul's drunken mind, the word conjured an image of himself in his office, soaking wet, with Ramona Buck and Lawrence Filby standing over him, shaking their heads. YOU'RE FIRED, PAUL. FIRED. "I don't need to go to the hospital," Paul said, slurring his words.

Another lightning strike illuminated the little world under the bridge, and for a brief second, Paul could see the policeman's face and, in Paul's periphery, what looked like another figure walking this direction, about twenty or thirty feet away. By the time Paul turned his head to look for the other figure, darkness had reclaimed the area.

"I can't leave you here, man. You're all wet and you're shivering. It's not even cold out. Something's wrong. You need to come with me, okay?"

Just let me fucking die, Paul was about to say, and then another voice—coming from the darkness where Paul had thought he saw someone—said, "Let me take care of him, officer."

The flashlight's beam swiveled to frame the new approaching figure, but somehow the light didn't show anything more than a dark shape, as if the light itself was repelled by the figure.

"Hold it right there," the policeman said, drawing his sidearm with his free hand.

"I've got this covered, my friend," the dark figure said, and then a pair of golden eyes shone out from the darkness.

The policeman holstered his pistol, turned, and began walking toward his patrol car. His movements were stilted and mechanical, as if his limbs were being pulled by marionette strings. Without another word or even so much as a look back, the policeman entered his car and drove away.

Paul pushed himself to his feet, holding on to the concrete column as the world threatened to spin out from under him. "Hello?" he said into the darkness, but the darkness didn't respond. He began to wonder if he had hallucinated the entire thing—the policeman trying to take him to the hospital, the dark figure intervening—and then the lightning flashed again, and the figure was right next to him.

"You look like shit, *dongsaeng*," it said. "Let's get you cleaned up. You've got a lot of work to do."

"Min-woo?" Paul said.

"It's me, neighbor. In the flesh. I would've gotten here sooner, but, you know, the whole death thing got in the way. I hope you still have my notebook. I've got a lot of stuff to add."

Paul's legs gave out, and his back slid down the column until he was on the wet ground again. With the police car and flashlight gone, the area under the bridge was near pitch black. All Paul could see of the nearby figure was how its silhouette blocked the light of a distant streetlamp.

"Min-woo?" Paul repeated. His confused mind rambled on, "Notebook? Shit. I forgot it in the hotel. I don't have a laptop anymore, and I..."

"Easy come, easy go," the figure interrupted in a voice that certainly sounded like Min-woo's. "Like life, right? One minute you're alive, the next you're dead. And then, sometimes, against all odds, you're alive again."

Golden eyes glowed like before, only now the figure must have squatted down because they were only a foot away from Paul's own eyes. The light grew so bright that it burned away the darkness and left a white nothingness in its place, where only Min-woo's voice existed.

"Sleep now, Paul," the voice began, but as it continued speaking, it became another voice entirely. A deeper voice, ancient and heavy with a thick accent. "And when you awaken, we can begin preparing for your return."

CHAPTER 6
TALK OF DEBTS AND JOURNEYS

The two women sat in the *gardistaro*'s chamber of white marble and light, surrounded by statues on pedestals that all seemed to be waiting for one of them to break the silence.

Corinne reached out a hand to Supriya, who was on the floor, breathing heavily, still recovering from the effects of the *Koŝmaro*'s gaze. But Supriya ignored the offered help and pushed her tall, muscled body upright, favoring her mechanical leg.

A fountain ringed by stone benches commanded the center of the chamber. Corinne sat on a bench and began using the fountain's cold water to wash away the paint on her face. It would come back—it always did—but she needed the paint gone while talking with Supriya. She needed to be Corinne and not Skull Girl.

Supriya sat on the neighboring bench with a look of curiosity and perhaps concern, a departure from the glassy, expressionless gaze of the *gardistaro*.

"Why are you here, Corinne?" Supriya finally said. "Why did you come back? You didn't have to."

Corinne rinsed the paint from her hands in the fountain and watched as the black, white, and red dissolved until only crystal-clear water remained. "I did have to."

"But you aren't drawn here. You aren't trapped like we are. You haven't taken on a role."

"Haven't I?"

Supriya didn't respond, and the two stared at each other until Corinne lowered her eyes, looking instead at Supriya's hands. Those hands were covered with dust and char from the floor of the burning church. Without understanding why, Corinne reached out both of her own hands, palms up, and waited until Supriya in turn put her hands in Corinne's. Then Corinne began to wash them clean with the fountain water.

It took a minute or two, and neither woman spoke. The intimacy of the act was almost too much for Corinne, and she had to focus on the mechanics of the washing itself to quiet the dissent in her head. This felt right, just like it must have felt right to Supriya, who was letting it happen.

Finally, Supriya pulled back her hands. "Thank you."

Corinne dried her hands on her jeans. "I don't know why the *Kôsmaro* told you to help me, but I did come here to ask for your help."

Supriya started to say something and then made a little shake of her head. Then she straightened her back and looked in Corinne's eyes as she spoke. "You just saved my life, and it's not the first time. I'll do whatever I can. But I have to warn you. I lose myself in her, sometimes for hours. I can only speak for Supriya Reddy. I can't speak for the *gardistaro*." Supriya suddenly pursed her lips and began looking around the room as if searching for something. "How did you get in here, anyway? I only use gateways to enter my chamber. It never occurred to me that there was another way in."

Corinne gave a dismissive shrug. "The statue of the winged woman, there." She pointed. "The alcove behind it has a false wall. On the other side is a courtyard with more statues."

"I know about the courtyard, but I didn't realize there was a door."

Now it was Corinne's turn to give the other woman a confused look. "Don't you use that alcove for your gateways in and out of the chamber? Your gateways need an existing door, right?"

"Huh. I guess using the *gardistaro*'s powers has become so

natural to me that I don't think about it." Supriya's look became serious. "I'm glad Jay doesn't know about that door. And there are no dark shadows in here, so whatever he's doing to move between the shadows...I'm sorry, I took us on a tangent. You said you wanted my help."

Whatever he's doing to move between the shadows? Corinne had encountered other *stelistos* before. They reminded her of the scorpions back home that would get into your shoes and folded blankets and then stab out at you when you least expected it. But what Jay seemed to be doing was different, different in a way that made him especially dangerous. Not like a scorpion that could be stamped out with the very shoe it had hidden in.

Corinne hadn't come here to talk about Jay. "I have a favor to ask," she said. "Will you take me into the Ruins within the Gray Waste?"

At the mention of the place, Supriya stood and began to take on the expressionless gaze of the *gardistaro*. With the shake of her head and a few rapid blinks, Supriya was back. She crossed her arms and began pacing, the hem of her gown coasting along the marble floor like a morning fog. "Say that again. I'm sure I misheard you."

"You heard me just fine. If I understand your story correctly, you were on an elevator that took you down instead of up, and the elevator's doors opened in the cave by the *masinisto*'s mansion. That's how you found yourself here, in the Between. Is that right?"

Supriya nodded.

"That's similar to what happened to me. The door from my world opened in the Ruins near the lair of the *malespero*, in the second world of the Between. If I want to go back home, I need to go through that same door." Corinne paused, rubbed a hand on her cheek, and saw that no paint had yet returned. That gave her the strength to say something she hadn't yet said to anyone, including herself. "I want to go home. I want to go home, Supriya. I don't want to be the person I'm becoming. I don't want to be the person I was, either. I want to find my fucking life, or make a new one, or whatever. I want to live a life, not just survive, and that's all

I've been doing for... for my entire adult life. Does that make sense to you?"

"More sense than you know."

"So, you'll take me, then? And maybe you can help open the door home if it's closed?"

Supriya's stare carried the *gardistaro*'s iciness. It seemed that inside her, a battle for control was raging, and Corinne's words were shifting the tide in favor of the role over the human playing it. "I will do this, but you have no idea what you're asking me."

"I think I do, Supriya. I've spent what seems like years here. I know the danger."

"Yes, the Ruins are dangerous. I'm sure you know that as well as anyone. But there is more that you don't know. The *malespero* has taken a special interest in us. In me and Jay. She—it is a *she* under that armor, a young girl, even—she takes newcomers into her ranks and sends them out to kill us. But she does it one or two at a time, in a way that she must know will fail. She's pulling us deeper and deeper into our roles. I don't know why, but I feel like whatever her game is, we are playing it. Her game within this greater game. She is turning Jay into the darkest form of the *stelisto*. I no longer trust myself around him."

A hiss escaped Corinne's lips.

"You think you know Jay, but you don't. You have no fucking idea who he is." Every bit of Supriya's tall, muscled body seemed to hum with a quiet anger. "I see you judging him every time you see him. Discarding him with your eyes. I hear what you say about him. And the threats. I hear them, too."

"I've been around my share of the *stelistos*." Corinne tried to keep her words calm, but she could hear the impatience in her voice. "It doesn't matter who he was. That person is gone. He's a killer now. The *stelistos* are all killers. His fate was sealed when he picked up that knife."

"I won't discard him like that!" Supriya yelled, her voice seemingly amplified in the small stone room. "You're projecting your own self-loathing on him."

Corinne stood and felt the cold rush of adrenaline wash over her. Even without looking at her reflection in the fountain's water, she knew the painted skull had returned to her face. The room seemed framed by the darkness of the skull's black eye sockets.

"I shouldn't have come here," Corinne said. Under her coat, she had three knives in a belt resting on her right hip. The fire and force wands were tucked into the coat's inside pocket on her left. Could she get to any of them, much less use them, before Supriya carved her in two with a few waves of her hands? Probably not. Corinne raised her hands to visibly signal that she, at least, had no desire to initiate an Old West style duel. She slowly turned her back on Supriya and walked to the hidden door in the alcove behind the carved angel.

"I shouldn't have said that," Supriya said. "I will go with you to the Ruins and help you get back home. Come back and sit down. Please."

Corinne took a deep breath and closed her eyes. She didn't turn around. Supriya's words had stung because they contained truth. "Maybe it's best that I go alone. I can do it. I've done it before."

"But you can't do it without me. Your door home...It won't open for you again. It's been too long. Maybe I can open it, just like I've been able to reopen the door to the Prentices' backyard." Supriya let out a deep breath. "And I'm sorry for what I said, Corinne. I'm not sorry that I still want to believe in Jay."

To Corinne, Supriya's words sounded sincere, but as she knew all too well, sincerity and delusion were often dance partners. All the Between's roles were dangerous—even the *gardistaro*, the welcomer of new players.

"If you walk out that door," Supriya said, "I'll follow you and help whether you want me to or not. I have a debt to repay to you, and I am repaying it right now. Like it or not. You asked. I accepted. No takebacks."

"No takebacks? Are we on a playground or something?"

Supriya let out a chuckle. "We are most certainly on a playground. A bloody doomsday playground. So, playground rules apply. And if you think you're more stubborn than I am, oh, are you in for a surprise."

Corinne walked back to the benches and, with a resigned huff, threw her backpack on the ground. She glared at Supriya, who might as well have been one of the mythical statues that ringed the room—a lioness in human form, chin held high, looking down at Corinne with confident yet strangely playful intensity. There was, indeed, no winning a battle of the wills with this woman—not a playground, nor anywhere else for that matter.

"Let me refill a few water bottles, and then I'm ready to go." While kneeling at the fountain, Corinne asked, "Why were you fighting the *Koŝmaro*? It was the *Koŝmaro*, right? I've never seen it look like that. It knew my name and demanded that you help me. That's the strangest part of all of this. I've never heard it talk before, and the first time I do, it wants you to help me. What the hell is that?" Receiving no answer, Corinne looked back over her shoulder at Supriya.

"Do you wish to have the answers?" Supriya said in an icy voice that matched the sudden change in her posture and presence.

Corinne realized immediately what was happening. The *gardistaro* asked all newcomers if they wanted answers—all newcomers that lived long enough to encounter her, that is. It was not exactly a trick question, but the answer carried far more weight than most realized. Paul had been fortunate when he had met Supriya's predecessor, because Corinne had warned him.

"You'll eventually run into a woman in a white dress with gold eyes," Corinne had said to Paul back in the field with the broken colossus, shortly after they had met. "She's the *gardistaro*. She's your only hope of escape. Don't threaten her and pay attention to everything she says. She'll ask you if you want to stay. You have to answer *no*."

"Why would anyone answer yes?" Paul had asked.

"Because they don't realize what she's asking."

Later on, Paul had encountered the *gardistaro*, who in turn asked the very words that Supriya now asked Corinne. *Do you wish to have the answers?*

"No," Corinne said. And then louder. "No. I do not wish to have the answers."

As easily as it had come, the glassiness of Supriya's demeanor vanished. She blinked several times as if to clear her vision and then said, "Never forget who I am, Corinne. Never forget *what* I am." She traced a rectangle in the air, and in the alcove behind the winged statue, a glowing, framed gateway appeared—a gateway leading to the beginning of the Grand Staircase. "Now, let's go find your door home."

CHAPTER 7
MOZ IN THE GRAVEYARD

Jay drifted through the graveyard like a forgotten memory, moving unseen from the shadows of one headstone to the next. The grave-yard's strange skeletons, made of old automotive parts—junklings, Jay had named them—were oblivious to the *stelisto*'s presence. He passed silently, so close to one that he was able to reach out and disconnect a little hose from its ankle. A few seconds later, when Jay was already next to a crypt more than twenty feet away, the junkling took a step forward and crumpled on its limp foot.

"Have a nice trip, gears-for-brains," Jay muttered under his breath a little louder than he had intended. A nearby junkling turned from its fallen companion to look toward the sound with its single headlamp eye, but the *stelisto* was invisible in the shadows. He could have fought every single one of them and won without breaking a sweat. Probably. But he didn't come here to fight, although he was angry enough to.

Corinne was back in the Between, and that condescending bitch had taken Supriya away. Granted, Corinne had saved Supriya from the *Košmaro*, but saving Supriya was his goddamn job! And he'd been just about to do it, too, but the fucking *Košmaro* was Julie, so what the hell was he supposed to do? Kill his best friend's wife? And now Corinne had Supriya in the *gardistaro*'s chamber, which might as well have been the moon.

He calmed himself with a breath of the cold cavern air and became one with the darkness. He *shifted shadows*—that's how he thought of it—and was instantly on the other side of the crypt's closed door of iron bars, sitting on its lone contained tomb. Supriya had asked him recently how he moved between shadows. "It's exactly like what you do with the gateways, except different." She wasn't amused by that answer. He hadn't amused her much as of late. Supriya had been losing herself to the role of the *gardistaro*, becoming all detached and aloof. So cold she could've crawled out of the very tomb he sat atop now.

He, on the other hand, was the same old Jay. Sure, his jokes had become darker, but he was still making people laugh. Making himself laugh, anyway. If you don't have your sense of humor, what do you have?

The tomb was long enough for him to stretch out on his back and cross one boot over the other. In all of the Between—or at least in the parts he had been in which, granted, wasn't all that much of it—there was no place more serene and relaxing than this particular crypt within the dark cavern that contained the *masinisto*'s mansion. The mansion itself was nice and all, in a Victorian haunted house kind of way, but it had two problems. The first was the *masinisto* himself. Or maybe herself. There had been so many *masinistos* lately that Jay had lost track, which led right into the second problem. Someone or some*thing* was always attacking the damn place. All its defenses seemed to invite rather than repel unwanted guests. When he and Supriya had briefly lived there for a few weeks, when Supriya was the *masinisto*, it seemed that an assault on their home occurred every few days. Those assaults all failed, of course.

Laying on top of this tomb, his thoughts turned to those past fleeting moments when the mansion was theirs. His relationship with Supriya—if he could even still call it a relationship—was now ice. Back then it had been pure white-hot fire, a fire that at times threatened to consume them both. More than anything now, he wanted that fire back, even if it meant immolation.

A song came to him, a tragic song, and in his head, his singing voice sounded exactly like Morrissey's.

Oh one-legged woman,
Incinerate me with your love!
You only have one leg.
But it's okay,
Because I only have one heart.
Oh one-legged woman,
Cover me with your flames!
Your flames of... looooove.

He closed his eyes and let the absurdity of the song mingle with the warmth of the memories. The Knife of Undoing at his side was quiet and satisfied for now. A sad smile spread across his face, and then the smile vanished. Corinne's words echoed in his head.

He'll kill you, and me, and everyone else he meets. They all do it. All of the stelistos. *Until someone finally kills them, or they kill themselves.*

What a rotten woman. It was all her fault. Julie being the *Koŝmaro.* Supriya almost dying—again. Supriya being locked away from him. Everything from the beginning had been Corinne's fault. If she hadn't been fighting them in the field that day, Paul never would've accidentally shot Supriya, and the *Koŝmaro* wouldn't have chased them and destroyed Paul's house. A nagging voice in his head pointed out that it had been Jay's own idea to follow Corinne after being warned not to. The voice also expressed some vague confusion about how Julie being the *Koŝmaro* could have been Corinne's fault, but he ignored it.

Suddenly the knife came alive, sending a wave of energy through him. Someone else had entered the graveyard. The knife could feel them, could sense their beating heart, and so Jay, the *stelisto,* could sense them as well. He silently got to his feet and slid into a shadow next to the crypt door. Through the door's bars, he saw junklings creeping through the graveyard, faintly illuminated by the few gas streetlamps lining the nearby path up to the mansion. Despite their clunky appearances, the junklings moved almost as silently as Jay did. Their focus was on the hatch at the center of the graveyard, one of only two ways into this cavern.

A figure was standing next to the hatch in the glow coming from the room below. Another climbed up and another after that. They kept coming, each carrying long spears and wearing armor that looked like it had been assembled out of mismatched museum pieces. One had a rifle. If Jay had any doubt of who they were, the ash dog scrambling out of the hatch confirmed it. Soldiers of the *malespero*.

Jay had encountered more than his fair share, and for each of them, human and canine abomination alike, that encounter had been their last. Those fights, though, had been against small numbers. Already a dozen or more had emerged from the sitting room maze below.

The *masinisto*, in the mansion above the graveyard, was in for a bad evening. And Jay had a front row seat to watch. *Looks like we're gonna have a job opening in the Between shortly*, he thought with a silent snicker. *No experience necessary. Must be comfortable working in extremely dangerous situations and likely dying within the first week.*

The rock walls of the cavern reverberated with every blow of the battle. The swarms of junklings made an impressive stand; they really were terrifying, moving like the 1980s Terminator with its stop-motion jankiness. But there were too many soldiers, and several had flashlights of some kind. The junklings' main weakness was that they became immobilized when a beam of light shined directly at their headlamp face, which, according to Paul, had been demonstrated rather poorly by Min-woo.

Min-woo. I miss that goofy little guy.

And then a stray flashlight beam cut through the crypt and briefly melted away the shadow Jay had been hiding in. He pulled back deeper into the crypt and redoubled his efforts at being as silent as death.

At the fight's conclusion, Jay expected the soldiers and the ash dogs—several dogs now, haloed by the glow of their ember hearts —to begin their assault on the mansion. But instead, they seemed to mill about within the graveyard as if waiting for something.

I've got a bad feeling about this, Jay thought, preparing to shift shadows out of the crypt to make his escape. The crypt's shadows vanished before he could use them, and a soldier standing nearby was suddenly covered by radiant blue flame. The blaze grew and grew until the whole graveyard, the whole cavern itself, became saturated by blue light.

The other soldiers and even the dogs hid their faces from the glare. Jay blocked as much as he could with an outstretched hand. Through his fingers he saw the radiating figure walk slowly and deliberately toward the crypt. Toward him. Unlike the others, this soldier's armor was covered with thorn-like spikes, and in place of a helmet was a black mask of a face frozen in agony. The *malespero*.

With the shadows gone, the crypt had become a jail cell. Jay's watering eyes went to the thick lock on the crypt's iron door. The Knife of Undoing could slice through it. The knife could slice through almost anything.

"A little mouse is caught in a trap. How tragic," came a voice from in front of him, a voice so unexpected that at first Jay didn't realize it had come from the *malespero*. The light dimmed a bit— not enough to be of any use to Jay, but enough for him to see the person before him. A gloved hand pulled the mask aside, revealing the face of a young woman, perhaps no more than fifteen or sixteen years old. She looked strangely familiar. Jay had seen her before—he was sure of it—but he couldn't place where or when.

"You're the *malespero*?" he said. "You're the fuckwit who's been trying to kill me and Supriya this whole time?"

"You sound disappointed." Her voice had the hint of a Southern lilt, hopping through some words and meandering slowly through others. "Like maybe you were expecting someone different?"

Jay started to respond but thought better of it. He was already caught in one trap; no need to step into another. She was right, though. Without having given it much thought, he had envisioned the mysterious and powerful *malespero* as a Hollywood bad guy type, a Bond villain: male, older, brooding, disfigured in some way —probably with a scar cutting across his face, leaving one eye colorless. The girl in front of him looked nothing like that. Her face had no scars, and her eyes looked, if anything, kind and inquisitive. Her hair was tightly pulled back in two French braids with tails hanging behind each ear, framing a youthful face so at odds with the wicked, thorned armor she wore. The casualness in the way she stood and talked, as if the *stelisto* posed no threat at all, deeply unsettled Jay.

He gave his best evil grin and said, "You know what they say about cornered animals, right?"

The *malespero* narrowed her eyes in consideration. Then she turned and spoke to a nearby soldier. "Tell the *masinisto* that we are not here for him. As long as he stays in the mansion and stops sending his rust wraiths after us, his life will be spared."

"Rust wraiths?" Jay said. "Damn that's a cool name. I call them junklings."

The *malespero* turned back toward him. "You were saying something about being a dangerous animal needing to be put down?"

"Uh... I'm pretty sure I said nothing like that."

"Jay, if I had intended to kill you, one of my dogs would be eating the face off of your corpse right now."

"Eating my face? Ugh. Now I've got that image in my head. No dog's gonna be eating my face, because the dogs and your goons and you will all be...Wait. You aren't here to kill me? And how the hell did you know my name? Where have I seen you before? I have seen you before, haven't I?"

An explosion followed by yelling came from atop the hill near the mansion. The *malespero* rolled her eyes and called out, "Juan Carlos? Where is Juan Carlos?" A soldier made his way to her and said, "Aqui." A mechanized voice came from a little attachment wrapped around his ear: *Here.*

"Juanca, do you want to be the *masinisto*?"

"Si mucho, si le place." *Yes very much, if it pleases you.*

"Then take Andrei and Hattie over there and like three or four more and eliminate that distraction, please." She took a large handgun from a bag at her side and handed it to him. "If he tries to use any of those gadgets of his, shoot him in the chest, okay? Be safe, Juanca." After Juan Carlos trotted off with several of his comrades, she turned her attention back to Jay. "Where were we? Oh, yes. You said I looked familiar. I'll let you figure out why on your own. But *we* haven't met until this moment. As for why I'm not planning on killing you and how I know your name...I have been the *malespero* for...a long time. You look surprised. You have a very expressive face. You must be terrible at poker. Anyway. You don't age here, Jay." She seemed to reconsider her words. "Not physically. However you come here, that's how you'll look until... well, until you die. Because no one escapes. Not really."

Jay scoffed. He could escape any time he wanted to, from the Between and from this little trap she thought she'd laid. His leg muscles twitched with nervous energy as he felt the moment of action nearing.

The *malespero* droned on, oblivious to her approaching death. "I've been here longer than most of the others. Cole lasted a while as the *nenio*, but your gang dropped a cathedral on him. I've seen several *stelistos* come and go and thought it was the weakest Chaos role by a wide margin, but you've convinced me otherwise. I've been testing you. Testing all the others, really. And what I've seen—"

The great bell rang, echoing in the cavern, and Jay used the split second of distraction to act. His right hand flashed out with the knife, cutting through the iron lock like it was made of paper. With his left, he threw the door open. He started to run, but before he made it a single step, his right hand felt like it had been hit by a sledgehammer. Bones cracked and he cried out in pain. The knife flew out of his hand, tumbled in the dirt, and collided with a headstone in a loud clang.

The *malespero*'s left arm was extended, palm open and covered in blue flame. She then pointed her palm toward Jay and a second blast of invisible force hit him in the chest, sending him back into the crypt, and he narrowly missed the tomb. At the nod of her head, two soldiers trotted to the crypt door and leveled their spears at the opening.

"And what I've seen," the *malespero* continued as if nothing had happened, "fits into a plan to break this place, Jay. To break the Between once and for all. And it just may be that the little mouse trapped in a cage is the key to it all. I hope that makes you feel special. It should. You work for me now, little mouse." Then, to a soldier who had walked near the Knife of Undoing, she said, "Antwon, if you touch that knife, I will liquefy your organs. Am I understood? Good. The *Koŝmaro* will be here soon. Grab our little mouse. We leave for the Ruins now."

CHAPTER 8
A REUNION, OF SORTS

Paul found himself inside a house, sitting in a velvet chair in a familiar living room. A giant painting hung on the wall across from him: a Warhol-esque depiction of Muhammad Ali in a bank vault, sitting atop a pyramid of cash. Min-woo's living room.

Paul didn't remember waking. In fact, he wasn't even sure he had fallen asleep, or passed out, or whatever. The world had simply turned a blinding white, and now, just as sudden, he was sitting in Min-woo's living room, wide awake but still drunk and dizzy.

Min-woo walked in carrying a small silver tray atop which sat two glasses of water. Paul's first thought wasn't that it was, undeniably, Min-woo here in the flesh; his first thought, instead, was of the silver tray and how no one would carry two glasses of water with a tray in their own house. No one but Min-woo Kim, of course.

"Holy shit, it is you," Paul said, his words slurred and clumsy. "And your house. It looks just like it did."

Min-woo glanced around at his own living room and then turned his brown eyes toward Paul. "The house was sitting here waiting for me. The cleaners and landscaper kept coming, as if I had never left, or, I suppose, as if I were just away for a long vacation on a remote but not too remote beach somewhere, like maybe the Canary Islands. Someplace with a Ritz-Carlton. I have standards." He took the smallest of sips from his glass of water. "Who knows if my parents ever would've gotten around to selling the place. In their house—my childhood house in Waco—my bedroom still looks the same way it did when I left for college some disgustingly large number of years ago."

Paul followed exactly none of that. He stood, braced himself against the arm of the chair while the lingering whiskey haze threatened to topple him over, and surveyed his surroundings. It had been months since Paul had last been in Min-woo's living room, but that time now seemed to belong to a bygone era. The room's details were all correct: the linear, beautiful yet uncomfortable furniture; the Ali painting; even Min-woo himself, with his corduroy pants and purple plaid shirt, and the way he sat stiff-backed and cross-legged in his chair. But it also felt surreal, which Paul attributed to the entire bottle of whiskey he had consumed. He stumbled to the street-facing window and twisted the blinds until he could see out. The chain-link fence and warning signs still surrounded the site of the former Prentice house, although a section of the fence looked to have been torn apart. He wondered about that briefly but then heard himself ask, "Who's been paying your cleaners and landscaper this whole time?"

Min-woo chuckled. "Of all the questions you could be asking me right now, that's what you want to know first?"

Paul twisted the blinds closed again and went back to slump in the chair. *Of all the questions*...None of the answers mattered though. He looked down at himself. Dried mud caked on his jeans, and flecks of it dotted the velvet chair like sprinkles on a cupcake. Grime covered his palms and ringed his fingernails. He didn't belong here in Min-woo's pristine house.

"I can't believe you're alive, Min-woo," Paul said. "I don't understand how it's possible, but nothing makes sense to me anymore. Did you come looking for me? You shouldn't have. I'm sorry, but I want to be left alone. In fact..." He pushed himself up again and began toward the front door.

"Hang on, Paul," Min-woo said. "Paul?" When Paul ignored

him and continued toward the front door, his voice grew deep and heavy as he commanded, "Stop!"

Paul halted and turned back toward the unfamiliar voice, the same voice he had heard briefly under the bridge. Min-woo's eyes were gold and glowing, and the trademark kindness in those eyes was gone.

"Who are you?" Paul asked. "You're not Min-woo. Is this even Min-woo's house?"

Min-woo's eyes returned to their friendly brown, and he laughed like they had just shared a great joke. "You're still alive in there after all, *dongsaeng*. I wasn't sure. You look like death. The scar on your forehead...The *Kôŝmaro* really did a number on you. But not as much as you've done to yourself since then. You're like an animal. A scared animal covered in filth. I don't know if my upholstery will ever be clean again, but easy come, easy go. Like life, right? One minute you're alive, the next you're dead. And then, sometimes, against all odds, you're alive again."

Paul started backing away toward the door, his mind spinning. "Easy come, easy go? You said the exact same words to me under the bridge. Same exact words, same intonation and everything. Who or what the fuck are you?"

Min-woo's smile vanished. He didn't look angry, exactly, but more... disappointed. "I did repeat those words, didn't I? Well, it's hard to have more than one soul-form in a single body." With that, he began changing. Min-woo's jet black coiffure thinned to wisps of gray on a bald head. His skin became ghostly pale, peppered with liver spots. Tailored clothes were replaced by a sweater and wool slacks, both worn and moth-eaten, and easily a size too large for the bony frame underneath.

In front of Paul now sat an old, withered man with watery eyes and a constant body tremor. The man's skin was rice paper thin, and through it, Paul could see the snaking paths of veins, all seeming to softly glow with a golden hue. Even the man's heart shone through his clothes.

When the man spoke again, it was with choppy English and a heavy accent. "Sit down, Mr. Prentice," he said.

Paul's body followed the instruction on its own, clumsily taking him back to the chair across from the man and plopping him heavily down in it.

The old man nodded, seemingly to himself, as if a piece of machinery had functioned as intended. Then he leaned back in his chair and took a long, slow breath. "The soul is like a software program," he said. "In my youth, long ago, I was a computer engineer. This body"—he pointed a shaky finger at himself—"is hardware meant to run a single software program, so to speak. The software for Rezső Simko. That was the name my mother gave me. But you see, this hardware can run other software also. I am also running your friend Min-woo Kim right now." His physical form shifted back to that of Min-woo, the glowing veins vanished, and his voice shifted to Min-woo's amused Southern lilt. "Paul, it's really me in here. I'm just not... alone. Or in control." Again he shifted back to become the old man, Rezső Simko.

It shouldn't have made any sense, especially not to Paul's drunken mind. But it did. "Min-woo's revenant form," he said. "That's the *software* you're talking about."

The old man smiled, showing jagged, yellow teeth. "You are a smart one, Mr. Prentice. I found Min-woo's revenant form after you smashed my city."

"*Your* city? I didn't smash—"

"You did. And you destroyed the *Košmaro*." The toothy smile faded. "All fine. It has happened before. Will happen again. But"— he pointed a gnarled finger at Paul and his eyes flared—"you've been staying out. You are the *serĉilo*. You wear the Silver Spiral on your arm. You have a role to play. Play now or die and give it to another. But do not stay out. The Between needs the *serĉilo*."

Paul pushed his sleeve up, exposing the twisting metal that wrapped around his forearm. Seeing it made his head spin. "I don't care what the Between needs. If you can tell me how to get the damn thing off, you can have it back. It doesn't do anything anymore. And I don't want it." He accidentally knocked the water glass onto the floor where it bounced, its contents spilling all over a geometric patterned rug.

The old man steepled his fingers and leaned toward Paul. The gold veins glowing through his skin turned amber and then red, and his eyes became cruel and crimson. "You talk and look like a broken man." Then he gave a wicked laugh that turned into a coughing spasm. When he regained control of himself, the red cast that had briefly overtaken him was gone. "You think she has forsaken you, don't you?" When Paul didn't answer, he said it again, this time using her name. "You think your Julie has left you?"

Paul wondered what kind of god or demon sat across from him. The moment he heard his wife's name, nothing else mattered. "I ruined everything. I destroyed our lives. It's all my fault. Of course she fucking left."

The thing calling itself Rezső Simko held his hands in the air and wiggled gnarled, illuminated fingers. "I am tired, Mr. Prentice. Very tired. But I am still capable of performing magic tricks. I will repair a broken man with magic words. Are you ready, *serĉilo*?"

"What the fuck are you talking about?"

"She did not forsake you. While you have been wallowing and hiding, she has descended to the deepest world of the Between. Are you hearing me? You look pale, like you've seen a ghost, as they say. Mr. Prentice? You look worse than me, and I am nearing my own end." The man frowned and transformed back into Min-woo. "There we go. I'm sure it's much more comfortable to look at your devilishly handsome neighbor than that leathery ball sack of a man." Min-woo then seemed to argue with himself, or rather, with another voice inside his head that Paul couldn't hear. "It's true. All you have to do is look in a mirror. Loose, wrinkly skin with random whiskers jutting out everywhere. You look like a ball sack."

Paul reached for his water on the side table and then remembered he had knocked it on the floor. He stood, wavered about in his lingering drunken haze, and grabbed Min-woo's water out from his hand. He drank half and poured the other half on his head. Julie was in the Between? In the deepest world of the

Between? He stumbled toward the front door. If Julie was somehow in the Between, he had to go to her.

"Hang on there, Mr. Hero," came Min-woo's voice from behind him. "You keep trying to leave, but we aren't done here yet."

Paul's drunken mind thought only of Julie, of getting across the street to the remains of their old house and descending into the Between through the iron door in their backyard.

"STOP."

This time, it was Rezső Simko's voice, or rather, several overlapping layers of Rezső Simko's voice. The command froze Paul's body, his hand reaching for the door. "COME BACK AND SIT DOWN."

Like a marionette, Paul swiveled and began walking stiff-legged back toward the velvet chair. Rezső Simko's eyes flared like two giant red stars directing all of their energy at Paul. As he heavily sat down, the light of the stars vanished, and the red glow of the old man once again turned gold. Paul's body returned to his control. He felt like he had just run a marathon.

"Please do not make me expend such energy again. I have so little left, and you are wasting it."

"What the hell are you?" Paul said.

"A man, like you. Transformed, like you."

"I'm nothing like you. Let me leave. I have to get to Julie."

"In good time. Your Julie is in no immediate danger." The old man got a faraway look in his eyes and then nodded. "Even the *Malluma Sinjoro* is not so reckless as to attack her after so much time without a *Košmaro*. He had grown weak. We all had grown weak. The soul-furnace was cold. Now it blazes again as the harvesting of souls resumes. Yes, Julie is safe for now."

"What the hell are you talking about? *Malluma* what? The *Košmaro*? We destroyed it. I saw it die in white fire. What does this have to do with Julie?"

Despite the old man's obvious fatigue, a lively twinkle flashed in his eye. "Indeed you did destroy it. And this morning, your Julie found the *Košmaro*'s artifact, the Thorned Loop of the Ever-Dying. Like Jay found the Knife of Undoing, she picked it up without knowing what it was or what it would do to her. Now she is the *Koŝmaro,* and she shows great promise. Like you show great promise, Mr. Prentice. Too much promise to be the mere *serĉilo.*"

The room began to spin. Paul gripped the arms of his chair hard, but the spinning wouldn't stop. Julie was the *Koŝmaro*? The creature that would fuel a lifetime of nightmares? He wanted to run to her, no matter what dangers stood in his way—but what happened when he reached her? The only sure way to escape a role was death. "You motherfucker. You wanted this to happen, didn't you?"

His host had become Min-woo again. "That chair was a Saarinen original from the '60s, Paul."

Paul looked down to see that the arms of the chair had been crushed under his grip. He felt the *serĉilo*'s bizarre layering at work, many Pauls all combining their strength. He hadn't felt that since their fight with the *Koŝmaro* weeks ago. The past *Koŝmaro.*

"Don't worry about the chair. I was about to say easy come easy go, but I caught myself," Min-woo said with a chuckle. "Same thing with your house and all the rest of it. It's done. The house is destroyed. Julie is the *Koŝmaro.* You can't change any of that, so all that matters is what you do next."

"I want to be free of this shit, Min-woo or whoever you are, and now you're telling me Julie is caught in it as well? I want us out. Both of us. I want us to go back to the life we had."

Min-woo ran the fingers of both hands through his hair, but somehow his mini-pompadour was left undisturbed. "Like I said, that is simply not possible. I hate to be this blunt with you, my friend, but the life you had was doomed. You needed a good shakeup. Granted, this particular shakeup is full of death and monsters. Couples therapy and some self-work is what Dr. Kim would have prescribed. But it wasn't up to me. So, what are you going to do, Paulie-boy?"

Instead of answering, Paul looked for something else he could crush.

"When I asked what you're going to do, it was a rhetorical

question," Min-woo said. "You know that, right? You're going to play the game. There's no escaping it."

"What if I refuse?"

"You are free to refuse, of course. Anyone who tells you there is no such thing as free will in this life has made a choice to live in a very small and dull universe. Go ahead and choose to do nothing. It's your right as a free-willed mortal, but you will never see Julie again. Or Jay, for that matter. He has been captured by the *malespero*, who has something planned for him that I'm sure is not good.

"Then there's Corinne. You have a soft spot for her, I know. She wants to go home, which would be a nice, happy ending for her. But she is headed down the wrong path and will soon find herself in a deadly position.

"And then there's me, the best neighbor a boy like you could ever have. I am stuck cohabitating with this old man, but there may be a way to restore my body and free me." He shifted into the figure of the old man. "Mr. Prentice, returning to this world exhausts and ages me, and I have so little energy left. We must conclude our conversation, and you must make a decision. You are free to abandon your wife and your friends. Crawl back under the bridge. That is certainly an option. But I suggest the other. Embrace your role as the *serĉilo*. Return to the Between."

Paul walked back to the window and looked out at the empty space where his house once stood. "You're trapped in a role as well, aren't you?" Paul asked. "The most powerful one. *Dio Ordo.* That's my guess. But you're just as trapped as the rest of us are."

The old man suddenly roared with laughter. "I am Rezső Simko, born in Budapest in 1958. But I am also, as you guessed, the one called *Dio Ordo*, the Order God. That is not why I laugh. I have not hidden my abilities from you, so it is no stroke of brilliance that you are correct. What is unexpected, Mr. Prentice, is your recognition that I, too, am a prisoner of the Between. I have gilded its walls. Indeed, almost every element of it reflects my conceptualization of what this amalgamation of many-worlds means. But, still, I am its servant...until..."

"Until someone replaces you."

"Precisely."

"Which is what you want me to do," Paul concluded. It wasn't a question.

"You see how weary I am. My time is nearing its end. I can either choose my successor or leave it to chance. I prefer the former." His strange inner glow flashed red briefly, and a scowl appeared on his face. The change reverted so quickly, Paul wasn't sure if he had imagined it.

"You're insane if you think—" Before Paul could finish his sentence, his subconscious mind finally connected the puzzle pieces scattered throughout the old man's words. "Hang on... You grew up in Budapest back when they taught Esperanto. And you were a computer engineer. Inside of the Between, you're the Order God. Jesus, it's so obvious, why am I just now realizing it? The computer game. You're the one who programmed it." Without waiting for the old man to respond, Paul asked, "Did you create the Between?"

With much effort, the old man stood. "I do not know who or what created the Between. I built the *game*, as you called it, to be a simulation of the strange world I found. You see, I stumbled into the Between in much the same way as you, as all of the outworlders. I first became the *serĉilo*, like you, and while I was able to escape back home from time to time, the Between possessed me, as it now possesses you. Everything I learned I added to my simulation. I believe it helped me survive. Over time, I played many of the roles, and ultimately became *Dio Ordo*. Then an...unexpected...thing happened. As the Order God, the Between itself evolved to resemble my own conceptualization of it. My conceptualization, as I have already explained, was framed as a computer program. So, you see, the Between's reality became a real copy of its own computer simulation. Fascinating, is it not? If you become *Dio Ordo*, the Between will again transform to become your conceptualization of it."

"I don't want to become a god of anything," Paul said. "I want to be free. I want all of us to be free."

Rezső Simko gave Paul a wry grin. "To achieve the latter, you must abandon the former. Become *Dio Ordo*, and the Between resets. All roles except yours are released."

"You mean…"

"Yes. They all become free."

"Everyone but me." Paul's mind reeled. He was the reason they all were trapped. He was the reason Min-woo was dead—or something like dead. It seemed like such a small price, to trade himself for everyone else. And wouldn't they be better off? Julie could find someone else. She could finally have a—

The old man interrupted Paul mid-thought. "I am tired, Mr. Prentice. Our discussion must end, and I must return." He hobbled to a burled walnut desk and from a drawer pulled out what looked like Min-woo's notebook. "Do not lose this again. I no longer have the strength to conjure another, and it is the only gift you will receive from me. Stay or go. Succeed or fail. It is you who will determine your fate…and that of the others."

Question after question burned through the whiskey haze in Paul's mind, but before he could ask a single one, the old man's eyes flared—one gold and one red. "Rest now, Paul Prentice, for you will soon need every bit of strength you can conjure and more." A laugh, equal parts amused and sinister, filled the room.

Paul began to protest, but then everything became weightless: the glass in Paul's hand, the chair he sat in, the table beside it. All the furniture and knickknacks in Min-woo's living room floated and drifted from where they lay. Only the old man, Rezső Simko, stayed fixed in place, his eyes shining painfully bright. And then the glow from those eyes vanished and took all the light with it, leaving Paul in a thick, smothering darkness.

"Mr. Prentice has the strength, but I am not sure he has the fortitude to succeed me," Rezső Simko said to the now empty room. He walked slowly toward the front door, pausing briefly to rest with a hand on a lacquered entryway table.

"To succeed *us*, you mean," said the voice of another Rezső

Simko, though it came from the same, withered body. That yellow inner glow had shifted red, and Rezső's expression became mischievous and wicked. "If I had my way, we would bring everyone together and announce that the last one standing becomes the next god. Let them sort it out."

"Of course you think that. You are the half of me who is *Dio Kaoso*," the Order embodiment of Rezső Simko said. "Leaving it open-ended risks the Between itself. If the Between vanishes, no more outworlds will be formed by the branching of chance, and the existing outworlds will become disconnected and drift apart, never to be joined again. Reality as we know it may slowly disintegrate into nothing. Does that not terrify you?"

Chaos-Rezső laughed. "All of reality is at stake? You have quite the imagination, brother. I doubt very much that the Between can be destroyed. However, I must admit I am tantalized by the promise of oblivion."

Order-Rezső scoffed. "I will never understand you." He stood as straight as he could and proceeded to the front door. From Minwoo's elevated porch, he could see over the safety fence to the Prentices' backyard, where a rectangle of black iron stood out against the surrounding grass. "Enough talk. Let us return. What will happen will happen."

"Now you sound like me."

"No one is perfect. Not even a god."

CHAPTER 9
A CHILD IS (NOT) BORN

Julie knew, even before she felt the first of those awful cramps, before the waves of nausea came, that she was pregnant. She and Paul had been married less than a year and had planned the next decade of their lives together, free of responsibility. She wanted to see Paris and Rome, to bicycle across Vietnam, to climb Kilimanjaro. At twenty-six, she had already become the director of the Blanton Museum's annual fund, and she saw a career taking shape that she wouldn't have dreamed of just a few years before. Paul had agreed when she said she wanted to wait until thirty to try to have children. His mind leaped to the financial benefits of delaying, of course, but she knew him well enough to know that a lifestyle change as big as having children was something he would put off until she forced the issue. And she wasn't ready to force the issue yet. She had a life she wanted to live first.

Except the pregnancy test said otherwise.

Paul had reacted with confusion, wanting to analyze how such a thing was possible when she was on the pill, and she had yelled at him. Called him unfeeling and robotic. She had never talked that way to him before, and it had surprised her as much as it had surprised him. Worse, his reaction was almost identical to her own, except she had been alone and in the bathroom when she learned the life they had dreamed about together wasn't the life they were going to live.

Paul came around almost immediately. Faster than she had, if she were being honest with herself. Either that, or he was a damn good actor. Paul, a good actor? Not a chance. He had hugged her and smiled. The first tears had been his. "It will be wonderful," he had said.

And in less than a day's time, her mind seemed to have transformed. It would, like Paul said, be wonderful. Daydreams of exotic travel destinations gave way to those of family Christmases. To the faces of her parents when she told them they would be grandparents. To new shared memories of first words and first steps.

It was, even with the morning sickness, the happiest time of her life for the next two months. Until the miscarriage. No one talked about miscarriages, the grief of losing the life growing inside you, of losing the dream of what that life would become. People gave more sympathy to the loss of a fucking cat than they did a miscarriage.

It hurt their marriage. They should have talked more, should have seen a therapist. Paul seemed to take his emotional cues from her, and if he didn't see her grieving, then he didn't show his own, assuming he felt grief beyond that first week or so.

For the next few years, the miscarriage became a silent but ever-present ghost that occupied a space between them. Their previously healthy sex life seemed like it had been left behind on the other side of an ocean. What made it worse was that Julie had stopped taking birth control pills. The hormones didn't work well with her body and mind. They never had, which is why she wasn't always good about taking them on schedule...which was how she had accidentally become pregnant in the first place. And so, sex brought with it a threat of repeating the event they no longer spoke of. When they did speak of children—often when nosy relatives or friends brought the subject up—they reverted to their old, pre-miscarriage plans, but the words sounded hollow and rehearsed to her ears.

On the night of Julie's twenty-ninth birthday, they celebrated with friends downtown until the bars closed at 2:00 a.m., rare for them even when they had been in their early twenties. Back home, some combination of the wine—easily two whole bottles worth for her—and the now-visible age of thirty and all it meant looming before her, Julie acted in ways she hadn't in years. She climbed on top of Paul, who had already fallen asleep, and began kissing him and taking his clothes off. He awoke, drunk and confused, but his body responded quickly and then he was in the moment with her. When the excitement became too much for him, he tried first to get her to slow down, and when she didn't, he tried to pull out, but she tightened her legs around him and wouldn't let him go. He panicked and his eyes went wide, and then, after a shudder, he stopped resisting.

Afterward, they lay silently next to each other, awake and suddenly feeling sober. When Paul finally spoke, it was to ask her how she would have felt if he had done what she did. Making the decision for both of them without discussing it first. "It's not the same," she had answered. And while that was true—if that night led to a pregnancy, it was her body that would carry their child, not his—it didn't change the fact that she *had* made the decision for them both.

The next morning over coffee, she apologized, but she felt like she had broken something in their marriage that an apology couldn't fix, that maybe nothing could fix. Paul said, "If you had asked me, I would have said no, and it would've been the wrong answer."

Whether it was bad luck or a cruel twist of fate, that night did lead to another pregnancy and another miscarriage. In Julie's mind, it was the same child as before trying to come into the world. Her body had failed it, or maybe it had sensed that its conception was somehow wrong, and it retreated into the darkness. She hid this second pregnancy from Paul, telling herself that she did it to protect him. When it ended, she felt like the world split between her and Paul. On his side, the pregnancy had never happened, and he went about his Paul-life in oblivious Paul-style.

Her side of the split held all the hope and the loss, all the pain, the failure, and the deception, which she bore alone. She hid it all as best she could, but she couldn't hide it from herself or from the child who she so desperately wanted to bring into the world.

The great bell echoed through the eight worlds of the Between. Its sound hit Julie like an ocean wave that knocked her loose from her body and sent her spinning back into a dark corner within the space her body had occupied. A void in the shape of a minotaur stood in Julie's place. She peered out from the void, seeing the world warped by the *Kosmaro's* aura, reality diffracted like light through a prism. Far away, outside the aura, things *were*. Within, things *might be*.

The *Kosmaro's* beast form moved in giant steps in the direction of a corpse, driven by the command of the bell. She knew now how the *Kosmaro* harvested souls, how *she* harvested souls. She had delivered basket after basket of souls to the Underworld where they fueled the giant machine at the bottom of the Between. Each time, when she collected the souls and carried them down, she believed it was a manifestation of her unborn child's soul. Once the delivery was complete, once the soul was imprisoned in iron, the delusion vanished, leaving behind guilt and a feeling of emptiness that rivaled the void.

She knew all this, yet still the bell brought back this delusion again, and as she approached the corpse, she felt a mother's anguish at what had been done to her child. She vowed to protect it so that it would never be in danger again. And then, her perception began to dissolve until she became lost in the void, and the beast acted on its own.

Sometime later, with no memory of the intervening time, Julie found herself as *herself*, no longer as the beast, standing on a pathway of crushed stone, flanked on either side by a sea of colorful flowers. The void still clung to her like an oily film. That feeling receded over the next several seconds but never fully vanished—a reminder that her time in this form, as herself, was limited.

She knew this to be the Garden of Before, the Between's fourth world. She had seen it in flashes while passing through it as the beast, but she had never been here in her own body until this moment. A thorn from the basket's handle, woven of bramble, dug into her palm. The basket was heavy with the weight of a soul.

My poor child, she thought while knowing the soul came from the body of the dead man in front of her and didn't belong to her own unborn child. As the *Kosmaro*, she could believe two different things at the same time. She could *be* two different things at the same time.

A cliff far in the distance called to her. Behind the waterfall streaming down the cliff's face of sheer rock was the *Kosmaro's* tunnel, bridging the Between's worlds. The World Tunnel would take her to the Underworld where she could deliver the soul and protect her child from all future violence.

The void started to spill out of her, beginning to form the beast, but she suppressed it, and the void retreated. It had rarely worked when she'd tried this before, to stay herself through force of will. But now it had, and for the next few fleeting moments, her choices were her own.

She picked a flower from the Garden in front of her. A single, ruffled bulb of yellow the size of her fist sat atop a thick stem covered with downy white fuzz. She brought it to her nose and took in its sweet and earthy scent. Other plants in the Garden that she had seen looked like things from alien worlds, but this flower and all its ilk in the small field before her were marigolds of a type she remembered from her honeymoon with Paul, in Mexico.

With the marigold in hand and the warmth of the sun on her cheeks, the memory of that trip became so vivid she felt like she had stepped into the past. The crushed stone path became the soft white sand of the beach. Bare feet replaced her running shoes. The field of flowers waving in the wind became the ocean, bringing with it the surf's churning growl and the scent of salt and seaweed in the air.

But before she could lose herself in the memory, a tall, night-black thing interrupted the scene. It looked like a pointed obelisk, towering out of the water, but whether it was close or far, she couldn't tell. The scene from her memory vanished, returning her to the Garden, but the obelisk remained.

Smaller, mirror-like obelisks were everywhere, marking each intersection of the Garden's grid of paths. But this single obelisk that had marred her daydream stood much taller than the others, and instead of a mirrored exterior, it appeared as a void silhouette. Like the beast form of the *Kosmaro*.

As she approached, voices in her mind began to whisper. These voices she had heard before. At times they sounded like they were talking to her, but the more she listened, the more it became clear that they were fragments of the memories of those who had preceded her as the *Kosmaro*, triggered by something she had seen. The dark obelisk caused a flurry of these memories.

The nexus. The center of the Between, where all the outworlds intersect.

Everything is here.

Nothing is here. If you enter it, you will become nothing.

Inside the nexus I see them all. Everyone I have lost, alive again!

The flower fell as she pressed her hands against her ears, as if that could stop the voices of the memories. She knew that the Between existed, somehow, at the intersection of parallel worlds, what Paul had referred to as outworlds. The Corinne and Supriya she knew were not the Corinne and Supriya of her own outworld. They had come from other outworlds. Were the voices saying that this obelisk—the nexus—was a connection between all of the outworlds? If so, maybe the nexus offered another way home. But the last voice had suggested something different.

Inside the nexus I see them all. Everyone I have lost, alive again!

What did it mean to *see them all*? To look into other worlds and see living versions of those who had died? Julie thought of Min-woo. Could she step into this obelisk and see Min-woo, alive and well, in a neighboring outworld?

She looked at the basket in her hand. The voice, like the others in her head, had been from a prior *Koŝmaro*. Had it stood in front of this obelisk carrying a soul like she did now? *Everyone I have lost*, it had said. What if she took the soul into the nexus? Could she restore it somehow?

Her right hand reached to touch the obelisk, as if upon its own volition. She recoiled but decided to follow her instinct and touch its darkness. Upon contact with the obelisk, her mind split into a million minds, but the *Koŝmaro*'s aura sprang forth as a reflex, like it had when she tried to sever her finger from her hand in the car door. Her many minds cohered into one, but the overlapping worlds did not. She knew that if she had not been the *Koŝmaro*, the nexus would have torn her apart.

Within the nexus, she found herself in an unexpectedly mundane place: a bathroom, the type found in a modest apartment. Within the bathroom stood an unfamiliar man staring intently at himself in the mirror as he ran a razor across his face. The man looked to be in his late fifties, hairline receding past the crown of his head, a loose belly hanging over the towel wrapped around his waist. Every action he took seemed to blur and then cohere. Small, seemingly insignificant decisions—to make another stroke down the left cheek, to move to the jawline—split the scene into branches, into new, overlapping worlds. Julie found that she was subconsciously using the *Koŝmaro*'s aura to force the divergent paths to become singular. She was following a single version of the man in a single outworld.

She tried looking at herself in the mirror but saw no reflection. The man didn't seem to notice her, either.

Who was he? As soon as the question formed in her mind, the answer became obvious. She looked at her basket. The soul within glowed like a tiny star. The dead man on the path...She was watching the lives of that man's parallels. The soul had guided her to him within the nexus...as if it was searching for its home.

She gently took the soul from her basket and held it close to the man. The soul recognized its body and cried out to be united with it. Its cry tore at her heart. Before she knew it, she was reaching with her other hand, the beast's dark hand, into the man's outworld.

The man sensed something was wrong. He turned and saw the monstrous hand coming toward him out of thin air. He panicked and dropped the razor but was too overtaken by fear to move.

My child needs this body! Julie screamed out in her mind. She grabbed him by the throat and pulled him out of his world, into the nexus. His eyes rolled back, and his body went limp. The soul in her other hand flared and cried with anticipation. But the man's body had another soul within it! She would have to tear it out and... and, what? Discard it?

What am I doing?

Julie threw the man back into his world and, with a single step, took herself out of the nexus obelisk. Back on the Garden's rocky path, her legs threatened to give out. The soul in her hand continued to cry, but its cries had weakened, and it had become so dim it could barely be seen. She steadied herself and put the soul back in her basket.

In the nexus, she had found a way to restore a soul, to bring the dead back to life, but it required an equal and offsetting act of wickedness. Thinking about it made her legs go weak again. The man's look of terror kept flashing in her mind. But even more disturbing was the thought that, for the right person, in the right moment, the price might be worth paying.

As if her own dark thoughts conjured it, the void began to emerge from within her. This time she couldn't resist it. She took on the minotaur form that resembled *First Mother*. Before returning to the World Tunnel and answering the call of the Underworld's bell, she let out a roar that echoed into the far reaches of the Garden.

CHAPTER 10
THROUGH THE GRAY WASTE

"One hundred and twenty-eight," Supriya announced, her voice echoing off the obsidian floor and walls of the Grand Staircase.

"More than that, surely," Corinne said. "It feels like it's been an hour or more."

"What? I don't mean the stairs. You had asked earlier about the number of"—Supriya searched for the right word—"*destinations* within the Patchwork World's maze. Like the field with the big, broken statue where you made your camp. There are one hundred and twenty-eight destinations." A hint of the *gardistaro*'s unnatural smoothness permeated Supriya's words. "Jay and I explored them all, and until you and I entered the staircase just now, I could visualize each of them in my head and know whether they were empty or occupied by someone... or some*thing*."

"I had no idea there were so many. I wasn't in the habit of exploring for exploration's sake. The field, the graveyard mansion, the old church, the surgery theater..."

An involuntary shiver ran through Supriya at the mention of that last room. Bags of blood hung from IV poles next to a rusty metal bed with worn leather straps meant for securing arms and legs. Supriya was familiar with surgical tools from her time in medical school, but the dirty blades and clamps presented on a rolling table beside the bed looked more like devices of torture than of healing. Three rows of seats filled a gallery above the operating floor. But what kind of operations occurred there?

"I hate that place," Supriya said.

Corinne, ahead of her on the steps leading down into darkness, looked back up briefly with her painted skull face and gave a nod. "I found it by accident, back before I knew more of the maze's patterns. I grabbed several useful tools but made it a point to never go back. It's creepy."

"You know which place I think is even creepier? The larder," Supriya said.

"The place with all of the food?"

"Yeah, and the jars of formaldehyde with strange animal parts and big insects with hairy legs and pincers. The worst thing about the larder is the footsteps on the floor above. Someone is always walking around up there, but they are invisible to my *gardistaro* sense. Like a ghost or something. Jay called out to them, or it, or whatever, and the footsteps stopped for a few seconds, but that was it."

"Of course Jay called out to them."

"His curiosity has gotten us into trouble on more than one occasion."

"Curiosity? Is that what you call it?"

Supriya did her best to ignore the question and the unhidden disdain in Corinne's voice. They descended in silence for several more minutes in the cold darkness.

This time, it was Corinne who spoke first. "How well do you know the Ruins beyond the Gray Waste?"

"I've never been."

Corinne stopped unexpectedly, and Supriya nearly ran into her.

"Never been?" Corinne asked. "You and Jay never went to other levels? The Between's other worlds?"

"Only the time when we were trying to escape the *Kosmaro*, and I was unconscious during much of that, as I'm sure you remember. You and Paul dragged me through the Gray Waste, after all. Assuming these stairs ever end, this will be the first time I have laid eyes on the second world."

"So, you don't know for sure if your powers will work." Corinne had an annoying habit of framing her questions like accusations.

"Of course they will work. I am the *gardistaro*," Supriya said with an unruffled certainty. In her mind, though, she began to wonder. How would she create a gateway between doors in a desert without doors? What about the Ruins? She cleared her throat and added, "Ninety-five percent certain. Eighty. Make it seventy-five. I'm seventy-five percent certain my powers will work there. We'll see soon...if these fucking stairs ever end. The one thing that still doesn't feel natural even after wearing a prosthetic for years now is stairs. I hate stairs, and I particularly hate these stairs."

"Supriya, if you can't create a gateway to somewhere in the Ruins, we'll have to walk through the Gray Waste. I brought water and a cloak. I even have sunglasses. You didn't bring anything."

Supriya rolled her eyes and gave Corinne a dismissive wave as if she were shooing away a pestering insect. "I'm upgrading my certainty to ninety-nine percent."

"Based on what?"

"Based on I'm done with this conversation. When we get to the platform below, I'll use the exit to open a gateway to your tower. And just like that, we'll be there."

Corinne stared blankly at her, then shrugged and continued down the stairs.

"Just like that, huh?" Corinne wore some stolen convenience store sunglasses she had pulled out of her backpack. Nonetheless, she shielded her eyes from the overwhelming sunlight pouring in through the platform opening at the foot of the Grand Staircase. "'Just like that, we'll be there,' you said."

"I know what I said!" Supriya waved her hands around the

perimeter of the exit, and when a shimmering gateway failed to appear, she marched around the platform angrily as if looking for something to throw or break.

"Any idea why it isn't working?"

"It works, Corinne. It works just fine, thank you. I can make a gateway right here, right now, if you want me to."

"But..."

"But I have no idea where it will lead to."

"That's a problem."

"I'm aware it is a problem. I don't need you to tell me it's a problem." Supriya stopped, closed her eyes, and smoothed the front of her gown, which hadn't needed smoothing at all. When she opened her eyes, they flashed with a hint of gold, and her voice again had the *gardistaro*'s unnatural iciness. "All space is adjacent. Distance is merely a matter of perspective. When I know two places well, I can *rotate* them in my mind, rotate them in planes you can't see, until I find the positions where they are adjacent. My gateways expose that adjacency. It is a bit like manipulating a Rubik's Cube."

"A Rubik's Cube? That makes a strange kind of sense, I guess. It sounds like you need to be pretty familiar with the locations you're trying to connect."

"Correct. And unfortunately, I don't know the tower in the Ruins at all beyond your description. Which apparently isn't enough."

Corinne took off her backpack and began digging through its contents. She handed a rough sand-colored cloak to Supriya and then a bottle of water, one of six she had stolen along with the sunglasses from a Walgreens on her way to the remains of the Prentice house that morning. "We walk, then. From here on, you need to follow my instructions, or you'll get both of us killed. Our first enemy is the sun. Put the cloak on and drink that entire bottle."

"Do you have another cloak for yourself?"

"Do I look like Cloaks-R-Us to you? No, I don't have another cloak. My jeans and this coat will have to do. I didn't think to pick up sunscreen or a hat, either."

Supriya tried to hand the cloak back, but Corinne pushed it away.

"You'll get scorched in that dumb cheesecloth gown without cover, Supriya. Now put it on, and let's go. If we get lost in the Waste, we're done for. So keep up. Once we get to the Ruins, there will be cover." Without waiting for a response from Supriya, Corinne stepped out from the shade within the Grand Staircase and onto the platform. The sunlight instantly felt like a fast-food heat lamp cooking her through her clothes.

Supriya followed. Rolling dunes of sand extended in all directions from the platform. Somewhere out there was a lone spire of rocks, the only landmark in an otherwise endless and uniform desert. The rocks were the key to navigating the Gray Waste. Keeping them directly behind you led to the next segment of the Grand Staircase, the segment leading down to the third world, the City Above. Walking toward the rocks led to the Ruins.

The wind whipped sand in all directions, making it difficult even with Corinne's sunglasses to see where they were headed. She had survived the Gray Waste several times before, most recently with Paul helping navigate using tips from that strange notebook he had. But her past successes gave her little comfort under the Waste's unrelenting sun. In each of her prior crossings, she reached a point where the sand, the sun, and the monotony ground down her will until she was convinced she would die out here, lost in an oblivion that seemed as empty as outer space. A nothingness of light rather than a nothingness of darkness.

She had begun to feel that familiar tug of despair when Supriya started talking again, as if they weren't facing certain death, as if the middle of an endless desert were the perfect place to carry on a conversation. Corinne told her to stop talking, that talking wasted energy and water. But Supriya kept on.

"You don't always have to be such an asshole, Corinne."

Corinne made no response, focusing on her footing as she climbed a dune that seemed to be never ending.

"Particularly to Jay. He doesn't deserve it. Even with the knife, he's a good person. He's fighting it with everything he's got."

"We've been over this, Supriya. It's not personal. The knife will win. It always does."

"It hasn't won yet."

"Tell that to the people he's murdered. Your role blinds you, Supriya."

"And your fatalism blinds you, Corinne," Supriya shot back. "Yes, Jay has killed... many people. That is true. But none of them—except perhaps my *gardistaro* predecessor—were innocent. They all had attacked us...or would have, given the chance."

"How convenient that they all deserved to die." The image of Matt Waggoner flashed in Corinne's mind, his eyes wide with astonishment as the car Corinne drove struck him. Over and over again she saw those eyes and felt the sickening satisfaction of that moment. What right did she have to judge Jay and Supriya, or anyone else for that matter?

Supriya, oblivious to the moral handwringing in Corinne's mind, continued, "Do you think that's all Jay and I have been doing for the past however long? Killing everyone we meet? Don't forget what role I play, Corinne. It's true that most of those we encounter want to kill us. Some sent by the *malespero*. Others... This place makes it easy for people to revert to savagery. But not everyone. I am the *gardistaro*. Those who want my help receive it. And Jay helps me help others. Just yesterday he found a boy who couldn't have been older than ten encircled by the *malespero*'s ash dogs, and he rescued that boy and took him to me and... Hey, are those the rocks we're looking for?"

Supriya pointed somewhere in the distance, but Corinne stared instead at Supriya. The heavy cloak draped over her couldn't hide the stature of a warrior goddess carved from stone. The burning sun of the Waste, the buffeting sand, the maddening endlessness, death all around them—none of it seemed capable of bending Supriya's will. Corinne almost believed Supriya when she claimed that she, and perhaps even Jay, could overcome the artifacts of the Between and remain themselves. If anyone had the strength, surely it was Supriya.

But no one had that strength. Jay was inches away from being lost, and soon after him, Supriya too would fall despite her will. If she wasn't already dead by then.

"You are making the same mistake I made," Corinne said.

Supriya turned toward her with a fire that rivaled the sun above. "Did you not hear a word I said?"

"I heard every word, Supriya. You're trying to convince me—or maybe yourself—that you and Jay are good people. But it doesn't matter who you are. A failed ballerina hooked on pain pills like me, or the strongest woman I've ever met who can't say no to the promise of being stronger, of being a goddess." Corinne paused and looked to where Supriya had been pointing. The hazy, heat-warped air did its best to obscure the stone spire in the distance, but it was finally visible. "The stronger this place makes you, the more it tricks you into thinking that strength is your salvation. It isn't. It's what binds you here. If you truly want to leave, you have to be ready to leave that strength behind. If there's a way to give up your artifacts and be free of your roles, you have to want that freedom first. I'm not sure that you and Jay do. I want it. My freedom is past those rocks ahead, and I intend to take it. There has to be a way for you and Jay to do the same, but you'll have to find it on your own. Then you can leave for good."

After a few seconds, Supriya said, "Lead on, Skull Girl."

CHAPTER 11
THE RUINS

As the two women approached the rocky spire, the ground beneath them began to change from ever-shifting dunes to weathered stone. Visibility decreased as if they were entering a light fog. They found themselves on the ridge of a canyon, overlooking the remains of a once great city now known only as the Ruins. Supriya followed Corinne to the shadow created by the rocks, where they could view the city without being exposed on the ridge.

Supriya had expected broken and collapsed buildings, and of these she saw many: once proud skyscrapers that had become husks like something left behind by giant, molting insects, and countless smaller buildings in various states of collapse. What she had not expected were the branching capillaries of lava criss-crossing between the piles of rubble. One wide river of lava flowed where water must have once bisected the town. It looked like a modern city had been placed in a crater of Hell and left to the unrelenting elements for a thousand years. It looked strangely beautiful. A peculiar twilight caused by snowy ash hung over the Ruins. At the very least, the Ruins offered an escape from the unrelenting sun of the Gray Waste.

With her *gardistaro* sense, Supriya felt the presence of a hundred or more humans below, most within a huge, surprisingly intact oval structure beyond what would have been the downtown area of the city. It might have been a sports arena of some kind, but it now looked like a fortress that had weathered centuries of attacks and still stood strong.

Corinne, seeing the focus of Supriya's gaze, said, "The *malespero*'s lair. We want to stay far away from that place. My tower is over there to the right." She pointed her finger at a lone building near the lava river, a small clock tower with gaping holes on each side where the clock faces used to be.

"I sense a lot of people here but not the *malespero* or the *Koŝmaro*." While Supriya continued to probe the area with her mind, she scanned the streets with her eyes, looking for doorways she could use to assist their travel. A pack of what looked like ash dogs—although it was impossible to tell for certain through the debris from up on the ridge—emerged from the inside of one building, crossed a street, and disappeared into a shadow created by a broken skyscraper. She was about to point them out to Corinne when she saw something else moving on a nearby street. Something that looked human, or, at least, walked upright with two legs and two arms. But it was too big to be human—three or four stories tall, stretched out like the reflection in a funhouse mirror. Its torso seemed to glow ember-red, visible even from this distance.

"What is that giant thing?" Supriya asked.

"The *burning ones*," Corinne said. "That's what I've heard them called. There's another over there. See? I don't know if they're controlled by the *malespero* somehow or if they walk around aimlessly, if they're guarding the Ruins or if they're hunting. What-ever they're doing, we want to stay clear of them. If you start smelling sulfur, that means one is nearby."

Supriya saw the one Corinne pointed at and another on a nearby street. She wished she had Jay here. The burning ones wouldn't have worried him one bit, and if they did, he would have cracked a joke so unfunny that it became hilarious. But Jay wasn't here, so she had to be the brave one. "If we can get down to that nearest building, I might be able to jump us from one doorway to the next. If I can see it, I can probably make a gateway to it. Better than walking down the middle of the street."

Corinne tightened her backpack and double-checked the knives and wands she kept hidden under her jacket. She pulled out the gray wand and held it so tight her knuckles turned white. Supriya had seen the shockwaves that wand sent out.

"We'll keep to the buildings as much as we can. If we're attacked, we run. We can't hang around and fight. There's a lot more crawling about in the Ruins than what you can see from here, and it will all be on top of us if we make a racket." Corinne looked down at Supriya's prosthetic leg.

"Yes, I can run, Corinne," Supriya said. "Faster than you."

Corinne nodded. "I believe you."

"Lead the way," Supriya said, expecting Corinne to set out along the ridge toward an area where the canyon wall had been ground down to a gentle slope, either by sand and time or by a civilization long since vanished. Instead, Corinne put one hand on the ground near the edge, pivoted, and dropped over. Supriya scrambled to the edge and found that Corinne had merely jumped down to an outcropping about five or six feet below and was now descending the canyon wall with almost mountain goat-like ease, hop-stepping from rock to rock.

"It looked like you jumped off the edge," Supriya said as she scooted over it with far less grace. "I'm wearing a gown and sandals. Great for climbing. No need to wait for me. I'm sure I'll be fine." *Fucking ballerina*, she added in her head.

Corinne, already another thirty feet below, looked up at Supriya with her expressionless skull face and said, "I'll slow down."

She didn't slow down—at least, not that Supriya could tell. Supriya did her best to keep up, losing her footing repeatedly, tearing up the palms of her hands to catch herself over and over again. As they got deeper into the canyon, the heat from the flowing lava below rose up to meet them. Unlike the scorch of the sun in the desert, this was all-encompassing, like they had climbed into the mouth of a giant beast. At least the sun didn't seem to have its same oppressive power in the canyon. The deeper they climbed, the more the light seemed to come from the floor of the canyon rather than from the sun above. By the time they reached the bottom, they were in the twilight section Supriya had seen from above. A thin layer of ash covered every surface, motes of gray floating in the air like dirty snowflakes.

Supriya almost asked Corinne if something was burning somewhere in the city to produce all this ash. By now, though, she knew better than to expect simple cause and effect within the Between. The sky over the Ruins was full of ash and locked in perpetual twilight because that's how it was here. No other reasons were necessary.

She followed closely behind Corinne to the hollowed-out corner of a building at the perimeter of the Ruins. The building— the two walls that were left of it—was made from reinforced concrete. No glass or wood anywhere. The windows had no metal frames. The doorways had no rusted, broken hinges. Had the doors and windows ever been functional? Were these so-called ruins ever anything more, or had they been created within the Between in exactly this state? The questions seemed academic, but Supriya had a feeling the answers were anything but.

When Supriya made gateways between two locations, she connected already-existing doors. Not door-shaped spaces, not suggestions of doors, but actual human creations that served to divide and link separate spaces. Something about the human conceptualization of a door was what enabled it to be used as a *gardistaro* gateway. If these door-shaped spaces in the Ruins were never really doors, could she link them at all?

She scanned the nearby buildings until she found what looked like another doorway. This one—another open space in a concrete wall—was on the exposed interior of one of the broken skyscrapers, six stories up. She closed her eyes and tried to visualize the doorway in her mind. In the Patchwork World, this had never been a challenge. She did it without consciously trying to. But here, it took effort, almost more effort than she could muster. The instant her mind's eye saw the doorway, it started to dissociate, like the surrounding wall was made of smoke and could be blown apart by a breath. She tried again, and again the image in her mind came apart just as she saw it.

"Are you trying to get us up in that tall building?" Corinne whispered.

The unexpected sound of Corinne's voice broke Supriya's concentration, and when she opened her eyes, it was with a glare.

"If it doesn't work, we need to find another way. And quick," Corinne added and then nodded in the direction of the adjacent street. A pack of ash dogs were approaching, perhaps a block away. The dogs hadn't noticed them yet—or at least, the dogs made no sign that they had. But if she and Corinne didn't move soon...

"It will work," Supriya said, eyes closed again. She had spoken a little louder than she had intended, and Corinne's resultant growl indicated that Supriya's words had been too loud, indeed.

Instead of focusing on the doorway in the skyscraper, Supriya visualized the Ruins as a whole, as she had seen the area from up on the ridge. In her mind, she saw the collapsed structure she and Corinne now hid in, and she saw, too, the skyscraper. Between them she imagined a yellow thread, its ends loose and moving like a snake with a head on each end of its body, searching and searching. She placed her hand on the rough concrete of the doorway next to her, and that doorway immediately appeared in her mind near one end of the thread. Before the doorway could dissolve, she made the thread strike and attach itself. In her mind, the nearby doorway turned yellow and became one with the thread. At the other end, she tried to do the same with the doorway in the skyscraper, but the thread wasn't long enough, and the doorway began to break apart.

Next to her, Corinne was talking. A hand on Supriya's shoulder, pulling at her. And something else as well—the *gardistaro* awareness that someone new had entered the Ruins. Not through the Gray Waste like they had, but directly from outside the Between. A new outworlder.

She shrugged all of this off and focused on the doorway high up in the skyscraper again. When it tried to dissolve, she reset its image in her mind. Over and over again, as it broke apart, she replaced it. Faster and faster, until the image of the doorway held. With all her might, she compressed the space between the doorway and the loose thread.

A gateway flashed into existence, and immediately she stepped through it with Corinne close behind. Once Corinne was clear, Supriya released the gateway. A wave of exhaustion briefly made the world dark, and before Supriya knew it, she had fallen into Corinne. Both of them ended up on the floor, but it was the floor within the skyscraper. In the distance, the grinding, metal-on-metal howls of the ash dogs filled the air—anguish at the loss of their prey.

Supriya tried to get to her feet, to hide her sudden exhaustion from Corinne, but the skull-faced woman held her down.

Shhhh, Corinne mouthed with a finger at her lips and then gestured to their left with a slight nod of her head.

A man sat in the window of the neighboring building only twenty feet from them, scanning the Ruins with a spyglass. Like all the *malespero*'s soldiers, he wore makeshift armor, pieces of leather and metal bound together with rope and rags. A tattered wide-brimmed hat sat above a face smeared with char. Everything about him looked gray and dirty like the building he was in, like all the Ruins. A crossbow of some kind sat in his lap, and strapped to his back was a baseball bat with nails driven through the end.

Luckily, he hadn't noticed them and seemed intent on something happening near the base of the building in which Supriya and Corinne now sat. The soldier stood, placed his thumb and forefinger in the corners of his mouth, and made a piercing whistle. A series of similar whistles came from all over the Ruins, followed by a crash from below.

With the man distracted, Supriya pulled herself to her feet and leaned out the window to see what was happening. Several dogs and more of the *malespero*'s soldiers were chasing someone through the street between the two buildings. Their prey had a lead of a city block or more, but the dogs were closing in quickly, and other soldiers were converging from a street to their right.

The fleeing man was the new arrival Supriya had sensed seconds ago. The poor fool had stumbled into the Between in the worst possible way. As he ran, he kept yelling as if he was pleading with someone for help. It sounded like, "Oberon! Oberon!" The name meant nothing to Supriya, but his newness and his desperation called out to the core of her role as *gardistaro*. The man hadn't yet been given a choice.

Without thinking, she created tiny tears in the space in front of the man's pursuers, little gateways to elsewhere that acted like razors suspended in the air. She had discovered this type of attack by accident while in Jay's kitchen and had used it several times since.

The dogs seemed to sense something wrong in the air ahead of them and nimbly avoided Supriya's trap. Two of the pursuing men, however, ran directly into the tears. Their armor did nothing because there was nothing to block, but that nothing—that elsewhere in space—tore through them like the sharpest of blades. Another soldier, seeing two of his comrades fall, stumbled to a stop and began looking for their assailant in the nearby buildings.

Supriya had begun to trace the outline of another tear, this one destined for the stopped soldier's brain, when Corinne pushed beside her at the window. The gray wand in Corinne's hand let out a hollow thrum, and a cone of rippled air struck the soldier in the neighboring window just as he pointed his crossbow at Supriya's head. The crossbow flew one way, the man's hat flew another, and he was knocked to his back. A second later, the crossbow hit the ground with a crack.

A much louder crack—this one like a thunderclap—came from below. Broken pieces of concrete peppered Supriya's face. A bullet had struck the wall next to her. On the ground below, a soldier deftly reloaded a bolt-action rifle. Supriya dove back from the window.

"We're about to have visitors," Corinne said. "Can you create another gateway? If not, we're in trouble. We can't fight them all."

Supriya's mind kept pulling her attention toward the fleeing man. "Did you see him?"

"Him? There were a bunch of them."

"No, I mean the man they were chasing."

"The man they were chasing? They're always chasing someone. We can't be everyone's hero, Supriya. Let's focus on saving ourselves. A gateway would be nice right now."

"Make it yourself, then," Supriya snapped and instantly regretted it. She turned her attention to the landscape of broken buildings. She thought she saw a door on a strange bridge connecting two buildings but realized it wasn't a bridge at all. The top half of a tall building had broken off and now leaned into one of its neighbors. It looked ready to collapse at any moment. Most of the structures were in such disrepair that jagged holes were the only suggestions of where doors might have been.

"There's a stairwell over here," Corinne said. "And it looks more or less usable."

"What? You want to go downstairs?"

"No, I don't want to go downstairs! I'm going to blast anyone who comes up it. Unless you can provide an alternative."

"I'm working on it!"

In the middle of the city, about halfway to the tower, Supriya saw an open space with nothing but rubble and intersecting lava rivulets. Maybe it had once been a park. It didn't look like a park at all now, unless it was a park in hell. Beyond the park, the buildings were too obscured by the ashy darkness for her to make out their details.

"Supriya?"

She ignored Corinne and kept scanning for anything resembling a doorway, but her eyes kept trailing over the park until something at its center caught her attention. Was that a doorway, right in the middle of the park, on what looked like a small island in the lava? She squinted.

"Supriya! They're coming!"

It was a doorway under a strange arch. If the arch had been part of a larger structure, that structure was now gone, leaving only the arch and the door.

"I found a place," Supriya said, "but I don't think you'll like it."

"It can't be any worse than staying here," Corinne said as she made her way back to Supriya from the stairwell. Corinne looked where Supriya pointed and then her skull-painted face scowled. "Never mind. You've managed to find someplace worse. We'll be out in the open. Find someplace else."

"There is no *someplace else!*"

Sounds came from the stairs. Voices. Heavy footsteps.

Corinne moved back toward the stairs and began studying a wall. She mumbled something to herself about the odds of the building collapsing. The whole structure shook. Dust rained down from the ceiling above them.

"What did you do?" Supriya asked.

"That wasn't me!"

Another rumble, more dust. This time the building groaned, and the floor felt loose for a moment under Supriya's feet. She held on to the concrete opening and continued looking for a viable doorway. Would she even be able to create another gateway here? The last one took almost everything she had. Before she could tail off into doubt, she saw movement in the area she thought of as the park. It was the new arrival, still running. He was almost to the park's edge. She didn't see any human pursuers—maybe they were all climbing the stairs under her—but she did see several dogs, a pack nimbly jumping the lava streams after him.

Yet another rumble, worse than the previous two. A crack ran through the ceiling above.

"That one was me!" Corinne yelled, her wand aimed at the space where a wall once was—a wall that she had just knocked down into the stairway up to their floor. A plume of dust rose from the stairwell. "Should slow them down a bit." No sooner had Corinne said those words than out of the cloud lunged a dust-covered ash dog, striking her in the chest. She tumbled backward, and her wand bounced along the floor.

The dog saw Supriya moving toward it, and in its brief moment of hesitation between targets, Supriya traced a small gateway in the air. The top half of the dog's head fell through the gateway and emerged out of a linked portal a couple of feet to its right. Its body collapsed, and what looked like molten metal poured out of the gaping hole in its head.

Corinne pushed herself to her feet. Instead of thanking Supriya, she asked, "Where did my wand go?"

"It's right over..." Supriya pointed to where she saw the wand bounce and roll, but there was a large missing portion of the wall where the wand should have been.

The skull-faced woman narrowed her eyes and then turned back toward the stairwell, where they both could hear voices and the sound of rubble being moved. Corinne took the red wand out from her jacket and sent a jet of fire into the dust and collapsed concrete. A voice cried out in pain.

Another voice, this one gruff and accented, as if English weren't his first language, said, "You're trapped up here. Give up. You can join us!" Other nearby voices laughed.

Corinne responded with another blast of flames.

"We've got a spicy one, lads!" came the voice from the stairs.

"I'll get us out of here," Supriya said. *I hope*, she added silently. She went to another window and continued scanning for doorways while doubt clawed at her. What if her *gardistaro* energy was too depleted to form another gateway—or at least a gateway large enough for them to travel through? She and Jay had discovered early on that their role abilities had limits. The more they used those abilities, the more fatigued they became, but it was a unique form of fatigue, not physical and not mental, either. Nani, her grandmother, used to speak of *shakti*, the energy within everything. Whatever it was—*shakti*, *chi*, or the Force from *Star Wars*—Supriya's fuel tank felt dangerously low.

She closed her eyes and recited the words of Rabindranath Tagore that she had taken as her personal mantra. "Let me not pray to be sheltered from dangers but to be fearless in facing them. Let me not beg for the stilling of my pain but for the heart to conquer it." She repeated the final words over and over until she felt full again, full of the energy of those words.

...the heart to conquer...

...the heart to conquer...

She opened her eyes and looked again across the ruined hellscape. Except for the strange arch in the park, there were no other doorways. It would have to do. She began tracing the air around the doorway near her and in her mind reached for the doorway in the park. Even if she hadn't been exhausted by her previous effort, connecting the two should have been an impossible task. Cocooned in the words of her litany, she refused to acknowledge the impossibility. She refused, as well, to accept her body's physical limits. Darkness consumed her vision, but she didn't need her eyes because she saw her destination with her mind. The strength drained from her leg of muscle and flesh, so she leaned on her leg of metal, and it stood strong. She felt the gateway snap into being, and everything she had ignored came rushing back.

She collapsed, but not due to her own weakness. The floor had cracked, and the wall to the left of her crumbled as a large hand grabbed ahold of it. The smell of sulfur became so overwhelming that she could barely breathe.

The head of a burning one raised over the floor next to her, pits of fire where its eyes and mouth should have been. Its other hand grabbed the ceiling above, and it pulled itself up to reach in for her.

Another crash, this one heavier than the others. The building shook and then listed toward the burning one. As she had done hours before, Corinne dragged Supriya through her own gateway right as the entire structure gave way.

"The best I could do," Supriya said. The stone beneath her was hot —Delhi asphalt in summer hot—but she lacked the strength to do anything about it.

Corinne tried to pull her up, but while the skull-faced woman was more than capable in many areas, brute physical strength was not one of them. Supriya outweighed her by at least fifty pounds and might as well have been made of lead.

"I'm not complaining," Corinne said and nodded in the direction they had come from. A cloud of dust was expanding from the fallen building and had already covered half of the Ruins. "But you can't rest here. We have to keep moving. The tower is close."

The great bell rang. It had become a familiar sound to Supriya in the Between, but instead of becoming numb by familiarity, the bell sent her heart racing. She could feel it shaking the bones within her body as if it had come from deep inside her. The great bell of the Underworld had once rung for her, summoning the *Koŝmaro* to come for her soul. The *Koŝmaro* would be here soon. She tried to warn Corinne and felt herself speaking but couldn't hear her own words.

Corinne looked at her strangely. "Julie? Julie, who? Julie Prentice? Why did you just say Julie's name?"

Supriya had no answer. She wasn't sure she had spoken at all, much less said Julie's name. She opened her mouth again, to tell Corinne what had happened to Julie, but the words were gone. *I do not wish to have the answers*, Corinne had said. The icy cool of the *gardistaro* washed through Supriya, pushing her consciousness to the back of her mind—an observer in her own body. She rose to her feet, fluid like a spirit rather than a body made of flesh and bone.

Supriya's sudden transformation was enough to alarm and distract Corinne. "Stay with me, Supriya. We're almost there."

"I'm with you," Supriya said with a voice that suggested otherwise.

Corinne gave her a look of skepticism but set out, nonetheless. What choice did she have? They wordlessly navigated the little streams of glowing lava and eventually made it to the other side of the area Supriya thought of as the park. From there, they slipped from building to building, seeing only a single *burning one* lumbering in the direction of the collapsed building.

When they reached the tower, Supriya felt control of her body begin to return. "We made it," she said. The structure before them was a tower in name only. Compared to the other buildings in the city—what remained of the buildings, anyway—the tower was short and unimpressive. Fifty feet tall, if that. A blocky column with barely enough space inside for a staircase. Atop the tower, each of its four sides had the same circular opening where perhaps a clock face once had been. Unlike the other buildings, which were all made of the same drab concrete, the tower was entirely constructed of ruddy brown brick.

As if reading Supriya's thoughts, Corinne said, "Back home, down by the river at the edge of town, there's a clock tower that looks exactly like this. I never paid much attention to it, so I can't be certain, but I think this is the same tower."

"The same tower? What does that mean?"

Corinne thought for a minute and then said, "I'm done trying to figure out what shit here means. Come on." She entered the tower. Supriya followed.

At the top of the tower was a small, square room illuminated by the circular holes at the tops of each of its brick walls. None of the walls had any features or distinctive marking.

Corinne looked from wall to wall with confusion. "I'm not sure which one it was."

"I can tell you," Supriya said. She held her hand up to the nearest wall and closed her eyes, but she felt nothing. The same with the other three.

"Maybe you need to rest a bit," Corinne said.

"I'm sure that's it."

A bit turned out to be at least an hour, most of which was in silence, both women sitting leaned against a wall. Eventually the silence began to grate on Supriya. "Let's get you home," she said. She could feel the energy, the *shakti*, within her, not as full as if she'd had a night's sleep, but enough. Once again, she examined each of the walls, reaching out with her mind for the invisible door that had once been the connection to Corinne's outworld. It had been a long time—Corinne had been vague about just how long—since the door had been used. Still, Supriya should have felt a trace of it. Whether that trace would be enough to reopen the door was another question entirely. A question she didn't have to answer because she felt nothing.

She looked at Corinne, and that look communicated everything. The skull-faced woman merely nodded.

"Consider your debt to me repaid," Corinne said.

"I'm sorry. When I was the *masinisto*, I understood how all this works. Now, though... Maybe it's been too long? Or maybe if I rest some more—"

"No," Corinne interrupted. "I shouldn't have gotten my hopes up."

They sat in silence. Supriya wracked her mind for something, anything, she could do for Corinne. "I'm familiar with this place now, so I can at least get us out of here, open a gateway between the door to the tower and the Grand Staircase. Beats walking back through the desert."

"You go ahead."

"And leave you here? Why would you stay?" To Supriya, staying was suicidal. "We're not out of options. Jay and I could force the *masinisto* to make a new connection to your outworld." She wasn't sure it actually worked like that, but at this point, all she cared about was the defeated look on Corinne's face, made doubly dire by the painted skull. "Or I could become the *masinisto* again. For a little while, anyway."

Corinne didn't seem to be listening.

Supriya was about to try another approach when she sensed that Jay had entered the Gray Waste. Jay had nearly died in this desert several months ago. He had told Supriya his tale of survival more times than she could count, a tale that became more harrowing and heroic with each retelling. But apparently even the Gray Waste wasn't enough to keep Jay from following her like an abandoned dog. How would Corinne react to the news that Jay was on his way here? As she was about to tell Corinne, she sensed others emerging in the Gray Waste near him. Many others, and one of them in particular radiated with a presence she recognized —another of the Between's canonical roles. The *malespero*.

"What's wrong?"

Supriya looked at Corinne with confusion. How long had the skull-faced woman been staring at her? "It's Jay," she said. "He's here... and he's with the *malespero* and dozens of the *malespero*'s soldiers. They've captured him." Her irises flashed gold, and she took on the steely look of the *gardistaro* before gliding toward the stairs.

"There's nothing you can do, Supriya," Corinne said, but if Supriya heard her, she showed no evidence of it.

———

After Supriya left, Corinne sat in the tower, mind empty of thought, body empty of energy and purpose. She might never have stood had movement not caught her eye through a hole in one of the tower's walls. The outworlder, as Supriya had called him—the man who had been running from the ash dogs and the soldiers before she and Supriya diverted their attention—had climbed up in the remains of a building near the tower and was huddled in a corner. She knew the confusion and fear he now felt. She also knew that she couldn't save him, or herself, or anyone else, but she stood and went to him anyway. What was the name of the Greek character who kept pushing the boulder up the hill only to have it roll back over him time and time again?

CHAPTER 12
A CAGE OF BLACK IRON

The *malespero*'s soldiers threw Jay face first into the hardscrabble ground. With his wrists shackled behind his back, he couldn't catch himself, so he got up and personal with every bit of grit, every grain of sand. He spat, or at least tried to, but his mouth was so dry that all he could do was blow and cough. Something thudded next to him, so close to his face that it knocked sand into his eyes.

"Where the fuck did you get a bottle of Dasani?" he said and then wormed his way to it. The label on the bottle had been bleached by the sun, but it still carried the incongruity all objects from home had when they unexpectedly showed up here. He was so thirsty that he tried to untwist the cap behind his back and then drink from the bottle while lying on the ground. A good third of the water ended up somewhere other than in his mouth.

One of the soldiers finally took pity on him and removed the shackles. In the process, the bottle got kicked aside, and the rest of the soldiers laughed as Jay scrambled to the bottle and tried to suck out the remaining moisture.

"That's enough. We didn't bring him all this way to let him die of thirst," came a voice that was now all too familiar, a young voice that seemed to dance between friendly innocence and mean-spirited haughtiness.

Jay rolled over and saw the *malespero*'s silhouette standing over him. Spiked armor and braided ponytails eclipsed the perpetual noonday sun. He had a dozen insults ready but instead heard himself say, "I want my knife back."

"Soon enough, Jay. I need to show you to your room first."

They had dragged him across the desert and to the remains of a city of fire and unending twilight within a canyon. He paid attention to little along the way—little except for the oppressive sun and the backpack that the *malespero* carried slung across one shoulder. The backpack held the Knife of Undoing, the *stelisto*'s artifact. It called to him, pleaded with him to regain it. Shackled and surrounded by the *malespero*'s soldiers, all he had been able to do was watch and follow.

Until now, he hadn't really seen the structure they had entered. A partially collapsed stadium, like the Roman Colosseum but more modern, duller. Two decks of seats, a hundred rows or more, stretched up to the ash-clouded sky. Whatever had been in the stadium's center was long gone, and now all that remained was a vast expanse of hard ground in the middle of which someone had built two large geodesic domes of black iron, one inside of the other. A cage of some sort.

"That's your room," the *malespero* said, nodding toward the domed structure. It was fifty or sixty feet across and about half that tall. A soldier moved and twisted several of the outer dome's iron rods, and a section of it seemed to unfold and open. He repeated the process with the inner dome. "Never seen doors like that, have you?" She didn't wait for Jay to answer before continuing. "The problem with doors in the Between is that they can be used by the *gardistaro*. I'm not a fan of unexpected guests. I'm told that she's here, somewhere in the Ruins already.

"You'll also notice the cage is completely open to what limited sunlight makes it through the haze. It wouldn't be a very good cage if you could escape it, and I know what you can do with shadows. When you're done training each day, you'll be provided a bedroll. You'll need your rest."

"Training? I'm not doing anything for you," Jay said.

The *malespero* gave him a blank stare through her iron mask and then said, "Walk into the center of the cage." After several seconds passed with no movement from Jay, she said, "Walk into the center of the cage... and I will give you your knife back."

At the mention of the knife, a cold wave of desire ran through him. He could have resisted if he had wanted to. Probably. But he heard truth in the *malespero*'s voice; she really meant to give it back to him. So, he did as she instructed and trudged to the cage, leisurely and cool, as if going to the cage had been his idea all along. Then he ruined it by looking back over his shoulder, over and over, not at the *malespero*, but at the backpack she carried. He was being led like a dog on a leash in front of all these watching soldiers. Soon he'd have his knife back, and none of it would matter. Soon he'd carve out each and every eyeball that had witnessed this humiliation. When he reached the center of the cage, one of the soldiers folded the opening of the inner dome back together, closing Jay inside.

The *malespero* walked inside the outer dome and stopped at the bars that stood between her and Jay. She playfully dangled the backpack in her hand before pitching it through the bars. Jay caught it before it hit the ground and tore the zipper open to get at the knife. Once it was in his hand, energy flooded him, erasing his exhaustion and filling him with hate and the lust to slaughter everyone around him, starting with the *malespero*. He moved in a flash, striking at one of the cage's iron bars, expecting it to give like paper under the knife's blue blade.

A jolt struck him. It was as if a giant snake made of lightning had come through the knife, through his arm, and sunk its fangs into his heart. He staggered backward and fell hard.

"The knife did that to you," the *malespero* said. "It commanded all your focus. You didn't notice the cables running from the cage to the generator. You didn't notice when Esther over there threw the switch and the generator started up, electrifying the cage. Do you hear the generator now, grinding and belching smoke? How did you miss that? The knife, that's how.

"During your training, it will be the knife compelling you to do as I say. Not me. You were the one that picked it up. You became the *stelisto*. You became a powerful *stelisto*. I haven't seen one who could travel through shadows like you. But you need to be more powerful still."

"Let him go," came Supriya's voice.

Jay felt a tangled flash of joy, pride, and love, and then it all soured into despair. "No, Supes! Get the fuck out of here! It's a trap! The whole goddamn thing is a trap!"

The *malespero* tilted her head a bit, and despite the mask covering her lips, it was clear from her narrowed eyes that she was smiling. "I was wondering how I was going to capture you, Supriya Reddy. You've made my work easy. Thank you." The *malespero* swiveled and walked out of the cage.

Supriya, eyes blazing gold, stood at the edge of the arena floor, arms outstretched like a Greek goddess about to call down a lightning strike. Two soldiers had rifles trained at her while others carrying clubs and spears began walking slowly toward her.

"Consider your next action very carefully, *gardistaro*," the *malespero* said.

In spite of the *malespero*'s words, Supriya made sudden gestures with her hands, and each of the rifle-armed soldiers collapsed. While the others backed warily away, the *malespero* began sprinting toward Supriya, thorned armor suddenly ablaze with blue flame.

Supriya directed her razor gestures at the *malespero*, but all that resulted were static pops and flashes of light within the flame surrounding the *malespero*.

"That doesn't work on me, girl!" the *malespero* said in a voice that radiated hatred and menace.

It was the first show of anger Jay had seen from the *malespero*. Even with the Knife of Undoing in his hand, dread and panic suffused him. He tried again to chop at the bars separating him from Supriya. The jolt seemed worse this time even though he had braced for it. By the time he gathered his wits and sat up, the fight, such as it was, was over.

The *malespero*, still ablaze, stood over Supriya, a rippling wave of force emanating from her left hand, pinning Supriya to the ground.

All Jay could do was scream.

The *malespero* looked at him over her shoulder and then, in a loud voice that contained none of the venom it had seconds before, said, "It would be so easy for me to crush every bone in her body and leave her as a whimpering puddle of flesh. Seeing her in *that dress*"—she spat the words as though they pained her—"makes me want to do it." She let the weight of her words hang in the air and then continued, "But I won't. Do you know why, Jay? Because I don't have to. Because torturing Supriya is your job." With her right hand, the *malespero* beckoned the soldier standing near the generator. "Esther, come over here."

A woman with jet black hair who looked to be in her forties ran quickly to the *malespero*. Like all the soldiers, Esther wore mismatched armor that had been collected, assembled, and pieced together from whatever had been handy. Unraveled soda cans riveted into thick canvas. A set of shoulder pads that looked like they had been stolen from a high school football locker room. Pants of canvas and denim with leather patches along the thighs.

Esther kept her head bowed, eyes trained on her own feet. "Yes, *malespero*?"

"Take her gown off."

"Yes, *malespero*."

The soldier named Esther had difficulty navigating the force wave emanating from the *malespero*'s left hand. Supriya, despite everything, struggled so hard that it took two more soldiers holding her legs before the deed was complete.

The blue fire around the *malespero* vanished, and she turned away from Supriya as if the naked woman on the ground no longer mattered. She held and inspected the *gardistaro* gown. "It really is exquisite, as beautiful as my armor is wicked. But it didn't belong to you, Supriya." The *malespero* turned toward Esther. "Take your clothes off."

Esther glanced confusedly at the other soldiers.

"Esther, do I have a habit of asking for things twice?"

"No, *malespero*." Esther quickly removed her armor, leaving her in an old Levi's T-shirt and faded yellow cotton shorts. How quickly she looked transformed. Some of the other soldiers turned away as she stripped completely.

"Now give your clothes to Supriya. Good." She tossed the *gardistaro* gown to Esther. "Congratulations, Esther. You are the *gardistaro* now."

CHAPTER 13
HELLO, LITTLE ONE

Near the edge of the Ruins, on the far side opposite of the rocks leading to the Gray Waste, a lava spring began to bubble. A small four-legged creature covered in glowing molten rock climbed from the pool on unsteady legs and then shook itself in the same way that a wet dog shakes itself dry. This creature was a sort of dog but with a smoldering ember at its core instead of a heart. It made eye contact with the person watching nearby and began to wag its stump of a tail.

"Hello, little one," the *malespero* said. She beckoned for the newborn ash dog to come to her with a gesture from both her hand and her mind. The ability to command the creatures of the Ruins was something that emerged over her time as the *malespero*, like the *stelisto*'s new ability to shift shadows. Sin described the emergence of latent role abilities as *awakening*. Whether that was a term he came up with or not, she had no idea.

Sin would be visiting soon. He always seemed to know when something eventful happened, and capturing both the *stelisto* and the *gardistaro* easily qualified. He always, also, brought death with him when he visited. The *Malluma Sinjoro*. The Dark Lord of Chaos. Her taskmaster.

When the ash dog came near, she could feel its heat radiating out as if it were a little furnace. It would grow to full size within a few hours. Only by coming here could she see the creatures when they were small and not yet the monsters that they would become. She scratched it behind the ear with a gloved hand.

"Your name is... Otter," she said. "Do you like your name, Otter?"

It responded with a wag and leaned into her hand. This little act of affection broke through all her emotional walls, and tears welled up in her eyes. She had lost her ability to feel, first by pushing the feelings away, and then by becoming the *malespero* and having the role's warlord persona cover her own thoughts like its black armor covered her skin. But at this spot in the Ruins where the ash dogs were born of fire, those lost feelings broke through. She didn't know why—perhaps it was the connection she had with the creatures—but the feelings were never happy ones. Only loss, grief, and, most of all, loneliness. But they were hers and they were real.

Otter put one paw on her lap and then the other. When he tried to climb into her lap, his heat became overwhelming. She gently nudged him back to the ground.

"You don't want to be a monster, Otter. Do you?" she said and then added, "Neither do I."

It stared at her with its fire-pit eyes. She gave it another few scratches and then her gaze caught the mask sitting on the rock next to her. She turned the mask over and studied its face—agony cast in iron. Who had it been modeled after? She had found the mask in the Between's sixth world, the Skytower, where it had been sitting in the middle of a giant lotus leaf, as if waiting for her. Her sister had been with her then—it was before they went their separate ways—and had urged her not to touch it. Thoughts of her sister kept her tears flowing.

Against her sister's wishes, she had kept the mask...and then she had begun wearing it.

"I know this mask," Sin had said when he first saw her with it on. "Long ago, a powerful *masinisto* journeyed to the Underworld and took one of the iron statues back to his mansion to study. He cut the face off the statue and made this mask. Then he took the soul the statue had carried and worked it into the metal of the mask. That is why it is always cool to the touch. He created the mask to trick the Between into thinking its wearer was already dead. Whoever is dead cannot be killed again. Or so the *masinisto* thought."

"How did he die?" she asked.

"Oh, he didn't die," Sin said. "He took another role, a greater role, and no longer needed the mask."

She had asked if Sin had been this *masinisto*, but Sin did not answer. Sin only gave when giving suited his needs. He never spoke of the mask again, and she knew better than to ask. She told herself she only wore the mask to prevent others from judging her, from seeing her youth and mistaking her for a child. But with her sister gone, in the absence of her near constant touch when they were next to each other, the mask gave her the feeling that she wasn't alone. Another soul, trapped in the iron, touched the skin of her face. She talked to the soul when her soldiers weren't around, chatted with it mindlessly like she used to with her sister. It never answered.

Another ash dog crested a nearby pile of rock; they liked to sit up there to survey the area. It saw them and made two staccato barks. Otter looked up at her and tilted its head.

"Yes. Go join your brother, Otter. You have a job to do, and so do I. No use putting off the inevitable."

She watched Otter trot away, stood, and put the mask on.

"Why am I so much angrier than my sister?" she'd asked the therapist so many years ago, in a different lifetime, in another world.

"Let's not compare people, Lauren," the therapist replied and then drank from a mug of something steaming that filled the room with a cloying honeysuckle odor. "Everyone is different. Let's focus on you. Are you feeling angry right now?"

"But we're not different," Lark said, ignoring the therapist's attempt to channel the conversation. "We're twins. We have the same DNA."

The therapist made an audible *hmm* and nodded her head slowly in a pattern Lark had seen countless times. "You do have the same DNA, but that doesn't make you the same person. We're all products of both nature and nurture. Our genes and our experiences. From the moment you and Zenia were born, you have diverged in your experiences, and you have developed as distinct people. Have you talked to your sister about how you feel? You're very close. Do you feel comfortable sharing your feelings with her?"

"That's a dumb question," Lark said. "We share everything." She looked around the room, at the shelves filled with untouched books and meaningless knickknacks. Everything about the room felt artificial—props for a performance. One item in particular caught her attention: a black wooden mask with carved feathers atop its head and a shiny beak. Lark stood and walked to it. The therapist showed a moment of surprise and then cocked her head in curiosity.

"Go ahead and look at it," the therapist said after Lark had already taken the mask off its display stand. "I got it in Mexico. It's Mayan."

Lark picked at a little golden sticker on the inside of the mask that said, plain as day, *Made in China*. She took the mask back to her chair and sat. The mask had elastic bands crudely stapled to its edges. She pulled them back over her head and slid the mask to cover her face. The eye holes were small, framing her view with a ring of darkness.

"Do you mind if I wear this?" Lark asked.

"I guess go ahead, Lauren. We were talking about your feelings of anger. Who are you angry at?"

Lark leaned forward and rested her elbows against her knees, her hands clasped together, fingers interlaced. With the mask on, she felt it was easy to stare at the therapist, as if Lark were looking into the room through a two-way mirror. "Everyone," she said. "I'm angry at everyone. My parents. My teachers. You."

"What about your sister?"

"No," Lark said, quickly and emphatically. "I'm not angry at Zee at all. Why would I be?"

Again the therapist pretended to give Lark's response deep consideration. "You said *everyone*. You said *I'm angry at everyone*."

"I didn't mean her." But she was angry at Zee, and until this moment, she hadn't admitted as much to herself. The mask made the lie easy. With it on, she felt like she could say anything. But that didn't mean she believed it.

She was angry at Zee for finding a way to be happy again, for forgiving their parents. For feeling the way Lark wanted to feel. Lark could make the bad feelings go away by running until she lacked the energy to feel anything at all. But she couldn't force herself to move on, to stop imagining Ross in their burning house, to stop hearing herself gut her dad with her words.

"Lauren?" the therapist said.

Therapy hadn't changed anything. Not for her. What she wanted in that moment was to become someone else. To put a mask on and never take it off.

"Can I keep this?" she asked.

"The mask? Lauren, I told you... It's special to me. It's Mayan."

Lark took it off and tossed it to the therapist, who splashed out half of her tea attempting to catch it. "It's not Mayan," Lark said. "It's made in fucking China. It's all bullshit." She walked out even though there were twenty minutes left in the session, and she never came back.

CHAPTER 14
RETURN OF THE SERCÎLO

When Paul woke up, his head throbbed like a naval battle was being fought within his skull. Every part of his body hurt. Behind him, the concrete column from the bridge pressed hard into his back, and his legs ached from hours spent on the rocky ground. The previous night must have been a dream, the product of an exhausted and lonely mind mixed with a bottle of whiskey. The dream explanation survived for a few seconds—long enough for Paul to reach back to the concrete column, to work his way to his feet, and find that it wasn't the bridge's concrete column behind him. It was a smooth wall. And the dark expanse before him wasn't the shadowed area under the Rosewood Bridge. He seemed to be submerged in a chalky twilight that he could taste with every breath. A bitter, metallic flavor that made his lips and tongue tingle. He coughed and then covered his nose and mouth with the sleeve of his shirt. Little black dots freckled the skin of his hands.

The floor beneath him was hard to see, covered with the same ash that floated in the air. He pushed his way across the floor until he reached a jagged edge. He was atop a broken building of some kind, towering above a ruined city with rivers of glowing lava.

"So, I guess the talk of it being my choice was all bullshit," Paul muttered. He promised himself that, if he survived, he would swear off whiskey for life. Not a drop more. Not even the good

Japanese stuff. He had never been so hungover. His body felt like it had been used as a crash test dummy, and his eyes were so sensitive that even the perpetual twilight here made them burn.

Yet despite his misery, he felt unexpectedly calm. For months he had dreaded a return to the Between and had become paranoid that every door he encountered—at the hotel, at work, while shopping, even the goddamn bathroom stalls—would lead to the sitting room maze. Now that he was here again, it was as if the weight of anticipation had been lifted, replaced instead by the *serĉilo*'s insatiable curiosity and the all-consuming need to find Julie. If only he had a fucking clue what to do next...

He tried to focus on Julie—what else mattered?—but he couldn't make any sense of what had happened to her without considering who or what had given him the information. He had seen Min-woo back in the flesh somehow, but it wasn't really Min-woo, or if it was, then it was Min-woo's soul inhabiting the body of a decrepit old man. And the old man, Rezső something—Paul couldn't remember his full name—talked as if he had not only created the computer game version of the Between but that he was also *Dio Ordo*, the Order God himself, one of the Between's two pinnacle roles. It occurred to Paul, then, that Rezső might be the Chaos god as well. Like the two-faced Roman god, Janus. God of beginnings and endings, of war and peace. Min-woo's FAQ notebook had little to say about either of the Between's god roles—and they *were* roles, Paul had discovered. But the way the old man's eyes and skin oscillated between a gold and crimson glow seemed consistent with the Janus theory, so Paul saw no reason the roles had to be separate.

Whatever god-role the old man played, he wanted Paul to return, using dire proclamations about Julie and the dangers facing Corinne, Jay, and Supriya as a motivational cudgel.

And now here Paul was, atop a broken building in a fiery city that could only exist in the Between. Assuming this wasn't another of the waking dreams he had been experiencing. Over the last few months, something strange had happened when Paul played the computer game version of the Between. The first change—or at least the first change he noticed—had been subtle. His eyes began to see different colors in the green-on-black ASCII text. Descriptions involving blood became red. Text of shadows and night took on a dark gray tint. And so on. Then he began to hear background sounds and atmospheric music that matched his room or location. When he stopped and tried to focus on the sounds, they disappeared, but minutes later, while engrossed in the game again, they returned. And then came the waking dreams.

"After a while, you could get used to anything," Meursault, the title character of Albert Camus' *The Stranger* had said. Was Meursault providing a warning or was it a simple statement of fact? Paul pressed his palm against the dirty concrete floor and took in a deep breath of hot and bitter air. *Am I dreaming?* he asked himself. He put the tip of his thumb between his teeth and bit down until he felt pain. *Not a dream.* It wasn't the pain that convinced him. It was the chalky taste of the ash from the floor, the type of detail that was unlikely to be present in dreams.

"Get out of your head and do something, Paul," he said aloud.

He felt the *serĉilo's* strength flowing into him from the Silver Spiral on his arm. That strength gave him the determination to run out from the building and into the Ruins in search of Julie, to smash anything that got into his way. But if months of playing the computer game version of the Between had taught him a single thing, it was that recklessness always invited death. If he died here in the flesh, he wouldn't see a black screen with the words YOU HAVE DIED. He wouldn't see anything at all.

What he needed now was Min-woo's notebook. On the concrete floor nearby sat a plaid leather backpack that he hadn't noticed until then. A Burberry backpack that probably retailed for over a thousand dollars. Only one person Paul knew would own a backpack like that. Min-woo Kim. Inside, the backpack contained several bottles of water, some protein bars, and, like the Phoenix arisen from its ashes, the FAQ notebook with a message taped on the cover.

Dongsaeng,

Time is short, so I must be uncharacteristically brief. You hold in your hands the new and improved version 2.0 of my FAQ notebook. Sanon! (That is Cheers! in Esperanto. Don't ask me how I know that. Rezső Simko's mind may be leaching into mine and vice versa. The thought makes my stomach turn... Or is it his stomach? Oh, Paul, whatever you do, don't die and cohabitate in the gray matter of an octogenarian demigod. So much for brevity...)

In addition to some helpful new notes I have scribbled in the margins, you'll notice a new chapter at the end called "The Game." I encourage you to read this chapter whenever you face something especially dangerous, which I fear will be frequent. I wish I could give you all the answers you will need, but alas, not even Rezső Simko has all the answers. He told you he wanted you to succeed him as Dio Ordo. This is only partly true. His mind is divided in two, one side serving Order, the other serving Chaos. Do not trust him!

Now, go forth and try not to die, serĉilo. Mia kusenveturilo estas plena je angiloj! (I'm either wishing you good fortune on your adventure or saying that my hovercraft is full of eels.)

Min-woo

P.S. I almost forgot a very important detail. This notebook contains my soul, so don't let this one get destroyed. If you find a way to impart my soul in a new body, please make sure the body is up to my standards.

Ah! So, Paul's suspicions were correct: the two supreme gods of the Between, presiding over Order and Chaos, were the split faces of a single Janus god. A god Min-woo stressed could not be trusted. As for Min-woo, his soul was somehow contained by the notebook itself. What that meant precisely, Paul had no idea. But it made him think twice before dog-earing a page.

He carefully leafed through the notebook. If this was a recreation, it had every wrinkle and taped-together tear of the original. Min-woo's scribble handwriting populated the margins. The colored tabs separating the notebook's sections were all bent, and the clear plastic sleeves had yellowed with age. All except for a new tab, the last tab, labeled "The Game."

I think my current situation counts as facing something especially dangerous, Paul thought as he turned to the new section. The blocky, ASCII text on the page almost caused him to drop the notebook.

```
[2] Top of a Ruined Building
   You are on the top floor of a ruined
building. From here, you can see the Ruins
stretching out in all directions. The roof
is missing. The sky is covered by a dark
haze that the sun can barely penetrate. On
the floor is a backpack. Stairs lead down.
There are no other exits.
   >
```

Paul scanned the concrete walls and then stared at the backpack lying on the ground as if it were a large, offensive insect. He turned to the next page in the notebook. It was blank. As was the page after and every remaining page.

"What the fuck is this, Min-woo?" he said under his breath. The blank pages reminded him of the books on the shelves of the false library, the buried chamber in his backyard. Those books had been lures, designed specifically to pull him into the Between. But the blank pages in Min-woo's notebook must have been left empty for a different reason. On a whim, Paul closed the notebook and took the stairs down to the next floor of the building.

Like the floor above, the room was made of bare concrete. If there had once been flooring, wiring, plumbing—anything else at all—it was long gone. The room did have one unique feature that looked to Paul to be recent: a large bloodstain in the middle of the floor with tracks to suggest that whatever had been killed had been dragged down the next flight of stairs. He had the immediate desire to go back upstairs, but he forced himself to wait while he reopened the notebook to the first page of the final tab. The look and layout of the computer text was the same, but the words had changed.

```
[2] Inside a Ruined Building
   You are near the top of the building. A
large bloodstain covers much of the floor.
Stairs continue up and down.
   >
```

He shook his head in disbelief. "The Game" section of the notebook wasn't a guide like the rest of the pages within it. It seemed to be a paper version of the computer game itself, updating the page based on Paul's location. As miraculous as that was, Paul struggled to see how it could be useful to have a static, brief description of the place he was already at. But if that was all the new section provided, it only needed a single page. Why have all the blank pages that followed?

What if the pages weren't always blank?

He reread the description of the room and focused on the little greater-than symbol beneath it. Was it a cursor, waiting for input?

He needed a pen! That thought sent him patting his jeans pockets, front and rear, despite never having carried a pen in his pants pockets in his life. And he, of course, found no pen there. However, the pouch pocket in the front of the backpack did have a thoroughly impractical and expensive-looking fountain pen with a screw-on lid, spare ink cartridges, and MWK engraved in its ebony case.

The pen's flat nib made some dry scratches before he shook it a few times and sent ink onto the concrete floor. With the ink flowing, Paul wrote a *D* next to the cursor. When he turned the page, instead of finding it blank, he found the description of the next floor down in the building.

He scribbled another *D* next to the new cursor to continue down the stairs and turned the page again. Another block of ASCII text greeted him.

```
[2] Floor of a Ruined Building
    You are on the bottom floor of a tall
building. The walls are made of concrete.
Here and there scratch marks and other
gouges decorate the walls. The doors and
windows are all missing. The doorway to
the north leads to the main square of the
Ruins. The south exit leads to an alley-
way. Stairs climb up into the building.
    >
```

"Holy shit," he said. He smiled so wide his cheeks hurt.

Min-woo had given him an item as powerful as any of the Between's artifacts. More powerful, perhaps. With this notebook, he could see around corners. He could test various courses of action until he found the right ones. He could see into the goddamn future. Even better, he could force the various possible futures to be the one future he wanted.

When was the last time he had felt this confident? This in control of his own life?

He quickly skimmed the notebook's entry for the Ruins, mentally inventorying the monsters and environmental dangers awaiting him when he left the building. The real danger of the Ruins was the *malespero*, the Warlord of Despair, the most powerful of the lesser servants of Chaos. The *malespero* was a killing machine, with a spiked suit of armor and the ability to send out shockwaves of powerful, sledgehammer-like energy. As if those weren't enough, the notebook described an ability to control the creatures of the Ruins, although it provided few useful details. The one bright spot, if he could call it that, came in the form of a handwritten note that Min-woo had scribbled in the margin.

The serĉilo's strength-of-many power might be an effective counter to the malespero's shockwave attack.

Let's hope I never find out, Paul thought to himself. He ate one of the backpack's protein bars in three quick bites and washed it down with a full water bottle. He crushed the bottle and tucked it neatly into the backpack. Then he descended to the bottom of the building and prepared to step out into the Ruins.

His heart raced. Seemingly half of the water he had just consumed was already streaming down his forehead as sweat. Using "The Game" section of the notebook, he explored the area outside of the building, scratching notes with the fountain pen, turning pages, and periodically shutting the notebook and reopening it, which allowed him to start again anew.

His plan, thus far, was straightforward. He needed to escape the Ruins and return to the Gray Waste. Then, he needed to find the Grand Staircase leading down. Down, down, down, he would go. Through the Between's lower worlds and ultimately to the Underworld and the shore of the Black River where the iron statues stood. It was the one place he knew for sure where he could find the *Koŝmaro*. Where he could find Julie.

Through the *paper game*, as he thought of it, he saw that a pack of ash dogs was approaching from the neighboring alleyway. Fighting the ash dogs was a disaster. Even if he could win, more would quickly appear, followed by soldiers and a giant shambling creature the notebook called a *burning one*. His path out of the Ruins wasn't one of destruction or even stealth. It had to be timing, enabled by the notebook.

He was about to step out and begin a sequence he jotted down on the notebook's cover when the sight of Min-woo's written name made him pause. *Remember what happened to Min-woo*, he said to himself. Min-woo's game knowledge became his undoing when the Between in-the-flesh presented complications beyond what he had seen in the computer game. In his mind's eye, Paul could still see Min-woo's flashlight bobbing up and down while he ran through the graveyard, pursued by a horde of metal skeletons.

Paul looked down at the notebook and pen in his hands. Was he about to walk out carrying them like this? Did he think he could pause the world around him while he found the answer to whatever unanticipated challenge came his way?

As his confidence began to wane, the great bell rang, echoing through the Ruins.

The *Kosmaro* was coming here.

Julie was coming here, right now.

He stuffed the notebook and pen into the backpack and, without a second thought, ran out into the street toward the sounds of fighting in the distance. A voice in his head began screaming *NO! NO! NO!* while another, calmer voice said, *Go, serĉilo. Go to her.*

He jumped over little streams of lava that cut through the streets like branching veins and made for a wide thoroughfare that intersected the street he was running down. Ahead he saw several soldiers, also running in the direction of the gunshots, screams, and... was that a roar? In their hurry, the soldiers didn't see him, but one of the ash dogs bounding alongside them did. It stopped and lowered its head, back arched to raise hackles that the beast's charred flesh didn't have. It let out a rumbling growl, causing the other dogs—six of them—to join by its side.

Paul's mind flooded with memories where he fought packs of ash dogs as the *serĉilo*, something he was certain he had never personally done. He didn't resist, and instead let the memories guide his actions. He ran at the lead dog, pulling power through the Silver Spiral. He felt the strange sensation of becoming one with additional Pauls from neighboring worlds. His feet hit the ground with several multiples of his own strength, propelling him forward faster than he had ever run before.

The lead dog took two involuntary steps backward as its intended prey sped toward it with impossible speed. The dog made a feeble lurch, but in a single motion, Paul caught it by the neck and used his momentum to hurl the dog. Paul's arm moved with such force and speed that the dog's head snapped clean off its body before it had even left Paul's hand. The headless corpse slid across the sandy road, and its head struck a wall on the road's far side and burst into a gray cloud.

The other dogs scattered and ran. A nearby soldier that Paul hadn't noticed stared wide-eyed and slack-jawed before turning and running as well. Paul picked up a rock that easily weighed ten pounds or more but felt like a pebble with his multiplied strength. He reared back to throw the rock and then, with a quick shake of his head, dropped it. He wasn't here to fight the soldiers. He wasn't a killer.

More gunshots echoed from somewhere ahead and to his right. Where there was fighting, there would be death. And where there was death, he would find the *Koŝmaro*.

He cut through the husk of a building and climbed up a pile of concrete that let him run atop a raised, bridge-like structure. From his vantage point, he could see the fighting in a clearing no more than a football field's distance away. What he saw caused him to slow to a stop, confused. The overlapping Pauls slipped back into their own worlds.

Below, a dozen bodies or more littered the ground. Bodies of the *malespero*'s soldiers. Four remaining soldiers and two ash dogs seemed to be fighting each other. Not as teams, but all of them individually fighting, recklessly, as if driven mad with bloodlust.

Paul watched for several seconds trying to make sense of what he saw. Near the battlefield, a lone figure walked casually, as if it had strolled through the fighting without any concern for what was happening. Stranger still, the figure's white hooded robe seemed too bright in the Ruins' dim sunlight, yet he was sure it wasn't glowing. Instead, it, and the figure wearing it, looked superimposed on the world.

Paul ran along the edge of the fallen building, following the figure. A voice in his head, a memory from a *serĉilo* long dead, screamed at him to stay away from the figure. *Malluma Sinjoro! Malluma Sinjoro!* the memory kept repeating. The words felt familiar, but Paul's mind was too clouded by the memory of others that he couldn't tell if he, Paul Prentice, had seen or heard them before.

Whether the figure knew Paul was following it from above or not, it gave no sign, still ambling down the middle of a wide road. As Paul drew closer, he could make out more details. The skin of the figure's hands and face was an unnatural pitch black, a stark contrast to its bright white robes. Every part of the figure that should have been shadowed was instead lighter, as if Paul were seeing a film negative rather than the real thing. As this thought occurred to Paul, his body crossed a threshold of some kind, and suddenly the whole world became color inverted. The muted dusk-orange sky of the Ruins became blue instead. The sun, now a deep indigo that was almost black, radiated blue darkness. Paul stopped and almost lost his balance. The skin of his own forearms also now looked dark blue and covered with white hair. The Silver Spiral had turned a gunmetal gray.

The figure, still walking, now wore an almost black robe and had ghostly white skin. The world around Paul had inverted, and only the figure seemed normal. No, normal was the wrong word. The whole world had become wrong, and only the figure was right. *Malluma Sinjoro!*, the voice in Paul's head screamed again. Or had Paul screamed it? The figure's gait slowed, and its head tilted so slightly that Paul couldn't be sure he had imagined it. After this hint of hesitation, the figure didn't turn and instead kept walking. Paul felt a strange compulsion to protect the dark figure. To serve it and destroy anyone that came near it. And others were near it, weren't they?

Paul turned toward the battlefield and saw that only one of the *malespero*'s soldiers was still alive—the apparent victor, breathing heavily, clutching his side. Filled with sudden rage, Paul tightened both hands into fists and pulled the strength of ten and then a hundred Pauls through the Silver Spiral. He dropped down twenty feet or more from the fallen building and landed as if his body were light as a feather. Then he ran at the soldier, wanting to tear the man limb from limb. He had only taken a few steps when the world snapped back to its normal colors and the bloodlust vanished.

Paul sank to the ground, suddenly overcome with dizziness. He looked back over his shoulder at the figure still walking away, color-inverted once again. Right there on the ground, Paul pulled the notebook out of his backpack and flipped through its pages, looking for the entry on the *Malluma Sinjoro*. He needed an explanation of what that creature was and why he had been overcome with the all-encompassing desire to kill. He paused at Min-woo's hand-drawn table listing all the Between's known roles and became momentarily distracted.

	Order	Chaos
Gods	Dio Ordo	Dio Kaoso
Greater Servants	The Kôsmaro	The Malluma Sinjoro
Lesser Servants	gardistaro	malespero
	klaro	nenio
	masinisto	songô
	serĉilo	stelisto

So many names. The Chaos roles were the more obvious

threat, but all the roles twisted their players toward unique and often dangerous ends. Some, like Supriya's *gardistaro* role, Paul knew well. Others, like the *klaro*, the *malespero*, and the *songo*, he had not yet encountered—and there was nothing more dangerous in the Between than the unknown.

He had read the notebook's entry for his own role, the *serĉilo*, over and over again. Min-woo had highlighted two sentences in bright yellow and, as if that weren't sufficient, used a ballpoint pen to underline them and to add little stars in the margins.

> *The* serĉilo's *hunger for knowledge and understanding is the role's Achilles' heel. Over time, the* serĉilo *tends to grow numb to nearby danger as the pursuit of knowledge becomes of singular importance.*

And that's what had just happened. Paul followed this figure, this *Malluma Sinjoro*, without even considering the danger of what he was doing. He was about to continue flipping through the pages when he realized he was making the same mistake yet again right this very second, sitting in the open, attention on the notebook in his hands and not the Ruins around him.

He stood and spun around, expecting attacks to come from all directions, but the only other creature he saw was the remaining soldier, crawling through the sandy, blood-soaked ground next to his fallen companions, crawling through the aftermath of *Malluma Sinjoro*'s Aura of Chaos. *Aura of Chaos.* The phrase hung in Paul's mind. Had he read those words in Min-woo's notebook, or were they fragments of a foreign memory? He ducked into a partially obscured area to his left and paged through the notebook again until he found the section he was looking for. Min-woo had circled *Malluma Sinjoro*'s name and drawn a line to the margin where he had written: *Esperanto for "Dark Lord."*

> *Malluma Sinjoro* emanates an Aura of Chaos that fills its current *location or room. All mortals except the servants of Chaos (the* stelisto, *the* malespero, *the* nenio, *and the* songo) *who find themselves in this*

aura will be filled with an uncontrollable rage toward everyone and everything except for Malluma Sinjoro.

Malluma Sinjoro was the Chaos demigod of the Between. On equal footing with the *Koŝmaro*. And Paul had been running toward it without any caution whatsoever. He read through the notebook's entry twice more, but it contained nothing else of use: nothing about *Malluma Sinjoro*'s purpose or function within the Between. Paul would have to learn that on his own, either through the game section of the notebook or through direct observation.

Frustrated, he shoved the notebook into his backpack. He didn't need more information about *Malluma Sinjoro*, not now and hopefully not ever. The knowledge seeker side of the *serĉilo* kept getting the better of him, distracting him from the task at hand. That task was finding Julie.

He stepped out of his hiding place and saw the giant space-warping form of the *Koŝmaro* standing in the middle of the battle-field, surveying the dead. The *Koŝmaro*'s distortion field made it hard to look at, but even still, Paul could make out the pregnant minotaur shape of the beast. The shape of *First Mother*, the wooden statue he and Julie had in their living room.

Without a second thought, he yelled, "Julie!" and the beast turned toward him.

CHAPTER 15
A MOMENT TOGETHER

From within the maelstrom of blurring probability, Julie looked out at the man standing on the edge of the bloody battlefield. Instead of seeing Paul, her husband of almost five years, she saw a young boy. The boy's appearance shifted rapidly, as appearances did within the *Kosmaro*'s aura, but Julie could see the unchanging spirit within the boy, which she recognized as her lost child. He called to her with a voiceless cry that made her heart resonate in pain and her eyes fill with tears. Her child had been lost in the real world before he could be born, and now he was trapped here, confused and alone.

Julie's body, in the form of the giant pregnant minotaur, walked toward the boy seemingly on its own. Why didn't her child come to her? Why was he here now, where the dogs would tear him apart? Where the *burning ones* would grab him with their giant hands and devour him?

From within her pocket of extradimensional space, she retrieved the basket made of thorny branches. The basket was full of the souls of this child already. All souls here were her child's soul. The dead men and women nearby, the ones who had turned against each other. In life they looked different, but in death they were the same. Her child.

And here her child was again, on his knees, waiting for her. But this child seemed different than all of the others somehow.

She picked him up in her monster hand, careful not to let her sharp claws dig into his flesh. She lifted him into the air until his eyes were level with her own. In those eyes, she saw her own reflection, both the beast and the woman at the same time. She stroked her child's hair with her free hand and then let the claw of her index finger trail down his forehead until it was pointing directly into his skull, where the soul of the child resided. The only way to protect the child was to free him from this false vessel.

"CRY NOT, MY CHILD, FOR I AM HERE TO TAKE YOU AWAY," she said, the voices of the beast and the woman echoing in unison.

As she was about to begin digging the figure of a spiral into the child's forehead, she saw that the scar of a spiral was already there. Confusion pulled her out of the moment and let her see the child anew. The child's face had become Paul's. And then she saw, in her mind, the image of the past *Koŝmaro*, holding Paul in the air among the wreckage of their house, its finger pointed at his skull as hers now was.

She dropped him and backed away. The minotaur form shuddered and vanished, leaving Julie staring in disbelief at her hands, her now normal and small human hands, and what they had been about to do.

"Paul!"

He struggled to his feet, and after a few seconds of disorientation locked eyes with her. Tears welled and his lips trembled. She blinked away her own tears and embraced him, holding him as if his physical presence was the only thing keeping her moored to the ground. He held her just as tight.

"I thought you had..." he started, but he couldn't finish the sentence. The cold wetness of his tears spread across her cheek.

He thought what? That she had left him? Walked out, leaving him alone in that hotel? She pulled back and grabbed his face with both hands, hands that suddenly seemed so tiny and delicate.

Staring into his eyes, she said, "Listen to me, Paul Prentice. I'm not leaving you, and you aren't leaving me. Ever. Till death do us part. If we have to make our way through hell, we'll do it together."

He pulled back, took a deep breath, and nodded. She saw his expression steady as he pushed his emotions back and switched to problem-solver mode. If they had been in any place other than the fiery ruins of a demon-haunted city, she wouldn't have let him turn off his feelings so quickly, but an extended emotional connection would have to wait. She could feel the echo of the Underworld's great bell still resonating within her, pulling at her and her basket of souls. They only had a brief moment together before the pull would become too strong and she would again transform into the beast.

"What do we do, Paul? How do we escape?"

He narrowed his eyes, studying her face. "You have to go, don't you?"

"Soon, yes."

"My role sometimes possesses me also. I understand." He blinked rapidly and seemed to search for something with his eyes. "Even if we find a way home, if we're still in these roles, it will draw us back in. Like it did with Jay and Supriya. Like it did with me, eventually."

"I can't take the ring off." Her mind flashed back to the instant when she had her finger in the car door jamb, slamming it over and over, trying in vain to sever her finger. Bile rose in her throat. She swallowed hard. "I tried."

"You can change roles, and you can have your role taken from you, but from what I've learned, there's no other way, besides death, to leave the roles behind."

"Dying is off the table," she said, surprising herself with a wry grin, but it slipped away as another wave of the bell's echo rolled through her. "What about the nexus in the Garden of Before? I entered it recently and found a way it could restore life. Is there a way we could use it?"

"The nexus? I... uh..." He must have known their time was almost at an end because his words came urgent and quick. "Jules, I think you're onto something. The nexus is where the outworlds all overlap. You entered it? Maybe the rules inside the nexus are different." His eyes widened. "Or maybe the rules themselves are projected out from within the nexus. Yes! That would explain so much! We're bound to the rules of the Between here, but within the nexus those rules... We might be able to change them!" He started rambling through hypotheticals, talking rapidly, incoherently, cutting off his own sentences, his eyes now far away. She knew he was slipping into his role as the *serĉilo*, mind flooded with the memories of those who had played the role before. Like the foreign memories growing louder in her mind with each echo of the bell.

"Paul, we don't have time to solve it now. Should I meet you there?" She shook him. "Paul! Should I meet you at the nexus in the Garden?"

The faraway look in his eyes vanished, and he straightened, seeming to become bigger somehow. More substantial. Calm. Confident. She had seen this before, his *serĉilo* power like a camera's image coming into focus. "I will be there," he said with a voice so pure and firm that it drowned out the echoes of the bell. "I will be there," he repeated, "and I will have figured out how to free us."

She grabbed him and pulled his face down to hers, kissing him hard, and then she pushed him back. "I love you, Paul Prentice. Now, run from me. RUN!"

Her lips on his briefly pulled him back from the *serĉilo*'s detachment, but the words were no longer spoken with her voice alone. By the time she had yelled *Run!*, the beast's voice had taken over. Paul spared a half second to nod, and then he did as she said, vanishing behind the shell of a ruined building.

In the form of the reality-warping beast, Julie let out a roar that shook the third world of the Between.

CHAPTER 16
THE AURA OF CHAOS

Through an antique telescope from atop the wall of her makeshift castle, the *malespero* watched the encounter between the *serĉilo* and the *Koŝmaro* with morbid fascination. She had thought that Paul was about to have his soul ripped out through his forehead. That would have been a problem for her plan—Sin's plan, really. But then something happened that she hadn't seen in her many years trapped here. Paul and his wife—Julie, Sin had said her name was—had overcome their roles, if only for a moment.

Perhaps if she'd had their strength, things would have been different with her sister. The thought came with a bright, hot pain in her heart like she had been stabbed. But the pain quickly faded, leaving a numbness in its place.

She scanned through the Ruins with her telescope until she found the *Malluma Sinjoro*—the Lord of Chaos she simply called Sin—walking casually and slowly toward the stadium. The fighting between her soldiers had been Sin's doing. That much was obvious. But had he orchestrated it to draw Paul and Julie together? To test them? More specifically, to test Paul?

She didn't know what irritated her more—that Sin would take such a risk or that he had been right to force a test. In the Between, all tests that didn't kill you made you stronger...but most killed you. Without taking her eyes off Sin, she yelled out to her soldiers that the *Malluma Sinjoro* would soon be here. "Everyone out of the stadium. Now!" As an afterthought, she added, "And bring Supriya Reddy to me." A half dozen voices responded with their quick assent, and she heard their footfalls as they ran to convey the messages to the others.

She followed Sin with her telescope as he approached, twisting uncomfortably as sweat began to make her armor, normally an unnoticed, second skin, stick like a cheap plastic costume. Watching Sin, she felt like a girl in a costume and not the feared destroyer she supposedly had become. The artifact collar she wore usually shielded her from most of the feelings that would get in her way as the *malespero*: sadness, guilt, and to some extent, pain. But it didn't prevent the deep unease and the fear she felt when she saw Sin. She had never seen him angry, had never seen him directly harm anyone or anything. Yet every agent of Chaos in the Between seemed to wear marionette strings handled by his fingers. Whatever Sin was planning, it would happen soon, and her utility to him would come to an end. What happened then?

Her thoughts were interrupted by an itching sensation in the back of her mind, a nearby presence. She reached to pull her mask back down but, with a sense of who was standing behind her, changed her mind. *Let her see my face*, she thought.

Indeed, it was Supriya Reddy with her arms crossed and her head tilted back slightly. No longer with the godly glow of the *gardistaro*, she was dressed in Esther's ill-fitting clothes that had likely been worn by more than one corpse. Still, Supriya had the presence of a Valkyrie. A Valkyrie with a metal leg.

"Someone wants to meet you," the *malespero* said before turning back around and again looking out into the Ruins with the telescope, making it clear that Supriya was so little a threat that she could be ignored.

"Someone wants to meet me? Sure, they do," Supriya said, voice dripping with sarcasm. "Someone may *want* something from me. I can't imagine what that is. I have no powers anymore."

The *malespero* lowered the telescope. The thought of losing her powers should have been terrifying, but instead, it seemed freeing. She fought the impulse to tug at her collar, which suddenly felt tighter than usual. "What's it like? No longer playing the role? Getting to be yourself again?"

"Two friends chatting about their feelings? Is that what we are now?"

"You and I both know there is no such thing as friends here."

"You're wrong," Supriya said.

The *malespero* turned and faced Supriya again. "I wish I were."

Another several seconds of silence passed before Supriya said, "For a time, Jay and I went back and forth between his world and here. The role became weak when I was gone, and I could feel all the guilt from the things I'd done."

"Is that what you're feeling now? I'm genuinely curious, Supriya."

"Yes," Supriya answered. "Does that make you happy? That I feel guilty now?"

The *malespero* frowned. "No, it doesn't make me happy. It's a shame, really. You're free, which means you could theoretically escape. You and your *friends* destroyed the exit atop the Chaos Cathedral. But rumor has it there are other exits. If you traveled through one, alone, you would go home. At least, I think so. Isn't that what we've all wanted? To go home? But you can't go home, can you? Not after everything you've done."

"No. I don't think I can," Supriya said.

The *malespero* looked at the sky above them. The haze created a perpetual dusk of red and purple around the dim circle of the sun. It occasionally struck her how beautiful the Between could be despite its brutality. "It's good that you're honest with yourself," she said, looking back at Supriya. "I know I can't go home, either. But that doesn't mean we're doomed to be the bloody tools of this world and no more."

"What do you want from me?" Supriya asked coldly, arms now crossed in front of her. "You kept me alive for a reason. Whatever that reason is, say it."

"Fair enough. Follow me," the *malespero* said. She led Supriya down a set of switchback stairs under the stadium's upper deck. The stairs were especially treacherous, with missing walls and gaps in the steps where the ground was visible far below. "You can help destroy this place, Supriya. That's my goal. I want to destroy the Between so that no one is ever pulled here again. Watch out for this part here." She waited while Supriya navigated a section of broken stairs. She wanted to hate Supriya. It would have made everything so much easier if she hated Supriya the way she hated Jay. "There's a transition of power coming soon. The old gods are dying, and before new gods can replace them, we will kill them all. There will be no transition, and the Between will collapse."

"Why do I have the feeling I'm not going to like my part in all this?" Supriya said.

The *malespero* lowered her mask. "There is no happy ending for any of us, Supriya. Now move faster. We can't keep our guest waiting."

As they crossed the threshold into the twilight glow of the arena, the *malespero* wondered, not for the first time, if this arena had ever been a real place, with a crowd roaring as athletes entered. No crowds sat in what was left of the bowl ringing the sand and dirt covered field. The only other person here was Jay, in the cage specifically built to contain him at the center of the field. Several dead bodies lay on the ground within the cage and the dirt was stained by fresh blood.

Jay sat cross-legged and stiff-backed in the center of the cage. His black *stelisto* garb seemed darker than before, almost like a void in space, except for the peculiar, embroidered flowers on his chest and ankles. His cage was positioned so that he had no shadows to fuel his *stelisto* abilities. If he continued to grow in power, if he further *awakened* as Sin wanted, what additional powers might he gain? Would his soul become so dark that he no longer needed shadows? Would he create his own darkness? The *malespero* didn't know. But she would soon find out.

Jay tilted his head up slowly and stared at them with chaos-red eyes.

Supriya stopped. "What are you doing to him?!" she exclaimed as she ran to the cage.

"The cage is electrified," the *malespero* said. "Touching it will only bring you pain."

Supriya turned back toward the *malespero* with eyes of venom, and her hands balled into fists that looked like they could pound through brick. "What the fuck are you doing to him?"

"I'm helping him grow stronger, Supriya. Every kill elevates him in his role as the *stelisto*. I told you that we have to kill the gods in order to break the Between. To kill a god, we need a god-killer. That's what I'm helping Jay become."

"A god-killer?" Supriya echoed. The rage in her voice had given way to confusion and then to panic. A second later, realization rippled through her, and she stumbled back, bracing her metal leg with both hands as if she suddenly doubted it would hold her. "You... you brought me here to put me in the cage with him!"

"Yes, Supriya. That's why you're here."

"He's going to kill me," Supriya said. "If I go in there, he's going to kill me."

"He might," the *malespero* said. "Or he might break the role's hold on him and become its master."

"Is that possible?"

"I don't know. Only minutes ago, when you found me watching the Ruins through the telescope, I saw Julie Prentice overcome her role as the *Koŝmaro* and spare the life of her husband. We will soon see if Jay has Julie's...fortitude."

"And if I refuse?"

"He can hear us having this conversation. You are going in that cage, either under your own power or with my...assistance."

Supriya seemed to consider this. Then, with a deep breath, she stood tall and said, "I'll go in. Under one condition. You answer a question."

Each second that Supriya delayed brought Sin one step closer to the stadium. The *malespero* forced herself to relax her jaw and let out a deep, slow breath. "Ask it."

"What is your name, *malespero*? Who were you before you

became"—Supriya gestured with her hand at the *malespero's* spiked armor—"this?"

The *malespero* took her mask completely off. "Maybe I have always been *this*," she said. "Maybe the Between chiseled away everything that had been covering the real me." She heard her own words but didn't believe them. Why, then, did she say them?

Supriya didn't appear to believe her, either. She crossed her arms and tilted her head a bit, communicating as much.

Something about the moment reminded the *malespero* of the sessions in the therapist's office. The weight of the air. The lack of any separation between her and the woman awaiting her response. The feeling that time had stopped and wouldn't resume until she spoke. "My name is Lauren, but I've always gone by Lark." The sound of her name seemed to hang in the air. When was the last time it had been spoken aloud? She knew the answer. It had been her sister who had last said her name, pleading with her to snap out of the destructive haze of her role. "This is not an invitation for you to use that name, Supriya. You asked, I told you, and that's that. Now it's time to put Jay to the test. I will open the cage and..."

"I have another question," Supriya said.

The *malespero* pushed down the surge of anger that flared inside her. It would be easy, so very easy, to break that strong body, to put an end to Supriya Reddy here and now. But to do so would ruin the plan. If Sin found Supriya already dead, what then? Lark might find herself in the cage instead. She tried to take the bite out of her voice and mostly succeeded. "You are trying my patience, Supriya. What is it now?"

"Who or what is the *Malluma Sinjoro*? I heard the others say the name before they left. They said he's coming here. That's who *wants to meet me*, as you put it."

It was as if the damn woman were reading her mind. "He is the greater servant of Chaos, the counterpart of the *Koŝmaro*. A man, a mortal, just like us, but playing a role more powerful than the one you used to play. Or the role I play now." The *malespero* waved off Supriya's next question before she could ask it. "If we want the

Between to collapse, Chaos has to win. I've been testing *stelistos* to find one who could become the god-assassin we need. The others failed. The *Malluma Sinjoro*—Sin, as he likes to be called—believes Jay can succeed. But I believe Jay's power comes from you. Your partnership allowed him to survive. Your belief in him made him stronger. So, you see...You are the one who can bring about his transformation." She lowered her mask once again, and said, "Enough talk. Walk into the cage under your own power, or I will break your remaining leg and throw you in."

———

Supriya walked toward Jay's cage and her own probable death, but for the moment her mind was on the young woman—the young girl—next to her. This young girl had been the cause of much of the danger she and Jay had faced in their time in the Between. Supriya already knew this. What she began to suspect but hadn't understood until now was that these dangers had been tests of a sort. It was easy to think of the *malespero* as a force of evil, killing for the joy of killing, killing to spread chaos. This young girl was certainly that, but perhaps there was more. She also looked familiar, but if Supriya had seen her before, she couldn't place where.

Supriya met Jay's eyes and saw the fire behind them vanish, his expression softening into the somber longing that pierced her heart more easily than the *stelisto*'s blue-bladed knife ever could have. Those eyes knew there was no future for them but sadness. Even the *malespero*'s unexpected future, in which Jay the god-assassin would help bring about the end of the Between, was no happy ending for the two of them. Only more death and more destruction awaited.

The *malespero*'s gloved hands worked the mechanisms of the cage's inner and outer doors with no visible effect from the electricity coursing through the metal. Once the way was open, Supriya entered with her head held high.

"Welcome to the penthouse suite, baby," Jay said, forcing a crooked smile. His eyes were sad, tired. "The view sucks, the amenities are shit, people keep trying to kill you, and it's got a bit of a scorpion infestation going on, but other than that..." He sprung to his feet and gave a disappointed look to the *malespero*. "I know you're from the South, little lady. Can't hide that accent. How about a little Southern hospitality?"

"My hospitality is letting the two of you determine your own fates," the *malespero* replied dryly after closing and locking the inner door behind Supriya.

"I guess that's something, given the circumstances," Jay said. Then his smile turned into a glare that gave Supriya chills even though it was directed at the *malespero*. "It's more friendly than I'll be when our situation is reversed, which it will be. I promise you that."

The *malespero* seemed to ignore this, but after she locked the outer door, she turned to Supriya. Despite the mask, it seemed the young girl named Lark—and not the *malespero*—spoke to Supriya.

"I'm not doing this to torture you. It will feel like that, but as I've told you, there is a purpose in the pain you're about to feel." Then she turned toward Jay. "For you, on the other hand, the torture...The torture is a side benefit." She walked to the edge of the arena floor, turned, and stood, her right hand holding her left wrist, waiting.

The torture is a side benefit? Supriya had only a split second to consider those words and the malicious change of tone that accompanied them before Jay had her wrapped up tightly from behind. Panic shot through her. With both hands, she grabbed his shirt at his sides and torqued hard in a judo-style throw. She pushed against the ground with her leg of muscle, spinning them both off their feet.

"Whoa, now!" Jay landed back-first on the ground, with Supriya's weight crashing down on top of him, and he let out a long, wheezing groan.

Before Jay could move, Supriya grabbed both of his wrists and used her shins, both flesh and metal, to pin his arms down. Her eyes shot to his empty right hand, and then his left—also empty. His knife was still in its sheath at his waist.

"I know it's been a while, but you gotta wine and dine me first," Jay said, wincing from the pain of her weight on his arms.

Her heart thudded in her chest, and beads of sweat covered her exposed skin. She had been convinced he was finally trying to kill her like Corinne said he would. Supriya looked at his sheathed knife two more times to be sure it wasn't already buried in her back.

Below her, she saw the sad, familiar smirk and those puppy dog eyes of his, now clear and fixed on hers. Within her, animal terror fought with pity and love. For the time, anyway, love came out on top, and the tension drained out of her all at once. She got off him, pulled him to his feet, and kissed him on his dry, sandy lips as she hugged him.

"I'm sorry, Jay. I'm sorry for what she is doing to you. But we can beat this, together. You can triumph over your role. Become its master. She said it's possible. I think it is." Supriya stepped back and grabbed both of his hands. She wanted so much to believe her own words.

Jay looked down at their clasped hands and then gave Supriya an arched eyebrow.

Supriya had never been one for holding hands or other forms of touchy-feely affection. Was this a sudden change of heart, or was it simply a means to keep his hands free of the knife?

Before she could say more—not that she had any idea what more to say—Jay shrugged and said, "Babe, ain't no magic knife in this world or any other that's as powerful as my love for you. Consider my role already broken. The test, passed." He looked over Supriya's shoulder at the *malespero*, who stood silently with the mask of agony covering her face. "Hey, spikey lady! It's gonna get really boring if you're waiting for me to break!"

The *malespero* didn't respond.

Supriya and Jay continued to stand there awkwardly in the center of the cage, hand in hand. Supriya was about to say she believed him when movement in her periphery caught her attention. She turned and saw a man in a white cloak emerging from the dark entry hall of the arena. The whiteness of his cloak and the unnatural obsidian black of his skin appeared hyper-real against the sand and concrete of the arena, almost like the man's image was superimposed on the rest of the surrounding reality.

"The *Malluma Sinjoro*," the *malespero* announced. She nodded her masked face at him and said, "Welcome, Sin."

"Who's the albino dude?" Jay whispered.

"Albino?" Supriya said, confused. "His skin is as black as night."

Jay gave her a sideways glance and frowned. "Are we not looking at the same guy? Black cloak, skin whiter than my ass?"

Black cloak? White skin? Supriya let go of Jay's hand and backed away as far as she could from the approaching man until the electrified dome blocked her retreat. Why was she seeing something different than Jay?

Jay, for his part, hadn't backed away and didn't seem the least bit intimidated, fists at his hips, the fingers of his right hand twitching, brushing the Knife of Undoing. "Have you come here to be bored, also? What kind of dipshit name is Sin?"

As the cloaked man neared, Supriya saw a bluish glow in his eyes that confused her even further. The eyes of those in Chaos roles sometimes glowed red as if burning. With Order roles like the *gardistaro*, the eye glow was gold. But blue?

The man, now halfway to their cage, addressed Jay in a voice that somehow combined the harshness of gravel and the calming smoothness of honey. "I see through you, *stelisto*. I see the lust in your heart, the hunger in your soul. Give in and become more."

Jay turned away from the man and rolled his eyes. He made a joke of some kind, but Supriya lost the words as the colors of the world around her inverted. The sandy brown of the ground and the hazy amber of the sky became shades of blue. Jay's black clothes and the spiked armor of the *malespero* turned an almost painfully bright white. And the man called Sin now appeared exactly like Jay had described him—black cloak and albino white skin. Now Sin's eyes burned a deep, chaos red.

Jay hadn't seen or felt any sort of shift as the *Malluma Sinjoro's* Aura of Chaos swept over them. In the role of the *stelisto*, Jay was inoculated against its effects. Chaos already inhabited him like a ghostly possession, intertwining its lust and hunger with his, until he no longer knew which desires were his own.

Supriya either didn't catch his joke or didn't find it funny. No matter. No one cracked up their audience one hundred percent of the time, not even Jay motherfuckin' Lightsey. He gave her a wink and turned away before allowing his eyes to fixate on the pulsing jugular vein in Supriya's neck. His mind lavished in visions of that vein torn open, hot blood spurting out onto the dusty ground, onto his hands and face. The bitter, salty taste of it. The—

He shivered, shook loose those thoughts, and tried to put on his best Clint Eastwood *Man with No Name* face as he met the eyes of the approaching Mumbo Jumbo, or whatever the albino douchebag was called.

"If you want to see the real me, *friend*, why don't you let me out of this cage? We can get up close and personal." Jay knew full well that taunting another role character in the Between was a dicey gambit, and this man certainly was playing some sort of role. But Jay had killed his fair share of role characters and then some: a couple *masinistos*, a *gardistaro* (that one still felt a little wrong, but you can't make an omelet without breaking a few eggs, right?), and even the goddamn *Koŝmaro*. "Have you heard about my fight with the *Koŝmaro*? My mega-junkling? It was epic shit, man. Hollywood level—"

Supriya smashed into him from behind, sending him hard into the metal cage. A jolt of lightning tore through him, scrambling the world in blistering white pain and a loud *POP!* that sounded and felt like his heart exploding. He staggered, trying to keep himself upright, and then Supriya was on him, and they were on the ground, her fists and claws pounding, tearing into him. The scrambled world snapped back into focus with a new shock of pain. She had bit him in the fucking neck!

With her on top, she created enough shadow on him that he could *shift* enough to be loose of her grasp. He rolled free. Something akin to muscle memory took over. The knife was in his right hand while his body turned sideways, left arm probing out like a boxer establishing distance as he stayed light on the balls of his feet.

A line of red leaked down the left side of Supriya's face, her blood mingling with his on her lips and teeth. He must have nicked her with a backhand slash. She didn't seem to care. She looked like a deranged animal, hate and death in her eyes.

She charged, reckless and wide open to a counter from his knife. But he held the weapon back even as it felt like it was tearing his arm from his socket. In the split second before she hit him, he cataloged all the places the knife would have struck. Her neck, first. Then her right inner thigh, opening the femoral artery. Three stabs to the gut. Then one up through the chin. He saw it all happen in his mind, the Knife of Undoing demanding that it be done. But Jay held, which left him open to Supriya's bull charge.

Again they were on the ground where Supriya's extra twenty pounds of muscle gave her all the advantages, and again Jay had the wind knocked out of him. The knife flashed out, but he caught it, its blade only an inch away from her exposed side. While he struggled with the knife, Supriya positioned herself so that she was sitting on his stomach. She punched him hard in the face twice. He felt his nose break on the first strike and his head smash into the hard ground beneath him on the second. His whole body momentarily went limp, and when his senses returned, she had both hands tight around his neck.

Her side! Gut her! Slice her fucking arm off! Voices in his head screamed at him to fight back—voices that sounded like his own, but still he held the knife away. Darkness filled the edges of his vision. The knife fought for control, but as his body's strength drained away, so too did the knife's.

Is this so bad? he thought as the world's light dimmed to almost nothing. *Going out... being ridden cowgirl style?* A little shudder rolled through him that was as much of a laugh as he could muster. *Reverse cowgirl... would be... better,* his fading mind added. *No more stranglin'... with reverse cowgirl.*

What should have been his last conscious thought—a memory of Supriya straddled backward on him in the bedroom of the *masinisto*'s mansion—triggered an idea so stupid and immature that it had to work. With Supriya leaned over to squeeze the final ounces of life from him, she blocked out the light of the sun above, covering him in weak shadow. He couldn't vanish completely into it, but it was enough for him to *shift* underneath her. In an instant, his feet were where his head had been as he recreated the position from that memory. *Reverse fucking cowgirl!* his mind screamed as he took in a gulp of air. Before Supriya could adjust herself, he sat up and slid his arms under hers, the knife still in his right hand. He had her in a Full Nelson, his big brother Cal's favorite torture position. Supriya squirmed and almost broke free, but with each breath his strength returned. The nasty thing about the Full Nelson was that it took a lot less strength to hold the position than to break out of it, which he had learned at age twelve when he had fifteen-year-old Cal trapped in it for almost an hour.

Now he was on top of Supriya, her stomach pressed to the ground. The butt of the knife was right above the base of her neck. It vibrated in his hand but had no way to strike from this position. The blade was even a little too close to Jay's own face for comfort, but at least he could keep his eye on it and, with a glare, remind it who was in charge.

"What the hell got into you, Supriya?!"

She writhed and struggled but didn't respond.

Jay twisted his head back and yelled at his observers. "Hey, dumbshits! I can keep her in this position all day. All fucking day. That good enough for you?" It was a lie. He could keep this up for a while, but all day was out of the question.

Neither Sin nor the *malespero* said anything in return. Jay could only see their still silhouettes near the cage's outer wall.

"You want to wait around all day? Fine! I've got nothing better to do!" he yelled. Then, with his arms starting to quiver and his grip slipping, he silently whispered, "They're calling my bluff, babe. We're fucking dead if you don't snap out of it."

"I told you he would be hard to break," the *malespero* said quietly as Jay continued spewing taunts and insults at her and the demon-man standing beside her.

Sin, for his part, made no response. He had been unusually quiet as he watched, which the *malespero* took to be a very bad sign. Sin's visits were normally brief and filled with instructions intermingled with his brand of patronizing praise. There was nothing she could tell him that he didn't already know—that he hadn't in some way personally orchestrated.

"I have things to do, little bird," Sin finally said, turning toward her, his eyes like smoldering coals. "I expected him to break by now."

She was so taken aback by his admission that she didn't know how to respond. Or had it been an accusation? Was he blaming her for Jay's resilience? "He can't hold out forever," she said. "The longer he resists, the greater his break. Isn't that what you said?"

The fire in Sin's eyes grew so hot she could feel the skin of her face begin to burn even through her mask. "I did say that," Sin said.

"I will stand here until he does break," the *malespero* said. "I'm sure you have other places to be."

"Are you trying to get rid of me?"

Within Sin's Aura of Chaos, she couldn't lie to him, so instead of answering she turned her attention back to Jay and Supriya. Jay returned her look with a glare from eyes that burned almost as deeply as Sin's, and his rambling taunts became increasingly vile—all the things he would do to her with his knife, the ways he would make her feel pain once he got loose.

Sin gave a growling chuckle that did little to lighten the mood. "I wanted to be here when it happened. The Between has never seen a *stelisto* reach the second awakening. But more than that, I wanted to protect you, little bird. No matter how powerful he becomes, he can't harm you if I'm near."

"I have survived this long by not underestimating anyone."

"We are making a god-killer, Lark, and you are not a god."

A wave of revulsion came over her, hearing her name spoken by his voice. Had he said her name before? Not since she put on the collar, surely. "I am prepared for whatever comes next. My soldiers now occupy the *gardistaro* and *masinisto* roles. For a time, they will remain loyal."

"That was either good thinking or good fortune. I have a feeling those two roles in particular will become very useful." He turned to Jay and said, "*Stelisto*, don't disappoint me. Kill your lover, kill your best friend, kill the god who rules this place... and then kill yourself." With that, he walked to the arena's tunnel exit and toward the Ruins beyond.

When Supriya's rage vanished, it left behind a wake of exhaustion and emptiness. She stopped struggling, thinking that Jay would ease up, but he didn't. His arms were shaking, and he kept mumbling something to himself, although Supriya couldn't make out the words. Was he saying, *I'm in control I'm in control I'm in control?*

"Jay," she said. "Whatever came over me... It's gone now. Jay?"

His mumbling and writhing continued as if he hadn't heard her.

"JAY!"

He stopped. She felt him twist on top of her to look back at their observers.

"The creepy albino guy is gone," he whispered.

Jay released her and moved to the opposite side of the cage so quickly that by the time she turned her head to see him, he was already there. He tried to put his knife in its sheath twice before it finally slid in. The knife wanted to fight, to kill. Jay had somehow overcome both the knife and Supriya's animal rage, but the toll on him seemed severe. His eyes were bloodshot and sunken in. His cheeks looked gaunter than ever. His nose was crooked, dried blood caking his nostrils. And the continuous mumbling...It made

Supriya think of a homeless man she used to encounter on the bus during medical school. Most days the man would get on the bus muttering, unsteady feet shuffling to a seat. He seemed to be experiencing some other reality, fueled by untreated mental illness and whatever chemical cocktail he had ingested to numb the pain. One day the man stabbed another passenger, and Supriya had to administer first aid while other passengers held the man down. The out-of-focus look in the man's eyes...It looked just like Jay's eyes now.

Supriya pushed herself to her feet. Her neck and her arms ached from what had seemed like eternity in Jay's Full Nelson hold. She ignored the pain and ignored the voice in her head screaming about how badly she had hurt Jay, how close she had come to killing him. The only thing that mattered, now, was that they were both still alive.

The *malespero* stood watching, arms folded, agony mask still covering her face. She hadn't moved the entire time. The man called Sin, the *Malluma Sinjoro*, was nowhere to be seen. Whatever had come over her, whatever had inverted the colors of the world, it had to have been his doing.

"It didn't work," Supriya said to the *malespero*. "Jay fucking beat it. He passed your test."

The *malespero* turned her masked face to look at Jay. "That was an impressive display of willpower, *stelisto*. I knew you could do it. Sin thought otherwise. You're used to people underestimating you, aren't you, Jay?"

Jay glowered at her. His mumbling stopped, but he still shuffled back and forth like a spinning top starting to wind down.

"Let us out," Supriya said. "Jay passed your test like you wanted."

The masked face swiveled. "Look at Jay, Supriya. Does he look transformed to you? Does he look, all of a sudden, more powerful? Like a god-assassin?"

The questions took Supriya by surprise. She looked at Jay, who was back to mumbling again. His body shook with a tremor, and then another a few seconds later. He had passed the test holding himself back, fighting the knife when Supriya had been taken over by Sin's power. But it hadn't steeled him, and in fact had done the opposite. He looked, now, like a man suffering a psychotic break.

"Well, Supriya? Is our work here done?"

"Take your fucking mask off, Lark. Speak to me as a person, not as a monster."

The *malespero* stood motionless for a few seconds, and then she took off the mask and tossed it to the ground. Her face—Lark's face—looked so young and sad. She touched the spiked collar at her neck, and the black armor covering her seemed to liquefy and retract into the artifact. Now Lark looked younger still, wearing a thin tank top and nylon shorts loose on a lanky body. It was hard for Supriya to imagine a greater transformation—the armored destroyer to this young girl.

"Is that better?" Lark said. Her voice sounded different as well. Softer.

"Yes. It is better," Supriya said. "Now tell us what happens next. When are you going to let us out?"

Lark looked down at her hands and then began rubbing them together. "I've done terrible things as the *malespero*, Supriya. There's a kind of veil over my heart that keeps me from feeling the full weight of what I've done, but I know." She looked up at Supriya and frowned. "You're not getting out, Supriya. Not now. Not ever. You're going to die in this cell, and Jay is the one who will kill you with that knife in his hands. Maybe he'll stab you through the heart." Her lips curled into a sneer. "Just like he killed my sister."

CHAPTER 17
PAY ATTENTION, SERĈILO

As he walked among the husks of long-dead buildings, Paul fought the urge to turn back and look at Julie. After feeling so lost and abandoned, to see her eyes brimming with love… it overfilled his heart with an emotion he couldn't name. It should have been joy, right? To know that he hadn't lost her. And there was, indeed, some aspect of joy, elation at being in Julie's presence, but it was a joy wrapped in a dizzying, heartbreaking sadness. Wrapped again in guilt for his lack of faith in her. Wrapped yet once more in disgust for not truly knowing her heart after years together.

If he turned back now, he would see the monster she had become, and he didn't trust himself to look away before the trance took him again. It was his fault that she was trapped here. That Jay was trapped here, too. And that Min-woo had died and now had his soul stuck in a notebook.

The notebook… The answers to this whole mess lay somewhere in its pages—either in the FAQ entries Min-woo had supplemented with his own computer game knowledge, or in the new section that provided a paper game testing grounds. The standard Paul Prentice modus operandi for dealing with complicated emotions was to push them aside in favor of analysis. The *serĉilo* role turbocharged this MO, bringing to bear the babbling memories of *serĉilos* past and what felt like overlapping minds of additional Pauls inhabiting his head, dissecting the problem du jour.

While walking vaguely in the direction of the rocks demarking the edge of the ruined city, Paul leafed through the notebook, looking for hidden subtext in entries he had perused many times over. The entry to the Garden of Before described a "nexus" at its heart that was "the point within the Between where all outworlds intersect." Min-woo had scribbled a comment in the margin.

Nothing to do here. Maybe just a thematic element.

Just a thematic element? Paul thought for a moment about Min-woo's comment, and then it all seemed to click. The computer game version of the Between had a *Home* location where adventurers began and where they could return to resupply. The game didn't allow you to explore Home, because Home existed outside the game, and outside the Between. Similarly, if the nexus truly was the location within the Between where all the outworlds intersected, then, like Home, its representation within the game would be highly limited because the outworlds existed outside of the game.

Minutes ago, Paul had told Julie that the rules themselves might've been projected out from within the nexus. This idea hadn't come from the notebook, nor was it the product of Paul's countless hours playing the game on his work laptop. The idea must have come from the memories of past *serĉilos*.

Hey in there! Paul yelled in his head. *How does the nexus work? Is it a gateway back home like the Altar of the Sky, or is it something more? Is there something within the nexus that makes the Between what it is?* He waited for a response, but the only voice he heard was his own.

He thought about his *serĉilo* power and how it seemed to work. It pulled aspects of other Pauls together so that he, briefly, possessed their convergent strength. But who were these other

Pauls? As the *serĉilo*, he could use them but not interact with them. He could feel them but only distantly. Maybe the nexus was more than where the other Pauls overlapped. Maybe the nexus functioned as a prism, reflecting the overlapped Pauls into the Between in exactly the way Paul experienced them as the *serĉilo*.

If the reality of the Between was a projection out of the nexus, was there a way to change how that projection worked, thereby changing the rules of the Between? This thought had such a ring of familiarity to it that Paul was convinced past *serĉilos* had explored it as well. But if they had discovered any deeper truth, they weren't sharing it through the strange echo-memories that filled his head. If he and Julie were to escape, he would have to discover that truth.

And if he couldn't... Well... The only surefire way to free everyone was for Paul to replace Rezső Simko as the dual-faced god, causing the Between to reset. He thought he was ready to do it if it came down to it. But between now and that moment, he vowed to do everything he could to find another way.

As he walked through the Ruins lost in thought, motion ahead brought him back to the present moment. A cloaked figure darted between buildings. Was that a skull-painted face under the cloak's hood? He almost yelled out but caught himself, and in doing so recognized that once again he had been wandering in the open, lost in thought, in a world that could see him dead in an instant.

"Pay attention, Mr. Prentice," he said, imitating the voice of a dour finance professor whose lectures had bored Paul to tears back in undergrad. He scanned his surroundings, following his own advice. Apart from a few fire moths fluttering about near a lava stream, he saw no movement. Beyond the buildings ahead where he thought he had seen Corinne, the beginning of a rocky incline led up to the bowl of the crater and out of the Ruins.

No sign of the *malespero*'s soldiers. No metallic growls from ash dogs. Things seemed strangely empty and peaceful on this side of the Ruins, aside from the smell of rotten eggs. A smell that seemed to have intensified as he stood there.

A cacophony of memories of that smell came to life in his head as something massive and scalding hot wrapped around him and lifted him into the air. He twisted and saw the hulking figure of a *burning one* staring at him with flame filled pits where its eyes should have been. Its mouth widened as it lifted Paul higher. Twenty feet, now thirty feet in the air. The pressure from its grasp made it almost impossible to breathe, and Paul could feel his skin burning from the contact.

Reflexively, Paul pulled on his *serĉilo* powers. He felt his own presence multiply as more and more Pauls filled him, layering him with protection and strength. But as he was about to use his amplified power to push free from the *burning one*'s grasp, the thick sulfur fumes surrounding the creature filled his lungs, starving him of oxygen. He wretched, and his multiples began to slip away. He pushed with all his might against flesh as hot as a sizzling iron skillet. The *burning one*'s hold loosened a bit, and if Paul had a few seconds more he might have gotten free, but it was already cramming him into its hot, putrid mouth.

Teeth as big as a person came down to cut Paul in half. He narrowly avoided them by diving into the oven that was its mouth. It let out a deafening roar of surprise and anger. Then the mouth slammed closed, and in the blistering darkness, he felt its huge tongue pressing him backward to swallow him whole.

In the darkness, Paul's mind created a new landscape of the thing's mouth, where the abyss leading to its stomach became instead the well from Paul's nightmares. A familiar cackle came up from the well.

"NO!" Paul screamed. "I DESTROYED YOU!"

A hundred and then a thousand Pauls filled him, steeling him against the heat. He held on to a tooth, resisting the *burning one*'s attempt to swallow him, and then he grabbed the base of the tooth and pulled. It came loose, all three rotten feet of it with two pointed roots like devil horns. Paul rotated the tooth like it weighed nothing and rammed its roots upward into the roof of the *burning one*'s mouth.

The creature staggered in pain, and the world around Paul shook. Light poured in as it opened its mouth and inserted its finger, trying to pry Paul out. He grabbed the finger, arms wide like he was holding a barrel. Bracing one foot against another tooth, he drew in every ounce of power from every remaining multiple. The *burning one* tried to pull its finger free, but Paul anchored himself firmly, and with a loud pop, the finger tore loose. Paul jammed it in the thing's throat.

He held on to another tooth as the *burning one* fell to its knees. Then Paul threw the massive creature's jaw open with such force that the top half of its head tore completely off. It slumped forward. Before its lifeless torso crashed into the ground, Paul jumped. He used the last of his summoned strength to catch himself when he landed on the hard ground.

His skin burned. He was covered in reeking slime. And he felt almost consumed by the emptiness that followed such an intense use of the *serĉilo*'s power. But he was alive.

An ash dog watched him with wide eyes. It turned and ran when he looked at it, bolting past a skull-faced figure who looked like a ghoul watching from the shadows.

Corinne stepped out into the open, holding a spear with dried blood on its long, kite-shaped blade.

"We've got to stop meeting like this," Paul said, wiping sulfurous muck off his face.

Corinne stared blankly at him with those black-ringed eyes, and then her painted teeth curled into a smile. The smile lasted only a second before it vanished. "Still getting into trouble, I see. Speaking of trouble...You've seen your wife?"

He nodded and wanted to say something more but found himself at a loss.

Corinne held up her hand. "This is not the place for a reunion, Paul. That stunt of yours made a lot of commotion. Every soldier and monster in the Ruins will be here soon."

He followed her to the edge of the Ruins, where the rocky bowl began its climb to the ridge bordering the Gray Waste. Here, the top of an isolated three-story building provided the perfect place to rest and catch up.

As Corinne had predicted, the area where Paul fought the

burning one was now prowling with activity. Two more *burning ones* towered above the nearby structures, their heads swiveling in search of Paul. They were a few hundred yards away, but Paul could smell their brimstone stench in the air. How had he let one get so close?

"So, you saw Julie also?" he asked, his voice cracking on his wife's name. "You know..."

"What she's become?" Corinne finished the sentence for him. "Not at first. Supriya knew, but she kept it from me. It wasn't hard to connect the dots."

They sat there, legs dangling over the edge of the building for several minutes, sharing the silence. Corinne wouldn't offer consoling or sympathetic words. It wasn't her style. The Corinne that Paul knew in high school was never one for small talk or throwaway gestures. This hardened, world-weary version of Corinne even less so. To know Corinne was to be able to translate her silences. And right now, this silence was a shared moment that conveyed everything it needed to.

"I have a plan," he finally said, ending the silence.

"You always do. I hope it works better than mine did."

"My plans don't have the best track record, if we're being honest," he said. "So, what happened with you?"

She recounted it all: finding Supriya in the church with Julie and Jay; the narrow escape from the *malespero*'s soldiers; the failed attempt to open her door back home; Supriya leaving, convinced that Jay was in danger; and the newcomer who she had found hiding in the top of a building, much like Corinne and Paul were now. Corinne had tried to help the man—Esteban was his name—but he had seemed deranged, rambling about this being a simulated world run by an artificial intelligence named Oberon.

"Oberon? The fairy king from *A Midsummer Night's Dream*?" Paul said. "I think the truth is weirder than this all being a computer simulation. A lot weirder. What happened to the guy?"

"I gave him a knife and a banana," Corinne said. "And then I left him."

The blunt, remorseless statement made Paul laugh. A fucking

knife and a banana? Hilarious, in a dark, dark way. But also a reflection of how detached Corinne had become. Even without an artifact and one of the Between's canonical roles, Corinne had been transformed. That was anything but funny.

"There are other ways home for you," Paul said, changing the subject. "The Altar of the Sky on top of that crazy cathedral. The blood portal that let us escape to my house. Maybe it's been rebuilt, or the Between has regenerated it. This place does that, right? Resets itself periodically?"

"I think so," Corinne said. "Maybe."

"Maybe? Well... I'm meeting Julie at the nexus in the Garden of Before. The cathedral is on the way, so we can go together to check." He saw Corinne's eyes narrow at the mention of the Garden, and his mind became filled with memories from the last playthrough of the Between's computer game on his laptop. The Dead-Paul chasing him. The little flying *diableto* that speared him through the heart. He cleared his throat and continued on, as much to prevent Corinne's questions as to head off his own thoughts of doom. "And if the Altar of the Sky is still in a pile of rubble, there's another altar not too far away."

"Where, exactly?"

"Not far." He pulled out the notebook and flipped to the section that described the altars, which was under the *Saving Your Game* entry. "Uh... Here it is. The Altar of the Abyss. Apparently, it's on a hidden floating disk under something called the Sacred Nothing."

"Sounds pleasant. Where is it?"

"The Between's fifth world. The World in Pieces." He waited for her to say something about how dangerous that area was, how getting there would be impossible.

Instead, she said, "We have to leave Jay and Supriya behind. Can you do that, Paul?"

She could just as easily have stabbed him with one of her throwing knives with how the words pierced right through him. Rezső Simko had said something about Jay and Supriya being in great danger, and Corinne's story confirmed it.

It was just a matter of time, I guess, before you abandoned me, too. Jay had said those words back in the sitting room maze after Paul had let his frustrations get the better of him. Jay hadn't been wrong. At every opportunity since then, Paul had chosen others before his best friend. And he was about to do it again.

"I can't save everyone," he said, more to himself than Corinne. "Jay and Supriya have survived this long on their own. They can survive without me."

"No, Paul. They're not going to survive, and there's nothing you or I can do about it. Trying to save them means losing Julie and getting yourself killed, and you'll still fail. You have a hard enough task as it is."

"Fuck." Paul stood and grabbed the backpack. In the hazy distance, he could see the stadium that was the *malespero*'s lair, and then he turned his back on it and began to climb down.

The ridge above the Ruins felt like a demilitarized zone, or a respite spot in a video game, a safe space under the shadow of rocks where you could catch your breath. While both Paul and Corinne had moved quickly to climb up and leave the Ruins behind them, neither were eager to step into the Gray Waste and under the sun's laser-eye of death. Corinne offered Paul a bottle of water from her backpack. He shook his head and made to get his own bottle from his backpack, but all five of his bottles were empty, smashed in the grip of the *burning one*. He pretended to drink from one while running his hand through his hair to block Corinne's view. He felt like an idiot.

"I'm going back for Jay and Supriya," he said. The decision swept through him all at once, knocking aside the reasoning and consideration that had filled his head during the climb up to the ridge.

Corinne gave him another of her silences. This one roughly translated into: *Indeed, you are a fucking idiot.* Then she said, "Fine. Lead the way, hero."

CHAPTER 18
REVENANTS

The dark minotaur silhouette of the *Kosmaro* stepped out of a cave high atop the mountains of the Underworld. Its presence startled a crab-like creature that had been picking for insects among the rocks near the cave's entrance. The crab scurried away through the *Kosmaro*'s distortion cloud, changing with every step—seven legs, now six, now twenty. Two large claws, now one; twitching eyestalks, now a single cyclops eye, now eyes that looked almost human.

Within the cloud, Julie's presence shifted, too. At times she felt that she and the giant void-beast were one and the same, bonded by a warped sense of motherhood. Other times, Julie was merely a passenger, looking out from within the cloud but not in control of the beast's actions. And other times still—becoming worryingly more common—she was lost entirely within the void, oblivious of the world around her and the passing of time.

She closed her eyes and willed herself to become only Julie. The rippling distortion cloud and the void silhouette at its center faded until only Julie in her human form remained. Jeans, Nikes, and a twisted black metal artifact encircling the middle finger of her right hand. A look of calm determination on her face.

The air was cold and carried with it the acrid smell of ammonia. Her eyes watered, and her throat itched. With every breath, her body wanted to retreat into the safety of the distortion cloud, but she held firm.

At a glance, the Underworld looked dead and barren, but she had noticed on her previous trips here that life gained footholds everywhere, even in the bowels of the Between. The little crab-things hiding in the rocks on the mountain. The angry bristles of brown and purple vegetation that somehow extracted sustenance from the Underworld's yellow sky and rocky ground. The occasional ripples in the Black River suggesting something swam in its inky waters. The leathery flying creatures that from a distance looked like birds lazily gliding on thermals.

She wiped at her eyes and coughed. There was only so much air her body could take, and she was quickly reaching her limit. She let herself become the beast again.

The *Kosmaro* walked down the mountain path toward the Black River, where the ferryman sat in his boat, head covered by his shroud, skeleton hand gripping his long steering pole. Barefoot pilgrims were gathered near the shoreline, kneeling with their foreheads pressed to the earth. The distortion cloud swept over the pilgrims as the *Kosmaro* passed them. From within the void, Julie watched them with confusion and horror. What is it they thought they achieved, suffering the environment of the Underworld to come so close to a creature with a penchant for tearing souls from bodies, dead and living?

The question vanished from her mind as if it had been one of the fleeting permutations created by the distortion cloud. As the *Kosmaro*, she waded through the dark waters of the river, growing steadily in size so that the water level never rose above the middle of the minotaur's distended belly. In his boat, the ferryman appeared to give the *Kosmaro* no notice, although he did use his pole to brace the boat against the incoming waves.

On the far shore, the army of iron statues welcomed the *Kosmaro* with faces permanently in agony. Thousands of them, all unique, each representing a person who had entered the Between. Some were filled with the soul-forms of the dead, their constant anguish fueling the giant machine hidden by the fog past the bell tower. Others were empty, waiting for the inevitable deaths of those whose images they shared. The statues were the only ending the Between offered.

As the *Koŝmaro* walked among the statues, a new one rose out of the ground, filling an empty spot on a mound near the bell tower. The *Koŝmaro* paid it no mind. New statues were always being created as more people found their way to the Between.

The time had come to finish the duty ordered by the great bell's beckon. Julie felt her presence *pull forward* within the *Koŝmaro*. She raised a right hand in front of her that was both the beast's and her own, acting as one. With that hand, she reached into the pocket of extradimensional space at her side and pulled from it the basket woven of thorned black branches.

Her heart broke at the sight of the basket, radiant and full of the lost souls of her children. She had to protect them, to hide them away where they could never be killed again. One by one she found their matching statues and guided their ethereal forms into the cold iron skin that would hold and protect them forever. They cried out to her as she left them, but she had to leave them. There were always more. So many more.

Until her basket was empty and there were no more. The enchantment faded, leaving her standing encircled by agonized faces, their accusatory iron eyes all trained on her, their sole jailer and torturer. She retreated into the *Koŝmaro*'s void to escape.

The *Koŝmaro* tucked the empty basket into the hidden pocket and began walking toward the bell tower. The tower stood at the edge of a fog-filled chasm, forty or fifty feet tall, a spiral of ascending stones that looked like scales. The tower's spire curled forward as if it were instead a giant finger scratching at the dying sun above. Atop the tower was the great bell, made of the same black iron as the statues fanning out around it. Even when silent it seemed to radiate power. When the bell tolled, all material and space within the Between shook with its resonance. There was no corner, no hidden part of the Between where the bell's ring did not reach.

The *Koŝmaro*'s destination was not the bell tower itself but the round pedestal next to it. When not acting in service of the bell, the *Kosmaro* stood like another of its statues, awaiting the next call. As the beast stepped onto the pedestal, the fog in the chasm behind the tower shifted, and Julie saw a glimpse of the Great World Engine. A machine the size of a city, fueled by the suffering emanating from the statues. The machine that bound all the *outworlds* to the Between.

Before reaching the center of the pedestal, the *Kosmaro* stopped. Paul would be waiting for Julie soon in the Garden of Before. She couldn't let herself be stuck here, waiting on the whims of the bell. The beast wanted to step to the middle of the pedestal. She wanted it also, felt compelled to do it, but she resisted.

In the many-layered, thunderous voice of the *Kosmaro*, she said, "IF IRON IS WHAT IS POWERFUL HERE, THEN I WILL BE IRON ALSO." Her words seemed to vibrate the air and the statues themselves, creating echoes within their empty cavities, so that it sounded like the whole hillside chanted along with her.

...THEN I WILL BE IRON ALSO...

The *Kosmaro* turned from the pedestal and began walking toward the river, toward the mountain path leading out of the Underworld. Toward Paul.

A door at the base of the bell tower opened, and from within, a small and withered old man emerged. He glared at the void creature with eyes that were twin golden suns.

"RETURN TO YOUR PEDESTAL," he commanded, a heavily accented roll on each hard consonant.

As if the words had been a tether, the *Kosmaro* was immediately drawn back toward the tower. Halfway there, it stopped.

"NO," it said.

NO, all the statues echoed.

The sunfire in the man's eyes doubled, then doubled again, until the entire Underworld was bathed in blinding light. The light pierced through the *Kosmaro*'s cloud as if it weren't there. The blacker-than-black void became filled with light. There was nowhere for Julie to hide. No way to resist.

The beast began walking again. Julie was aware of the movement but couldn't see or feel anything. The light was devouring her, burning through every aspect of her being, every thought and dream that had ever entered her mind. *This is what the souls in the statues feel*, she thought. *I did this to them!*

She reached out with the beast's hands, not at the old man—because the light would not let her—but to a nearby statue. Her claws dug through the iron, and then with a tear, the statue burst open.

The light flickered.

She grabbed another and tore it apart as easily as if it had been made of paper. This time, the light *shuddered*.

"RETURN TO YOUR PEDESTAL," the old man commanded again.

The *Koŝmaro* continued to do as it was commanded, but the shuddering light gave footholds for Julie to resist. Instead of fighting directly against the old man, she tore apart another statue, and the footholds grew.

Using the *Koŝmaro*'s size and might, she smashed and tore at the statues. Dozens, maybe hundreds were destroyed before she realized she could see again. Wisps of bodies floated among the statues. A wave of grief almost as intense as the light had been came over Julie. They were her children, and now they would be lost forever.

"You don't realize what you are doing, Julie!" the old man yelled, looking feebler than ever. "You have to play your role!"

Despite the grief, despite knowing that the man's words were true—she had no idea what she was doing—she grabbed the broken husks of several statues and squeezed them together until they became a makeshift wrecking ball in the palm of her huge beast hand.

"I AM PLAYING MY ROLE," she said in the *Koŝmaro*'s booming voice, "BY MY RULES AND NOT YOURS." Then she threw the wrecking ball at the bell tower, striking it dead in its center. The top of the tower wavered. The bell let out a droning off-key note that threatened to shake the entire Underworld apart, until the tower collapsed in on itself and all became silent.

Julie turned in the direction of the mountain pass and was about to run when she saw dozens of ethereal human forms among the broken statues. Some ran from her beast form, others appeared dazed. One, who looked like a young girl in her early teens, stepped forward. Her face was twisted in pain or maybe fear, but the look in her eyes made Julie think she could see the woman behind the beast's void-silhouette.

"Help us," the girl said in a hollow voice.

Revenants. The word appeared in Julie's mind, but whether it had come from a foreign memory or from Paul's story of what had happened to Min-woo, Julie didn't know. The revenants were soul-forms like those the *Kosmaro* collected, but they were transformed by their imprisonment in the iron statues to appear as they had in life. Like all soul-forms, they would soon fade to nothing without a body of iron or flesh to inhabit.

"Please," the girl implored.

"I WILL SAVE YOU, MY CHILD," Julie heard herself say in both her beast and human voice. She couldn't restore their broken statues, and even if she could have, the thought of imprisoning them again of her own volition felt wicked and wrong. With her basket, she gathered first the girl's revenant form and then as many others as the basket would hold. Then she ran from the field of statues toward the Black River and the mountain pass beyond. She ran as fast as the beast could go, but she couldn't outrun the cries of the revenants she had left behind or the guilt of what she planned to do to save those she carried.

CHAPTER 19
BLOODLETTING

Jay squatted low on the ground near the electrified cage, away from Supriya and away from the bodies of those he had slain. He could hear the cage buzzing, as if its metal tubes were full of wasps, angry and ready to sting. He couldn't look up at Supriya without seeing the juicy vein on her neck or the lattice of veins under the skin of her forearms, all begging to be opened. In his mind's eye, he could see her arms with the veins exposed, with the skin peeled back delicately with his knife, as if he had peeled off the skin of an apple. He could peel her. Every inch of skin, without opening a major vein or artery. If she wanted to stand there staring at him—THEY WERE ALL STARING AT HIM—let her do it without skin...

He tried to push the images from his mind. Why would he do those things to Supriya? He loved Supriya more than he'd loved anyone in his whole life! He went to cover his eyes with the palm of his right hand, but he found it was holding the Knife of Undoing, even though he had put it back in its sheath.

"Fucking knife," he muttered.

It glinted blue in acknowledgment.

"Hold out a little longer," came Supriya's voice from the other side of the cage.

"I can hold out all fucking day!" Jay yelled, still staring at the ground. If he looked anywhere else, if he made eye contact with anyone—a soldier, the *malespero*, Supriya, it didn't matter who—if he saw the vulnerable parts of their body where the knife wanted to cut, he wouldn't be able to stop himself, even knowing what the cage would do when he struck it.

The knife needed blood. He needed blood. He rolled up the sleeve on his left arm and saw his own forearm, lined with thick veins under the spread of tally marks that inventoried his kills. A little cut might help, might subdue the knife for a few minutes so he could think of a way to get out. There had to be a way out.

"He's going to kill himself."

He'd never heard such horror in Supriya's voice, even when they had been trapped in the mansion, surrounded by junklings. He started to say something to console her, to reassure her that he wouldn't harm himself, but his forearm was now covered in blood. Heavy, fat drops of blood landed in the dirt, finding cracks and spreading into a ruddy brown slurry. The stain on the ground looked like a face. A devil face made of dirt and his own blood, staring back up at him. Or was it his own face?

"Save her from the pain. Kill her now and save her!" the blood-face in the dirt said before its features ran together.

"NO!" he yelled. "NO! I won't break!"

He looked up at the *malespero*, but she wasn't there. He spun, searching for her. Several soldiers had returned and stood in even intervals around the cage, but the girl in the black spiked armor, the girl he wanted to slice into ribbons, was nowhere to be seen. "I will never break! Do you hear me?" He turned this way and that, screaming. "NEVER!"

CHAPTER 20
TO BE FEARLESS

While Paul ran through the streets of the dead city, his *serĉilo* mind provided an ongoing commentary as if it were a narrator in a nature documentary. It marveled at his speed. A few additional Pauls allowed him to maintain a sprinting pace that otherwise would have lasted only seconds. Even as the *serĉilo*, Paul couldn't keep the pace indefinitely. The Pauls he pulled into himself through the Silver Spiral on his forearm grew tired quickly and had to be replaced. His pool of replacements slowly refilled, but it wasn't endless. If he used all his power getting to the *malespero*'s lair, he'd have nothing left for what he found there.

The remains of several automobiles, including what had once been a transit bus, served as a mini obstacle course, slowing him down as he zig-zagged between some and leaped over others. His inner documentary narrator pointed out that these weathered vehicles—their paint long since bleached away by the sun, tires turned to powder that had blown away—were the source of the material for the *masinisto*'s scrap metal skeletons, the creatures Jay had named *junklings*.

For a moment, Paul became lost in thought about the automobiles. *How long had they been there? Who once had driven them?* He almost turned and ran back to them when it occurred to him that they might still have license plates, and that he could learn more about their origin and the city that had become the Ruins by looking at the plates. But a clock was also ticking in his head, reminding him that Jay and Supriya were in danger and that Julie would soon be expecting him at the nexus within the Garden of Before.

He ducked behind a jagged wall when the dilapidated arena came into view ahead. It looked like it had been a college football stadium, easily double the size of the Colosseum in Rome. The stands had once extended almost two hundred feet high, he guessed, although most of the high seating had crumbled away. In its original state—assuming anything here had ever existed in any non-ruined form—it might have held a hundred thousand screaming fans.

And again, he caught himself distracted by the *serĉilo*'s constant analysis. What had happened to Corinne? She had been following, angry at him for running out in the open, but there was no way she could've kept up. He looked back at the path he had taken, dreading to see emptiness where Corinne should have been.

Instead, he saw a pack of ash dogs running toward him. The leader of the pack let out a metal-grinding snarl, and then the whole pack filled with yips and howls, the celebration of the hunt. Corinne was nowhere to be seen.

Indecision ensnared him like a spider's web. If he kept running, he could stay ahead of them, but they'd soon catch up. And what about Corinne? He had left her alone in this hell. If he fought the dogs or tried to scare them off, he'd create a commotion and waste more of his power.

He might have stood there, mind gridlocked by the pros and cons of each choice, had Corinne not emerged from the automotive graveyard beyond the dogs. Her skull-painted face looked grimmer than usual, and even from this distance he could see venom in her eyes.

He picked up a chunk of the broken wall that surely weighed twenty pounds, and with the power of ten extra Pauls, he hurled it at the dogs. Nimble as the canines they resembled, they avoided it easily, but the heavy impact startled them enough to disrupt their pace. Paul used that moment to charge directly at them. *Predators of all sizes,* his *serĉilo* mind commented, *tend to react with surprise when other creatures act as the aggressor.*

The dogs scattered and barked. With three quick steps, he caught one. Its skin was so hot that if he hadn't pulled in another several Pauls, it would've burned him. He threw the dog and took out two more like bowling pins.

Corinne caught up and was every bit as angry as Paul expected.

"This was not the plan, Paul! Not the fucking plan!"

"Sorry," he said. Now she was ahead, running straight toward the stadium. He turned to the dogs. Four remained, nervously pacing at a safe distance, that metal-on-metal growl coming from each. "No! Bad dogs!" he said, feeling ridiculous for saying such a thing. But the dogs took on a chastised look, ears pointed back, haunches squatted defensively.

He ran after Corinne, knowing the dogs would soon give chase.

Supriya's body ached, and she felt so exhausted she could barely stand. The skin on her thigh had been rubbed raw where sand had worked its way under her prosthetic sleeve. She had sand in her hair and mouth. She went to spit but her mouth was full of cotton, dry and swollen.

How many hours had they stood there? Soldiers came and went. That bizarre black-and-then-pale man who had radiated madness had come and gone. The *malespero* had gone as well, but now she was back, as still as a statue watching them, somehow even more malevolent without her iron mask on. *When would this end?* Supriya wondered, and then a more ominous question came to mind. *How would this end?* But Lark had told her.

Jay was on his knees, swaying back and forth, mumbling. He looked almost childlike, the way he seemed to be carving images into the ground with his knife. And then, every so often, he stabbed at the images, and his mumbling became loud and angry, and he didn't look childlike at all. He looked mad.

Supriya had tried apologizing to the *malespero*. No, to Lark. The role of the *malespero* may have amplified the hate and anger, but the drive for vengeance came from the girl who had lost her sister to the pair of them. That moment at the graveyard mansion replayed itself over and over in Supriya's mind.

The *gardistaro* had been watching them, then appeared unexpectedly through her gateways to call to them. Supriya knew now, having been the *gardistaro* herself, that the woman meant them no harm. Lark's sister had come to them, as the *gardistaro* came to all newcomers, offering a choice: knowledge or escape. But how could they have known at the time?

Jay had stabbed Lark's sister through the heart, and Supriya's response hadn't been horror or guilt. *Good*, she had said. *The bitch is dead.*

Supriya had stripped the woman naked and taken the *gardistaro*'s dress for herself without a hint of remorse. *And when I was stripped of the dress myself, I deserved it*, Supriya thought. *I deserve to be in this cage now.* She watched how the blue knife in Jay's hand seemed to catch the light of the sun above and throw it at her like a glare. *I deserve what is coming.*

Without the role of the *gardistaro* crowding her mind, the guilt of her past deeds filled the space of her thoughts. She had felt this before, in Jay's kitchen, still the *gardistaro* but far enough from the Between that the role's hold on her had weakened to near nonexistence. The guilt had been crushing. Enough to send her back to this world of death and doom.

Now she had nowhere to hide. Nowhere except the path the *malespero* had laid out for her. And for Jay.

She turned to the *malespero* and was about to say, "You win," when it occurred to Supriya that her death need not be a victory for the *malespero*. She turned then to Jay, fighting the *stelisto*'s murderous urges with everything he had. The *malespero* wanted him to fight, to resist until Jay was truly lost and all that was left was the killer. The god-assassin, the *malespero* had said.

But what if Supriya took his hand and guided the knife to her own neck? What if she gave her life instead of waiting for Jay to break and take it? If she saved him, at least in part, from the responsibility—the guilt—of killing her, would it ruin the plan the *malespero* and her demon lord had devised? Their plan was to destroy the Between—at least, that's what Lark had said. Didn't Supriya want that as well? Yes. Of course she did. But she didn't, for a moment, trust either one of them. Lark was mad with need to avenge her sister. And Sin...Supriya had no idea what he really wanted. All she knew was that Lark was just as much of a pawn in Sin's game as Supriya and Jay were.

So, fuck him.

Fuck their plans.

"Let me not pray to be sheltered from dangers but to be fearless in facing them," Supriya said aloud. "Let me not beg for the stilling of my pain but for the heart to conquer it."

She walked toward Jay with the words of Rabindranath Tagore echoing in her mind, accompanied by the ghost of her Nani repeating them alongside her. The familiar words became new again in her ears, as if they had been written and taught to her for this very moment.

"What are you doing, Supriya?" came Lark's voice, not the *malespero*'s.

Supriya repeated the mantra, let it carry her to Jay. Lark said more, but Supriya no longer heard her. Jay spoke as well, his eyes red with fire and pain. A moment of clarity, cutting through the madness.

"Stay away, babe," he said, eyes full of tears. "Please. I can't help myself."

She took his empty left hand and guided him to his feet. And then she took his right hand and guided the knife to her neck.

CHAPTER 21
IN THE ARENA

It wasn't until the blade met Supriya's neck that Lark understood what the woman was doing.

"No!" Lark screamed. She needed to see Jay break, and Supriya was trying to take that away from her. And what if that kept Jay from becoming the monster he had to be? Sin would hold Lark responsible and see to it that she was the next to die by the Knife of Undoing.

The spiked armor ignited with cold blue flame. She ran along the perimeter of the cage, searching for the right angle to separate Supriya and Jay by force. What else could she do? As she lifted her arm to send a shockwave into them, flames roared out from the hall leading to the arena floor. One of her soldiers—Thomas, it looked like—flew out from the hall and rolled like a rag doll almost all the way to the cage. His chest had been caved in by whatever had struck him.

Her other soldiers rushed to the arena entrance while a moment of indecision overtook her.

Jay and Supriya had their foreheads together, eyes locked, oblivious to what was happening outside the cage. The knife was at Supriya's jugular. It quivered and flared with its own blue light.

A woman with the face of death came out of the flames, red fire wand in her left hand and a silver knife in her right. Lark had never seen the woman but had heard rumors of her, a survivor without a role. A ghost.

One of her soldiers aimed a rifle at the woman, but a spear struck him in the chest with such force that it punched a hole clean through him. He stood in disbelief, looking down at the cavity in his chest before collapsing.

The thrower of the spear stood in the hall behind the skull-faced woman. It was the man named Paul, the newest *serĉilo*, who —if Sin's rumors were true, and they usually were—had been handpicked by *Dio Ordo* to be his successor. Lark had watched the *Koŝmaro* nearly kill him, and then it seemed he had left the Ruins. Clearly, he had doubled back. Lark had killed one *serĉilo* herself. Sin had warned her that Paul was exceptionally strong in his role. But the plan was not to kill him. Not yet, anyway. If he died now, the Order God would simply find another successor.

Her mind searched for a way to salvage all the pieces of Sin's plan, but as the last of her soldiers fell, survival became the only priority. A glimmer of red and silver streaked toward her—one of the skull-faced woman's knives. The radiating force of the spiked *malespero* armor redirected the knife harmlessly into the dirt in the center of the arena. With an outstretched left hand, Lark chan-neled a shockwave of that force toward the skull-faced woman, sending her tumbling and sliding.

The *serĉilo* was running directly toward her. She directed another shockwave at him. She didn't expect it to have the same effect on him as the skull-faced woman—this was the *serĉilo*, after all—but it didn't knock him off his feet at all. His progress slowed to a stop, and then he pushed through the shockwave, his eyes flaring with golden light.

She put everything she had into the shockwave and called out with her mind to the nearby burning ones. *Help me!*

It wasn't the force emanating from the *malespero* that Paul had to worry about; with his presence filled with all the Pauls the neighboring worlds had to offer, that force felt like little more than a heavy wind. No, it was the sand under his feet, causing him to slide back with every step. If he could just get traction, he could be on the *malespero* in a heartbeat. He could tear the artifact collar from her neck and end this. He could stop whatever was happening with Jay and Supriya in that cage.

Paul half-turned his head to look at the cage, but any lack of focus caused him to slide more. The ground beneath him began to shake and the sound of booming footsteps came from behind him. Corinne, on the ground past the *malespero*, wasn't moving, but she would have to wait. He put all his focus on the *malespero* and closing the gap between them.

His shoes slipped, but each leg possessed the strength of a thousand legs—at least for the moment. He pushed pits into the ground and accelerated forward. The demeanor of the *malespero* had broken. Instead of a warlord demigod, she looked now like a scared girl, helpless in the face of a closing freight train. Paul was that train. If not for the waves of force emanating from her outstretched hand and the spiked armor she wore, she would have been turned to paste when Paul smashed into her, his shoulder lowered like a linebacker's. The spikes on her armor tore away several of his multiples but couldn't touch the real Paul nested within.

The *malespero* tumbled backward albeit with a surprising amount of control, using projected force to keep from crashing on the ground and impacting the wall behind her. Paul moved to follow, but the stench of sulfur hit him as hard as the *malespero*'s shockwave, and a shadow darkened the sky above. He looked up to see a giant, filthy foot stomping down.

Paul rolled clumsily to the side as the *burning one's* foot slammed down and filled the air with a plume of dirt and sand. He scrambled back to his feet, uncertain which way was which. With the air opaque, he couldn't see the *burning one* and be ready for its next attack. He held his hands above his head, feeling his multiples and his strength draining away—he had held too many for too long. He thought he still had enough left to catch the *burning one's* foot and keep from being crushed, but he wouldn't know until it happened.

The stomping attack he had braced for didn't come. The dust plume tore apart as the *burning one* took two long strides through it and scooped up the *malespero* with its hand. For a second, Paul thought of his own experience in the oven that was these creatures' grasps, and he expected it to lift the *malespero* to its mouth and to bite her in half. But it was her monster. It lifted her as it kept running and held its hand out with a loose grip. The *malespero* knelt on the platform of its palm, watching Paul as the giant ran to the edge of the arena and climbed through a broken V-shaped opening in the wall.

"Leave her, Paul," came Corinne's voice behind him.

He had been of such a singular focus that he was about to chase the *malespero* and the burning one into the Ruins. He went to help Corinne stand. She had almost as much dust on her face as paint, and her hair looked like a Jackson Pollack painting. She slapped his hand away and nodded toward the cage.

Oh, God, Paul thought as he saw what Corinne had directed his eyes to. A single figure lay on the ground in the center of the cage. He ran to the cage and tore its outer fence apart, though not as easily as he might have a few minutes before. He was so focused on the figure within the cage that he didn't see the wires running to it. Electricity jolted through him, but he ripped through the inner fence just the same even as it drained him further. Many Pauls slipped away with the shock. He was so exhausted that he wanted to let the few remaining go, but what he saw at the center of the cage was more than he could handle by himself.

It was Supriya on the ground, half her face visible, the other half pressed into a circle of blood that extended two feet in every direction around her head. The one open eye Paul could see stared out into nothing.

He dropped to his knees next to her, soaking his jeans in her blood. "Supriya, you're going to be okay," he said as he turned her over. "You're going to..." His words caught. The side of her neck on the ground was cut clean open, split into a gap so wide he could have put his hand inside. He fumbled at his pockets with the nonsensical notion that they might hold a pair of golden obols in them, like those he had used in the field when his errant gunshot had struck Supriya in the chest.

"Jay?" He looked about. "Jay, where did you go? I'm sorry, Jay. I'm so sorry. I tried to get here. I tried... I..."

Corinne came up next to him. "Oh, Supriya...Jesus," she said, her voice catching. And then, "Where did Jay go, Paul?" She shook him, and when he didn't respond, she shook him harder. "Get up, Paul. Now. Where did Jay go?"

The voices in Paul's head came alive at this question, arguing with each other.

Where is the stelisto?

He's gone!

Vanished in a shadow.

There are no shadows here.

The smoldering wood, do you smell it?

Paul indeed smelled the smoldering wood, and it triggered memories of Jay recently, smelling like he had been standing next to fire, his eyes red. "He's still here," Paul heard himself say aloud.

As he said those words, a swarm of black ash in the air coalesced next to him and a flash of silver and blue struck out, biting at Paul's neck. He felt his skin grow hot and wet with blood. He grabbed at the dark form, but it became diffuse again.

"RUN!" Corinne screamed, backing toward the hole that Paul had torn in the cage.

"What about Supriya?" Paul said, holding his neck. It was a question that needed no answer. Supriya was dead, and the slice to Paul's neck nearly caused him to join her. The blade—the Knife of Undoing, Jay's *stelisto* blade—had sliced through each of the remaining multiples that still overlapped with Paul and reached his vulnerable body beneath.

The darkness swirled into a silhouette on his other side. This time the knife cut Paul across the forearm as he tried to block the attack. Again, it cut through all the layers with bright hot pain.

"Die, you fucking traitor," came the echo of Jay's voice from the silhouette as it broke apart into a smoky cloud that circled Paul within the cage.

Two jets of fire came from the red wand in Corinne's hand. The cloud of darkness split apart each time, avoiding the flames and reforming after.

"You abandoned us... You let her die..." Jay's voice emanated from the swirling darkness—everywhere at once. Then came an agonized wail. "She's dead! Dead! No! I was holding on... I wasn't going to do it..."

"I'm sorry, Jay!" Paul yelled. "I..." He wanted to say that he couldn't have saved them. He couldn't even save himself. But it felt like a lie. He stumbled backward, toward Corinne.

The darkness spread so thin that it vanished, and then it came together. First behind Paul, where a slash caught him across the back, from his waist to the nape of his neck, and then again to his left. He pulled away, but the blade clipped the tip of his left ear off and cut into his scalp. Blistering heat seared the side of his face, as if the blade had left behind some of its angry curse, a poison spreading from where it had severed flesh.

More jets of fire came from Corinne, but whatever Jay had become was too diffuse, too nimble to hit. A sound came from the swirling darkness that oscillated between sinister laugh and agonized wail.

Paul pulled through the bloody Silver Spiral on his forearm, but he had exhausted the neighboring worlds of his parallels and only a few remained. Enough to keep him standing, but not much more. He stumbled toward the hall leading out of the arena with Corinne nearby. The look she gave him was as grim as he had ever seen on her face, and that was saying something.

Before they reached the hall, the darkness congealed again. A slash caught Paul across the left hamstring, and a second slash might have finished him had Corinne not scorched the nearby air with her fire wand, singeing Paul in the process. He fell to the ground, each laceration screaming like white-hot metal pressed against his skin. He managed to push himself to his feet, back near the arena wall, and stretched his arms out wide. There was no running from Jay, not in Paul's condition, not with the form the *stelisto* was now able to take.

"If killing me is what you want, Jay, then do it!" Paul yelled.

The darkness arced and twisted like a flying serpent, dissolving and reforming while Jay's laughter and cries grew louder and louder. Through Paul's periphery, he could see Corinne backing away. There was nothing she could do.

Jay appeared before Paul, his face visible for the first time as the darkness solidified. The Knife of Undoing stabbed out like a scorpion's barb, catching Paul in the chest. Jay leaned in, pushing the knife toward Paul's heart as the *serĉilo's* multiples vanished, and the flesh gave way. A quarter inch deep and then a quarter inch more. They strained against each other in this moment bordering death, both men's hands locked around the knife's handle. In Jay's glare, Paul saw the hate fueled by the knife, but beneath the hate was a profound sadness, a terror at what he was watching himself do. Paul surged with a final influx of strength, less to protect himself than to put an end to this agonizing moment. To save Jay from what was about to happen. He grabbed Jay by the front of his shirt, hands crumpling the embroidered flowers, and then slammed him into the wall.

Jay's face showed only shock as some part of him that was solid and real struck stone, but he also seemed to turn ethereal upon impact, screaming in pain in all directions as the dark shadows spread across the wall. The darkness and the screaming faded into nothing, carried away by the wind.

"Did I..." Paul began, and then he was falling. The world became distant, as if he had become one of the voices deep in his mind and no longer occupied the rest of his body. He twisted and hit the ground, the world now sideways before his eyes. He tried to blink away the blood as it clouded his vision, but after two slow blinks, the world stayed dark.

CHAPTER 22
THE NATURE OF THINGS

The man who had once been Rezső Simko stood among the broken statues and watched as the Underworld's bell tower slowly reassembled itself. The *Košmaro* had smashed the tower, but nothing in the Between could ever truly be destroyed. Given time, everything reverted to Rezső's initial conceptualization; it'd been that way since he'd claimed the artifact that now took the form of a ruby amulet worn around his neck. But this state of the Between was transitory. It had existed as something else before him and would change to become something new once he relinquished his role.

Despite serving as the Between's overseer and indeed as both of the supreme deities within its domain, he understood almost nothing about the Between's fundamental nature beyond the layer of abstraction that he now inhabited. He wondered if there even was a fundamental nature buried within the nested layers of abstraction. He was no closer to answering this question than he was the first time he had asked it, when his body was young and not the feeble, dying thing it had become. A lifetime ago, in the outworld he had come from. A thousand lifetimes had passed here.

"So slow," came a deeper and perpetually amused copy of his own voice. "The last time the bell tower was destroyed, it reassembled itself within minutes. It still has hours left to go. Our power is growing weak. Our time is coming to an end."

"We have grown old," Rezső said. He said *we*, but he didn't think of the other voice as belonging to someone else. It was his voice, coming from a second version of himself inhabiting the same body. The artifact had split him in two, joined but forever opposed. One side governing all order and structure in the Between, the other presiding over chaos and destruction. Separate yet singular. "It is time to pass this role to another and to let the cycle begin anew."

"It is a shame that our time has to come to an end. I have liked existing, and the thought of not existing pains me. Endings are too clean," Chaos-Rezső said.

Order-Rezső thought on this. In his mind, endings were anything but clean. Systems began to fail and spill out their contents. Bodies withered and lost control. Hopes and plans unraveled into the frayed edges of regret. Beginnings were clean and filled with promise, but endings were rotten, dirty things. He said none of this. Now was not the time for an esoteric argument. "What pains me more," he said instead, "is this thing we have created. It is an abattoir. We saw the Between as a game, and so it has become a game that serves no purpose other than to inflict pain."

"Purpose is something we project onto things. There is no fundamental purpose to anything in the universe. Things are. We are. And then they are not. And then we are not."

"I don't believe that," Order-Rezső said.

His Chaos twin chuckled. "The nature of things is not dependent on your beliefs or mine."

"You're only saying that because you are the embodiment of me that presides over chaos."

"And you're only looking for purpose because you're the embodiment of me that presides over order."

It was Order-Rezső's turn to chuckle. "Then let us play our respective roles to the end."

His twin's voice took on an even more amused tone. "Very well.

To the end, then. With the tower broken and the *Koŝmaro* running rogue, we are too weak to do much more than watch."

"So, we watch. That should make you happy."

"It indeed does make me happy. Tell me... Did your chosen successor survive? The *stelisto* was gravely wounded in their fight but will soon recover. No *stelisto* has achieved the second awakening before, yet there is something holding him back. If he can master his new power, he will be unstoppable. If your successor lives... his remaining life may be short."

Order-Rezső hesitated, watching as the broken pieces of a stone came together in the air, and then, once whole, moved into place on the wall of the tower. "Congratulations on your accomplishments thus far. The *stelisto* is a force of chaos unlike any we have seen. Even the *Malluma Sinjoro* will not be able to control him. But don't claim victory prematurely. The *serĉilo* lives."

His twin scoffed. "Bah. Mr. Prentice is proving to have more lives than a cat. Is he still headed to the nexus within the Garden of Before?"

"The nexus? Why would he go there?"

Chaos-Rezső let out a deep laugh and the nearby dusty air took on a crimson hue. "I can hear the uncertainty in your voice. You're worried he will find a way to use the nexus to escape his role... and escape the future you have planned for him."

"If the nexus offered such a thing, we would have discovered it and used it years ago. No one understands the nexus better than we do."

"And yet..." Chaos-Rezső said, drawing the words out.

"And yet, what?"

"And yet we understand so little."

"If you're trying to get me to admit there's a chance he might find a way to escape, then fine. Anything is possible."

"So, Mr. Prentice *is* headed to the nexus?"

Order-Rezső hemmed and hawed. There was no use trying to keep secrets from his Chaos half. Information bled across whatever membrane separated their personas. "He was gravely injured, and at the moment, he is incapacitated. But, as you know, the *serĉilo* heals faster than any other role. And Julie Prentice is on her way to the nexus as we speak. Paul will do everything he can to meet her there, but many obstacles remain for him, not the least of which is the Garden itself."

"The tower will soon be restored. We could ring the bell and draw the *Koŝmaro* back. Mrs. Prentice is strong-willed, but no one can resist the great bell."

"Draw her back to what end? We agree that the time for transition has come. Why put off the inevitable?"

"Why, indeed?" Chaos-Rezső said with a teasing singsong to his voice.

"If you wish to make a bargain, state it plainly."

"You're always in such a rush. Fine. I will not interfere with the reunion of Mr. and Mrs. Prentice provided we can ring the bell one final time and have it call to *all* the servants of Order and Chaos. Summon them all to the center of the Garden of Before. To the nexus."

Order-Rezső let out a huff of annoyance. "Bring them all together? You want a grand battle to choose a successor. That is far too chaotic for my taste."

"A battle is not predestined. They could negotiate. Play eeny-meeny-miny-moe. Flip coins. Hold an election. There are any number of non-combat solutions."

It was now Order-Rezső's turn to say, "And yet..."

"And yet, they will probably fight. Fighting does seem to be human nature. The uncertainty appeals to me, but a singular, final event is also a thing of order that should appeal to you. I am compromising here."

"A singular, final event does indeed appeal to me. More than that, I feel compelled to bring about this very ending. Why is that, do you suppose?"

Chaos-Rezső chuckled. "We saw this world as a game, as you said earlier, and all games have endings. All games have winners and losers. This is how it must be."

"You're right, I am sure. Don't let it go to your head. Fine. We will bring them all together."

"Splendid! Shall we leave now?"

"Not just yet. I want our last sight of the Underworld to include the tower standing whole one final time. I want to be here for the final tolling of its bell."

CHAPTER 23
THE FINAL TOLL OF THE BELL

In the cavern within the Patchwork World, the Between's first world, the *masinisto*'s pen began to quiver, ruining the journal entry he had been meticulously crafting. Two lenses twisted down from his crown to cover his right eye like a jeweler's loop. He tried to study the pen as he would any misbehaving machine, to understand whether its malfunction was due to a design flaw or a need for maintenance. But the pen shook too much to be studied. He set it on the table where it bounced and quivered, as did the inkwell and the paperweight one of his predecessors had made from a human skull. He stood and found the floor of the study shaking under his feet. *An earthquake?* he wondered, but he had experienced earthquakes before, and this was something different. He felt it in his teeth and his bones; a sound, too deep to hear, struck at the fundamental resonant frequency of everything. A sound that shouldn't be possible. *The bell!* A foreign voice in his head exclaimed. *Only the great bell of the Underworld could make such a sound!* The sound grew until it became all-encompassing, shattering the glass vessels on his shelves, cracking the solid wood desk in front of him. When it stopped, the world felt fuzzy and out of focus. The only clarity was the imprint left by the sound of the bell on his mind: *The end is here, and I am being called to witness and take part.*

When he trusted his hand to remain steady, he reached and touched his crown with his index finger and called out to the rust wraiths in his mansion and in the graveyard beyond. "Sígueme al Jardín de Antes, mis creaciones. Nos vamos y nunca volveremos."

Before he could set off, however, a knock came from the front door of the mansion. Whoever it was had avoided the detection of the rust wraiths. Had the *stelisto* escaped? No one else could move through the graveyard with such stealth.

The *masinisto* wearily left his study and made his way to the staircase leading to the mansion's entry hall. Halfway there the colors of the mansion around him inverted, and he almost lost his footing. He felt a sudden hunger for violence come over him but saw no one at whom to direct it. He swung open the mansion's great front door and found himself standing before the *Malluma Sinjoro*, the devil-man the *malespero* called Sin.

The *masinisto* fell to his knees. "¿Cómo puedo servirte, mi maestro?" A winding, seashell-like device wrapped around his ear translated his words to English.

"The bell calls us, Juan Carlos, so we must go," Sin said. His bone white face took on a wolfish smile. "But before we leave, there is a thing you must build for me..."

———

"I, your shepherd, have been called," said the *nenio* from the altar of the partially restored *Katadralo Kaoso*, in the floating city within the Between's third world. "And so you, as my flock, have been called, too." She descended into the nave, her crimson robe flowing behind her and the Twilight Scepter in her raised hand crackling like a Tesla coil. Her adepts followed next, and as she passed, those in the pews joined in the procession. Some human and some that were something else, with their too-long arms and too-long legs, with their sharp teeth and bulging eyes.

"Oblivion is coming," the *nenio* said. "Let us go to the Garden of Before and welcome it."

In the middle of a great stone leaf extending into the clouds from the Skytower within the sixth world of the Between, the *klaro* sat unmoving, legs crossed, back straight, hands steepled together in front of her in a meditative state that made her body immaterial. Even artifacts could not touch the *klaro* in her trance. Yet when she opened her eyes and the veil of the trance fell, she found a thought floating in her mind that had not been there before, a seed that had been planted and that had grown into an understanding, a certainty. This world between worlds was nearing its end, and she had been summoned to witness its death and rebirth.

She became ethereal and passed through the Skytower's stone exterior. Waiting for her inside, perched in the middle of a massive web, was the *araneo*, the orb weaver who guarded the Skytower's topmost reaches. The spider moved quickly on its spindly legs toward the *klaro*, but as it came near, it crossed into the *klaro*'s Aura of Calm, and its animalistic hunger vanished.

The *klaro* put her palm flat against the *araneo*'s head and it let out a mellow hum in response. "I must go, my beautiful friend," the *klaro* said, looking at the *araneo*'s many eyes in turn. "Perhaps we will see each other again in another life."

On a small island floating in darkness, the *songo* rifled through the pockets of a corpse impaled on wooden spikes. The *songo*, the Dream of Chaos, had many such traps hidden among the archipelago of The World in Pieces, the Between's fifth world. This trap had ensnared one of the strange pilgrims who ventured down to the Underworld in search of a transformational encounter with the *Kosmaro*. The pilgrim's coarse robes contained only some stale bread, and a strange golden coin stamped with the impression of a bee.

The *songo* was twisting the coin before his examining eye when the bell's toll shook him and the island beneath him. With a thought, he dismissed the illusions hiding all his traps, and he exposed the true path that led to the Grand Staircase. He spared one look at the little hut on a neighboring island. It'd been his home within this broken world surrounded by the void. And then he set off to end his isolation, and to bring his dreams to those he would meet in the Garden.

The *stelisto* drifted as a cloud of shadow in a semi-conscious, dreamlike state. If he felt anything, it was pain—pain that had splintered him into a million motes of darkness. The toll of the Underworld's great bell sent each of these motes vibrating with purpose. They came together and first formed a silhouette, and then the silhouette became the solid presence of man, curled on the dirty ground, whimpering, struggling to breathe.

He tried to push himself up with his right arm, but that arm only hung limp and wouldn't move. Then with his left. He saw a mark on his forearm that he, himself, had carved. It was bigger than the other kill-tally marks, and a slow trickle of blood ran from it like a crimson tear, staining his flesh, further staining his already stained soul. For a moment, while the bell's echo still reverberated through every part of his being, his mind was insulated from the horror of what he had done, of the kill that was signified by that mark. And so he began shuffling in the direction of the Grand Staircase with only one destination in mind.

At the far edge of the Ruins, opposite of the rocks that led to the Grand Staircase, the *malespero* had gathered several of her soldiers and was relaying instructions when the tolling of the bell filled the air and made the sand on the nearby dunes sizzle. All heard and felt the bell, including the ash dogs and the two nearby *burning ones*, but only the *malespero* and the newly made *gardistaro* were gripped by its compulsion.

"Change of plans," the *malespero* said. "We're going to the Garden of Before. Grab whatever weapons you can, but make it quick." To the *gardistaro*, she said, "Sin told me we would all be called. He was right, as usual. He said he wanted you to get there first and to meet him for further instructions."

"Me? Why? What further instructions?" the *gardistaro* asked, her voice breaking in and out of the smoothness that was characteristic of her role.

"I don't know, Esther," the *malespero* said, "but what choice do you have? What choice do any of us have?"

"Do you trust him?"

The *malespero* laughed—a full laugh, the first she could remember since Zee had worn the dress Esther now wore. "Do I trust Sin?" she echoed. "I trust him to use and discard us. Once you're able, get out of his aura, get as far away from him as possible."

Back at the arena, Esther used a storage door to create a gateway to the Grand Staircase. It took all the *malespero's* willpower and then some to keep from following her through. Once the gateway vanished, the *malespero* and her soldiers began the journey on foot.

She had to go to the nexus within the Garden. She was compelled by the bell. But she was in no hurry to get there because she knew, at least in part, what Sin had planned. Lying to Esther had been easier than she had expected.

CHAPTER 24
THE FIRST TO REACH THE GARDEN

Traveling through the World Tunnel felt to Julie as natural as a neighborhood stroll. As long as she didn't think too much about it. The pitch darkness. The impenetrable stone walls. The knowledge that this was not an underground passageway as it appeared but a tunnel through some extradimensional space adjacent to all eight worlds of the Between. A space like the one where she kept her basket.

What is on the other side of these walls? she wondered, dragging the claws of her beast hand across the rough stone of the tunnel.

Nothing and everything! answered a foreign voice within her mind.

More voices from those who had been the *Kosmaro* before her chattered in her head like a theater audience impatiently waiting for a show to begin. The voices had grown louder and more numerous with every hour Julie spent as the *Kosmaro*. When would she no longer hear her own voice? When would she become smothered by the crowd amassing in her head? What scared her more, though, was when the voices went silent. In those moments, she became only the beast, and her voice became silent as well.

She had to be the beast, now, to navigate the tunnel and see in the darkness. But she had to be Julie as well, first and foremost, controlling the beast as if it were a vehicle—like Ripley's power loader from the movie *Aliens*—a shell surrounding her true self and nothing more. With the bell tower smashed, the beast had become pliant. *How long until—*

As if it were listening to her thoughts, waiting for her to lower her guard, the bell rang but with an unfamiliar, primordial resonance. The walls of the tunnel quivered. The *Kosmaro's* reality-warping field flashed on and off like a television losing its signal and going to static. Every bone in Julie's body seemed to ring in unison.

The echo of the bell tapered and faded away, but it left in Julie's mind an idea. The idea didn't take the form of words, but she understood it so well that it was easy to translate it into an instruction: *go to the nexus within the Garden of Before, where you will witness and take part of the end and the beginning.*

She was Julie now, and Julie alone, standing in the cold darkness of the tunnel but neither disoriented nor scared. The bell had commanded her to do exactly what she was already doing. At the nexus, she would save the souls she carried within her in her basket, and she would meet Paul. Together they would relinquish their roles; he had promised to find a way, and no person in the world was more reliable than Paul. Then they would go home.

It sounded simple in her mind, naively simple. But the bell had provided its validation. The end and the beginning. The *Kosmaro's* aura came to be again, illuminating her path. At its center, the beast's void silhouette stood, as always, but it was behind Julie as if it were her shadow.

She ran forward, faster now and with renewed purpose, trying to ignore the voices in her mind that had all begun to laugh at her.

The World Tunnel opened into a chamber filled with life. Mosses of orange and green covered its walls. Ahead, daylight filtered in through the sheer curtain of a waterfall. A six-legged salamander-thing puffed up bright red cheeks to woo a nearby mate.

A beautiful, hidden room. Julie released the *Kosmaro's* aura to prevent it from disturbing the place and its inhabitants. She stepped through the waterfall, shocked at how cold the water was, and found herself on the side of a cliff overlooking the Garden of Before.

From up high, the Garden appeared to be a patchwork quilt of rolling colors and textures extending out in all directions. Paths separated each square, forming a giant grid. It reminded Julie of a piece of graph paper she had filled in square by square with markers during math class in middle school. She still had that paper in a memorabilia box in their attic back home.

No. The box had burned with everything else.

She began to climb down the cliff. It wasn't steep, but the rocks were wet and so was she. Before reaching the ground, she paused briefly to study the obelisks that stood at each intersection of the paths. One obelisk, at a seemingly random spot off to her left, stood much taller than the others. And unlike the others, which shined like mirrors reflecting the sun, this larger obelisk was the same void-black as her minotaur form. An absence rather than a presence.

She didn't see Paul waiting there for her, so she must have arrived before him. Good. It gave her time to use the nexus to find bodies for the souls she carried in her basket.

Why? Why would we do such a thing? a memory asked in a pained voice.

To save them! another said.

Ah, but at a price.

She tried to ignore the voices and the uncertainty they fed. She counted the intersections between herself and the nexus. Eleven forward and then nine to the left. She had been to the nexus before and expected it to be easy to reach again. What could be simpler?

At the bottom of the cliff, the cascading water flowed into a wide stream that curved to her right in a grove of trees. Little ornate bridges carried the path over the water. Some were made of wood, some of stone. But none were in the direction she was headed, so she ignored them and moved on.

On the path forward, she was flanked by red poppies on one

side, and on the other, a sea of wide, tall blades of grass undulating in the wind like seaweed. She moved quickly, trying not to get distracted by every fantastical sight the Garden of Before offered. Julie Prentice's superpower, so to speak, had always been her ability to *get shit done*. She used this ability to shut out everything but the path before her. She passed three, four, and then five obelisk-demarcated intersections on her way to the eleventh. But the path to the sixth presented something she hadn't seen from her vantage point on the cliff: an ornate bridge crossing a stream.

The world she had blocked out came rushing back in. A group of sail-backed monkeys hooted and chirped from a small grove of immaculately pruned trees. Every few seconds, a monkey jumped from its perch on a tree and landed with a splash in the stream. They beckoned at her to join them.

Her attention, though, was on the stream and the bridge, not the monkeys. She had seen them neighboring the cliff where she had climbed down from the World Tunnel. Or was this another bridge crossing another stream next to another grove of trees? She turned to look down the path behind her and felt her stomach tighten. She should have been several hundred yards from the cliff, but somehow, here it was, no more than twenty feet before her, water splashing so close it almost reached her feet. More alarming, she saw another figure climbing down the cliff near the waterfall... a figure that looked identical to her.

Are we lost in the Garden again? a voice in her head asked.

We're not lost!

Yes, we are. We always get lost here.

She put her palms flat against her ears, but the arguing voices came from within her head and couldn't be blocked out. She hadn't been paying attention and had gotten turned around. That's all. Seeing herself was unsettling, but the chattering memories seemed to know this was part of the Garden's Escher-like nature.

"Lost in my own thoughts," she said aloud, as if speaking it made it true. Then she added, "Like Paul." The sound of his name lingered on her lips as if he had just softly run a finger across them. She said his name again, and with a shiver, set out.

She ran along the path next to the cliff until she reached her starting point. It looked unchanged. She kept the cliff to her back, not wanting to see herself even if she understood why. Red poppies to her left. Tall grass on her right. Forward to the eleventh obelisk, then left six. Same as before.

Julie walked with purpose, head up. Even without the *Kosmaro*'s aura surrounding her, she could reach into the extradimensional space at her side. She did so and touched the basket, to reassure herself that it was still with her. Through her touch, the revenants in the basket cried out, and a wave of guilt came over her. To save them was to doom others.

She jogged past two obelisks before something made her stop. A feeling that she was being followed. She spun. The path behind was clear, leading all the way back to the cliff where the waterfall glimmered in the sunlight. She thought she saw another Julie to her left, but when she turned that direction, the path lay empty. As she was about to continue toward the nexus, something moved within a square of land covered with ivy and then seemed to disappear. It was large. Too large to hide in the ivy. Where had it gone, and why couldn't she describe anything about it? Aside from a pair of butterflies dancing in the air, and the swaying of flowers and branches in the wind, she saw no movement. So, she turned and continued on.

She saw it again in a field of what looked like person-sized daisies. What *it* was, she still couldn't say, but it had gotten ahead of her. Was it following her? Or hunting her?

Become the beast, a voice in her mind whispered.

No, she replied. If she stayed the beast too long, she would lose herself in it.

Become the beast or the naĝanto *will eat you!*

The what? She peered between the tree-like flower stems, scrutinizing every shadow and every hint of motion. But again, whatever she had seen had vanished. If she kept stopping like this, the end that the bell foretold would come before she reached the nexus. As she was about to continue, *it* moved again, this time directly before her.

A *bulge* in space—that was the only way she could describe it —swam out from the daisies and across the path. It darted through a stretch of white ferns to her right, a huge form with a body like a whale and a tail that whipped back and forth. Then it stopped, becoming completely invisible in its stillness.

Become the beast!

"No!" she screamed.

Under the single tree atop the cliff, Rezső Simko stood and watched as the world behind Julie rolled and shifted toward her. It reminded him of a cat he once had that liked to sleep under his bedsheets. Each night, the cat would burrow near his pillow and crawl its way to the foot of the bed as a moving lump. The thing approaching Julie was a similar moving lump, something that swam under the fabric of space, bulging it out rather than occupying it as matter. And so, it made no noise as it neared and then launched itself toward her. Julie vanished in a ripple when it swallowed her, and then the thing swam off through a lilac field toward the sun.

"She let herself be eaten by the *naĝanto!*" Rezső's Chaos twin exclaimed.

Order-Rezső tsked and spat on the ground. "She was careless. I expected more from her."

Suddenly, the *naĝanto's* moving lump of space tore open, and the *Koŝmaro* exploded into being, its void-form so tall its head eclipsed the sun. A half second later, a shockwave swept into the cliff, kicking up a typhoon of water and air and knocking Rezső to the ground. He covered his head as ripples in the air rained down all around him, and chunks of the *naĝanto* came flying at him.

"Ah," Order-Rezső said as he rubbed his forearm where a sharp rock had struck his skin. The rock had not injured him; he couldn't be injured in his own world. "She was not as vulnerable as she appeared. Look how she controls the *Koŝmaro's* form. She has awakened."

His Chaos twin grumbled. "Now I'm the one who is disappointed. I expected the *naĝanto* to eat several of our guests. It appears we have been knocked to the ground."

"We are growing weak. Let's end this quickly."

"Not much longer, I think," Chaos-Rezső said.

Julie reeled from what just happened. She had felt herself being swallowed. The world turned into a translucent bubble that shrank, tightened, and became suffocating, and then she was moving with it, inside of it as it swam away with a full stomach. She panicked. The *Koŝmaro*'s aura sprung into being, but as the beast stepped forward within her, she fought to hold it back. Even as the *naĝanto* began to crush her, she refused to let the beast take control.

The beast broke first. She felt the *Koŝmaro* succumb, becoming an extension of her rather than a role that she filled. She transformed into the void version of herself, growing titan-sized in an instant, bursting the *naĝanto* from the inside. Then she looked out across the Garden of Before, not from within the void but as the void itself.

Have I ascended? came a voice within her head that she did not recognize, but the term the voice used—ascended—seemed to describe almost too perfectly how she now felt. The Thorned Loop of the Ever-Dying still bit into her finger. The *Koŝmaro*'s role still filled her body like an impossibly deep breath. Yet the role had become both more mighty and more pliable to her control. She, as the *Koŝmaro*, had evolved. *Ascended.*

She walked through its flowers and trees, crushing them under both her own feet and the cloven hooves of the minotaur. The Garden tried to lead her away from the path she traveled, as it had done before, but the *Koŝmaro*'s aura contained the permutation of the Garden that led Julie directly where she wanted to go.

The void darkness of the nexus obelisk reflected no light at all, making it seem to float out of the frame of its surroundings. Julie found that if she walked directly toward it, she couldn't tell if it was hundreds of feet away or so close that she risked accidentally walking into it. In the end, she reached it by blocking out the sight of it with one hand and focusing on following the Garden's path until it reached the intersection where the dark thing stood.

Others would be here soon. She looked back across the Garden, still towering over the land. Strangely, at the limits of her vision, there was no horizon. Instead, the faraway stretches of the Garden faded into the blue of the sky in a wide, blurry band that made it impossible to tell where land stopped, and sky began. There was no curvature to the earth here, and the land extended endlessly.

What she was looking for, however, was close by. Both entrances to the Grand Staircase looked to be within a quick jog of the nexus. The stairs leading up—a column that disappeared in a hole in the sky—was about a half mile from the cliff with the waterfall where she had come from. The stairs leading down sat in a ring of blue-leafed trees perhaps two miles to her right. She saw no movement near either. Paul hadn't reached the Garden yet, but neither had the others. Before returning her attention to the nexus, she looked again at the cliff. No one but her would come from the World Tunnel hidden behind the waterfall, yet she felt like someone or something was watching her from there. And then she saw a figure standing under the single tree atop the cliff. If it had been Paul, she would've known from the way he stood, even from this distance. But it wasn't. Someone else was watching her.

It was the old man from the Underworld.

She had ignored him once and decided to ignore him again. She shrank to become her normal height but kept herself wrapped in the void and shielded by her aura. With her hand holding the basket within its extradimensional pocket, she stepped into the nexus.

CHAPTER 25

HUNTER AND PREY

Jay crouched within the rusted husk of a station wagon, his burning red eyes fixed on the main gate of the stadium where he expected Paul and Corinne to emerge at any second. Each breath Jay took was accompanied by stabbing pain. He had broken some ribs when Paul threw him against the wall, and his right shoulder drooped and was probably dislocated.

Corinne stepped out first, her skull-painted face scanning this way and that, looking for him. He quickly found the three shadows he would use to reach her. The first took him to a concrete pillar about fifty feet away, the limit of his ability. But when he emerged from the shadows, exhaustion and pain overcame his bloodlust. He slumped against the pillar, laughing. He wasn't sure whether he was laughing at Corinne and Paul and their doomed attempt to survive or at his own pathetic brokenness. The laugher brought with it more stabbing pain, and then the laughter turned to tears.

"Quit your fucking crying," Big Cal said, clear as day.

Jay had his eyes pressed closed, trying to keep out the pain. He knew if he opened them, his dad would be standing over him, a menthol cigarette hanging out of Big Cal's mouth, his expression that familiar mix of disappointment and disregard, his eyes masked by aviator sunglasses with mirrored lenses. "Only men get to hunt with me and your brother. Are you a boy or a man, Jay?"

In that moment, the pain in Jay's shoulder hadn't come from being thrown into a concrete wall. It came from the savage recoil of an Argentine Mauser rifle rechambered for 30-06. He had wanted to shoot that gun as a rite of passage after watching Little Cal take down a doe with it at age thirteen. But Jay's ten-year old frame—all toothpicks and rubber bands, as Little Cal teased—got knocked back like he'd been hit by a sledgehammer.

"Quit flinching and lean into it," Big Cal had said, but all that did was make it hurt more. And after the fourth shot, tears streamed down Jay's face, and he gave up.

"I can't do it, Dad. I can't," he said, and then he opened his eyes and saw the hazy air of the Ruins where he expected Big Cal. Near the stadium's gate, Paul had joined Corinne. Paul's clothes were covered by blood. Most of it his own, let loose by Jay's knife, but some must have come from—

No! No! No!

Now it was Supriya's face, pale and dead, looking at him with disappointment.

"Why, Supriya?! I was holding out. You didn't have to. You—"

The knife in his right hand throbbed, pulling him back to the moment, reminding him of who he was and what he needed to do. Paul and Corinne had to die. That was the only way to gain Big Cal's respect. He had to make them pay for what had happened to Supriya. They were responsible for Supriya's death, not Jay. He knew these thoughts were nonsense driven by the knife's thirst, but the longer they lingered in his mind, the more they found root and grew like invading vines. The more he followed the knife's lead, the more it rewarded him by stripping away his pain. If he didn't keep killing, the pain would come back. He felt it coming back.

Paul walked with a limp and a hand on Corinne's shoulder. His face showed only stubborn determination and no sign of pain.

The serĉilos heal quickly, a voice in Jay's mind said. *Kill him now before he regains his strength!*

"I can barely fucking move, you idiot," he mumbled. "I ain't killin' nobody right now."

It took all he had to follow Paul and Corinne through the Ruins. The voice in his head had been right: by the time they were near the rocky incline that led up and out of the Ruins, Paul's limp was nearly gone, and his pace had quickened. They would've left Jay behind, just as Big Cal had left him behind on those hunting trips years ago. But fortune, or more likely chaos, intervened.

One of the *malespero*'s soldiers, a young man of no more than twenty, wandered aimlessly with blood in his hair. Concussed, confused. The soldier appeared to have followed the *malespero* as she made her escape, riding on the hand of a *burning one*, but the man fell behind. Bad luck for him; good for Jay. As silent as a thought, Jay came up behind him. With a quick stab in the back—an act of compassion, really—Jay eased the man out of his suffering. The knife flared with blue light upon its fatal impact, and through it, a soothing heat flooded into Jay, into his shoulder and chest, healing him or making him oblivious of the pain. He didn't know which, and what did it really matter?

One more kill would make him as good as new. He scanned for another soldier, for anyone, really. But all he saw were Paul and Corinne, now halfway to the ridge. There were no shadows he could use on the rocky incline to catch them, and the rocks atop the ridge were too far for him to shift to. He could have used his new ability, which rendered his body pure shadow—so thin and diffuse as to be invisible. But it took so much out of him, and they were too far ahead. They would reach the blinding sands of the Gray Waste before he caught them, and he would exhaust himself again by trying.

It didn't matter. He knew where they were going because he was going there as well. The bell had called, and its compulsion made the knife's lust feel like mere suggestion.

Paul scanned the sea of dunes behind them, shielding his eyes from the blinding light of the sun over the Gray Waste. "Do you see the *stelisto*?" He didn't ask if Corinne had seen Jay; Paul couldn't let himself believe that Jay was capable of doing those things back in the *malespero*'s lair. Whatever was hunting them was no longer his friend. At least, that's what Paul kept telling himself.

Corinne had on a pair of knockoff wayfarers with neon yellow arms. "No," she said. "For once, I'm glad this place is so bright and miserable."

They had heard Jay laughing and crying within the Ruins as he stalked them. Once, Jay had pleaded with someone, although Paul couldn't make out what he was saying or to whom. It would have been easier if Jay had taunted them and acted more like the creature of darkness he had become. Instead, he sounded both mad and wounded. Paul had no idea what to expect from Jay other than more pain.

"Wait..." Corinne said. She had created a visor over her eyes with both hands and was leaning forward. "Shit. The *malespero*. Let's hurry."

With the heat warping the air, Paul couldn't make out anything in the distance at first. Then he saw a single figure running toward them in slow motion. Long, heavy strides that took several seconds each. A *burning one*, with smaller figures at its sides. A dozen or more soldiers and a pack of ash dogs bigger than he had ever seen.

A storm of sand swirled behind them. Paul had recovered more quickly than seemed possible, but he still felt weak. He could sense the pool of his parallels refilling, but it was shallow. If the *malespero* caught up to them out here in the open, they stood no chance at all.

He ran after Corinne, trying to mimic the way she used long strides to descend the dunes—a controlled slide with each step. His steps were clumsy and deep. Twice he fell. At the top of the next dune, he saw that the *burning one* looked much larger in the distance now. It was gaining on them, and quickly.

Its huge feet give it a lot of surface area on the sand, his *sercîlo* mind noted with fascination. *It doesn't slip with each step like you do, despite its size and weight.*

Good to know, he answered back, watching with annoyance as his own feet sank in the sand of the next incline.

"There!" Corinne yelled from the top of the next dune.

When he reached her, he saw the entrance to the Grand Staircase ahead. The *burning one* behind them had greatly outpaced the others but it couldn't catch them before they made it inside. On its outstretched palm, the *malespero* stood wreathed in blue flame. She wouldn't catch them before they made it to the Grand Staircase, but she was letting them know that the fight with her was far from over.

If the Gray Waste were any other desert in any normal world, it would have quickly buried the Grand Staircase's platform under sand. As it was, the platform's wood slats and the rugs bordering the entrance showed no effects from the harsh environment. Similarly, although the wind peppered their skin with sand even on the platform, no sand blew into the dark stairway itself, and when they entered it, the temperature seemed instantly cut in half.

"It's a good thing we got here before the *stelisto*," Paul said, looking down into the darkness surrounding the stairs.

"Are you sure we did?"

Corinne's question sent him into a tailspin that was half fear and half analytic confusion. The notebook didn't describe the *stelisto*'s new ability—the way that Jay became a shadow so diffuse as to be invisible. Could he have used that ability in the light of the Gray Waste's sun? Passed them by only to lay in wait here in the darkness?

"You can think and move at the same time, Paul," Corrine said, descending in rapid, seemingly weightless steps.

Paul followed and then stopped, swinging Min-woo's backpack off his shoulder. "Hang on. I have an idea. And don't get so far ahead of me."

"I wouldn't be so far ahead if you would keep moving."

He flipped through the notebook until he reached the new section. "We won't beat the *stelisto* and the *malespero* by running or by fighting, Corinne. We have to use every advantage we have. We have to know things they don't and do things they won't expect."

She let out an annoyed sigh and said, "Fine. But make it quick."

He held the notebook so she could see its pages.

```
[∞] The Grand Staircase
   You are on the obsidian steps of the
Grand Staircase. The stairs lead both up
and down into darkness.
   >
```

He scribbled a *D* next to the cursor and turned the page. "The *D* stands for down. It's from the computer game. Instead of pushing a button on the keyboard, you write the command, and the notebook updates the next page. Watch this," he said. The next page looked exactly like the one that had preceded it.

```
[∞] The Grand Staircase
   You are on the obsidian steps of the
Grand Staircase. The stairs lead both up
and down into darkness.
   >
```

Again, he wrote a *D* and turned the page. And again, he was greeted by the same text. Ten more pages and the pattern continued.

"You're wasting time, Paul. This isn't helpful."

"Be patient," he said. Before she could protest further, he lifted the next page directly in front of her. "Look now."

The text looked almost identical to all the pages that came before it, but one new sentence made Corinne's black-ringed eyes go wide.

```
[∞] The Grand Staircase
   You are on the obsidian steps of the
```

```
Grand Staircase. The stairs lead both up
and down into darkness. The stelisto mate-
rializes and attacks you with the Knife of
Undoing.
   >
```

"So, he has gotten ahead of us and is waiting to attack," Paul said. "But now we know where. Stay close as we go down. I'm guessing that each page represents about ten steps, so we should see him in about a hundred to a hundred and twenty steps. Plus or minus."

"Plus or minus what?"

"It's not an exact science, Corinne. I wish it were," he said. "But it's enough. Notice how the notebook said "The *stelisto* materializes and attacks *you*." *You*. That means he'll be attacking me, and I'll be expecting it."

"If you're wrong and he attacks me instead, I'm dead."

Paul stepped down first, leading the way, gesturing for her to follow close. "I'm not wrong," he said. *Please don't let me be wrong*, he added to himself.

Jay had followed much closer than Paul and Corinne suspected. As the *burning one* lumbered after them, conveying the *malespero* in its hand, Jay ran alongside it in its giant shadow on the sand. The shadow allowed him to maintain a constant half-shifted form; he was both difficult to see and so light on his feet that the sand didn't slow him down. Still, it took all the strength he had regained from his recent kill to keep up the pace across the desert. And the sulfur stench from the *burning one* left him lightheaded and queasy.

The thing lowered its arm, and the *malespero* stepped onto the Grand Staircase's platform. She had let the blue flame surrounding her vanish, but even without it, she cut an imposing figure in her gleaming black armor under the bright sunlight.

With her back to him, she appeared vulnerable, but he had underestimated her before and paid dearly for it. Did she know he was here? Was she baiting him into a trap of some kind?

"Quit being a sissy," Big Cal said.

Jay spun, looking for but not seeing his father. The *malespero*'s head tilted ever so slightly. Had she heard Big Cal, too?

"Don't call me that," he snapped, unable to stop himself.

The *malespero* stepped backward and the flame reignited on her spiked armor. "Even here you're able to hide," she said. "Do you see how powerful I've helped you become?"

Her eyes flickered from the *burning one* to the Grand Staircase's entrance, inventorying the only shadows that might be hiding him.

"You can kill them all, Jay. They're gathering now. Go and kill them, until there's no one left. No one but you, Jay... And then you can kill yourself and make all the pain go away. Wouldn't that be nice? That's what you want, right? Revenge and then darkness?"

The knife in his hand flared, enticed by what she described, and for a moment she saw him. He shifted to a small shadow made by the stone column that housed the Grand Staircase. She seemed to know where he had gone and turned to keep him in front of her.

"You can try to kill me, too. After the others," she said. "I was already a killer, but you made me worse, Jay. You took away the only person here I cared about. The one who might have saved me. And so, I did it to you. We both deserve to die, now. But not until we destroy this place."

In his mind he saw the eyes of the *malespero*'s sister, the *gardistaro* who he had stabbed through the heart. He saw those wide, shocked eyes now, and he had seen them every night since. Those eyes that asked "Why? Why would you do this? Why did you kill me?" He hadn't known who or what she was. He hadn't known that she came to help them. He tried blaming it on the knife. Over and over again he told himself that it wasn't him that had done it. The knife acted on its own. But he remembered how he felt in that moment when the blade pierced her breast. The joy of delivering a death of surprise. And that feeling—that rotten bliss—had haunted him as much as the look in her eyes. That act changed him, ruined him. The *malespero*'s words were right. That act ruined her as well. They both deserved to die.

The *malespero*'s soldiers and the pack of ash dogs crested the nearby dune. They would be here shortly.

"I could kill you now," he said, only half-believing his own words.

"Maybe. You only have a few minutes to try while I'm alone. But every second we spend chatting, the *serĉilo* gets closer to the nexus. He's the one who abandoned you. He's the reason Supriya is dead. And he will be the next *Dio Ordo*... at least, that's what I've been told." She turned her back on him. As she stared off into the desert, watching her approaching soldiers, Jay could see the pulsing blood rush through her carotid artery where it peaked out above her spiked collar. He began to salivate, and the knife trembled in his hand.

"You heard the bell," she said, looking back over her shoulder in his direction. "You know this is the end. If he gets there before the rest of us... If the Order God hands him the amulet... If Paul puts it around his neck..." She raised her hands and gestured at the sky. "Then all of this becomes his. Sin tells me you've been living in his shadow your whole life. I can see by your reaction that Sin is right, and of course he is. If you've been living in Paul's shadow, imagine what it will be like... to live in his world."

Jay couldn't listen to her any longer. He ran into the cold darkness of the Grand Staircase and started taking the stairs two at a time. The *malespero*'s laughter seemed to follow him, echoing off the obsidian walls and stairs. Then Big Cal and Little Cal joined in.

"Run, sissy!" they yelled in unison. "Run!"

He put his hands to his ears to try to block out the laughter and accidentally cut his own neck with the knife. It was just a nick, but with the taste of blood the knife wanted more. He held it with both hands as it tried to pull itself toward his neck again.

Above, he heard the first of the *malespero*'s soldiers entering the

Grand Staircase. *Carve up them, not me, you stupid fucking knife!* The knife relented, seeming to agree with the change of target. The knife let him sheath it, allowing him to climb onto the outside of the staircase where, between the candle sconces on the wall, the air was pitch black. He let himself become pure shadow and waited. With every passing second, he could feel Paul getting farther and farther away. But his knife needed blood now. He needed it, to feel the rush of the kill, to fill the emptiness inside of him with the energy of death.

A lone soldier came first, slender, carrying a rusty machete. The ash dog accompanying him stopped two stairs above Jay and began to growl, a percussive, grinding metal sound. It smelled him, even if it couldn't see him.

He leaped over the banister, solidifying out of shadow as he jammed the knife first into the dog's spine. Then, with a backhand slash, he severed the man's neck. While the head *thump-thump-thumped* its way down the stairs, Jay rejoined the shadows and climbed the outside of the spiral stairwell toward the rest of the *malespero*'s group.

When the next soldier came into view, Jay leaped straight toward him, reckless and filled with bloodlust. The soldier waved a hand in the air, and it wasn't until Jay felt sand hit his eyes and pepper his face that he understood what the soldier had done. A handful of tossed sand made Jay's form visible. A spear narrowly missed his side. He shifted as a rifle was aimed at his head. When the gun fired, filling the stairwell with its concussive boom, Jay was already emerging from a shadow two dozen stairs higher behind the group. He struck down two more soldiers and then vanished again in the shadows as the *malespero* began to flare with blinding blue light, like she had done back in the cave.

Fool me once! he thought with a silent cackle.

Filled with energy from his kills, Jay hungered for bigger prey. He *shifted* again and again down the column of the stairs toward Paul and Corinne below. He caught up to them in seconds and materialized directly in front of Paul, already stabbing out with the knife. It caught Paul in the stomach, but in an instant Paul had

Jay's wrist gripped in his own hand and squeezed so hard the bones crumpled. Jay screamed, and the knife fell from his hand, bouncing once off the stairs and then vanishing into the darkness. Paul's eyes shined with golden light so bright that Jay almost hadn't been able to turn to shadow.

How had Paul known? He had been ready, filling himself with his *serĉilo* parallels to slow the penetration of the blade. And the bright light from Paul's eyes! When the hell had he learned to do that? They were all out to get him! Every fucking one of them!

Cradling his crushed wrist, Jay shifted shadows as fast as he could until he reached the bottom of the staircase. Waiting for him was the Knife of Undoing with no sign of damage from the fall of hundreds of feet. He grabbed it with his left hand and immediately his confidence returned. Paul had gotten the best of him again. But the city outside the Grand Staircase was full of so many twisted alleys and shadows that Paul would never see Jay's next attack coming. Jay grimaced in pain as he ran out into the light. When he saw all the people walking about, all the blood that could be spilled to heal his wounds and give him strength, he began to laugh. Faces turned his direction, but he didn't care. Big Cal and Little Cal laughed alongside him, but he didn't care. There'd be no one left to laugh soon.

CHAPTER 26

ANOTHER TRIP DOWN THE STAIRCASE

Paul gripped the banister of the Grand Staircase so hard his fingers made imprints in the stone. Jay's knife had cut deep, deeper than he wanted to let on to Corinne. Every move caused the wound to throb in pain. But he had to keep moving. The sounds coming from above them were the approaching *malespero* and her soldiers. And while Jay had disappeared somewhere below them, he was hurt and unlikely to attack again soon.

"You're bleeding. Let me see it," Corinne said.

"I ain't got time to bleed," Paul said through gritted teeth. He winced with every step down, waiting for Corinne to respond to his near perfect use of Jesse Ventura's quote from the movie *Predator*.

But all Corinne said was, "Uh... okay."

Jay would have fired back another *Predator* quote—probably "GET TO THE CHOPPA!" in a lousy Arnold impersonation—and then the two of them would have spent the next few minutes lost in alien jungle combat nostalgia. They had seen the movie together at least a dozen times.

How was it possible that the fire-eyed, gaunt-faced assassin who had just stabbed Paul in the gut was the same friend he had known his entire life? The easy answer was that his friend was gone. That the monster wasn't Jay. But Paul knew from firsthand experience with the Between's roles that the truth was messier. And darker.

Paul focused on taking the stairs one at a time. Fortunately, they reached the bottom only a few minutes later. Jay and his knife were nowhere to be seen. A series of metal-grinding barks came from the darkness above, joined by human voices. Paul couldn't make out the words, but they sounded close.

"Let's go," he said, moving quickly for the platform and the sunlight ahead.

"He'll be waiting out there for us. And you're still bleeding."

Paul lifted his shirt and ran a finger over the knife wound. As Corinne said, he was still bleeding, but the bleeding had slowed, and the pain had lessened. This wound would have been lethal if not for the *serĉilo*'s power.

"You're not invincible." Corinne had an annoying ability to read his thoughts.

"Yeah? Well, neither is he. Let's get to the cathedral and hopefully send you home."

***

Stepping out into the City Above, the Between's third world, felt dizzying, as if they had teleported from one world to another—and in a way, he supposed they had. Here, in this floating city where buildings seemed to have grown like organic things and twisted into each other, the sunlight was every bit as bright as it had been in the desert, albeit without the face-melting intensity. The air in the city was filled with the scents of spices, food, and filth, creating a pleasant mélange one second, and with the changing of the wind, a foul odor of disease and death the next.

The City Above overflowed with the constant sounds of life. Everywhere else in the Between that Paul had experienced (firsthand or in the computer game), encountering life was rare, unexpected, and usually deadly. Monsters, carnivorous plants, swarms of flesh-devouring rodents, and the like—those encounters came down to: eat or be eaten, kill or be killed. Run-ins with other humans tended to feel like real life scenes from the Koushun Takami novel, *Battle Royale*. Which is why the City Above felt so surreal. Full of life and humanity, but without the ever-present feeling of impending doom... mostly.

Corinne knew the city well and led the way, hood up, head tilted down to hide her skull-painted face. She took a roundabout path toward the cathedral, avoiding narrow alleys where the shadows were heavy. Paul had no cloak and stood a head taller than most of the city's inhabitants, except for the oddly proportioned creatures Jay had named *ganglions*. One of them, wearing a bowler cap, with legs much longer than legs should be, had taken an interest in Paul and was tailing them. Was this the one Jay called Long Legs? Was it Ruki, the ganglion he had encountered in the game?

"Ignore him for now," Corinne whispered.

Up ahead, Paul recognized a twisted archway that marked the entrance to the city's central marketplace. In Paul's previous trip here, the marketplace had been the busiest part of the city. Now, though, the closer they got, the fewer people they saw. Initially, he felt relief. A dense crowd was a good place for Jay to lay in wait. But as they approached the marketplace, the silence and emptiness grew unsettling.

"Where the hell is everyone?" Paul asked.

Corinne pointed at the shops on the ground level leading up to the marketplace and then at the residences above. All doors closed. All windows shuttered.

Paul looked behind them and saw that their ganglion follower had stopped about a hundred feet back. It crumpled its hat in its hands as it paced nervously back and forth. It made no attempt to hide, watching them with its wide eyes. Paul was about to tell Corinne to be ready for anything, but he saw she already had her fire rod held in her right hand under her cloak.

The marketplace was empty, but all its stands were still filled with goods. Fruit of shapes and sizes never seen back home. Baskets, candles, spices. Flute-like instruments that looked impossible to play with branching loops and dozens of finger holes. But no people.

They walked between stands and carts warily, avoiding awnings and areas with even the slightest shadow. Ahead of Paul, Corinne stopped and then took two steps backward. Her weight shifted to her toes, and her stance widened. Ready to fight and ready to run.

"What is it?"

"Blood," she said, pointing at the ground ahead with the throwing knife in her left hand.

On the ruddy brown cobblestone was a wide smear of blood that ran forward and curved around a cart full of spiny white melons. Careful not to step in it, Paul followed its path. Another crimson streak ran on the ground to his left, between two stalls.

"That's a lot of blood," he said. "It looks like someone dragged bodies... but I don't see the bodies."

"The fountain," Corinne said.

In the center of the marketplace was one of the City Above's peculiar fountains. A stone torch sprayed water in the air. No pool caught the water when it fell. Instead, where a pool should be was open air, a hole straight through the floating island of the city where the land far below was visible. The stone railing surrounding the fountain had a dark red section where Jay—it could only have been Jay—had dragged the bodies up and over, and then let them fall from the sky.

"He couldn't control himself until everyone here was either dead or had run away," Corinne said. She began making her way toward the west exit of the marketplace, careful to avoid the bloody streaks on the ground, taking corners wide and slow.

Paul followed, trying to be equally diligent. "But why throw their bodies through the fountain?" he asked as he stepped absently into a puddle of blood.

"I can only guess," she said. "Maybe when it was over, it was like coming down from a drug high. The *stelisto* slaughtered everyone, and then Jay was left with the consequences of what he had done."

"So, he got rid of the bodies? Out of sight, out of mind?" Paul heard himself and was disgusted by the flippancy of his own words. Once he let in the reality of the nearby carnage, his stomach lurched, and the *serĉilo's* analytical calm slipped away. He stopped and let out a long breath into his cupped hands.

Corinne waited for him to collect himself, but no hint of emotion crossed her skull-painted face. When they began moving again, she said, "Some part of him still believes—or at least wants to believe—that he's a good person. So, he can't have a bunch of murdered bodies telling him otherwise. The addict's mind is a cognitive dissonance machine."

The farther they got from the marketplace, the more the city returned to life. As Paul tried to comprehend the wickedness of what Jay had done, a question occurred to him that made him distrust his own sense of morality. Were the denizens of the City Above actually human? Were they *real*? Paul studied the people without being obvious. Men and women alike wore what he thought of as smocks, big shapeless shirts that extended to their feet. The smocks were all variations of gray or beige, making Paul's faded jeans stand out like a chirping blue jay on a cedar tree. Their pale skin and colorless eyes would've made them appear almost identical if not for the rich variation in hair color. Golds, browns, jet blacks—no greens or purples or anything too outlandish. Enough detail to differentiate one from another, but not enough to make any one of them look unique.

"Hey!" Corinne said, jabbing a sharp elbow into Paul's ribs. "Pay attention or you're going to get us killed. That alley over there leads to the cathedral."

Paul absently shook his head. There seemed to be no way to keep his *serĉilo* mind from wandering. "Sorry. I was wondering if these people are NPCs."

Without looking back, Corinne asked, "What the hell is an NPC?"

"Non-player character," Paul said. "In video games, they help flesh out the story or a setting. But there are no humans playing them. It's just the computer. With these people here... I guess

I'm wondering if they're NPCs. The *Kosmaro* doesn't come for their souls when they die. Does that mean they don't have a soul?

"When we were here before and the cathedral collapsed, it must have killed dozens of them. And I haven't given them a second thought until now. I *have* thought about Cole—that was his name, right? The guy who was the *nenio*?"

Corinne was walking faster now, periodically looking back over her shoulder. She made an unexpected detour down an alley to their right and then across a footbridge that passed through a building, as if the building had grown around the footbridge.

"Yeah, Cole," she said. "He was part of the group I met at the beginning."

"I've thought about him," Paul said. "I don't know his story, but I know he had a story that ended at the church. As for the others... As for these people... Their deaths didn't register at all. And now Jay has butchered so many of them. And even still, even after seeing their blood everywhere in the marketplace, their deaths don't impact me like Supriya's does. It's not the same at all to me. I'm just wondering if..." He let his words trail off. Corinne had stopped and was giving him an inscrutable look with that skull face of hers.

"Sorry, I'm rambling," Paul said.

She surprised him with her response. "I killed someone, Paul." Her always rigid posture softened, and she began to fidget, holding the first two fingers of her left hand in her right. She kept looking over Paul's shoulder and then down at the ground.

Paul chose his words carefully. "Back at the Ruins? I brought you into that fight. I killed those soldiers, too. Are you talking about before? Corinne, you've done what you had to do to survive. We all have. This fucking place—"

"No. I don't mean here."

"What do you mean, then?" Paul could see the gears working in her mind as she continued to move about nervously, shifting her weight back and forth, fastening and unfastening the button on her cloak. Corinne had no patience for small talk. "I'm not going to judge you, Corinne," he said. "I'm the last person to judge you."

She stopped fidgeting and looked up at him and then off at a solitary cloud in the sky, a cotton ball lazily traversing the blue. "Back when I was staying with you and Julie... Back in your world, I mean. I used to go out during the day and steal things. Nothing important. Packs of gum. This shirt I'm wearing right now. Food from restaurants... I justified it because it wasn't my world. So, it wasn't real. The people I was stealing from weren't real to me. When you said that thing about non-player characters, it made me think of that justification."

"Maybe we're all NPCs in the lives of others. I've heard it said that life is, ultimately, a single player game." He had meant that to lighten the mood, but the words carried with them an existential darkness, like something Jean-Paul Sartre might have written had he written about video games.

"Am I an NPC to you, Paul?"

The question caught him off guard, but the answer was easy. "You're as real as they come, Corinne. You're more real than the rest of us. We're all playing a role here. Jay. Me. Now Julie. Poor Supriya. But not you."

She looked back at the solitary cloud. Paul let the silence sit. More than anyone he had ever met, Corinne made silence easy. She eventually continued, as he knew she would.

"The day before I left... Before I came back here... I killed someone named Matt Waggoner." She told Paul of her run-in with Matt in the convenience store. Of the strung-out woman waiting for him outside, the woman that could easily have been Corinne. Of stealing his car, hopping the curb, and running him over. "I didn't feel guilt at the time, and I still don't. Maybe the Between stripped away my humanity and turned me into a monster. Or it exposed who or what I really am. There's another Matt Waggoner back in my world. Maybe an infinite number of Matts out there. I feel like I killed a Matt-NPC, which is to say I don't feel anything at all."

As she spoke, Paul saw her skull makeup appear to spread. Her neck turned black with the white paint of a spine down its center. Her forearms and hands, extending out of her cloak, became painted bones. He grabbed her hand with his. She tried to pull away, but he held—not hard, but insistent. She looked down, saw the paint, and let out a long breath.

"You can't let me go back to my world, Paul. I'm a monster."

He had been rubbing at the paint on the back of her hand with his thumb, seeing if it would come off. But whether the paint came off right now or not didn't matter. He took her other hand and lightly squeezed.

"Look at me, Corinne. Please, look at me."

She tilted her head up. Corinne was taller than Julie but still a half foot shorter than Paul. In that moment, standing closer to him than she ever had, with her small hands held in his, the painted skull mask took on a new meaning to Paul. The Between had stripped Corinne down to her barest parts. That's what the skeleton was, or what it represented anyway—the core, diamond-hard unbreakable spirit Corinne carried within her. If only she could see it the way he did.

"When I look at you, I see… someone I care about. I never see a monster," he said, and then stumbled at what to say next. His *serĉilo* mind tried to intervene, reeling off all the ways Corinne embodied *Santa Muerte*, the Mexican folk spirit who guided and protected the nearly dead. But it was too much. He wanted her to see herself the way he saw her. He reached for something to say, but everything that came to mind sounded corny. So, he instead said, "You're a good person. When you walk back into your world, you'll do it with a clean slate. All of this will be left behind."

She looked up, maybe looking for the cotton-ball cloud, but it was gone. Then she nodded and gave his hands a quick squeeze before pulling them back. "Okay."

It was the little squeeze that told him that, despite his complete failure to articulate what he meant and how he felt, she understood. Or at least she understood that he was trying and that he cared. Before he could say anything else, she twisted so quickly that the back of her cloak nearly caught him in the face, and then she was off again, pointing this direction or that, checking behind them for followers, as if all the moral handwringing was done and gone.

He followed close behind, trying to make sense of the interaction they'd just had. Not the ethical quandary they had discussed, but the connection that the two of them shared. He cared about Corinne, like he had said, but "cared about" didn't do justice to what he felt at that moment. Maybe he loved her. Loved her in a way that didn't feel like it competed with his love for Julie. Or maybe *love* was a flawed word, an attempt to gather too many different feelings into a single category.

Thinking about feelings—particularly his own—made him feel as if he were a neanderthal trying to make sense of an automobile. Some things were beyond him, and feelings were part of that group.

They emerged from their maze of alleys to the familiar promenade in front of the cathedral where Jay had come out of nowhere to attack the *Kosmaro* and buy them enough time to escape. Where the hell was Jay, now? They had expected him to lay in waiting, to stab out at them from the city's shadows.

The *Katedralo Kaoso* towered before them, nearly fully rebuilt. Dozens of the creatures Jay had named *ganglions* took part in the construction. Some climbed on the scaffolding surrounding the cathedral, using long arms to reach down for stones and then to place them. On the ground, long-legged *ganglions* carried supplies here and there with big strides. A few with giant mouths filled with too many teeth barked orders. The red-robed *nenio* was nowhere to be seen.

Paul followed Corinne to a fountain in the promenade where they could get a better look at the cathedral without as much risk of being seen.

"No roof yet, so no Altar of the Sky. And a lot of goons," Corinne said.

"They're making good progress," Paul said. "It might be safer for you to hide out in the city here until it's done. The alternative is the altar in the fifth world, The World in Pieces."

"I'm coming with you. Someone has to make sure you don't die before you meet up with Julie."

Paul's mind shot to the experience of traveling through the Garden of Before. It had been in the computer game, yes, but the memories felt as vivid as if he had been there in the flesh. The memories of fear and panic, especially. Being followed by a walking corpse that turned out to be a dead version of himself—a herald of his own coming demise.

"Not a chance," he said. "It's too dangerous."

She laughed—an actual laugh. Had he ever seen this Corinne laugh before?

"I can't get to the fifth world without going through the fourth. I'm not asking for your permission, Paul. You're getting my help whether you want it or not."

"A knife and a banana won't suffice?"

"You're not in the knife and banana category, you big idiot."

He tried to hide the goofy smile wanting to spread itself across his face. "Not in the knife and banana category" was as close as it came in Corinne-speak to saying "I love you, too." What kept the smile from forming was the sudden certainty that Corinne would sacrifice herself to save him and Julie, just as he was ready to do the same by taking the god-role offered to him if it came to it.

"Corinne. Sometimes the only person you can really save is yourself. And when you get the chance, you need to do it. Don't be a martyr. Promise me that, okay? You deserve a happy ending more than anyone else I know."

The skeleton paint faded from her body, and even the skull on her face began to thin. "I promise you, Paul."

***

Ganglions lurked about the streets near the cathedral. As Paul and Corinne made their way to the next entrance to the Grand Staircase, Paul used the new section of the notebook to play-test alternate routes. Without it, they would have found themselves in several encounters, one in particular where they would've been outnumbered five to one.

"Feels a bit like cheating," Corinne had whispered. "I wonder if I can use this to help shoplift when I get back home." Seeing Paul's glare, she dryly added, "Kidding."

They passed one last alley before reaching the Grand Staircase, an alley neither of them had noticed until they were standing in front of it, so they hadn't used the notebook to ensure it was safe. In the alley, a person lay prone while a little red winged creature dug through their belongings. A barbed tail curled in the air behind the creature like a snake.

Corinne rushed to the other side of the alley opening without making a sound and then looked back with exasperation at Paul who stood out in the open. If the creature turned around, there would be no hiding from it. Corinne pointed at the ground next to her, but Paul held up a hand and shook his head.

It was the *diableto* that had speared him through the heart in the Garden. Not just the same type of creature, but the same actual creature itself. Even though its back was to Paul, he was certain. What was its name? Fiendbitch? Fangflower? Fangblossom! Yes, that was it. Fangblossom!

Paul cleared his throat.

The *diableto*'s head swiveled like an owl's, almost fully looking back at him without moving its body. It had big eyes and little fangs extending over almost human-like lips. It was simultaneously adorable and terrifying. He remembered thinking it looked like the birth child of a devil and a cherub when he had seen it before, and that description still seemed spot on.

"Fangblossom," Paul said.

Its big eyes became even bigger.

Paul remembered how angry this creature had become in the game when he hadn't known her name, and when he referred to her as *it*. He also remembered the *ganglion* named Ruki and how it had spoken to her.

"There's my beautiful little girl," Paul said, trying to make his voice sound as warm and authentic as possible. "I've been looking for you."

The creature—Fangblossom—turned its whole body toward him and tilted her head in confusion. She clearly liked being called beautiful, but suspicion filled those large eyes.

"Who are you, human? And how do you know my name?" she asked.

Next to the alley, Corinne had taken her red wand out and looked to be on the verge of attacking. Not that it would have done any good. *Diabletos* were immune to fire, Paul had seen in the notebook.

"My name is Paul Prentice," he said. "I am the *serĉilo*. Although I have not had the pleasure of meeting you myself, one of my predecessors has met you. Those memories are... delightful." He found, as he heard himself say the words, that they seemed to be somewhat true. One of his predecessors had indeed worked with this little fiend—or a creature who looked very similar.

"What is it you want from me, Paul Prentice? Can't you see that I'm busy?"

"Yes," Paul said. "I can see you're very busy. But I need your services, and I can pay you richly."

Fangblossom cackled and rubbed her little hands together. "I like being paid richly. What's the job, and what are you offering?"

Paul fished out a handful of protein bars from his backpack. "I need a guide through the Garden of Before."

"Trivial," Fangblossom said.

"For one as brilliant as you, I'm sure it is trivial." He waved the protein bars. "I have these delicious treats that I'm offering. They are..."

Fangblossom scowled. "You think to bribe me with food like I'm a monkey?"

"You know what monkeys are?"

"I'm looking at one," she said.

He was losing her. Worse than losing a guide in the Garden would be to have her following them. He racked his brain for helpful memories. An answer came to him.

"The treats are simply a gift of goodwill. I'm offering something I know you'll love... Murder."

"What the fuck?" came Corinne's voice from beside the alley.

Fangblossom seemed too pleased to have noticed. "MURDER!" she screeched and then let out a cackle. "I love murder! Who are we murdering?"

"Guide me to the nexus at the center of the Garden, and you'll see."

With two flaps of her wings, Fangblossom flew out of the alley and grabbed a protein bar out of Paul's hand. "Follow me!" she said, and then she noticed Corinne. Fangblossom's tail curled up with its barbed point ready to strike. "Who's this weirdo? Is this who we're murdering?"

"Touch her and you'll be the one who's murdered," Paul said before he could catch himself. "She's with us. Lead on," he added with a wince.

Fangblossom's eyes narrowed into a wicked glare, and for a moment Paul thought the *diableto* was about to start stabbing at them with her tail. But then she clapped her little hands in applause.

"Those creatures are horrible, Paul," Corinne whispered after Fangblossom turned and began leading onward. "What the hell are you thinking?"

"You've seen one before?"

"Yes. They're murderous, backstabbing weasels."

"Murderous, backstabbing weasels with very good hearing," Fangblossom said with a raised finger.

CHAPTER 27
THE NEXUS

Julie touched the inky surface of the obelisk and was pulled into the nexus. Unlike before, she was greeted by an all-encompassing gray. No distinct source of light. No ground. No sky. Only depthless matte gray.

She felt like she existed as a partially finished illustration, her figure drawn, inked, and colored, but with the background missing. A gray background could become anything, could it not? So many possibilities. But why gray, now? Why was it different than the last time she was here?

She looked to her basket to make sure it still held the revenant souls she gathered from the statues she destroyed in the Underworld. Eight tiny stars gleamed out from its interior. Last time, she had only come with one.

Out of the side of her eye she saw a tremor in the gray. When she turned toward it, the tremor was gone, but a new tremor came from her periphery in the other direction. After several seconds of twisting her head this way and that, trying to catch what was causing the blurring motion next to her, she realized it came from the gray itself. When she stared into it deeply, she saw a vibrating pattern that reminded her of the background of a peculiar painting by Carlos White that hung in the Blanton Museum. That painting and the gray surrounding her contained a moiré interference pattern, an optical illusion of movement created by the overlap of multiple patterns.

The gray around her wasn't empty, like the void; it was filled by the patterns of the eight lives radiating out in countless permutations from the souls in her basket. So many that, to see them all, was to see mostly gray.

With the *Kosmaro*'s aura, she suppressed all but one. She saw the overlapping lives of the young girl who had stood before her in the Underworld. The girl was running on a trail through the woods. Julie tracked alongside her without moving, looking in from outside the girl's world. Her figure blurred as different versions of her chose different paths. To the left of a tree versus to the right. To stride over a large rock in the trail or to step directly on it. Every version of the girl periodically looked back over her shoulder with wide eyes and a wider, mischievous smile.

"Can't you catch the rabbit?" one version of her yelled.

"The rabbit is escaping!" another version exclaimed.

Someone was running close behind the girl, but Julie couldn't see who. No matter which way Julie tried to turn, she still faced the same way. Then the permutations began to blur as the pursuer caught the girl here and there. With the *Kosmaro*'s aura, Julie tried to keep to the worlds where the girl escaped.

And finally, the girl slowed and rested. The moment had arrived. A single version of the girl in a single outworld. A body for one of the revenant souls Julie had promised to save.

She felt doubt begin to creep in and acted, out of reflex and out of desperation. She grabbed the girl, reaching out from the nexus and into the outworld with the beast's hand, because only the beast could do what had to be done. The girl screamed in terror as a figure of darkness emerged out of nowhere to seize her. And then Julie gripped the girl by the head and pulled her into the nexus. The girl writhed and thrashed, but in the beast's iron grip, no amount of struggling could free her. With Julie's free hand, she reached into the basket and scooped up the soul that matched the girl's body. She pressed the soul between the girl's eyes until it slid through the psychic membrane and vanished into her skull.

The girl's eyes rolled back, and her body convulsed. A part of Julie's rational mind understood what she was seeing. Two not-quite-identical souls were now in the girl's body, sending the body into shock.

You are killing her, a voice in Julie's head scolded.

Another voice: *No. We have done this before. Sometimes they live.*

Sometimes? To Julie, the writhing girl clutched in her beast hand was Julie's own child, the child who had tried and failed to come into the world twice before. Part Julie, part Paul. She pulled the girl out of the nexus and into the bright daylight of the Garden.

The girl hung limp in Julie's arms, no movement from her chest, no sign of life beyond the flush in her cheeks, which seemed to be fading. *Sometimes they live*, the voice had said. Sometimes? Julie couldn't let the girl die. Her daughter! Her child with Paul! She touched the girl's forehead with the *Koŝmaro* beast's long finger and felt the souls within the body struggling to cohere into one. She focused the *Koŝmaro*'s probability-warping aura on the souls in a way that felt instinctive, though she knew she had never done it before. She released the aura when she felt the souls were fully overlapped.

The girl's eyes blinked open. Julie, surprised at least as much as the girl, banished the *Koŝmaro*'s beast form, lest the girl see a monster and not her mother before her. Without the beast's strong arm to hold her up, the girl collapsed. Julie caught her, but as she did, the girl's face became foreign, and the illusion conjured by her role as the *Koŝmaro* dissipated. Julie stepped back, leaving the girl sitting on the Garden's rocky path.

"What? What happened to me?" the girl asked, patting her arms, legs, and torso as if to confirm her physical body was real. Her eyes focused on Julie. "Who are you? Where am I?"

Julie searched for words, her eyes filling with tears. How could she explain what she had done and why?

The girl scrambled back from Julie suddenly. "You! You

attacked me?" But as quickly as fear had overtaken her, it was replaced by confusion. "No, you saved me. You restored me! Why... why do I have two sets of memories? I was on the trail and... But I've been here, also, in the Between. And you saved me from the statue and... Are you the *klaro*? How did you do that?"

"I ..." Julie began. "I did something awful. I took a body of another you, and I... I gave it to you."

"Another me?" the girl said. She placed a hand over her chest and shook her head, seeming to marvel that her own heart was beating. Her eyes widened, and she pushed herself to her feet. "There are two of me in here!"

"I'm so sorry," Julie said. "I shouldn't have—"

"No," the girl cut her off. "I understand. At least, part of me does. The me that has been trapped here. I was the *gardistaro*. Then I was dead... The *stelisto* killed me. Stabbed me right through the heart. And then I became, like, a ghost or something, but I couldn't move, and the only thing I could feel was pain. And now I'm alive, and—" A look of alarm came over her. "Where's my sister? I need my sister."

"Your sister?" Julie asked.

"My twin sister, Lark. Lauren. She was the *malespero*. How did you restore me?"

"I haven't seen your sister, and I don't know what the *klaro* and the *malespero* are. I'm guessing they're roles. My husband is the *serĉilo*. I'm the *Koŝmaro*. I don't fully understand how I restored you, and I don't have time to try to explain right now. I have seven other souls needing bodies." Julie paused. "If your sister is still alive and in one of the roles, she will be coming here soon."

"Coming here? Why?"

"There's no time," Julie said. "What is your name?"

"Zenia. Zenia Montclair, but everyone calls me Zee."

Julie held the basket up. "I have seven other souls in this basket, Zee. They came from statues in the Underworld I broke, statues like yours. If I don't restore them, these souls will fade away, even in my basket."

"You have to save them, then. Just like you saved me," Zee said, as if it were a question so simple its answer was obvious. Then, as if the matter were settled, Zee said, "We're in the Garden of Before, aren't we? I'm not the *gardistaro* anymore. If you leave me, I'll—"

"I'll be quick," Julie said.

"I don't want to die again," Zee said. Her lower lip trembled, and she hugged herself while looking at the alien world around them.

"Sweetie, I'm not going to let you die. I promise," Julie said, taking Zee by the forearm, reminding herself that Zee wasn't her daughter—but that didn't seem to matter. The terror-wracked look in Zee's eyes tore at Julie's heart. "I need you to be strong," Julie said, as much to herself as to Zee. "Stay next to this obelisk. I'm going to restore the others and take them out one by one. They'll be scared, like you're scared now. I need you to keep them calm until I'm done. Can you do that? I'll go as fast as I can."

"And then you'll help me find my sister?"

The *malespero*. It was a name Julie had never heard until Zee spoke it, but it seemed to have a wicked ring to it. *Malespero*. Malice. Malicious.

"If she's alive, I have a feeling your sister will soon find us," Julie said, and then, without waiting for a response, she stepped back into the dark nothingness of the obelisk.

From the cliff, Rezső watched with amazement as Julie pulled person after person out of the nexus, restoring bodies to those who had been made into revenants.

"Julie Prentice has been here for such little time and is already accomplishing things we didn't know were possible," the Order part of him said.

"She may win this contest of ours," said the voice of his Chaos side.

"And become my successor?" Rezső crossed his arms and scoffed. "She is too rebellious. Too unpredictable. The Between needs a caretaker or a curator. She would dismantle it given the chance."

"Then I may root for her."

"Stop it."

"What?"

Order-Rezső growled. "You are goading me. I know what your plan is. You can no more hide things from me than I can from you."

"In the decades or more that we have coexisted, I have never once surprised you. Still..."

"Still... what?"

"There is a first time for everything."

Order-Rezső scoffed again. "Where are the others? They all should have arrived by now."

"Patience, brother. So quick to see our own ending?"

"I dislike the chaotic nature of this contest. The sooner it is over, the better."

"You are in luck, then. It has started." Chaos-Rezső pointed to a group of red-clad figures making their way through the Garden near one of the entrances to the Grand Staircase. "There is the *nenio* and her acolytes. And look. She has brought with her a ganglion to help them navigate."

"A ganglion? Again, you are attempting to provoke me...Using the absurd name that the *stelisto* calls them. Speaking of Mr. Lightsey... Do you see him?"

"I do not. But I see the *masinisto* with his rust wraiths."

Order-Rezső saw the *masinisto* as well because he and his Chaos counterpart shared the same eyes. As the *masinisto* walked down a garden path, he turned the handle of a little box full of gears. "Ah, he has created a device to help avoid the Garden's misdirections, clever man."

"One never knows what the *masinisto* will build," Chaos-Rezső said. "I suspect this is not the only device he has built for this occasion."

"I suppose we will see."

"And there is the *klaro*. Poor *klaro* She is hopelessly lost."

Order-Rezső huffed with impatience. "What about the *stelisto*?"

"You already asked about him not more than one minute ago, and I told you I did not see him. I still do not see him."

"You do not *see* him?"

"That is what I said."

"But do you know where he is?"

"All I know is that he is already out there. Somewhere."

CHAPTER 28

WHERE THE SHADOWS WERE
PLENTY

The eyes of creatures big and small looked out from their hiding spots within the Garden, watching the gathering humans. To some, the humans were prey, but to most, they were a danger. Where humans went, death always followed.

One of the many four-winged birds that made its nest in a cluster of berry bushes was particularly wary of the nearby humans. It darted back and forth between the vines by the big obelisk, where the fattest caterpillars could be found, and its nest where its hungry babies cried out. The humans had gotten too close for comfort, making the bird's little heart buzz like a toy motor.

It sat for a moment atop its bush, catching its breath, watching. A branch to its side snapped. A tiny sound, one that would not have registered if not for the bird's hyper-alert state. It turned in the direction of the snap and opened its mouth to let out a reflexive chirp of alarm. A hand materialized out of the shadow and grabbed the bird so that a finger and thumb held its beak shut. A sudden twist, and the bird's neck was broken without ceremony, without sound. Then the hand placed it softly on the ground, where several other four-winged birds lay dead.

The *stelisto* killed without thought as he slid from shadow to shadow, making his way toward the towering obelisk of darkness.

He touched the footpaths only when necessary, crossing as a swarm of almost imperceptible motes of shadow. Among the plant life, where shadows were plenty, he flowed through the darkness without effort and without physical movement.

He thought he saw Julie talking to a group standing near the obelisk, but when he shifted closer, she was gone. He circled around the obelisk looking for her, through groves of trees and seas of thick vines, traveling outward in expanding concentric rings. He had grown so sensitive to the presence of blood that he could taste it in the air even when it hadn't been spilled. He might have imagined seeing her—his vision couldn't be trusted with all the ghosts hanging around—but he knew the scent of Julie's blood, and he knew she had been there.

Maybe she was hiding somehow using her *Koŝmaro* power to elude him. A voice in his head laughed at him, told him he knew better than that. He was making excuses for his own failures, like he had his entire life.

"Get out of my head, Cal, or I'll cut you out," he said with a growl. Leaves rustled as animals fled from his unexpected nearby presence. His big brother's voice in his head laughed even harder.

He moved quickly, away from the obelisk, wanting to scream, wanting to slash every living thing to pieces with the Knife of Undoing. The knife didn't care for plant life. Animals only whetted its appetite. It wanted human blood, and it wanted it now.

A group passed next to him on the path, so close he could have reached out and touched the red robes of the nearest one without stepping out of the shadow of the tree that hid him. He recognized the *nenio*—a woman this time—and her acolytes. The last *nenio* had been crushed under a collapsing cathedral. This one's death would be so much less... noisy.

The group had grown confused and were arguing with their ganglion guide over whether they were going in circles and which way to go next. The *nenio* had the Twilight Scepter out, crackling with red electricity, as if that would provide any help. They didn't notice when the two at the rear dropped to the ground. The *nenio* herself only saw the *stelisto* because he made himself seen. He needed to witness the look in her eyes as the blade went in. The same look Julie would wear. The mix of pain and surprise and the profound realization that the end had come.

He could taste Julie's blood in the air again, even over the heavy taste of the blood he had just spilled. With the *nenio*'s entire party slaughtered, the voices in Jay's head laughed louder than ever, and he laughed with them.

CHAPTER 29
CALM BEFORE THE STORM

"I'm beginning to wonder if it was a mistake to trust her," Paul muttered to Corinne as the two of them ran to keep up with the little devil flying ahead on the Garden path. At each of the path's previous intersections, Fangblossom turned her head and stared down the four alternative directions with a perplexed look on her face, including the direction on which Paul and Corinne were frantically approaching. Then, Fangblossom confidently announced, "This way!" before streaking off in a seemingly random direction. Paul could find no pattern in the *diableto*'s choices. They didn't follow a circular route like the notebook recommended. He swore they had passed the octopus plants once before while going the opposite direction.

"I told you those things were trouble," Corinne replied with no attempt at all to quiet her voice.

Fangblossom spun and pointed a black-clawed finger at Corinne. "Did you just call me a thing?!"

"Ignore her," Paul said before Corinne could dig them into a deeper hole. "Have another protein bar."

The *diableto* caught the bar and stuffed it into her mouth, wrapper and all. She gave one more glare at Corinne and was about to fly off again, when Paul told her to hold on for a second.

"Please," he said. "I've been here before, and I don't think the path you're taking leads us to the obelisk. Not directly, anyway."

Fangblossom hovered in the air with both fists at her hips and her barbed tail swirling behind her. "You would think someone as big as you would have a big brain also," she exclaimed. "Come up to the top of this hill, meathead, and I'll show you what I have done." She flew off the path and into a pasture that sloped upward to a mound at the center of the Garden square.

Paul started to follow but hesitated at the edge of the path. "I read that it isn't safe to leave the path."

"It's safe," Fangblossom said with a dismissive wave. "Oh, but not there! Or there! And I think that brown spot is the sign of a burrowing slug monster. You know the type I'm talking about. All slimy with the rows and rows of chomping teeth."

"I'm officially an idiot for following her," Paul whispered to Corinne.

"And I followed you. What does that make me?" Corinne said dryly.

Paul made his way up the hill, avoiding the spots Fangblossom had identified as best he could. As he neared the top of the hill, he saw the Garden stretch out before him. The cliff in the direction he thought of as west. The night-black nexus obelisk a few hundred yards to the east, where several people had gathered—none of whom looked like Julie. But what caught his attention was the *malespero* with her soldiers and dogs, two squares over, headed away from them and in the opposite direction of the nexus.

"You see? Our pursuers are totally confused because of me!" Fangblossom gave a proud waggle of her head. "While we're off murdering people at the nexus, those buffoons will be getting digested by the *naĝanto*. You're welcome, helmet hair. Now, let's get to murdering people. Are those our victims?" She pointed at the gathering by the nexus obelisk.

"We're not doing the murdering, Fangblossom," Paul said with a wince at the word. As the devil's expression shifted to disappointment and then to anger, Paul backpedaled. "We're trying to stop the murderers by... uh... I guess probably murdering them first. Look. We're not killers." He said this while nodding his head at Corinne, who stood there with eyes of death and a bloody spear in her hand. "Or maybe we are. Shit. Let's just get to the nexus, where I have a feeling there will soon be enough bodies to loot to keep you busy for a week."

Fangblossom grumbled, but Paul didn't hear a word of it, because at that moment he saw Julie step out of the black obelisk.

"There she is!" Paul exclaimed. "We have to go!" He began running down the hill in the direction of the nexus, so overcome by the sight of Julie that he pulled in several multiples to help him run faster. He had only taken a few steps when something large, strong, and sharp grabbed ahold of his right foot. It looked like a brown lump of pudding had broken through the soil. One dinner plate-sized eye blinked at him. Its tooth-ringed mouth had him by the ankle, adding more blood to his already blood-soaked jeans. If not for his *serĉilo* multiples, the thing might have bitten his foot off.

"Ahhh!" he screamed, yanking at his foot, his head swiveling back and forth between Julie and the slug-thing trying to pull him down into the ground.

"I told you to be careful, moron!" Fangblossom orbited around Paul, stabbing out with her tail at the slug.

"Ow! That's my leg!" Paul yelled as the barb on Fangblossom's tail sliced across his shin. He pulled and pulled, but despite his multiplied strength, the slug-thing still had him. Panicked, he turned back toward Julie...

... and saw a cloud of shadow materialize behind her. Jay, with the Knife of Undoing in his hand, about to strike.

Julie kept one hand held firm on the arm of the man she helped out of the nexus, the last of the revenants whose bodies she had restored. She found the others strangely calm, unlike their state when she entered the nexus. Zee, for her part, had been trying to manage the group, more or less successfully.

A sleepy-eyed woman in a robe woven out of multicolored

flowers stood among the group. She smiled at Julie and said in a whispery voice, "Be at peace, friend. Does something ail your soul?"

The klaro's *Aura of Calm doesn't affect me,* said a voice in Julie's head. The who? What aura?

Julie quickly looked the woman up and down and decided she could be safely ignored.

Two others mingled about nearby, also without a care in the world. One was a man whose entire appearance seemed fluid, changing like images sometimes do in a dream. He met Julie's gaze with a smile of his own, although the way he held his head high and arched his eyebrows gave the look a wicked cast. Next to him stood a stout woman in a diaphanous white gown that looked identical to what Supriya wore as the *gardistaro.*

"Where did you get that dress?" Julie demanded.

The *gardistaro* smiled at her as if she had been given a lovely compliment and was about to answer when the flower-robed woman raised her hand and intervened. "Don't worry yourself over material things. Material things are of no consequence." Then she turned her sleepy eyes at someone behind Julie and repeated her earlier greeting. "Be at peace, friend. Does something ail your soul?"

Julie spun and found Jay standing only a foot away, the strange blue knife in his hand pulsing angrily. The beast tried to spring forth from the void, to attack, but she pushed it back and kept the *Kosmaro*'s aura at bay. Jay was looking at her with the same, dopey smile that he wore when he was stoned out of his mind—an almost ragdoll level of relaxation.

Come to think of it, they all looked like they came from the same college dorm room bong party.

"What are you doing here, Jay?" she said.

"I came here to kill you, Jules. To get back at Paul," Jay said in a mellow voice. "Then I changed my mind. The knife ain't too happy. See it squirming?" To the knife, he said, "Cut it out, man. That's not polite behavior. Bad knife." To Julie, as if all of this was normal small talk, he continued, "Killing seems like a lot of effort.

I don't think I'm into it anymore. In fact, I kind of feel bad about all the killing I've done."

Julie took two steps back and put her arms out as if to block him from those behind her. "Get away from me, Jay. And stay away from all of them, too."

"There's no need for anger. Be at peace," came the flower-robed woman's voice.

"Fuck off," Julie snapped.

Jay circled around Julie, holding up an innocent hand—the one without the knife—to show he meant no harm. His eyes moved to the woman in the *gardistaro* dress. "Esther?" he said. "That's your name, right? I don't blame you for what happened, Esther."

The *gardistaro*, whose name was apparently Esther, gave Jay a wide, sad smile. "Your words mean so much to me," she replied to Jay. And then the two hugged like they were the dearest of friends.

"What the hell is happening?" Julie asked. "Zee?"

The young girl put her arm around Julie and leaned into her as if they were mother and daughter. "There's no need to worry anymore. The *klaro* is here now, and everything is going to be better. Everything is already better. Don't you see? Oh. Who's that?"

Julie turned to follow Zee's gaze and saw Paul. His clothes were a bloody mess, and he was half-running, half-limping, flanked by Corinne in full Skull Girl paint on one side and a little flying devil creature on the other.

"Paul!" Julie yelled. The sight of him filled her with strength, almost like she had borrowed his *serĉilo* ability. Whatever the hell was happening here, they could handle it together.

"Everyone back!" Paul's voice was so loud and deep that it rumbled the ground. "Get away from my wife!" He saw Jay and his eyes flared gold. "You!" But then, as Paul and his little group got close, as Julie was about to run to him, Paul's steel-like intensity softened, and his pace slowed. "Oh. Everything's going to be fine, isn't it? We're all good."

"Yo, man," Jay said. "Dude, I don't know what came over me.

I'm sorry for stabbing you and slicing you and trying to stab you some more."

Paul shook Jay's hand and then pulled him in for a hug. "It's not your fault." He took the group in with a wide look and then settled his eyes on Julie with the same contented smile all of them wore. "It's none of our faults. We're all fine. We're going to be fine."

Julie turned to Corinne, whose dour and jaded nature had always seemed unassailable, yet Corinne had softened, too. For Corinne, anyway. She shrugged her shoulders and didn't look as if she wanted to kill anyone at that particular moment.

The flower-robed woman, who Zee had called the *klaro*, walked toward Paul with open arms. "Be at peace, friend. Does something ail your soul?"

Julie stepped in front of her, using every bit of her willpower to hold back the beast. "If you say that one more time, I'm going to strangle you with that robe."

The little red devil flew to Julie. "Yes! You're the only normal one here! These people should be murdering each other!"

Whatever had taken over the minds of the group, it hadn't affected Julie or this strange creature. "Do you know what's happening?" Julie asked.

"A lot of nothing!" Fangblossom said with a pout and her fists on her hips.

"I know what's happening," Paul said, walking toward her wearing that out-of-character smile. He pulled the notebook out of his backpack, and to Julie's surprise, it glowed with the same radiance of the souls she had collected as the *Koŝmaro*. "Look," Paul said, holding the notebook in front of her, open to the section describing the Between's canonical roles. "The woman in the flower costume is the *klaro*. She exudes the Aura of Calm." He tilted his head, like a dog in thought. "It must only affect humans, which is why Fangblossom is so angry. And you're one of the greater roles, Jules. So, it doesn't affect you, either."

Julie took the notebook from him, but before she could focus on its text, the soul trapped within it cried out to her. "Min-woo! It's Min-woo!"

"Oh yeah. I had forgotten about that," Paul said, as if possessing his neighbor's soul was a nice but trivial ordeal. "This sweet old man caught Min-woo's soul and stuffed it into the notebook. Maybe we can find a way—"

"To restore him," Julie interrupted him. "That's what I've been doing here, Paul. In the nexus. I can save Min-woo!" She looked at Paul and the others, the weird serenity they all shared. "But I don't want to go back into the nexus while this—whatever the hell it is—is going on."

"We're all calm, here," the *klaro* said. "There's nothing to worry about."

"She's right," Paul added. "Go get Min-woo's body back. It'll be great to see him."

"I love that goofy little bastard," Jay said.

The notebook throbbed in Julie's hands. She could feel Min-woo crying out to her, begging to be released, begging to be saved. "I'll be fast. As fast as I can," Julie said to Paul.

Fangblossom raised a finger. "Don't worry. If things get too weird, I'll start murdering people... starting with the flower-robed lady."

CHAPTER 30
THE CONNECTION WITHIN THE NEXUS

Even having entered the nexus several times already, even with the *Kosmaro*'s aura providing a buffer against the roiling waves of time and space, Julie still felt close to being lost in the nexus's maelstrom. The soul in her hand kept her grounded. It needed her. Min-woo needed her. She let herself take the form of the beast and sheltered in its void.

Next to her in the nexus stood a real-life Min-woo. She was so taken aback by his presence that she almost reached out to him. The image of his figure jittered, like a stuttering video feed, reminding her that what she saw was a composite, layers of separate Min-woos from separate outworlds. She followed the composite as it winnowed down to fewer and fewer overlapping Min-woos, just as she had followed the composite bodies of the others. She reached a single Min-woo in the familiar setting of his living room, and she prepared herself for the wicked deed that came next.

The souls she previously pulled from her basket had resembled tiny stars, bright but delicate like little fireflies that could go dim and vanish at any moment. When she took Min-woo's soul from the notebook, however, he emerged in full-sized revenant form. A shimmering ghost standing next to her.

Min-woo's revenant saw himself—or, rather, he saw the parallel Min-woo inhabiting the outworld they both observed. Min-woo's revenant face contorted in pain and longing, an expression Julie had never seen before on her perpetually effervescent neighbor. He reached for his body, driven by some innate need to rejoin his physical form, but his reach couldn't escape the nexus, and so it passed through his parallel without effect.

"I MUST RETRIEVE THIS BODY FOR YOU," Julie said in the beast's voice.

Min-woo seemed to hear and understand. He lowered his own hand and stepped back. Then he turned to her and did something none of the other soul-forms had done within the nexus. He spoke, and she could hear him.

"Julie," he said in a hollow voice like an echo carried on the wind. "I know it's you in there, my lovely friend. You freed me from my dirty, taped-together notebook. I love this notebook, but as a domicile for my soul, it leaves much to be desired."

As the hulking void-minotaur, she said, "YOUR SOUL-FORM WILL EXPIRE WITHOUT A BODY."

Min-woo nodded with a resigned look. "I hate to think of any Min-woo suffering. I've never liked suffering. I had my share of it early in life and decided it wasn't for me. But a little suffering is better than a lot of oblivion, so do what you must."

She moved forward and began extending her void arm, crossing from the nexus into the outworld. The Min-woo within the outworld saw the arm reaching for him from nowhere, panicked, and then fainted.

"That was a bit pathetic, wouldn't you say?" the Min-woo in revenant form said and then closed his eyes. "I can't watch this part."

Julie grabbed the outworld Min-woo and pulled his body into the nexus with them. Within the nexus, she repositioned the limp body, hooking her thumb and finger under the body's armpits and single-handedly hoisting it into the air as if it were a puppet. She moved the body forward, toward Min-woo's revenant form, and the revenant began to stretch toward the body as if pulled by a force of attraction. They became one, and the singular remaining Min-woo's eyes went wide open.

Julie had a sense of what Min-woo must be experiencing, because she had watched Zee and the others go through it as well. Two near-identical souls were now occupying the same body, a body built for one. She relinquished her beast form and softened her aura as much as she dared.

Min-woo convulsed and blinked several times but never lost his balance. After a long exhale, he looked at Julie and said with a half-smile, "I don't think the old tenant has fully moved out, but I'm in...and it feels wonderful to be real again!"

"Min-woo!" Jule exclaimed and then pulled him into a tight hug.

Min-woo squirmed in delight. "Oh, Julie, my sweet neighbor, my sister from another mister, the literal savior of my soul!"

She pulled back, her eyes full of tears. "No time for reunions. We need to get back to Paul."

He started to nod and then a curious look took his face. "Wait a minute."

"We don't have a minute," Julie said. "They're all gathering. Something is about to happen."

"But there's something I can do here. I can feel it."

Julie was about to grab Min-woo and yank him back out to the Garden when she remembered something Paul had said. "Maybe the world of the Between is projected out from the nexus. Paul thought there might be a way to change the Between's rules from within the nexus. He's right outside. Let's—"

"Your husband's a bloody genius!" Min-woo exclaimed. "Maybe genius is a bit much, but...I think he might be right, and I know just where to look." Min-woo held a hand in the air and then pushed forward as if he were opening a great door, and the world of the nexus shifted.

They stood in front of a grand building as wide as a city block. Regal, with castle-like walls, and an ornate red and green roof stretching above its five stories. It looked centuries old yet maintained with care. Beside it ran a wide river. A cloud of overlapping people moved all around the building's campus.

Julie's only experiences in the nexus had been dictated by the souls she carried with her. The souls linked to their counterparts in the overlapping outworlds. What Min-woo had just done wasn't linked to people; it was linked to a place. "How did you make us move?"

"We didn't move, sweet Julie. I shifted our perspective to another convergence."

Julie felt the seconds rushing by, but Min-woo knew things about the Between no one else seemed to. "Where are we?"

"I believe this is the Budapest University of Technology and Economics, where Rezső Simko slipped into the Between, and where he built his simulation. I know because I inhabited his body, and his memories flooded into mine. I lost myself in him for a time." Min-woo made the same pushing motion with his hand, and again the world of the nexus shifted.

Now they were in a cave of some kind with walls reinforced by carved stones. Julie had seen rooms within the Between's first world, the Patchwork World, made with these same stones. With more shifts, they moved through the cave's rooms and tunnels until they stopped in a chamber.

"It's here," Min-woo said. "The server."

In the middle of the chamber stood a wooden desk atop which sat a terminal and a keyboard. A huge cream-colored computer—bigger than any Julie had ever seen—was on the floor next to the desk, filling the room with a rumbling hum.

"We're in a forgotten room under the university," Min-woo said. It's part of a massive underground labyrinth beneath Budapest. If we weren't in such a hurry, and if I hadn't been recently beaten to death by rust wraiths in an underground room not unlike this one, I would want to explore a bit, but..."

He sat at the desk and began typing on the keyboard, the monitor's screen casting his face with a green hue. "It was in this room that Rezső found the entrance. When he entered the

Between for the final time, he took this server—this big, ancient computer here—and brought it into the entrance with him. That's why I can interact with it now, because it's actually here, not in an outworld." He pointed at a thick black cable extending from the computer. After several feet, the cable seemed to disappear into a blurry patch of air. "You see that? It's still connected back outside the nexus. This one computer connects back to *all* the outworlds. All of them, Julie. Do you see what that means? The computer game I played on my dorm room computer back in college... The game Paul connected to on his laptop... They were being served by this machine here, within the nexus, within the Between!"

Paul had spoken often to Julie about a strange connection between the computer game and the world he and Jay had slipped into. This machine here was that connection. "I get it, Min-woo. But why does it matter? Paul and the others are in danger. We have to get back."

"Yes," Min-woo said, nodding to her before turning his attention back to the screen. "You need to get back, but I'm staying."

"Staying? You can't stay. If I leave, if my aura is gone, the nexus will tear you apart."

"I don't think so," Min-woo said. "Not here. This room is real. It's not just overlapping outworlds. And the source code on this computer is shaping how the actual world of the Between functions. It's just like Paul said. I might be able to change things. Tweak a rule here or there. Maybe I can create a portal for us back home."

"Okay," Julie said. "I need to get back to Paul. I'll bring him here." As she said those words, all the pieces of a giant puzzle floating in her head—stories from Paul, her own experiences here, and now Min-woo's explanations—seemed to lock together into one complete image. If Min-woo successfully created portals home here, it wouldn't matter. They'd be pulled back by their roles. The name Rezső Simko hadn't meant anything to Julie when Min-woo had first said it, but she knew now that Rezső was the old man in the Underworld. The god of the Between forcing them all to play their given roles.

"Min-woo," she said. "Can we kill Rezső?"

"It's his world. I don't think so."

"Then that's the rule you should try to change."

"What a splendidly vicious idea," Min-woo said, cracking his knuckles like a pianist about to perform.

CHAPTER 31
SUCH A NOBLE OFFER

Paul tried to listen as Jay went on and on apologizing, but two things kept pulling him out of the moment. The first was Fangblossom, literally attempting to pull him out of the moment by yanking on his sleeve and then tugging with both hands on his ears.

"You're bewitched, you idiot!" she yelled.

The second distraction was his own mind. A chorus of *serĉilo* memories screamed warnings about the *klaro* and her Aura of Calm. He analyzed what they said and what he had read in Minwoo's notebook. The *klaro*'s aura made it impossible to fight and impossible to be angry, but it didn't charm those who were in it. In other words, one's thoughts were still one's own. Jay's words, while sincere, would mean nothing when they were no longer in the aura.

"Be patient, Fangblossom," he told his devil companion. "All this... peace... is temporary. You'll get what you came for. I promise." To Jay, he asked, "Can you give the knife to someone else?"

Jay held up the knife and made it dance and spin in his fingers. No matter how he twisted it, the point always ended up focused on Paul like an eye. "Now why would I want to do a thing like that?" he asked. "You're telling me to get rid of it. It's telling me to stab you in the throat. Can't everyone just enjoy the moment like ol' Jay here?"

This is where a chill should be running down my spine, Paul thought to himself. But since there was no chill, he found himself doing exactly what Jay had suggested, enjoying the moment.

"We have more guests," the *klaro* said, waving at the group approaching on the west path.

The head of the group wore a familiar crown, crisscrossed with wires and ringed with dozens of monocles as if it were the torture device of an evil optometrist. The man himself was unfamiliar to Paul, although the way Jay cocked his head suggested perhaps they had encountered each other before. Behind this new *masinisto* were several junk metal skeletons, what Jay called junklings. Again, Paul noted to himself that now was yet another time he should be anxious. Since he wasn't anxious, he instead studied the man and his group.

The *masinisto* was wary at first, clearly not expecting a calm gathering. The expressionless junklings, with swiveling headlights atop their rusted automotive junk bodies, looked from person to person as if inventorying their soon-to-be victims. But then the *masinisto* crossed the invisible line and entered the *klaro*'s aura. His face softened and became split by a wide smile.

"Juanca!" the new *gardistaro* yelled to him. In seconds they were catching up like reunited friends. The junklings showed no such change in demeanor, but a tap from the *masinisto* on his crown made them stand as still as statues.

"I remember that guy," Jay said, nodding toward the *masinisto*. "He helped capture me. He was a soldier with that spikey girl. The one with the dogs."

"The *malespero*," Paul said.

"Yeah, that's the one. I hope she's doing okay." Jay got a far-off look in his eyes as he continued. "It was a pretty good trick she pulled to get me to kill Supriya. But maybe Supriya got the last laugh by doing it herself. I wonder where the *malespero* is? I killed a couple of her soldiers on the way here. Probably slowed her down. I should apologize when she gets here."

As if on cue, the *malespero's* entourage crested a hill on the north path two obelisks away. Several additional soldiers and twenty or more ash dogs had joined her since Paul had last seen her in pursuit on the dunes of the Gray Waste. The *malespero* raised her hand, and her group stopped. She stood motionless, mask covering her face, and watched the group gathered by the nexus.

"She's avoiding the *klaro's* aura," Paul said.

"Little lady's a smart one," Jay said, giving her a look of admiration.

"Hey, that's my sister! She'll be so happy to see me."

Paul turned and saw a tall, lanky girl in her midteens that looked like an identical copy of the *malespero*. She had been one of the revenants that Julie restored. "Good for them," Paul said, as if being reunited with a dead sibling were an everyday occurrence.

"That's the *gardistaro* I murdered back at the mansion. Boy I felt bad about that. Glad to see she's alive again and doing okay. I should apologize to her, also. Man, I've got a lot of apologizing to do." Jay tried to sheath his knife five consecutive times, failing each. He took a step toward the girl but was interrupted by yet another newcomer.

A tree sprouted up in the east path about fifty feet from the nexus obelisk. Decades of growth occurred in seconds. The trunk thickened, branches extended in all directions, and leaves emerged, changing from red to orange and then brown before falling to the ground only to be replaced with new leaves. The gathered group all watched, transfixed, until moss covered the top sides of the branches, signifying in some way that the process was done.

The tree was magnificent. To Paul's untrained eye, it looked like an oak of some kind, but of a scale he had never seen in Texas. Its trunk had a diameter of at least ten feet. Its lower branches were as thick as trunks themselves and curled and twisted in the air like the snakes on Medusa's head. Several rested on the ground almost like bridges leading upward, where they formed a natural platform off the main trunk.

A man stood there, old and hunched, one hand braced against the trunk for support, a look of thoughtfulness and peace on his face. His eyes flared gold as bright as the sun for a moment, and then his face shifted ever so slightly. A contemptuous smirk replaced the soft smile. His eyebrows arched wickedly. Then his eyes flared again, this time with a dark crimson hue.

"We are the *Dio Ordo*," he said with eyes of gold, and then, "and we are the *Dio Kaoso*," he said with eyes of red. As he spoke, he continued shifting back and forth, his voice changing to match the appearance he wore. "We are the man Rezső Simko, split in two when I placed this amulet around my neck. Two humans in one body. Two gods in one form."

"Guy's a little creepy if you ask me," Jay whispered.

The *klaro* shushed him.

"We have lived a thousand lifetimes in this world of ours, and now our time is drawing to an end. Fitting that the end comes in the Garden." Rezső Simko opened his mouth to continue, but then froze in the middle of a grand sweep of his arms. His face took on a look of confusion, bordering on alarm.

Paul saw nothing that had changed around them, but clearly Rezső had seen or sensed something.

Rezső continued again. As he spoke, alternating between his forms, his voice regained the confidence of before. "We have been the gardeners of the Between. Its keeper and protector, maintaining the balance of Order and Chaos. Now we must give the amulet and our roles to one of you, who will take our place. Who should have it?"

"I will take it," Paul said without hesitation.

The group all turned to look at him.

Corinne, who had been quiet and keeping to herself, stepped up to Paul and whispered in his ear, "This wasn't the plan, Paul. I won't let you do this."

That last bit sounded colder than should have been possible in the *klaro*'s aura, Paul noticed, but because of the aura's effect on him, he let that observation quickly slip away. "I need to," he whispered to her. *It's good that Julie isn't here to hear this next bit,* he thought, and then he filled his lungs and spoke loudly. "I will take the role. I will send all of you home and turn the Between into something...else. Something that doesn't tear people from their homes, that doesn't pit them against each other. I'm ready."

"Look at Paul, being the big hero," Jay announced to the gathered group as if they were his audience. "That's fine with me. I'm not one for the spotlight, anyway. You got my vote, man."

"Such a noble offer," the *klaro* said, holding each hand out toward Paul as if she were receiving a gift from him. She turned to the old man standing on the tree's platform and said, "I support this as well."

The *gardistaro* and *masinisto*, with their arms around each other's waists, concurred. The *songo*, whose appearance had never stopped shifting, shrugged and said, "I am content with this outcome."

"Is it settled?" the old man asked as Order-Rezső.

As Chaos-Rezső, he responded to his own question, "We have not heard from all of the roles."

Jay raised a hand. "The *nenio* woman...Yeah, I murdered her on the path. So, if I get her vote, she votes for Paul also."

"We will accept that vote for Mr. Prentice," Order-Rezső said. "The *malespero* has chosen to stand apart and defied the bell. She abstains. The *Koŝmaro* has chosen to occupy herself within the nexus. She abstains as well."

"And what of the *Malluma Sinjoro*?" Chaos-Rezső asked, his wry grin growing wider, as if he had been waiting to ask this very question.

"He is in the Garden but has remained near the Grand Staircase. Like the *malespero*, he has forsaken the call of the bell. So, he abstains."

"Perhaps not," Chaos-Rezső said. "Look." He pointed at the *masinisto*, who had been quietly assembling something from the bag he carried.

Paul had been so focused on the Between's god speaking to them from his tree platform that he hadn't noticed the *masinisto*. On the ground before the man were two large rectangles made of pipes. The first rectangle was open, like a frame, with little feet standing it upright. The second rectangle was slightly smaller. The *masinisto* deftly stretched a tarp within its shape and connected the tarp to the rectangle. He stood this second rectangle on its end and slid two pegs from its long side into receivers on the larger rectangle.

"What are you doing? What is that?" Paul asked the man wearing the strange mechanical crown.

"It's a door," the *masinisto* said, looking pleased with his creation.

The *malespero* began running toward them, coming down from the hill on the path to the north covered in blue flame, ash dogs barking, soldiers yelling battle cries.

Memories in Paul's head screamed. He knew what was about to happen, but because of the *klaro*'s Aura of Calm, he only watched with detached fascination.

The *gardistaro* traced the *masinisto*'s newly constructed door with her hands, and a gateway sprung into being. Out of the gateway stepped the *Malluma Sinjoro*, the man called Sin.

"Sorry for being late to the party," he said.

The Aura of Calm vanished, replaced by Sin's Aura of Chaos. The blue of the Garden's sky became the color of flame.

CHAPTER 32
THE THREE AURAS

Julie stepped out of the nexus and into bedlam. The unnatural calm in the Garden had been replaced by something far worse. Everyone fought like animals, screaming and thrashing. Two women she had saved, who had talked like best friends only moments ago, now rolled on the ground, hands full of each other's hair. An arc of fire sprayed out from the red wand in Corinne's hand as she desperately fought off the junk metal skeletons that had surrounded her. The *gardistaro* was trying to cut the *songo* to pieces with little razor gateways in the air, but the man seemed to have multiplied into a dozen copies of himself. The *malespero*, flanked by ash dogs on both sides, sprinted toward the fray, her spiked armor covered in blue flame. Two of the *malespero*'s soldiers had rifles trained at the crowd and were snapping off shot after shot. Paul had one arm wrapped around Zee, restraining her, and one hand clutching his forehead. His fight appeared to be mostly internal, struggling against whatever madness had taken the rest. In the center of chaos stood a man Julie had never seen before, who hadn't been here when she'd entered the nexus. Black cloak, bone white skin, and glowing red eyes—he looked like a vampire lord radiating pure evil, which she suspected was not far from the truth. Voices in her mind whispered his name. *Malluma Sinjoro.*

She transformed. Her body became the void form of the minotaur. The aura of the *Koŝmaro* snapped into being, warping the space around her. Her aura counteracted whatever the pale man was exuding, but at a price.

"STAY CLOSE AND YOU WILL BE SAFE, BUT DO NOT LOOK AT ME," Julie said in the voice of the beast.

Paul had let go of Zee. Everyone near the nexus, within Julie's aura, had stopped fighting, including the women on the ground. But now they were all in the probability maelstrom surrounding the *Koŝmaro*, their appearances changing rapidly, their figures jittering as if disconnected from the space around them.

"NO!" she yelled as a man and woman she had rescued from the statues ran from her. Within a few steps they were outside of her aura and back into the chaos, and then at each other's throats.

Paul's form shifted less than the others, but even with the *serĉilo*'s ability to reinforce himself, the *Koŝmaro*'s power was yet greater. "I can stop him!" Paul yelled, eyes trained on the *Malluma Sinjoro*.

"PAUL!" Julie screamed, but Paul was already off and running. He crossed the threshold, slowed, and then fell to his knees. When he looked up again, the golden glow of his eyes was replaced by crimson red. She could almost feel the power of his multiples surging within him, but where would that power be directed? "MOVE FORWARD WITH ME," she said to the others protected yet tormented by her aura. Zee turned to look at her, and upon seeing the beast, was locked in a trance. One by one, they all became locked in the same trance she had felt that night when the last *Koŝmaro* had emerged from the iron door in her backyard.

She turned to the *Malluma Sinjoro* and let out an earthshaking roar. "NO ONE HURTS MY CHILDREN!"

Jay picked himself up off the ground and narrowly dodged the license-plate-bladed forearm of a junkling, arcing down at him like an executioner's ax. He collided with the metal fiend and tried to push it away, but his left arm hung limp, his strength all but vanished. The knife Skull Girl had thrown at him was still lodged in his back under his shoulder blade. He dissolved into shadow and slipped behind the junkling. The Knife of Undoing flashed out in his right hand, severing a few of the junkling's metal ribs, and a second slash cut the serpentine belt running through its core. Before its lifeless form hit the ground, Jay was already dissolving into shadow again, seeing attacks coming from every direction.

Dissolving into shadow took a heavy toll on him, especially with a knife stuck in his back, but he had to get out of danger. The *stelisto* was an assassin that attacked from the shadows, not a clumsy soldier who fought out in the open where any lucky moron could catch him from behind. As shadow, he drifted into a neighboring square of tall grass. He rematerialized in a crouch. Poorly hidden but hidden enough from the deranged fighters on the Garden path.

He yanked the knife out of his back, and for a moment the world was made of pain. Each breath he took felt like he was being stabbed again. He tasted his own blood in his mouth. The tip of Skull Girl's blade must have pierced his lung. Before he could wonder where she had gone, he saw a sweeping beam of fire cut through the crowd in front of him. The fire wand she had taken from a past *masinisto*. The Knife of Undoing pulled at him, wanting to bury itself in Skull Girl's heart. He shifted his weight to get a better look from the grass, but even that little movement had him doubled over in pain again.

What the hell was happening? One moment everyone was lovey-dovey—he and Paul had even reconciled—and the next, the Garden of Before had become Murder Central. He watched as the flower-robed lady—the one who only seconds before seemed to calm everyone with her slow-talking, New Age bullshit—brought a rock down over and over again on the *songo's* head, who had just before been about to run a spear through the *gardistaro*. The *gardistaro* thanked the *klaro* by portal-slicing her in half.

So much for saying *be in peace, friend*. More like, *be in pieces!* Jay's laughter caused him to bow over in agony.

The crowd shifted, and Jay saw the man standing in its middle, radiating chaos. Sin, the *Malluma Sinjoro*, a smile on his thin lips, his arms like an orchestra conductor directing a symphony of death. He gave a side-eyed look at Jay, somehow seeing him despite the shadow of the tall grass. The look oozed a mix of confidence and contempt that gave Jay the willies. No matter how badly Jay wanted the man dead, Jay couldn't touch him. His presence warped people's minds, some more so than others. Paul could have probably explained why, but the last thing Jay wanted right then was a lecture from Paul.

Jay needed his left arm to work. He needed to heal and to recharge. His knife vibrated in his hand. Only feet away, two of the *malespero*'s soldiers looked down the iron sights of their rifles at the crowd, out of Sin's range but very much in Jay's. As silent as a thought, he took one down and then the other with two neat cuts across their necks. The knife devoured their lifeforce and rewarded Jay with surges of healing energy. His shoulder felt looser. He could breathe deeply again without coughing up blood.

Not even a minute had passed since the fighting began, and already the crowd had thinned by half. Julie had returned and taken on the void-silhouette of the minotaur. Paul and several of the others were huddled close to her. *The reality-warping whirlwind around Julie must be stopping Sin's chaos*, Jay realized. But it couldn't stop the *stelisto*. He had fought with a *Kosmaro* before, had stabbed it despite its aura.

In three shifts, he cut across the nearby square of trees, behind Julie and Paul, behind the nexus obelisk. He took a deep breath and readied himself to run in when he saw Paul stand and walk out. What was Paul doing, leaving the *Kosmaro*'s aura? Paul collapsed as soon as he reentered Sin's aura, holding his head in his hands, trying desperately to fight it.

"You fucking idiot," Jay mumbled. "Trying to be the goddamn hero. Now you're dead."

There was no way for Paul to protect himself from Jay's knife—and Jay didn't even have to brave the *Kosmaro*'s aura to get to Paul.

Jay ran, half-man, half-shadow toward Paul, to put an end to

Paul's disappointed looks, to his unwanted life advice, to the friendship that had spoiled and soured and needed to die. Paul looked up at Jay as Jay reached him, the knife high and ready to stab down like a scorpion's stinger. Paul's eyes were red, the red of chaos that Jay saw in the *malespero's* eyes, the red he knew his eyes possessed as well. But there was no malice in Paul's eyes. He looked at Jay the way Supriya had looked at him in that last moment. No hatred, no judgment. Only sadness. *I'm sorry you have to do this*, Paul's eyes seemed to say.

The knife started to strike, but Jay pulled it back. The knife shook in his hand and several times jutted at his own chest, but again he overpowered it. How? With all the killing around him, with his knife compelling him to open rivers of blood, how was he able to hold back? He looked down and saw the weeping wound in his forearm—the tally mark for Supriya. That was how. She hadn't been able to stop what was inevitable, but she had found a way to let him keep an ounce of his humanity. And that ounce of humanity had prevented him becoming the pure killing machine that Sin intended.

"Get...out...of here," he said to Paul through gritted teeth. Then he turned to the *gardistaro*, bloodied and dazed. "That's Supriya's dress," he growled, and he shot out toward her.

A wellspring of anger had burst within Paul's mind, letting loose a flood of hatred, of chaos, of destruction. He held fast against it, hopeless as it seemed in the face of such a torrent. When he saw a color-inverted Jay standing over him, Paul didn't see someone who wanted to kill him. He saw a man about to put down a rabid dog, and a part of him—the hopeless part—welcomed the end.

But Jay had held fast, too, fighting his own internal battle that Paul watched in his friend's eyes. Jay succeeded, at least in directing his killer's blade elsewhere. But that left Paul, alone, drowning in the Aura of Chaos and its flood of death. He pulled on all the strength and willpower of the multiples filling him to fight against Sin's aura, but this wasn't a test of brute strength and will. The stronger he became, the more deadly he would be when the aura took him.

He stood and turned toward Sin, who was walking casually around the raging battlefield with a ghoulish smirk on his ghostly pale face. Paul tried and tried to channel the chaos within him toward Sin, but Paul's anger seemed to swirl around the man as if he were a smooth rock in a roaring river.

Sin raised an eyebrow when Paul made a single step forward. Then the demon-man turned, and with a voice as booming and mighty as the *Koŝmaro*'s, said, "*MALESPERO*, KILL THIS MAN."

Without any hesitation, the *malespero* ran toward Paul with a pack of snarling ash dogs in tow. Her armor was now a brilliant white alight with golden flame, her mask of agony covering her face. Finally, a target for his anger. He felt a hatred toward her unlike anything he had ever experienced—the combined fury of all the *serĉilo* parallels. He ran to meet her head on, and for a moment, lost himself in the torrent raging within him. But before the fight had started, he was already looking for his next target, the next person he would tear to pieces after he easily dealt with the *malespero*. He saw Zee, transfixed in the *Koŝmaro*'s gaze and completely helpless, and he hated her in that moment as much as he hated the *malespero* and...

And he pulled himself back. Right as the *malespero*'s first shockwave crashed into him, he put all his *serĉilo*-enhanced strength into fighting the anger, leaving none to brace himself against the blast. He tumbled backward, skin tearing on the rocky path, and crashed into the trunk of a nearby tree. Before he could so much as try to breathe, a second blast struck him, pinning him to the tree.

She had reached him in the next moment, arm outstretched, the air rippling between them. The dogs bit into his arms and legs as his chest threatened to collapse. The harder he fought back, the more he steeled himself against the assault, the more he lost himself to the chaos. The face of the *malespero*'s mask was unchanging, but the eyes, visible through two slits in the iron, showed the struggle within her as well. Every ounce of her power was flowing into Paul, and it would either crush him or make him lose control.

———

Corinne found herself, all of a sudden, strangely forgotten in the middle of the battle. Fights raged around her, but everyone else had targets other than her. She felt the bloodlust pouring out from Sin's Aura of Chaos but not as others felt it. The skeleton paint on her face now covered all the skin of her body. She was two women at that moment, just like when she looked at herself, naked, in the mirror in that cheap Austin hotel room and saw two superimposed forms: one, Corinne Pelletier, human and subject to all human weaknesses; and two, Skull Girl, the eternal survivor, untouchable by human desires. Sin's aura commanded Corinne like a drug pumped into her veins. But the aura slid through Skull Girl's bones and found no flesh to corrupt.

And so it was that Skull Girl, dragging Corinne Pelletier with her, walked up behind Sin, took one of her throwing knives, and stabbed it into his back.

The Corinne part of her felt Sin's aura flicker as he turned to her, confusion on his white-then-black-then-white face. She could almost hear the thought in his mind. *You're not even a role? You're nothing!* As he looked at her with those disbelieving eyes, he didn't see the hulking void minotaur charging toward him, lowering its horns. In two strides, as light and graceful as any steps she had taken as a dancer, Corinne moved away.

The monsters collided.

———

Julie found herself in a pit, an almost perfect bowl cut into the ground, exactly like back at the ruins of their home where the previous *Košmaro* had died, where its artifact ring had called to her. But she was neither dead nor free of the ring. The explosion had come from the death of the other demigod of the Between, the *Malluma Sinjoro*, run through the chest by one of her giant minotaur horns.

All she could hear was a shrill, endless ringing—not of the bell, but a remnant of the blast that felt stuck in her head. Beyond the pit, the air was heavy with dust, obscuring the aftermath of the blast. Bodies lay strewn in mangled heaps, some with missing limbs, all blackened beyond recognition. Near the nexus obelisk, a few figures stumbled about. She recognized Zee as one. The girl looked confused but otherwise fine.

The dust parted in front of her, and with a shock she saw a junk metal skeleton with its arm raised to attack. Two other skeletons stood nearby. Each had their headlight eye destroyed from the white fire blast of the *Malluma Sinjoro*'s death. Each remained unmoving, frozen like statues in the moment of their demise.

The dust swirled and parted again, and she saw Paul standing next to a young woman in black spiked armor. They were no longer fighting, and the armored woman had taken her mask off. Julie looked back at Zee—still near the obelisk—and then again at the woman near Paul. The two looked so similar that they had to be sisters. That meant this was Lark, the *malespero*, and the sister Zee had described immediately after being reborn from the nexus.

"Lark!" Julie yelled. She couldn't hear her own voice, but the *malespero* heard it, and with a confused look on her face, turned toward Julie. Then her gaze found Zee, and her entire body shook and threatened to crumble.

To Julie, the entirety of the world seemed to shrink into the little universe of brown dusty air they inhabited now, as if the destruction of the *Malluma Sinjoro* had created an insulated egg for this moment of reunion to happen. As she watched the two sisters run toward each other, Julie thought of a similar egg—the egg created by the previous *Kosmaro*'s death, when the heat warped the melamine tray on her bedside table into a protective shell around the engagement ring Paul had given her.

She stepped back to give the two girls space. The dust between them swirled and shifted...and then began to take a dark figure's shape.

Lark saw the shadowy figure of the *stelisto* a moment after Julie, but it was a moment too late. Lark extended her left hand toward him, palm out to send forth a shockwave. A flash of blue light came first, cutting through the air. Lark's hand fell to the ground like an inert thing knocked off a table.

Julie watched in horror, too stunned to act. She was caught in a slowing of time as Lark stared at her arm with disbelief, no longer as it was moments ago. She looked to her severed hand on the ground and then reached for it as if she was going to pick it up, as if the hand had merely been dropped and could be replaced.

Silent screams came from Zee and Paul. The knife-wielding shadow of the *stelisto* re-formed behind Lark. Another blue flash. Lark looked up, up, as if toward the heavens above, the real world beyond the Between. Her head lolled back, rolled off her shoulders, and fell to the ground. For a half second that felt like an eternity, the headless body of the *malespero*, of Lauren Montclair, stood there in the brown dusty air, in a little egg that had offered no protection at all. Then, it crumpled.

Too late, Julie turned back into the beast. Too late, the *Koŝmaro*'s aura burst out from her. The *stelisto* was already gone, returned to shadow, invisible to them except for his voice, laughing and crying.

"Is this what you wanted?" Order-Rezső said with an angry snarl from the tree's platform above, watching as the Between's final performance—*this* iteration of the Between, anyway—took place. "We have caused so much death and pain."

"Is it not fitting that our final chapter also be filled with death and pain?" Chaos-Rezső replied. "Look at the anguish on the *serĉilo*'s face. You wanted him to take your place. I think this turn of events will force him to."

"The *stelisto* will try to kill him first."

"For certain," Chaos-Rezső said. "As much as I don't like destiny, it seems that these two were fated to fight at the end. But, brother, as powerful as the *stelisto* has become, he is no match for the husband-and-wife pair, the *serĉilo* and the *Koŝmaro*. It is all but over."

"We're committed now," Order-Rezső said. "The ending must play out."

"Indeed. Let us enjoy this final moment where we are—" Chaos-Rezső's words caught.

The form of the *stelisto* materialized next to the dual-person form of Rezső Simko, the Knife of Undoing buried to the hilt in the god's stomach.

"The artifacts cannot hurt me," both of Rezső's voices said in unison as he doubled over in pain. "I am... the god... here! The Between's rules... are mine!" He turned his head toward the towering nexus obelisk, and his eyes widened with the realization of what must have happened.

The *stelisto*, his eyes burning red, his body more shadow than human, knelt down with the old man, keeping the knife in place in the man's gut. The *stelisto* stared into the old man's eyes for several seconds—a moment long enough to fit the perfect quip from Jay Lightsey, but Jay Lightsey was no longer there. The *stelisto* tore the knife upward, splitting the god of the Between in half.

Fresh from its supreme kill, the Knife of Undoing glowed brighter than it ever had before. Energy flowed through it and into the *stelisto*, god-energy that filled him until he overflowed, that healed every wound he had ever suffered, that made him feel like he had become a god himself. It felt radiant and blissful and then it burned into hot, iridescent pain. But it vanished as quickly as it had started, leaving him empty. Even the dark shadow that had accompanied him—that had become a part of him—was gone.

Jay looked at the knife in his hand. It no longer glowed, and its once mirror-like blade was now a dull gray. He had the sudden urge to throw the knife, something he had not felt since it had come into his possession. He acted on the urge and watched it spin end over end until it landed, point down, stuck in the middle of the path.

"What the fuck?" he muttered. "I'm...I'm me again."

In a daze, Jay looked at the dead shape of Rezső Simko at his feet and then at his own hands. He had killed with these hands. A wave of disgust rolled through him. It seemed impossible. How could he, Jay Lightsey, kill anyone? But the body was in front of him, and the memory of his hand plunging the knife into the old man was seared upon Jay's mind. A new scar was on his forearm, a mark already carved by the knife to commemorate the killing of a god. He ran his finger over the scar. It had been healed by the knife's final surge of death-energy, but the scar would remain on his forearm for the rest of his life. The biggest scar on his arm somehow remained unhealed, crusted with an angry, brown scab. The scab felt like an insect, burrowing into his skin. He tore it free, and blood came loose. Instead of washing away his pain, it stained his palm with it. No matter how he tried to wipe his hands, more and more blood seemed to cover them. The unhealed mark had been for Supriya. The wet blood on his hands, that would always be on his hands, belonged to Supriya.

It became too much for him to comprehend, and his mind—for a moment anyway—shut down. Too unfathomable to have killed the woman he loved, even if it had been her hand that forced the blade. To have killed the others. So many others. He turned, almost robotically, where he knew Paul would be standing, to ask his friend: How? How was any of this possible?

Paul, indeed, was right where Jay expected him to be, staring back up at Jay, eyes full of his own confusion. And next to Paul stood Julie, tears streaming down her face, holding a young, sobbing woman in her arms. Julie no longer had the Košmaro's reality-warping aura around her. Had her role vanished with the death of the old man also? Were they all free now? Had he just freed everyone?

If there was ever a moment for one of his signature wisecracks, it was now, but as his eyes drifted back over the young woman held by Julie, the words left him. Jay knew this young woman. He had killed her once before, with a knife through the heart when she was the *gardistaro*. And minutes ago, he had decapitated her sister. He leaned over and began to dry heave. Whatever rationale had driven him in those lethal moments was gone now, leaving only the grim knowledge of what he had done.

"What happened, Jay?" came Paul's exhausted voice from below. "Jay?"

The rage Jay had felt toward his friend was absent, and all the feelings the rage had been masking came loose. Jay had tried to kill Paul! Over and over. Jay had tried to kill Julie simply to hurt Paul. How could he ever look at either of them again? The dry heaves came again, and his legs threatened to give out.

Paul kept yelling at him, not with words of anger but confusion. Jay had no answers except the one: he had caused it all. He had pushed Paul to explore the chamber under the iron door in Paul's backyard. He had grabbed the Knife of Undoing, knowing even before it touched his hand, before having his identity warped into the role of the *stelisto*, that he was making a bargain with the devil. Only this devil wasn't a cloven-hooved, horned creature from fairy tales. The devil was inside him, had always been inside him. And he had let it out.

He had tried to kill Corinne for seeing who he was. That was Corinne's great transgression. And what about all the innocents? That's what they were: innocent. Even the *malespero* and her soldiers. He didn't have to kill any of them. He knew she was serving them up on a platter, and from that platter he ate generously, devouring life, his chin covered with blood. He only spared lives when Supriya made him.

Supriya... The look in her eyes at the end...Had he seen a golden light there? Even though the *gardistaro*'s dress had been taken from her, her eyes still shined in that final moment. Had that really happened, or was he imagining it now?

No, it had happened.

He could see the light from her eyes as if it had burned a

permanent hole in his own vision. Now that he acknowledged the hole, it seemed to get bigger, consuming everything nearby, washing away every sight and every thought in blinding, golden light.

That light receded, and he found that he held something in his hands, his bloody hands, that hadn't been there before. A simple golden square with a red jewel at its center—an amulet. Within the jewel was a delicate, twisted thread that looked at first like a crack. The thread glowed as if it were the filament in an incandescent bulb. A thin chain necklace connected to the golden square so that it could be worn around one's neck.

Jay had no memory of picking it up, but he knew what it was. An artifact, like the Knife of Undoing or the Silver Spiral that Paul wore on his forearm. But this was the artifact of the gods of the Between. Jay looked down at Paul, who had only minutes before announced he wanted to become the successor to the god-role.

Paul's eyes were darting back and forth between the amulet and Jay's eyes. "What are you doing, Jay? Don't even think about putting that on."

"Because you want it?" Jay said, with more of an edge to his words than he had intended.

"No! We're free from our roles, now. I was willing to take on that role when I thought it was the only way to free everyone else. I thought one of us had to be trapped here to free the rest. But our roles are gone. Don't put that thing on, Jay. We can escape now."

"I wasn't going to put it on." When Jay said those words, they were true. But why couldn't he? Paul was ready to be the hero. Of course Paul was. Paul always played the hero. The martyr. The designated driver when they went out. The voice of reason before they did something stupid as kids. The responsible adult.

Jay felt the amulet pulsing in his hands. All the power in this little object. Paul was right, of course. They were free from their roles. They could find an exit and go home.

But Jay couldn't go home. Not after everything he had done.

He looked at Zee, distraught but alive again. How had Julie brought her back? If Jay became the Between's supreme god, he could do anything Julie had done, right? He could bring them all back. He could fix all his mistakes. All the hash marks on his arm. All the scars on his soul. Make it as if they had never happened.

He lifted the amulet. The sun caught the giant ruby in its center, and the strange filament inside flared. Paul, Julie, and now Zee were staring up at him with looks of horror on their faces.

"Don't you see?" Jay said. "I can bring everyone back. It's all okay. I'll make it right."

Julie cried out, "It doesn't work that way! Jay, listen to me! Don't put that on!" She kept yelling something about souls, how Jay didn't have any of the souls, but he no longer heard her. He no longer heard any of them.

He closed his eyes, and the sunlight bleeding through his eyelids painted a red panorama before him. It started as the red of blood, the sea of crimson he had spilled with his hands. Then, as the sun warmed his face, the image shifted into the glassy surface of the ruby at the center of the amulet. A uniform red. A canvas on which he could transmute the pain he had inflicted into a new world full of new life. All he had to do was lower the chain around his neck and place the amulet flat upon his chest.

Something Julie yelled out broke through.

Supriya.

Julie had said Supriya's name. Jay didn't know the context, but the context didn't matter. Nothing mattered at that moment except for Supriya. It always came back to Supriya. He might tell himself that the amulet would allow him to right his wrongs, but the only wrong he truly cared about was the pain he had caused Supriya. He might, as the Between's new god, be able to recreate *a* Supriya, but would she be *the* Supriya he loved?

He thought of the night when he and Supriya had first escaped the Between, when Supriya had discovered that another Supriya already existed in Jay's world. Jay had described the *other* as "the wrong fucking Supriya" to Paul on the phone.

The red canvas transformed again into an eternity of torment. All the Supriyas from all the outworlds. Jay pulling them here, drunk on his godly power. Finding each Supriya to be wrong. And then discarding them. Over and over again.

Becoming the Between's god wouldn't save Supriya, it would multiply his sins against her.

He opened his eyes, and, after a few blinks to readjust to the sunlight, he saw the Garden of Before stretching out in front of him with corpses littering the ground and Paul and Julie staring up at him as if he were a monster.

He took one last look at the amulet and then said, "I'm not gonna do it. I've always chosen what I've thought was the easy path, and it keeps coming back to bite me. There's no easy way to fix what I've—"

<hr>

A crack like thunder interrupted Jay's words. An eye, red as the amulet's ruby, opened in the center of his forehead, and out of it poured a line of blood. His eyes rolled back, and he dropped in a single limp motion atop the corpse of Rezső Simko.

Paul spun and saw Zee holding one of the rifles, her eyes wide but cold and expressionless—a look Paul had seen on her sister as the *malespero*. Fangblossom hovered near the young woman with a self-satisfied smirk on her face.

"You promised me murder, Paul Prentice," the little devil creature said.

Paul ran to the tree and began climbing, slipping twice before catching a low branch and pulling himself to where he could grab hold of the platform. The voices of the past *serĉilos* were gone from his head, but his own internal voice took their place, screaming, "HE'S DEAD! HE'S DEAD!" But his body didn't hear. He moved as if there were a chance to save Jay. He couldn't have stopped himself if the world depended on it.

He lifted Jay and shook him as if Jay were only sleeping, saying his name over and over again. He might have gone on that way forever if someone or something hadn't stopped him, and that thing was the amulet, glowing like a burning ember on the platform next to him.

Julie had been right when she was screaming at Jay before. Unless they possessed the souls, like she had as the *Kosmaro*, there was no way to restore someone who had died. Jay couldn't have reversed what had happened to Supriya. Her soul had faded into nothing hours ago.

But, with the amulet, transformed into the Between's god, Paul could save Jay right now.

In the aftermath of the shot, Julie stood for a moment, overwhelmed by what had just happened. Jay was dead. Not the *stelisto* but Jay, who she had known for over a decade, who had slept on their couch more times than she could count, who had introduced her to Paul. She watched Paul run toward his old friend, toward *their* old friend, but she felt no urge to do the same. Julie had heard that the human mind couldn't feel pain from two different sources at the same time. One became dominant and the other muted. Whatever pain she felt for Jay was lost beneath the overwhelming sadness she felt for the girl holding the rifle who had shot him.

Being the *Kosmaro* had tricked Julie's mind into thinking that she and Zee were connected like mother and child. More than that, the role had switched on the mothering circuitry within Julie that had heretofore laid dormant. The role had vanished, but the circuitry was on fire now. Behind the girl's steely face, Julie saw the wounded soul underneath, and it broke her heart.

Zee didn't protest or even acknowledge that anything was happening as Julie took the gun out of the girl's hand. "Oh, my sweet young girl, no," Julie said, holding Zee tight, wishing she could take what Zee had done and make it hers. But the rifle shot would ring within Zee's soul for the rest of her life.

The stiffness went out of Zee's body, and she fell into Julie's embrace. Julie saw Corinne, suddenly alarmed at something behind them, but there was no capacity left within Julie to turn, no way that she would release Zee until Zee was ready to stand on her own. Whatever else was happening would have to happen without her.

Paul felt the sharp, cold edge of a knife press into his neck. His hands, holding the amulet, froze. He looked out of the corner of his eyes and saw Corinne's face without any sign of the painted skull. He hadn't heard her climb up on the platform. He hadn't seemed to have noticed anything except the amulet, humming in his hands. He didn't even remember picking it up.

"I won't let you put that on," Corinne said without a hint of compassion in her voice. Her other hand gripped his forearm tighter than Paul would've thought possible, as if the tips of her fingers were burrowing into him.

"If you're trying to get my attention, you have it," he said. "I can save Jay and several of the others here. The girl's sister, too. I don't want to stay. I don't want to become... whatever I will become. But how can I not save people if I have the chance, no matter what it costs me?"

The knife pressed harder. Paul felt it cutting into him.

"This isn't a debate," Corinne said. "If you bring that thing one inch closer, Julie will be a widow, and I will have your death on my hands."

"How can you—" he started, but she cut him off, her voice angrier than he had ever heard it.

"How can I what, Paul? How can I be willing to kill you to make sure this all ends? This is not the way to be the hero. Do you hear me? If you try to put that amulet on, you'll make me the villain. I'm willing to be the fucking villain right now, Paul, if it means this all ends." She cocked her head to the side and yelled, "Fangblossom, get up here!"

The little devil flew up and hovered before them. She saw the knife at Paul's throat, and her big eyes became even bigger before they narrowed, and a wide smile split her face. "Ah! More murder!" Fangblossom let out a cackle that gave Paul chills.

"Here's what's going to happen," Corinne said. "That amulet is going to be yours, Fangblossom. It's the most valuable thing in the Between. Everyone will want to steal it from you. But it will be yours and yours alone as long as you protect it and keep it safe."

"It will be all mine?" Fangblossom said, giddy with greed.

"All yours," Corinne said.

Fangblossom let out another cackle, this one somehow more bloodcurdling than the last. "Give it to me, Paul Prentice!" she cried, extending her little clawed fingers eagerly.

"Do you want to hand it to her or for her to take it from your corpse? Either way works," Corinne said. "What's it going to be, Paul? How does this story end for you?"

Her pupils had grown so wide that her eyes became like black pits. Staring into those eyes, he saw, for a moment, the well he had fallen into all those years ago. Just like then, he peered into the void and became seized by its promise of obliterating darkness. *l'Appel du vide*. He didn't want to wear the amulet, to become the god of the Between, no matter who he could save. But he didn't want to live with the pain of knowing he could have reversed everything—maybe, somehow—but chose not to. Corinne and her knife provided another option. Escape. Not from the Between but from everything. He stared into the dark wells of her eyes, waiting, feeling the blade press harder, wanting it to press harder still.

But then out of the darkness came something bright, a flash that caught the sunlight. A tear. He pulled himself out of the void and saw that Corinne was crying, and that he wasn't the one approaching oblivion with every second. It was her. Even though the knife was at his neck, he was the one killing her.

She spoke, voice unsteady, lips quivering. "Sometimes the only person you can save is yourself. And when you get the chance, you need to do it."

The words cut at him sharper than the knife at his neck. They were his own words, that he had spoken to her just hours before.

But more than that, they were spoken not by Skull Girl, but by Corinne, with eyes full of tears and love and fear. The paint had vanished from her face like his role had vanished when the Between's god had been slain.

"What am I doing?" he said, looking at the amulet in his hands. It pulled at him with what should have been a force so overwhelming that even the *serĉilo* couldn't fight it, but he turned again to Corinne's face—her unpainted, tear-stained face—and the amulet became powerless. "You're the hero, Corinne," he said. "It's always been you, not me."

"What? What are you saying?" Corinne said, the knife blade drifting away as her hand became unsteady.

In his mind it was so clear. He had been willing to play the martyr because that is what the hero ultimately does. And this whole time, he had thought of himself as the hero, as embarrassed as he was to admit it. But it had been Corinne who had saved each and every one of them, over and over, without the otherworldly strength Paul possessed as the *serĉilo* and without the cheat-code secrets of Min-woo's FAQ notebook. And here Corinne was, doing it yet again. Saving him, again. And she still couldn't fucking see it. The world became cloudy as his eyes, too, filled with tears. "This decision isn't mine. It's yours. I haven't earned this moment. You have."

He held the amulet out and felt Fangblossom's claws snatch it away.

The knife slipped from Corinne's hand, and she crumpled into a sobbing heap.

"You're free," he said, and he heard himself say it again and again, through his own shaking tears. "You're free. We're all free." He felt a hand on his shoulder and saw that Julie had climbed up with them. She sat herself between him and Corinne to hold them both, and they all cried together.

Every few seconds, the surface of the nexus obelisk flickered, and in its night-black façade, Corinne caught a glimpse of her own reflection. Dried blood caked the side of her face. Her shirt was stained and torn, and her hair looked rattier than an old, dried-up mop. Her skin had been burned, wrinkled, and mottled by the sun.

But the woman in the reflection had an immovable presence that rivaled the obelisk itself. That woman had seen some shit and was still standing. For the first time in...so long she couldn't remember... Corinne didn't turn away from what she saw.

Julie, who had walked up quietly beside her, said in that no-bullshit tone of hers, "Are you looking at your reflection?"

"I am."

"And what do you see?"

Corinne shrugged, which only served to encourage Julie. "Eh," Corinne muttered. "I see a woman who needs a bath."

Julie wrapped Corinne in a hug that started as a shared laugh but somewhere along the way turned into a farewell embrace. "We've cried enough. Go let Min-woo send you home. He's waiting for you. You're going to have a great life. You deserve a great life."

"I don't know about that," Corinne said. "I'll have *a* life. I'll try to make the most of it, and I won't forget you and Paul." As she said his name, she saw him over Julie's shoulder. Paul was sitting on the grass next to Zee in that awkward way of his where he knew someone needed him, but he wasn't quite sure what to do. He was trying, though. "Is he going to be okay?"

"I think so," Julie said, watching Paul with Zee as well. She got a thoughtful look in her eyes. "We all have lives yet to live. Let's go home."

EPILOGUE
THREE YEARS LATER

Something about the ease with which the knife slid through flesh triggered a wave of nausea, and Paul had to turn away from the butcher preparing rib-eye steaks behind the counter at the neighborhood grocery. How little effort it took to draw a line of steel through muscle. To a sharp knife, life provided no resistance at all.

Paul heard the cold slap of the steaks on the paper-lined scale, heard the paper being folded, the screech of tape unspooling and then fastening to the paper. He thanked the butcher with a quick nod and took the wrapped package even though he had lost all desire to eat its contents.

"Julie's missing out. Those are gonna be good," came a familiar voice next to him. Paul looked at his shopping companion, saw the smile of anticipation she wore. He put on his own smile, faking it at first, but how could he not be overwhelmed by happiness seeing Zee herself happy? After everything they'd been through, to be here now planning a celebration, any lingering sadness—and there would always be lingering sadness—was pushed to the back of his mind. He let the joy of the moment take over.

"A steak for me, a steak for you, and one for Uncle Min-woo," Paul announced. Then, in his best nasal French chef voice, he said, "Portobello kabobs for Jules." He stuck out his tongue and made like he was dry heaving.

Zee clutched at her stomach and used hand gestures to indicate a large quantity of vomit projecting from her mouth and splattering on the floor. "Fungus! Ugh." A nearby shopper scowled at Zee's antics.

Paul thought it was hilarious. "Okay, barfmaster. What about sides?"

"Mac and cheese!"

"Mac and cheese? That's all you eat. You can pick anything in this whole store. Get fancy. We're celebrating. It's our first night in the new house *and...*" He waited. When she didn't finish the sentence for him, he gave her another chance, "*And...*"

"And... I got into UNC." She tried to play it off cool, but a proud smile crept onto her face.

Paul pulled her in for a side hug and blinked away the tears forming in his eyes. The past three years had been hard. Full of guilt, unanswered questions, and absence. Deception and risk, too. It was no easy task to get Zee enrolled in a new high school, because in this world, another Zenia Montclair already existed. Uncle Min-woo had a solution for this, involving a thoroughly unscrupulous lawyer and a lot of money. For a while, Paul worried someone would dig into her records and unravel it all, but they hadn't, and they wouldn't. "Zee Smith" had a government-issued Social Security Number. She was legit as far as the Feds were concerned. The grades and the scholarships had been all her work. "I'm so proud of you, kid."

She tilted her head to rest it on his shoulder. "Couldn't have done it without you and Julie."

"And Min-woo," Paul said. "None of us would be here if not for Min-woo."

It was true, in more ways than one. Back in the nexus, Min-woo had found a way to manipulate a few key areas of the Between using the old mainframe computer at its center. The game's code proved almost indecipherably cryptic, written in some eastern bloc version of ALGOL 60 or Pascal with Esperanto syntax. To hear Min-woo tell it, his battle with the code was as deadly as the battle raging out in the Garden. Had his edits made

Rezső vulnerable? Min-woo wasn't certain. However, he claimed full responsibility for finding a way to get them all home.

While sifting through the code, Min-woo saw a name he recognized: *Altaro de la Ĉielo*. The Altar of the Sky, the exit Paul and gang had used to escape from the Between previously. Min-woo copied the code for the altar and added it to the chamber that neighbored the one with the computer. It worked. When they arrived, a new altar, a new exit, sat waiting for them.

Each of the survivors returned to their respective outworld homes. Corinne had said her goodbyes in the Garden, outside of the nexus, and when she was gone, it felt like a hole had been torn in Paul's heart. Inside the nexus, Julie helped each of those who had been restored from revenants as they placed their hands upon the altar and vanished.

Zee's turn was last. She approached the altar, stopped, turned to Julie, and said, "I can't. My brother is gone. Now my sister. There's nothing but a life of sadness for me back home."

"What about your parents? They'll be thankful to have you back," Julie said.

"They're already broken, and they'll be even more broken from losing Lark. I can't." She wiped a tear from her eyes, steadied herself, and looked at Paul. "What did Corinne say to you? When you were holding the amulet. What did she say to make you give it up?"

"Oh." A lump formed in Paul's throat. "She repeated something I had said to her before. Used my own words against me, I guess. But she was right. She said: *Sometimes the only person you can really save is yourself. And when you get the chance, you need to do it.*"

Zee walked to Julie, and the two held each other. Between deep breaths, Zee said, "This is me saving myself. I want to go back with you."

Julie kept her eyes on Paul's without blinking, waiting for him to answer while rubbing her hand up and down in soothing motions on Zee's back.

"We don't have a house or money," Paul said. "And there will be...complexities...with your records in our world."

Julie's stare didn't budge, waiting to see where Paul would end up.

Min-woo chimed in, "You've overcome bigger problems."

"We have indeed, Min-woo," Paul said. Normally, Paul's mind would have been racing through all the challenges ahead if they did this, but at that moment, his mind was quiet. Only once in Paul's life had he ever made a major decision without painstakingly analyzing his options: when he surprised himself by asking Julie to marry him. He hadn't bought a ring yet, hadn't made intricate plans to create the right moment to drop to a knee. He had simply been overcome by a certainty, seemingly out of nowhere, that it was right. Standing there in the nexus, Julie's eyes fixed on his, and for the second time in his life, the warm feeling of rightness swept over him. "Zee, if you want to come with us... *I* want you to come with us. It would make me very happy."

Back in the grocery store, Paul and Zee continued to fill their shopping cart. He and Julie had steady jobs, and their household budget was finally beginning to feel workable. Min-woo had a lot —everything, really—to do with that new level of financial comfort. Min-woo's last trick, before exiting the Between for the final time himself, was to hack the game's code to add another object in the neighboring chamber the same way he had added the altar. That new object was a 100-pound cube made entirely of 24-karat gold. According to Min-woo, it had taken more effort to move the object that weighed as much as he did than it had to create it. When presenting it to them, Min-woo said, "If you win a dungeon explorer game—and, my friends, this is absolutely a victory, all things considered—you have to end up with treasure. I didn't write the rules. Actually, I did write this particular rule and create this particular treasure, but that's neither here nor there. The Prentices need a new house, and Miss Zee could use a college fund. Congratulations."

In the bakery department, Zee couldn't decide between cake and pie, so she got one of each.

"And we can't have cake and pie without ice cream," Paul said.

In the frozen foods section, Zee loaded a tub of chocolate ice cream and one of vanilla into their cart. "You always talk about the value of options," she said. "These are delicious options." She looked to each end of their aisle, shook her head, and asked, "How long does it take to pick out some vegetables? Sheesh."

Julie had been gone for fifteen minutes or more. "Let's go get her," Paul said. They walked to the produce section but didn't see her anywhere. "She probably went looking for us."

After another few minutes walking from one end of the store to the other, glancing down every aisle they passed, they still hadn't found her. A creeping dread began to come over Paul, but then he saw Julie's unmistakable form at the end of an aisle with her back to them. Buzz cut, sundress, hands waving enthusiastically while she spoke.

"Of course she ran into someone she knows," Zee said.

"She knows everyone."

As they walked down the aisle toward Julie, Zee tapped boxes of cereal on the shelf as if she were playing a big percussion instrument. Zee could find a way to turn almost anything into a game or a toy for her imagination. Paul found himself lost in the moment, watching Zee absently amuse herself, until he saw who Julie was talking to.

"Corinne," he said.

"And there's the man himself," Corinne said, giving him a smile that didn't quite reach her eyes, her eyebrows arched ever so slightly.

Julie saw Paul's full shopping cart and held up the empty red plastic basket in her hand. "Lost track of time." She touched Corinne on the forearm and said, "So nice to run into you—I mean, meet you."

Zee followed Julie toward the produce section, saying something about potato chips being vegetables.

"Your wife is a hoot, Paul," Corinne said, still giving him that half-amused, half-suspicious look.

"A hoot?" He tried not to stare. This Corinne had been his high school girlfriend. He had described her as *my Corinne* to her skull-faced counterpart in the Between. But now, standing in front of her, fifteen years or so since the last time he had seen her, she looked more like a strange copy of his warrior companion. That Corinne—Skull Girl, survivor—had become his Corinne. The woman before him now had fuller cheeks and wore flip flops and jeans with pre-made fashion holes instead of holes torn by monster teeth. Still, her lack of any real greeting and her complete eschewance of small talk showed quite clearly that she was the same woman.

"Don't get me wrong. She seems wonderful. But I've never met the woman, and she greeted me like we were long lost best friends."

Paul thought for a moment about how to respond. "That's because we were trapped in an alternate dimension, and your parallel there was part of our little gang."

She leaned back and crossed her arms. "Sounds like something your goofball friend, Jay, would say. How's he doing? You two still close?"

"We're not close anymore. Haven't seen him in a while."

"That's a shame." When she said this, her face softened. She knew Paul and Jay had been inseparable when they were young. It was a shame that things withered, that things died. Friendships. People.

"Tell me, Corinne," Paul said. "Are you living a happy life? We're obviously not going to trade life stories while here in the grocery store. I'd like to leave knowing your life is going well. Who knows when or if we'll see each other again."

"This has been a very odd encounter, Paul." She let the sentence hang, still with that amused yet curious look on her face. It was as if she had come across a peculiar insect and found herself just interested enough to keep watching it. "Yes," she finally said. "I am living a happy life. Are you?"

He nodded. "I'm going to go find my family now. Be well, Corinne."

After the celebration that night, Min-woo walked the three blocks back to his house. His backpack, no longer filled with wine and champagne, felt as light as his spirits. The alcohol had gone to his head, but so had his emotions. The Prentices were happy. Zee had a life ahead of her. And Min-woo...well, he was going to get home before the main event started. What could be better in life than curling up on a French antique sofa, basking in the glow of a giant television, and watching two men wearing boxing gloves beat each other to a pulp?

"I'm just a simple boy with simple needs," he announced to the night.

In the back of Min-woo's newly constructed wine cellar, in the cool underground darkness, the knob of a closet door twisted. The door opened, and an otherworldly light poured out for a brief second before the door slammed shut. Something now inside walked within the darkness, sharp claws scratching the concrete with every step.

It came in through the unlocked back door and followed the noise and light of the television until it found Min-woo, so engrossed in the screen that he was unaware he was being watched.

It crept closer...

Closer...

And closer...

And finally, it leaped over the back of the sofa. Red splattered on the cushions' pristine fabric and on the rug.

"Damnit, Fangblossom!" Min-woo exclaimed, frantically dabbing at the spilled wine with a handkerchief.

The little devil creature had her eyes glued to the screen. Pumping her fists and dancing around on the sofa shadowboxing, she said, "Did I miss the battle? Did I miss them MURDER each other?"

"You didn't miss anything. It's about to start." He gave her an exasperated look. "Did you secure the portal this time? I don't want any more monsters in my backyard. Not after last time."

Fangblossom gave him a thumbs up and a toothy grin.

Min-woo abandoned his work on the stain and threw the handkerchief onto a silver tray on the coffee table. The announcer had just asked the crowd if they were ready to rumble. He slid the popcorn over to Fangblossom, who began shoveling it in her mouth with both hands.

Then, Min-woo tucked the ruby amulet back under his shirt.

ACKNOWLEDGMENTS

Lindsay Leslie, you inspire and encourage me. Somehow you haven't been scared off by the weird ideas floating around in my head.

Thank you to my wonderful editor, Alexandra Buchanan, as well as Sabrina Terry and the rest of the Parliament House team.

A special thanks goes to The Escapists for all the fun, laughter, and support. Life is so much better when shared with friends.

Last but certainly not least, thank you, readers. If you made it this far, you've spent 25 hours or more with me, Paul, Jay, Corinne, and the gang. You could have watched a dozen movies. Played the first quarter or so of Elden Ring. Driven across the country. Learned the basics of French cooking. Made a few weeks' progress on a new fitness campaign. Or slept. But instead you read these books. In the end, time is all we really have. That you spent some of yours with me is a treasured gift. I hope you had fun. I know I did.

ABOUT THE AUTHOR

Photograph by Patrick Larson

Ryan Leslie oversees research for a large health system, where making stuff up is generally frowned upon. His creative outlet has always been writing fiction. Ryan is the author of The Between (2021), its sequel The Garden of Before (2025), and Colossus (2024). He lives in Austin, Texas, with his wife, children's author Lindsay Leslie, and their two sons.

WWW.RYAN-LESLIE.COM